PRAISE FOR *THIS LOVELY CITY*

'Full of life and love, *This Lovely City* is a tender, at times heart-breaking, depiction of a city at once familiar and unrecognisable. It made my heart soar'
STACEY HALLS, *SUNDAY TIMES* BESTSELLING AUTHOR OF *THE FAMILIARS*

'I loved, loved, loved it, and desperately wanted things to work out for Lawrie and Evie'
CATHY RENTZENBRINK

'Superb... compelling storytelling, beautifully drawn characters and atmosphere that's deeply immersive'
HARRIET TYCE, AUTHOR OF *BLOOD ORANGE*

'*This Lovely City* is a beguiling, atmospheric and important novel, with wonderful, memorable characters and a vital message about love, loyalty and hope'
CAROLINE LEA, AUTHOR OF *THE GLASS WOMAN*

'Expect to be obsessed . . . [a book] you need to know about'
GOOD HOUSEKEEPING

'A thought-provoking and imaginative debut that conjures up the experiences of the Windrush generation in post-war London. Heartbreaking but full of hope'
WOMAN & HOME

'Louise Hare writes so effortlessly. It was a joy to read'
WOMAN'S WEEKLY

Louise Hare is a London-based writer and has an MA in Creative Writing from Birkbeck, University of London. Originally from Warrington, the capital is the inspiration for much of her work, including *This Lovely City*, which began life after a trip into the deep-level shelter below Clapham Common.

THIS LOVELY CITY

Louise Hare

ONE PLACE. MANY STORIES

HQ
An imprint of HarperCollins*Publishers* Ltd
1 London Bridge Street
London SE1 9GF

This edition 2020

1

First published in Great Britain by
HQ, an imprint of HarperCollins*Publishers* Ltd 2020

ISBN Hardback: 978-0-00-833257-0
Hardback (Waterstones): 978-0-00-839572-8
Trade Paperback: 978-0-00-833455-0

Printed and bound in Great Britain by
CPI Group (UK) Ltd, Croydon, CR0 4YY

For Mum and Dad, for everything.

'Ever so welcome, wait for a call.'
WEST INDIAN PROVERB

'It is like watching a nation busily engaged in heaping up its own funeral pyre.'
ENOCH POWELL

✳ MARCH 1950 ✳

'All fish does bite but shark does get di blame'
WEST INDIAN PROVERB

1

The basement club spat Lawrie out into the dirty maze of Soho, a freezing mist settling over him like a damp jacket. He shivered and tightened his grip on the clarinet case in his right hand. He'd best hurry on home before the fog thickened into a 'pea-souper', as they called it round here. The hour was later than he'd have liked; the club had been packed and the manager always paid extra if the band stuck around, keeping the crowd drinking.

'Done for the night?' The doorman leaned against the wall by the entrance, waiting for the last stragglers to leave.

Lawrie nodded. He'd been invited to stop for a drink with the band after the last set but he had somewhere to be. The night's moonlighting had been a last-minute call out. He'd already arranged to take Evie out to the pictures but he needed the money and his name was just getting known around town: *Mr Reliable. Able to fit in with any band at short notice. Call Lawrie Matthews, he's your man; he'll play anything for a shilling or two.*

It might be after three in the morning, but the street was still open for trade. Across the road a couple of girls loitered, hardly dressed for the March weather, their legs bare and their jackets open. They sheltered in a shop doorway, huddled together as they smoked. One of them called over to him but he pretended he hadn't heard. That sort of entertainment wasn't for him. A few minutes of pleasure taken in a dark piss-scented alleyway could not outweigh the guilt. This he knew.

Even back home in Jamaica, he'd never felt confident in himself, not like his older brother Bennie, but this city forced him even further inside himself. It was a chronic condition, like asthma or arthritis; he could go a day or so feeling perfectly normal and then just a word or a glance was enough to remind him that he didn't belong. He liked working the clubs because he could just play his clarinet and get lost in the music. His fellow musicians respected him; many of them even looked like him. He revelled in the applause that came when his name was shouted out and he stepped forward to give his small bow and a smile, just the right side of bashful. But as soon as he left the warmth of the club, things changed. People looked and decided what he was without knowing a single thing about him. Most of them were well-meaning. Somehow that was worse.

He walked swiftly down to Trafalgar Square, putting on a sprint as he saw his night bus approaching, leaping on the back just before it pulled away and clambering up the steps to the upper deck. He sat down, panting slightly through exertion and relief.

Settled, he looked out of the window at the desolate streets rolling by. The city appeared defeated beneath the weak glow of the late winter moon, which lazily cast its light down on the abandoned remnants of buildings that looked flimsy enough to blow over in the backdraught, if only the driver would put his foot down. Almost five years now since VE Day, almost two years since Lawrie had landed at Tilbury, and the city was still too poor to clean itself up. Austerity they called it, as if giving it a name made it more acceptable to those struggling to make ends meet.

The double decker wound its lethargic way south of the river and Lawrie tried to stay awake. His eyes were heavy but the draught through the window kept him shivering enough that he didn't nod off. He'd be home just in time to change into his uniform and swallow down some breakfast before heading out again to his proper job.

Jumping off at the Town Hall stop in Brixton, the last passenger left on board, he tugged his scarf up over his chin to ward off a wind that felt like icy needles stabbing against his face. By the time he turned the corner of his street his face was already numb and his gloved hand felt stiff around the handle of the clarinet case. He wiggled his fingers and looked down, checking they were still there.

Home at last; a chip of grass green paint flaking away from the swollen wood of the gate as he swung it open, the rough edge catching his glove. He let himself in the front door, careful to close it quietly behind him. Everyone would still be asleep; he could hear Arthur's less than gentle snores through the thin wood of the door that led to what had been the front room before Mrs Ryan had to let it out for much needed cash. He silently pulled off his shoes and shrugged off his coat, hanging it up by the door, his trilby next to it.

Upstairs in his bedroom he stowed the clarinet safely away at the back of his wardrobe. He trusted his fellow residents well enough, but his mother had always preached that temptation could befall the best of men. That stick of rosewood had been his father's before him. Irreplaceable. Maybe one day he would pass it on to a son or daughter himself. He'd dared to mention that dream to Evie only a few weeks ago, and her smile had given him hope.

It was a room that his mother would have been ashamed to offer her cook. Besides the wardrobe there was only space left for a narrow bed and just enough room on the floor for his friend Aston to sleep on when he was in town, which seemed to be less often in recent months. The small window, with a view from the back of the house, let in a little bit of light and a lot of draught. Lawrie had rolled up some newspaper and jammed it into the gap between the window and its frame, but that wasn't enough to stop the inside of the glass from frosting over.

His uniform was ready on its hanger, but the cold had stiffened his fingers and it was a slow process; shedding the suit of a professional musician and putting on his everyday postman's uniform. He blew on his hands, trying to get some warmth into them, but he already knew that only a hot mug of tea would work.

Down in the kitchen, he expertly lit the flame on the stove and stared out of the window as the kettle boiled. He fancied he could see the sky lighten slightly as the hour grew closer to dawn. The kettle began its low whistle, and Lawrie lifted it off the ring before it could wake anybody with a full screech. Mrs Ryan would be up early so he made a full pot, tugging the hand-knitted tea cosy around it so that she could have a hot cuppa as soon as she came down. He always let it sit a good long while. He'd never been a big tea drinker before meeting Mrs Ryan, so he'd become used to the way she brewed it. He kept one eye on the time as he clasped the mug, his fingers softening, the feeling returning, as he sat at the table and enjoyed the silence and warmth of the kitchen.

When the clock hands read half past four it was time to go. Lawrie wrapped up again in his heavy coat and the deep burgundy scarf that Evie had knitted him for Christmas. Reluctantly, he forwent his beloved lined leather gloves for the bobbled fingerless ones that did what they could to protect his precious hands against the elements while still allowing him to work easily. Pausing before unlatching the door, he took an extra few seconds to adjust his postman's cap on his brow before the long, age-speckled mirror, his forehead bisected by a crack in the glass, courtesy of a V-1 that had fallen in the next street in darker days.

'Oi!' Derek, Mrs Ryan's son, stood at the top of the stairs, just out of bed and wearing only an off-white vest and pants. His mother would have words if she saw the state of him. In his hand was a brown paper package. 'Take these over to Englewood, would you? Usual place.' He threw the package down and Lawrie caught it lightly, nodding his consent. More black-market stockings, he guessed. Rationing had made Derek a fortune. He tucked the package away in the hallway cupboard to collect after his shift.

The sorting office was only a ten-minute walk but Lawrie had to be early. He had to be the first to arrive. He glanced up at the house next door as he pulled the front door closed behind him, but Evie's window stayed dark. Not yet five and she'd be fast asleep. Last summer the early dawns had woken her, the sun rising to greet the city as he left for work. He'd pause and wait, turning when he heard the scrape of her sash window opening up. They'd never speak – she'd hold a finger to her lips and smile down at him worried that her mother would hear, even though she was unlikely to. Agnes Coleridge took sleeping pills and snored louder than any man Lawrie had heard, the rumble audible through the party wall. He'd smile back and Evie would blow him a kiss as she rubbed sleep from her eyes. And even though the dark mornings had put paid to this small joy, he couldn't help but pause for a moment beneath her window. Just in case.

'You!'

Lawrie stifled a groan. 'Sir?' He turned to face Eric Donovan who was waddling down the aisle in his direction, his creased shirt already coming untucked from trousers whose waistband looked to be on the verge of capitulation.

'Get a move on today, boy, you hear? Second lot's gone out late twice this week already.' The words were barked around an unlit Woodbine that perched on Donovan's narrow bottom lip; the slimmest part of him.

'Yessir.' Lawrie had never headed out late, but he'd learned there was nothing to be gained in talking back to the boss.

'And don't forget my order.' Donovan lowered his voice, Lawrie nodding to show he understood. Donovan's sweet tooth kept Lawrie in his good books, Derek supplying bags of white sugar to maintain Donovan's addiction.

Lawrie put his head down and got on with the sorting while his fellow postmen straggled in, the air filling with a cacophony of male voices. Joining in with the general banter cheered him up by the time he'd got his bag packed, hefting it across his back and adjusting his stance to accommodate the weight. His walk took him back down his own street – past Evie's house – so he didn't complain, despite it being one of the heavier routes.

Evie answered the door when he knocked at the Coleridges', a round of toast in one hand and a shy smile on her face that brightened his mood in an instant. He didn't deserve a girl this beautiful, not after what he'd done, and yet here she was.

'Anything for me this morning, Mr Postman?'

'Always.' He leaned forward and kissed her lightly on the lips, one eye checking over her shoulder in case her mother made a sudden appearance. He didn't take it personally that he was forbidden to cross the threshold. He was sure that Mrs Coleridge would have said as much to any man who was wooing Evie. After all, his skin was barely a shade darker than her own daughter's. Evie's father had returned to wherever he'd come from without knowing he had a baby on the way, leaving Agnes Coleridge holding a mulatto child. No wonder she had a disposition as bitter as quinine.

'Evie! Shut that door, will you? D'you want me to catch my death?' The kitchen door slammed.

'Don't mind her.' Evie pulled the door to behind her and wrapped her arms around her body, a flimsy protection against the cold, standing there in a plain blue cotton dress, navy jumper and her house slippers. 'You got time for a cuppa? I can bring it out.'

Lawrie adjusted his bag across his back so that there was space for her in his arms, pulling her off the step and holding her tight to keep warm. 'Not today.'

'Is it Donovan? You should tell him what's what.' Evie fussed with his scarf, making sure his tender skin was protected.

'I can manage him just fine.' Lawrie stole another kiss before letting her go. 'Just one letter today, ma'am.' She laughed and took it, pressing the palm of her other hand to his cheek. 'I'll call round tonight when you're home from work. You have a good day now.'

She leaned against the doorframe and watched as he made his way up the street, pushing envelopes into letterboxes, just as she did every day, whatever the weather. It was a miracle she'd never caught a cold, but Mrs Ryan reckoned that love did something strange to a body – that if it could be bottled or turned into pills it would make penicillin look like an old wives' remedy. At the corner, he turned back to wave and blow a kiss. She never went inside until he was out of sight.

Towards the end of the day, as he sat in the police station, he would wonder if in this moment he'd jinxed himself – walking around with that stupid grin on his face as if he were the luckiest man alive.

The morning followed its familiar rhythm. First man back at the sorting office, first back out with the next delivery, smirking at the look of disappointment on Donovan's face. He had a little gossip with Mrs Harwood as he gave her a hand carrying her shopping bags home and thanked Mr Thomson for a racing tip that he wouldn't use himself but would pass on to Sonny who loved a little gamble. Lawrie clocked off in the early afternoon, declining the offer to join the others in the pub down the street. He tried to go with them once or twice a week, but only because he felt he should. He liked a game of snooker or dominoes but he really didn't have a lot in common with these men: mainly married, mainly ex-servicemen, all white. Besides, he still had Derek's delivery to make.

He made a short detour home to pick up his bicycle and the package. Englewood Road was on the south side of Clapham Common, a place that was close to home; that green expanse of open land beneath which he had spent his first few nights in England. He remembered arriving there, that summer of 1948, and wondering how the sun could be so bright and yet so chill. And then they'd led him into the deep-level shelter, laughing at his terror at being underground, and fed him tasteless sandwiches along with the rest of the *Windrush* passengers who were unfortunate enough to have nowhere else to go.

The south side of the Common was busy with traffic, those famous red buses no longer a sight that thrilled him. At weekends the paths that cut across the Common would be much busier: couples strolling, children playing, fathers teaching their sons to sail boats on the ponds or feed the ducks. This was where he'd first set eyes on Evie, and where they'd had their first real kiss the summer before, sitting in the deep grass on a long hot Saturday afternoon. In better weather the air would be full of the shrieks of young children playing games, the chatter of their mothers as they exchanged gossip and pushed their progeny in huge Silver Cross prams that forced Lawrie from the path and onto the grass.

On this cold March afternoon, only the odd dog walker had ventured out. At this time of day he often saw these middle-aged women with their precious pets emerging from the large houses that surrounded the Common to walk their pampered animals in circles. Their children were grown and their housework managed by a housekeeper or a charlady, someone like Mrs Coleridge who did for a family over on the north side. They came striding along with an entitlement that Lawrie would never possess, letting their dogs off the leash and looking the other way as their beloveds squatted and left the mess for someone else to step in. Just before he reached Eagle Pond, Lawrie looked up and saw one such woman coming towards him, veering to one side as she walked briskly down the centre of the path; there was a Jack Russell trotting along at her heels, and if Lawrie had learned anything in his postal career it was to watch out for those little bastards. The woman stared as he rode past, and he knew that if he looked back she'd be watching him. Making sure he kept moving and didn't hang around like a bad smell.

The lady who answered the door at Englewood Road was no better. Barely two words to say to him, neither of them wasted on thanks, but the money felt comforting in his pocket. Lawrie's cut was twenty per cent, bargained up from ten the year before. Derek needed a trusted delivery man, he'd argued. Someone who didn't look suspicious knocking on a door and handing over a brown paper package. Who better than the local postman?

Maybe he should take Evie out, he mused. Not just to the pictures. The boss of the club where he'd played the night before, he'd mentioned a few times that he'd get Lawrie a good table if he wanted to bring his girl along. Lawrie always smiled back and thanked him for the offer, said that he'd let him know. He wasn't sure what he was wary of. There was no shame in playing music for a living. It wasn't as though Evie didn't know what he did but he liked that she was separate from all that. The women who frequented the club, not all of them but a few, they reminded him of his mistakes. They reminded him of Rose.

He cycled back the way he'd come, recognising the woman he'd seen with the terrier as he drew close to Eagle Pond, but the dog was nowhere to be seen. There was something strange about the way she was moving, and he found himself slowing down. She was pacing up and down in front of the pond, looking for something. Her gait was lopsided and, when she drew closer, he saw that her face was wet from tears that were blinding her. She didn't notice Lawrie until the last moment, suddenly aiming towards him and coming up short as she took him in properly. She held herself rigid, her mouth gasping for air that her lungs didn't seem to want to accept.

'Ma'am?' Lawrie swung his leg and dismounted, making his movements slow so that she didn't spook. 'You all right? Can I help you?'

She looked over her shoulder but turned back to him, fixing her eyes on his uniform. Whatever she'd seen was more frightening than one skinny black man. And there was no one else in sight. 'You – you're… a postman?' Her tongue tripped as she spoke.

'Yes, ma'am. Do you need help?'

She nodded and pointed in the direction she'd come from, a ragged sob creasing her body.

He couldn't see anything out of the ordinary at first. There was the pond, and there he spied the terrier. The small dog was soaked through. Barking urgently at him, it ran back towards the water.

'The pond.' The woman squeezed out the words and he noticed now that her hands were filthy, her coat spattered with mud.

'There's something in the pond?'

It was useless. She had begun to shiver, her teeth actually chattering as shock took hold. Lawrie laid his bike down on the grass and headed towards the pond on foot. The dog was still barking in a fury, running laps between the edge of the pond and the path.

'What you got, boy?'

The dog splashed into the water, checking back to make sure he was being followed. There was a bundle there, a dirty blanket that once had been white. Lawrie crouched by the edge next to a smaller set of footprints that must have belonged to the woman. It didn't look like much, this wad of sodden wool, but that didn't stop fear from squeezing his chest tight as he reached out with his right hand, the palm of his left sinking into freezing mud as he tried to keep his balance.

He strained his arm and caught an inch of fabric between two fingers. Pulling gently, the bundle moved closer and he grabbed a tighter hold. The wool was heavy with water. White and yellow embroidered flowers peeked out from beneath the pond filth. Daisies. When he lifted it the bundle was heavier than he'd anticipated, but it wasn't the weight that sent him crashing to the ground – only sheer luck landing him onto the bank rather than into the water. His heart pounded his ribs so hard that he glanced down at his chest, expecting to see it burst out through his coat, scattering buttons onto the ground.

The blanket lay there on the grass, the bundle coming apart. A baby's arm had escaped, along with a shock of dark curly hair and a glimpse of a cheek. It could have been a doll, but one touch had been enough to convince him that it wasn't. The hand was frozen stiff but the skin gave as his fingers had brushed against it.

Someone had left a baby in the pond to die. A baby whose skin was as dark as Lawrie's.

2

Typing had a rhythm to it that Evie enjoyed. When she was in a good mood, more often than not these days, she sang along quietly to the tapping of the keys as she transcribed Mr Sullivan's letters. He called her his little songbird and had been known to pat her on the head like a child, but he was a nice older gentleman and she knew she was lucky to have him. When his last secretary had left to get married, Evie had only been in the typing pool for a few months. Mr Sullivan's single stipulation for her replacement was that she should be the fastest and most accurate typist. Mrs Jones, the pool supervisor, had sent Evie upstairs with a sly smile on her lips, and Evie had braced herself for his polite excuse but Mr Sullivan's jaw had only dropped half an inch when he saw her, quickly masked by a smile, and it was Evie who had skipped back downstairs to whisk away Mrs Jones's smirk along with her coat and bag.

She loved her job at Vernon & Sons. A light and airy office on the third floor, a desk by the window so that she could indulge in the odd daydream, and her best friend sitting right opposite.

Delia was attached, professionally speaking, to the young Mr Vernon, the boss's son, and would fix a tight smile to her face each time she had to untangle herself from his wandering hands and their clammy palms, her head turned away from his halitosis. As Ma often said, thank goodness Evie had not been born pretty and blonde. Not that Delia was a bad typist, only the young Mr Vernon had his own set of requirements when it came to secretaries.

'I'll be off now, Evie.' Mr Sullivan emerged from his office, hat on head and overcoat slung over an arm. 'I'm taking a slightly longer lunch today but you won't tell anyone, will you?' He winked and grinned, in the manner of a kindly uncle to his favourite niece.

Evie smiled conspiratorially. 'I'll not say a word. Off anywhere special?'

'Just to see the kiddies.' His eldest daughter had two of her own now and lived just off Lavender Hill, only up the road. 'I'll be back by three if anyone needs me.'

She waved him off. It was one o'clock and the offices were all emptying out; she could hear doors opening and closing throughout the three floors that the company occupied, echoing up and down the staircase. The girls would be heading to the small staffroom, or outside if they were brave enough, to eat their sandwiches. The men would be going out to a café or home for a hot meal, to see their wives, or mistress in the case of the young Mr Vernon – he'd packed his wife off to Surrey during the war and never thought to bring her back.

'You almost done?' Delia whizzed a sheet of paper from her typewriter with a flourish. 'I'm starving.'

'Two ticks.' Evie locked her drawer. Things had a habit of going missing when she didn't.

'Off out are you?'

Evie looked up, stifling a groan. The suspected thief herself was standing in the doorway, her lip curling upwards in a sneer as she stared at Evie.

'Hello, Mildred,' Delia said, raising her voice. 'Can we help you?'

Mildred sidled into the room. 'We're having a whip round for Hilda. She's getting married a week on Saturday.'

'Hilda?' Delia pulled a thoughtful face, pretending she didn't know who she was. Hilda and Mildred were thick as thieves, each as spiteful as the other. 'Is she one of the typing pool girls? They all look the same to me.'

Evie saw Mildred's face flush.

'Are you going to put anything in or not?'

'I think I can spare a bit of change.' Delia reached for her purse and dropped a few coins into Mildred's palm.

Mildred scowled and closed her hand around the loose pennies. 'Don't worry, Evie, I don't expect you to chip in. I know you're hard up.'

Evie's jaw dropped as Mildred smirked, disappearing before Evie could think of a smart retort.

'I'd love to give her a good smack,' Delia said.

Delia had been Evie's best friend since the first day of school. All the little girls and boys had been dressed up in new uniforms, drowning in oversized clothes that their mothers prayed they would not outgrow before year end. Agnes Coleridge knew well by then what the other mothers would whisper about her at the school gates, and she wouldn't give them more ammunition than they already had. A talented seamstress, she had sewed Evie's hem so that she had a properly fitting skirt that could be let out as she grew. Evie had cried that morning as her mother cursed and plaited her hair, pulling tighter until she'd quashed its rebellion. Ma had wiped her daughter's tears with a damp flannel and kissed her forehead roughly.

At the school gates Evie had been unsure. Most of the children seemed to know one another but the Coleridges had only just moved to Brixton from Camberwell the week before. Ma had given her a little shove towards the teacher and told her she'd be back at the end of the school day. Miss Linton was young and smiley, her glasses making her hazel eyes look like giant marbles. She was too young to know what to do when Mildred had thwarted her seating plan by refusing to sit next to Evie. Delia was the one who shoved her hand straight in the air when Miss Linton asked for a volunteer to change places.

Like a bad smell Mildred had always been there in the background, impossible to get rid of. Nothing wound Mildred up more than knowing that Evie and Delia occupied privileged desks upstairs while she languished down in the typing pool with her poor WPM and tardy timekeeping. Evie had caught her before, sneaking around her desk when she thought that Evie had left for the day. She fingered the key to her desk drawer lightly and dropped it into her pocket.

'Usual?' Delia asked.

Evie nodded as they pulled on their coats and went downstairs, emerging onto St John's Road, just up from Clapham Junction station. The street was busy as usual, buses piling down in both directions, but they were only heading to the café next door.

'Egg and chips twice and tea for two, please.' Delia waved the menu away as they sat at their usual table, delivering their order to the waitress. 'Honestly, I don't know why she bothers asking. Are you seeing Lawrie tonight?'

Evie shook her head. 'The band got a regular Thursday night gig in Soho. It'll be just another evening in with Ma. She's taken on too much piecework again and I said I'd help out.' Not that she'd have been given a choice but it felt better to imagine that her mother was like anyone else's.

'What about tomorrow after work? Fancy coming shopping? I need to get some new shoes. These ones are worn through.' Delia stuck her leg out from under the table so that Evie could see the stretched leather, her big toe almost through at the front as she wiggled it around.

'All right but it'll have to be quick. I want to see Lawrie before he goes into town – Friday nights they play at the Lyceum.' She barely saw Lawrie during the week these days; a musician in great demand, their relationship was becoming a series of stolen moments between their day jobs and the band's growing popularity.

Delia smiled wryly. 'I see how it is. Lawrie comes first. You'll be getting married before long and I'll never see you no more. You'll be spending your days baking pies for Lawrie's tea and popping out beautiful brown children for him. And you'll remember that once you had a friend who you used to have fun with but now she's a dried-up old spinster and you don't have time for her.'

'Stop it!' They were both giggling now. 'Besides you're a long way off becoming a spinster. And if I do get married then you'll get to be my bridesmaid.'

'I've been a bridesmaid. Twice. It's not as exciting as you seem to imagine.' Delia's nose wrinkled.

They both fell silent while the waitress plonked down a heavy tray laden with teapot, cups and saucers, milk, sugar.

'Tell you what we should do.' Delia lifted the lid to check on the tea, determining that longer was required. 'Let's go to the Lyceum tomorrow night and see Lawrie play.'

Evie bit back her immediate response, to say that her mother wouldn't let her. She was eighteen after all. She could leave home any time she wanted, marry Lawrie if she felt like it without having to ask permission. And she'd rather face up to Ma than lie.

'Yes, let's do it,' she said, with more resolution than she felt.

Their food arrived and Delia wondered aloud if a dress the colour of her vivid egg yolk might not suit Evie. Evie laughed and shook her head, looking up to see their waitress standing at the door just behind Delia, deep in conversation with a local bobby. The policeman had popped in to grab what looked like a sandwich, parcelled up in paper, but something in the urgency of his manner made her stop and listen in closer, tuning out Delia.

'. . . don't know what the world's coming to,' the waitress was saying, holding out the bag.

'Not the sort of thing you expect round here,' the policeman agreed. 'Something's changed, and not for the better.' He glanced at Evie as he spoke, his face flushing crimson as she held his gaze. He grabbed his paper bag and left with a nod to the waitress.

'. . . and of course even bloody Mildred's waltzing round on the arm of a chap these days,' continued Delia, oblivious to Evie's wandering attention. 'Jack flipping Bent of all people.'

'You wouldn't want to be stepping out with him though, would you?' Evie turned back to her friend. 'Nothing much going on between them dirty ears of his.' It was Evie's turn to wrinkle her nose.

'But there's been no one decent since Lennie,' Delia complained.

'Really? You're saying *that* man's name in the same sentence as the word "decent"?' Evie laughed. 'You could do so much better, Dee. You'll see, I bet you, tomorrow night you'll be batting them away. And if not you can come backstage, meet the band.' She said it as a joke but regretted it immediately.

'Oh no, no penniless musicians for me, thank you,' Delia said, before quickly looking down at her yolk-smeared plate. 'I mean, Lawrie's one of a kind, ain't he? He's got a proper job, not just scraping by playing a few tunes.'

'Everything all right?' The waitress came to clear their plates and broke the awkward silence that had descended upon the two friends.

'Lovely thank you,' Evie told her, remembering what she'd overheard. 'Excuse me, sorry, I didn't mean to eavesdrop, but that policeman who was just in – did I hear him say that there's been a murder?'

The waitress leaned down to speak in a hushed voice. 'They found a baby drowned in one of the ponds on Clapham Common. Terrible, ain't it?'

The girls nodded, wide-eyed, and the waitress carried off their empty plates.

'Who'd do such an awful thing?' Evie exclaimed, as Delia pulled a packet of Player's cigarettes and a box of matches from her bag. 'I suppose it'll be in the papers tomorrow.' She took the cigarette that was offered.

'People shouldn't be allowed to have children if they aren't willing to do what's best for them.' Delia struck a match forcefully and held it out.

'Maybe some people don't have a choice.' Evie leaned into the flame, inhaling deeply.

'I don't believe that. Most of us know to do what's best. You know that.' Delia blew a smoke ring, thinking it over. 'That place is still open, isn't it? Where your mother went.'

'I suppose.' Evie didn't like to think about what might have happened if her mother had abandoned her there, at the home for unmarried mothers just off Clapham Common, not far from where this poor mite had been found. 'Either way, they deserve to suffer, whoever'd do that to a child,' she said finally.

As they packed up their things and prepared to head back to the office, Delia slid the topic of conversation back to the more pleasant territory of fashion. They decided to go along to Arding and Hobbs before they had to go back to work. Maybe she should think about buying something new to wear to the Lyceum. Lawrie might be working, but it would be their first proper night out together, and Evie wanted to look the part.

3

The room they'd left him in was inhospitable, but he supposed that was the point. Barely bigger than a large cupboard, it was windowless and even colder than outside. Lawrie watched his warm breath swirl like smoke beneath the harsh flickering of the bare fluorescent tube above him. Its relentless blinking made his head ache. The rectangular table before him was empty but for his own hands, fingers splayed across its dull scratched surface and his fingernails full of the same pond mud that coated his trousers and his coat. He wanted to change, to wash away the dirt on his hands that was making him itch. He'd asked for a glass of water but the policeman who'd left him in the room had not replied. Distant male voices could be heard along the corridor and he felt a coward for not going out there and demanding they give him something to drink.

The detective would be in soon. That's what they'd told him. And it wasn't like he was under arrest. He'd given a brief account by the side of the pond, his head turned away from that sad bundle on the grass. The constable had asked him to walk back to the station with him and give a full statement. Lawrie hadn't been able to think of a good enough excuse for not complying.

Eyes open, eyes closed, it made no difference. He could still see that tiny hand and the curl of black hair fixed in his vision, hear the hiccupping sobs of the dog walker. He'd turned away when the foolish constable began to unwrap the blanket that Lawrie had closed up out of respect, staggering back with a yelp as he discovered why the woman was so upset. Served him right for doubting them, but for a moment Lawrie had hoped – had prayed – that he *was* mistaken. The woman had been allowed to leave once she'd given her brief version of events. She reckoned she hadn't touched the body, though how she could have seen the baby without doing so, Lawrie didn't know. He could still feel the weight of the bundle in the muscles that ran up his right arm, could still feel the swift release of that tension as he'd let it fall to the ground.

The door opened. 'Lawrence Matthews?' Lawrie nodded as the man entered. 'Detective Sergeant Rathbone.'

The detective was smartly dressed, his jacket pressed and his dark navy tie neatly knotted. In his thirties, Lawrie guessed, with a narrow moustache and pockmarked cheeks that cried out for a beard. He sat down opposite and placed a manila folder between them. He didn't look at Lawrie.

Rathbone pulled out a notebook, a packet of cigarettes and his matches, laying them neatly by the folder. He took a cigarette from the pack, not offering one to Lawrie. Striking a match, he sucked the flame into the open tobacco before shaking it out and dropping the spent match to the floor. There was no ashtray, and Lawrie found the careless action irritating, his lips turning upwards a little as he realised how ridiculous it was to bother about such a small thing.

'What you smiling at?' Rathbone looked up suddenly.

'Nothing, sir.' Lawrie leaned back and swallowed, his throat dry. 'I just had a silly thought. That you could do with an ashtray.'

Rathbone cupped his hand behind his ear. 'I can't make out what you're saying, son. You'll have to speak more clearly if you're going to keep on in that accent.'

'Yes, sir.' He slowed the pace of his words, but not too much in case Rathbone thought he was trying to be funny.

The detective pulled a pencil from his jacket pocket. 'From the beginning then. Since this morning. I want to know exactly what you did, who you saw, everything. I'll tell you if I want you to stop.'

'Since this morning?' Lawrie's forehead creased as he thought back. 'I left the house just before five o'clock.' He paused and Rathbone waved him on. 'Went to work same as always.'

'You're a postman?'

'Yes, sir.' Could this man not see the uniform he was wearing? 'Sir, is there any chance of a glass of water?'

Rathbone arched an eyebrow. 'Don't change the subject. I said I'd let you know if I wanted you to stop talking.'

Lawrie blinked. 'Yes, sir. Well, after I clocked off, around midday, I decided to go for a ride to Clapham Common.'

'Why there? Why not Brockwell Park, somewhere closer to home?'

'The sun was out and I thought… well, the Common is where

I first stayed when I arrived in this country, see. I like it there.' His palms were sweating now, thinking about that damned parcel. Guilt must be written all over his face.

Rathbone put down his pencil and looked him directly in the eye for the first time. 'This all seems rather coincidental, don't you think? Way I see it, you had no good reason for being by Eagle Pond.'

'Wrong place, wrong time is all. I mean, do I need a purpose to use the Common? Does anybody?' Oh God, he was babbling now. 'Sir, it's just a park after all. I was just passing by, I go there all the time. At least twice a week.'

Rathbone stared; Lawrie looked away first.

'It is rather convenient though, you must admit.' Rathbone tapped ash from his cigarette onto the floor. 'A baby dies, through some manner or other, to be determined. Perhaps it's a loved child, perhaps it was an accident or the family couldn't afford a burial, perhaps at least the person responsible for her death regrets it. That's what it looks like to me. He doesn't want her body to go unfound. So he waits until dark before placing her body by the edge of the pond, knowing that people walk their dogs there. Then he starts to worry – what if she isn't found? He goes back to check and lo! There comes our Mrs—' Rathbone checked his notes. 'Barnett. Perfect timing. She panics and, seeing a man on a bicycle, she runs towards him seeking sanctuary. He steps in and rescues the body as planned so it gets a proper burial. Make sense?'

'The last bit, about her running towards me, yes.' Lawrie sat up and leaned forward. '*She* was the one who found the…' His tongue wouldn't form the word. He'd barely touched the child but he could still feel the slip of its – *her* – skin against his, the catch of her tiny fingernails as he'd snatched his hand away. 'You've got the woman's statement right there in front of you. *She* was there first. *She* was the one made me go and look.'

'Because there was no one else there.' Rathbone fired out the words. 'No one around but a nigger on a bicycle. You think she'd have gone to you for help if there'd been a single other person around?'

'I don't… I mean… what's that got to do with me?' Lawrie felt small all of a sudden, unprepared. He took a breath and tried to order his words. 'I just went there for some fresh air, not looking for trouble.'

'So when she says that you cycled past the pond once, then again not ten minutes later, you don't think that seems like odd behaviour?'

'No! And I did a good thing, helping that woman. I coulda just cycled off, you know? She was acting all hysterical, like a madwoman. And that dog of hers… But I could see there was something very wrong. I stopped to help.'

'So what? You're some kind of good Samaritan then?' Rathbone sneered.

'My mother brought me up to have good Christian values.' Lawrie fought the rising wave of humiliation that made his skin prickle. His mother would be horrified if she could see him now.

More notes were made with that sharp pencil. Lawrie tried to swallow but his mouth was too dry; he coughed uncomfortably as his breath caught in his throat.

'You saw the baby though.' Rathbone watched him keenly.

'Definitely one of your lot, wouldn't you say? Maybe it wasn't you after all, maybe you were just helping a pal?'

Lawrie looked down as his hands, clenching them together in his lap to stop the shaking. They'd told him he wasn't under arrest but he couldn't imagine that the interrogation would be any more severe if he had been. He understood now why they had brought no water to him. He was supposed to be uncomfortable. They thought he was a murderer. At best Rathbone had him down as an accomplice. The air around him felt as thick as the bright yellow custard that Mrs Ryan served up for pudding on Sundays, too dense to breathe properly. Should he just confess? Tell Rathbone about the parcel he'd been delivering? But what if the woman at Englewood Road denied it?

'You've nothing to add?' Rathbone paused before letting out a weary sigh. 'If I find out later that you've lied, things will go very badly for you, you know?'

'I've told you everything I know.' Lawrie blinked as more smoke was blown in his direction. Rathbone's cigarette, together with the nicotine haze hangover from the jazz club the night before, was making his eyes smart. At this rate he may as well take up the habit himself. 'I don't know what else I can tell you. Speak to my boss. He'll tell you that I spent the morning doing my job, not hanging around that pond like a ghoul. Talk to my landlady. I never been married, never had a child.' Just in time he stopped himself from mentioning Evie. He didn't want this man going round to the Coleridges', questioning Evie about him while her disapproving mother looked on. 'I'm not the only coloured person in London, you know.'

'You're speaking too quickly again.' Rathbone raised his voice. 'You seem agitated. Why is that?'

'I'm not agitated, I'm just tired is all.' He hadn't slept for over twenty hours and fatigue was dulling his mind. 'I'm hungry. And thirsty. I been here for hours and not even been given any water to drink.'

'This ain't The Ritz, son. We don't do silver service here.' Rathbone barked a laugh. 'Look, you was the only darkie any-where near the scene of the crime. No good reason for being there.' Rathbone leaned forward until Lawrie could smell the stale tobacco on his breath, overflowing like a used ashtray. 'Between you and me, I don't give two shits about some dead nigger baby. Too many of you around here already, but the law is the law. A suspicious death has to be investigated and someone has to hang for it.' He let the threat catch in the air before going on. 'Tell me what I need to know and I can make sure it don't come to that. I'll get you a bed. A hot meal. A fresh brew. I tell you something, our cells are far more comfortable than some of them places your lot live in.'

Lawrie felt his chest tighten as his eyes pricked with tears; he would rather die than shed them in front of this man. He thought of his brother; Bennie would never let a man like Rathbone get the better of him.

Rathbone opened his mouth to speak once more but was interrupted by a knock at the door. A younger man entered, also in plain clothes but less senior by the way he held his body as he nodded apologetically at Rathbone, who sighed and stood, following his colleague outside. Lawrie checked his watch again.

It would be dark out now. Would the evening papers have printed the story already? What if the police had given his name? Donovan would kill him if they mentioned that he worked for the Post Office. A journalist had already been snooping around outside the police station when Lawrie propped his bicycle up against the wall of the building, hoping that the location was enough insurance against it being nicked. The reporter had been too focused on firing questions at the constable to have really looked at Lawrie, but that had been hours ago now. Plenty of time for someone to let a name slip.

'Looks like you can go.' Rathbone reappeared, his face barely moving as he spoke. 'But don't think this is the end of it. I'll be seeing you soon enough, I expect.'

'Yes, sir.' Lawrie stood and made for the door before the detective could change his mind. Whatever had gone on outside that interview room, it had not pleased Rathbone.

A uniformed constable showed him to the spot where his bicycle had been moved to, dumped on its side in the yard at the back of the police station. Even in the dim dusk light he could see the slashes in the tyres without having to bend down. A glance over his shoulder showed Rathbone and the younger detective watching him out of the lit window. He wouldn't give them the satisfaction of a reaction.

He pulled his scarf up around his freezing ears and began to walk with his bicycle towards the main road, some sixth sense slowing him as he reached the corner, just in time to pull back. The journalist of earlier had multiplied into a huddled pack, puffing away on their cigarettes as they watched the front door of the police station. The bicycle wobbled beside Lawrie as he made a detour, discovering new streets that were both unknown to him and yet sadly familiar. Terraced houses with the occasional shocking rubble-filled gap. During the day these were children's playgrounds, the bombed-out buildings becoming forts and castles. Dens full of hidden treasure. In the darkness they were macabre ghosts of London's recent past.

Lawrie stopped off at a corner shop and bought a bottle of ginger beer. He'd be late for tea and Mrs Ryan would wonder what kept him. Evie too, when she arrived home from work before him. The thought of having to relive the whole experience again, seeing their faces fall in horror and pity, drained the energy from his legs.

He kept on going for the best part of an hour, but only three streets from home he wasn't sure he could make it. There was an alleyway on his right and he managed to bump the bicycle along the broken cobbles, shouldering open a wooden gate that was only half on its hinges, given up since it no longer had a house to guard. What had once been someone's backyard was overgrown with weeds and Lawrie slumped down into them, his back resting against the brick wall that still stood. A loose brick and a hard smack removed the bottle top, a helpful trick that Aston had taught him. The ginger beer burned his throat but it was a comforting fire, warm and familiar, and the sugar punched him in the face, waking him from his daze. He belched and wiped his mouth.

The skeleton of the house clung upright to the air, glass and debris littering the ground around him. The outhouse had survived almost intact, though its wooden door had decayed. Lawrie could see the porcelain bowl, the half-light of the distant moon glancing off its curves. This was a city marked by death, the darkness finally catching up with him. Everywhere you walked in London you could see tragedy through absence: construction sites that had sprung up to replace the missing homes, the widows who looked older than their years, that missing generation of men that had forced a desperate government to send their mayday overseas. Lawrie was only in the country because of the misfortune of others. He'd thought he was coming to help, same as Bennie had. 'Doing his bit,' as they said here.

The English just got on with life as if this was normal. Stiff upper lip, put on a brave face and pretend that if you can ignore the horrors of the past and think only of the future, then you too will be all right. This was an island of crazy people.

His mother had encouraged him to leave home but his brother had not warned him. Bennie Matthews had sent weekly letters home from his RAF base, addressed to their mother but always with a coded postscript for his younger brother. Never had he hinted as to what a dour country England was. Those postcards – what a dupe! Buckingham Palace in its pomp and splendour, the brilliant white dome of St Paul's, the famous Tower Bridge sitting regal beneath bright blue skies that could have been painted on. Bennie was a real-life hero, posting his tales of derring-do, camaraderie and local dances before flying back across the Channel to save the Motherland. He'd never said a bad word about the country he'd died trying to save.

Lawrie tipped the last few drops of liquid onto his tongue, laid his head in his hands, and sobbed until his ribs ached. The sky was clouded over in a reddish-brown smog, not a star in sight to wish upon, but he closed his eyes and prayed. He wanted to go home. That was it, a simple statement that he'd denied for so long because home, as he had known it, no longer existed.

He regained control and wiped his face, dampening the corner of his handkerchief with spit just as his mother had done when he was a little boy, hoping that evidence of his weakness would not be apparent to anyone when he got home. It was late, and he made his way carefully, keeping to the warren of alleyways before going in through the back gate of Mrs Ryan's house.

'Where on earth have you been, love?' His landlady called from the kitchen, opening the back door for him. 'I left a plate in the oven for you if you want it? You must be starving. Spam fritters and spuds.'

'Long story.' He propped the useless bicycle up against the wall and left his boots outside by the door. He rested his forehead on the cold bricks of the outside wall until he felt composed, then went in.

The meal was coming to an end, Arthur and Derek sitting there with plates that were empty but for the grease stains. Arthur was caught up in the full flow of conversation and Lawrie was grateful to slink past them all without attracting any attention. He hung his coat up in the hall and took his time about returning to the warm kitchen.

'I tell you quite honestly, Mrs Ryan,' Arthur was saying as he entered, 'I ain't never been so insulted. Not in all my life.'

Arthur shook his head vigorously to emphasise his point. Usually Lawrie would be fighting back a smile, since Arthur took offence to something or someone at least once a week; twice last Tuesday alone. God only knew why the man had bothered to leave Trinidad when he seemed so miserable in London. Lack of funds seemed to be the only reason he was still here. In his forties, Arthur never spoke about his long dead wife, and Lawrie only knew of her existence through Mrs Ryan: landlady, matriarch and confidante – as long as you didn't mind your secrets being shared within the boundary of her four walls.

'So what did you say to him?' Mrs Ryan asked, as she placed the teapot in the centre of the solid wood table that dominated her kitchen. She smiled at Lawrie, nodding to the cooker. 'Sit down, love.'

'What did I say?' Arthur continued. 'I say nothing. What else can I say? That man knows he can say whatever he likes to me. *I* say just one single word back to him, I'm out the door 'fore I can get my coat and hat on. He talks to me like I'm an imbecile 'cause he knows I just got to stand there and take it.'

'What happen now?' Lawrie asked Arthur, pouring himself some tea and cupping his hands around the mug.

'*My* father would have beat me half to death, I even dared to *think* what this fella say to me.' Arthur got into his stride. 'I mean, is this what they teach children in this country? To give cheek to their elders 'stead of respect?'

'Not in my day,' Mrs Ryan agreed, placing a warm plate in front of Lawrie.

'You should offer to kick the shit out of him,' Derek advised, fitting a filter-less cigarette into his mouth. 'I'll give you a hand if you fancy teaching anyone a lesson.'

'Derek!' His mother nodded towards the large crucifix that watched over them from the wall opposite, brought over on the boat from Cork not quite twenty years before, though they all went to the local C of E these days.

'Self-employed' was how Derek described himself. A businessman. He ran a stall on Brixton Market and at least half his income was legit. *A spiv*, Evie called him, and Lawrie could see that he looked the part. His luxuriant moustache was as styled as his hair, worn parted on the side and greased down. He wore more cologne than was welcome; it made Lawrie's nostril hairs twitch.

Don't trust him, Evie had warned Lawrie. *He'll say he's doing you a favour but he'll ask for double in return.*

He wasn't so bad, Lawrie had decided, and there had been benefits to living with a petty criminal. Derek was generous enough to share his ill-gotten gains. A whole extra block of cheese last week, a pound of bacon the week before. Arthur and Lawrie usually went halves on their monthly bottle of rum, which Derek gave them a good price on. They were still one of the few houses on the street to have a telephone installed, a lifesaver for Lawrie. A last-minute booking could only be accepted if the club could actually get hold of you. And, of course, running deliveries for Derek was adding to Lawrie's savings. He had almost enough saved up for a small wedding and a honeymoon – Mrs Ryan had reckoned on him needing seventy pounds plus a bit extra for spends. Except that because of Derek, Lawrie had been on

Clapham Common at the worst time possible and he couldn't marry Evie if he was sent to gaol. Or the gallows.

The fritters had gone hard in the heat of the oven, their undersides wet with grease that turned Lawrie's stomach. He tried to force down some of the mashed potato instead, washing it down with hot tea.

'Well, I heard something scandalous,' Mrs Ryan announced. 'I was at the butcher's earlier, trying to get a bit of beef so we can have a decent roast this Sunday. But no, they'd run out they told me. I tell you, I swear they keep back the good stuff. He's a mason, Fred Yorke, you know. I wouldn't be surprised if the best cuts go to his little friends from down the lodge. Them and their funny handshakes…'

'I tried to join once,' Derek reminded her. 'Bastards blackballed me. Can you believe the cheek of it?'

Lawrie could well believe it but he kept his mouth shut.

'While I was queuing, there were two women in front of me. Talking about a body being found up on Clapham Common. In one of the ponds. A child! And one of them had the ridiculous notion that it might have been there since the war. Kept hidden by the weeds. You do hear of it, people clearing away the rubble and finding people buried beneath, but not a child. The parents would have been going wild! Though the woman was ever so snooty with me when I pointed that out to her.'

'It wasn't a child. It was a baby.' Lawrie's voice sounded strange in his own ears, as though someone else was speaking through him.

'A baby? You heard about it on your rounds then?'

'No.' He tried to smile, wanting to reassure her, but his lips trembled and he pressed them together until they stilled. They'd find out soon enough. Better it came from him. 'I found it. I found the baby. In the pond.'

Mrs Ryan stared at him oddly, as if she was struggling to comprehend his words. 'Dear God.' She looked to the crucifix and crossed herself. 'Lawrie, you poor love! So is that why you're so late home?'

'I had to give a statement to the police and you know what they're like.' He tried once more to smile, still not entirely successfully. 'I was just glad to get out of there in time. I need to be in Soho for eight o'clock.'

'What? No, you can't, Lawrie. You've had a terrible shock and you've not slept since yesterday. You can't possibly go and play tonight. Your mother would never forgive me for letting you out in this state.'

Mrs Ryan was a similar age to his mother and they shared several things in common: both widows, regular churchgoers, recovering slowly from a war that had left their families irreparably damaged. They exchanged letters frequently, a few thousand miles of ocean unable to prevent them from finding a sympathetic friend in one another.

'I have to. Johnny's expecting me. I'll see Evie and then head out. I should be home by midnight so it's not all bad.' And then up at half four again to serve the Post Office. 'Besides, it's better to keep busy. Stop me thinking about it.'

'I don't know how you do it, I really don't.' Mrs Ryan shook her head. 'Well, at least clear your plate first. A good meal'll sort you out. Gosh, what a shock! You just never know what each day will throw at you.'

With that he had to agree. The only thing he did know for certain was that playing his clarinet, immersing himself in music for a few hours, would take his mind away from the day's events. He just couldn't dispel the prodding fear that he was going to be facing DS Rathbone again. This wasn't the sort of thing that went away with only slashed tyres to show for it.

Extract from the *Clapham Observer* – Monday 21st June 1948

'WELCOME HOME!': SONS OF EMPIRE DRAW CLOSE TO THE MOTHERLAND

Today, 492 men, women and children, from Jamaica and other parts of the Caribbean, will land at Tilbury in Essex, setting foot on British soil for what, for some, will be the first time. Others are returning from leave to rejoin our armed forces after fighting for their mother country during the most recent war. In preparation, the *Evening Standard* sent up a plane to greet them yesterday as their ship, the *Empire Windrush*, entered the Thames: 'Welcome Home!' its banner proclaimed.

What is unclear yet is where these men, for it is understood that the majority of the passengers are men of working age, are to be housed. The Colonial Office were unwilling to talk to this newspaper but an unofficial rumour indicates that a number of new arrivals are to be bussed to the Clapham area. Government officials appear to be unsure exactly why these men have been allowed to travel when no plans have been put in place for them. The Ministry of Labour has assured concerned MPs that all men who are not already bound for Air Force, Army or the mines will be interviewed and assisted in finding work. Suitable accommodation will be provided for them until they are in a position to find their own.

A Lambeth council representative had this to say: 'It is my understanding that these men are British subjects, invited here to help rebuild our great nation. Let the people welcome them into our community and be grateful that Lambeth has been chosen to benefit from a few more good, strong pairs of hands.

1948

Lawrie waited patiently, leaning against the rough brick of the pillbox wall and trying to look as though he belonged. He occupied his time by watching the people walking past, staring down the curious glances of the pale-faced Clapham locals as he tried once more to calculate how far his money would go until he found work. If the bus was four pence from here to Coldharbour Lane, then how many journeys could he make until he was broke? How much would he have to pay out for rent, and how much was a loaf of bread? Not to mention the expense of clothing. He was all right for now but once the seasons changed he'd freeze to death unless he invested in jumpers. He was already cold.

They called this summer because they knew no better. God help him when winter did come; he was shivering in the sunlight. People hurried along in their coats, umbrellas in hand, hats firmly pushed down and pinned into hairdos that had never been vexed by humidity like his mother's each Sunday as she fixed it up for church. Lawrie wore both the new jumpers she'd bought him as a leaving present, the arms of his jacket tight, unused to the bulk. He had thought of buying a scarf earlier in the day, only the shop assistant had made him feel anxious as he followed him around Menswear. Just as well.

Almost all of his savings, thirty pounds, had been spent on his ticket to England. On the dockside his mother had waved him off, pretending that it was a sneeze that sent tears scattering down her cheeks. As the boat was tugged away, he'd already had second thoughts, looking down into the water and knowing he was quite capable of swimming that short distance back to dry land. But then Aston had slung a loose arm around his shoulders and suggested they both go below deck and seek out some entertainment, by which Aston mainly meant gambling and drinking. If there had been more than a handful of women on board he'd have meant them too.

Here was the man now, Aston, his jaunty walk unmistakeable as he came out of the tube station, pausing to light his cigarette. Lawrie lifted a hand in greeting as his friend crossed the road.

'Where you been all day, man? I just come from the labour exchange and Moses said you never showed your face.'

Lawrie jabbed his right thumb upwards, indicating his injured eye, now swollen and ripe, a nasty cut below. 'I won't get me a decent job looking like this. I can leave it a day or two, go down there when I don't look like trouble.'

'Up to you, only don't be complaining if you end up cleaning out toilets or some such low-paid nonsense. You gon' miss out on all the good jobs,' Aston warned. He took a lengthy pull on his cigarette, as if he was trying to inhale all its nicotine in one lungful, then dropped it beneath his foot. 'Let's go. The boys are heading out into town tonight and I need to change me shirt.'

Lawrie had no intention of going out drinking again, not after the night before, but he followed his friend to the entrance of the shelter. He hated the place, hated that they'd been shoved down into the bowels of the city, unexpected guests that no one knew what to do with. His mother had said that Britain was an orderly place, that everything ran like clockwork compared to back home, but from what he had seen, this country was anything but organised. A plane had greeted them as they sailed up the Channel, Lawrie and his friends crowding onto the deck to look up in wonder. He had thought it an impressive gesture, excitement growing, until they'd arrived in Tilbury the next day to discover that nothing was ready for them.

One hundred and eighty steps led them down, a twisting helter-skelter; it could have been the entrance to Hell and he'd not have felt more terrified. It was getting easier, though. The day before, the first night down there, Aston had abandoned him, frustrated by Lawrie's slow two-footed progress as he clung to the railing, men flowing around him like a stream around a rock, the babbling of water replaced by the kissing of teeth. He still felt relieved when they reached the bottom, trying to forget about the tonnes of earth above his head and the rumble of the tube trains that passed close by, bringing commuters back from the city at the end of the working day.

The woman they'd nicknamed Rita Hayworth was carrying a pile of clean sheets along the corridor as they walked towards Fremantle, humming a popular song that he knew would be stuck in his head for hours. All the bunk rooms were named for naval captains, laid out like they were still at sea. Her heels clipped the concrete floor and he could barely see her face over the tower of linen.

'What on earth happened to you?' she asked, seeing Lawrie's eye.

'Oh.' Lawrie touched his wound gingerly. 'This? You'll think badly of me.'

'You were fighting?'

'Sort of.' He looked at Aston who shrugged and began to walk away. 'More like I got hit and didn't get back up. I wasn't expecting it though, the fella caught me by surprise. Mistook me for Aston. Since we all look the same...'

She looked him up and down: half a foot taller than her, lean and clean shaven. Then she looked over at the departing figure of Aston who was stocky with a neat 'tache. 'But you look nothing alike.'

'No,' Lawrie agreed, his face brightening into a wide grin. She blushed as she realised he'd been joking. 'The fool who hit me could barely stand, let alone see who he was hitting. I'm embarrassed, tell the truth, getting knocked over by a drunk.'

'What had Aston done to him?'

'Talking too much, as usual. To the girl behind the bar. This fella decided he didn't much like it is all.'

'And you took his punishment.' She nodded. 'Sorry, I didn't catch your name?'

'Mine? Lawrie.' He shook the hand she held out from beneath the sheets. 'Sorry, miss, I should be helping you with that load you got.'

'Call me Rose.' She let him take the bundle from her. 'If you could just pile them up over there. When I've finished later on I can take a look at that eye if you want. I'm not a nurse but we've got a first aid kit. You need that cut cleaning properly.'

Lawrie smiled and left her to it, dumping the sheets where she'd indicated before finding Aston, already on his bunk and reading that evening's *Standard*.

'What's news?' Lawrie climbed up to the bunk above.

'Maybe I should be asking you that.' His head poked out, grinning up at his friend.

'I was just being friendly.'

'Yes, well you shoulda checked her left hand first. You too late, my friend. But in more general news rain is forecast for tomorrow. Though that is an everyday state of affairs in this country, I must warn you. Buy an umbrella, you'll get some use out of it.'

Lawrie's head was beginning to ache as he rested it down upon a pillow that was barely thicker than a folded piece of cardboard. Damn that fool Aston, getting him into strife before they'd been a full day on dry land. He'd known as soon as they'd walked into that pub that it was a bad idea. They weren't welcome, no matter what that newspaper article said.

Sonny stopped by. 'You comin' out tonight, boys?'

Aston laughed. 'You only just met me?'

'No thank you,' Lawrie replied. 'I had enough excitement last night.'

'Boy, don't be like that. Come on out. We goin' to Soho. Johnny say there might be work there. They lookin' for musicians.' Sonny reached up and poked Lawrie in the side, making him squirm.

'You serious? He's still on about forming a band?' Lawrie sat up.

Sonny shrugged. 'Worth a look. If not then we go back to the labour exchange tomorrow, nothing lost.'

It was tempting. To earn a living from playing music… well, it was a dream that Lawrie had never thought might come true.

'Let me get my eye fixed up first but yes, then I'll come.'

'No problem.' Sonny winked as he saw Rose walking towards them. 'Man, I wish I get punched in the face if I get a woman like that tending to me.'

Lawrie ignored their sniggers and followed Rose into the first aid station, set up in what had been a makeshift infirmary during the war. Rose told him this as she sat him down on a wooden stool, turning to grab her standard issue first aid kit.

'Did you come down here then?' he asked. 'During the bombing?'

'No. We were living on the other side of the Common back then. We had our own shelter out the back, before we got bombed out. Not a direct hit, thank goodness.' She tilted his head up to the light. 'Did you make any attempt to clean this? It's a right mess.'

'A little.' His head had been throbbing and it had been so late when they'd arrived back the night before that even the rickety bunk had been too enticing. A splash of cold water after using the lavatory had been the extent of it.

'You could have fooled me. Hold still.' She held onto his head as she applied iodine to the cut.

'Jesus Christ!' That innocent ball of cotton wool felt like a poker straight out of the fire. 'What the hell is that?'

'Language! My mother would have given you a right piece of her mind if she'd heard you talking like that.'

'Mine too,' he admitted. He took a deep breath and held it as Rose carried on, making sure that the wound was clean before releasing him.

'So where were you last night?' she asked. 'Not round here surely.'

'Yes, actually. Just in that pub down the road, on the left.'

'I know the one. What did the man look like? The one who punched you.' She dabbed cool cream on his eye, the chill of it making him jump once more.

He thought about it for a moment. 'Shorter than me but not by much. Dressed pretty smart. Black hair. Sort of like Cary Grant in *The Philadelphia Story*. And he wore a ring on his right pinkie. That's what cut me.'

'Cary Grant, eh?' She busied herself tidying the supplies away. 'I don't know about him but there's quite a few chaps with dark hair round here.'

'True,' he agreed. 'And you lot all look the same to me.'

She laughed. 'Yes, well, I shall remember that when you walk past me in the street next week and don't give me a second glance.'

'As if that could happen!' Was he flirting with her? He'd never been much good at it before but she was smiling. Maybe some of Aston's charm was rubbing off on him.

'Have you found anywhere to live? After you leave here, I mean?'

'Not yet. I need to find a job first.'

'What job did you have back home?'

'Nothing. I mean, I was studying.' He glanced up at her, wondering if she thought him just a child. He wasn't sure how old she was. Probably older than his nineteen years if she was married. 'My mother wanted me to go to university but money was tight so, you know, here I am. Come to London, seeking my fortune.'

Rose giggled. 'You sound like Dick Whittington. And I'm sorry but these streets are more likely paved with rubble than gold.'

'I noticed.' He sighed. 'Still, a few of the fellas think maybe we can actually get a band together and earn money from it. I play clarinet. My father always wished he'd become a professional musician instead of working in an office. I suppose I'd like to fulfil his dream now that he's gone.'

'You're lucky,' she told him, 'to have something like that, something you love. I worked in a factory during the war, believe it or not, and I loved it. We had a right laugh and I felt like I was doing something proper, you know? Something useful. But Frank, that's my husband, he wanted things to go back to normal when he came home. Married women don't work, he says, not unless they need the money, it'd look bad on him. He doesn't even like me doing this only I insisted. So long as his tea's on the table when he gets home from work I reckon he can't really complain, and he's in the pub most nights anyway.'

'You don't look old enough to be married, you don't mind me saying.'

She smiled. 'No? I suppose not. We got married straight out of school. Frank was heading off to war and we knew there was a chance that…' Her voice trailed off.

'You were lucky,' Lawrie said. 'He came back.'

'Yes.' She took a step backwards, away from him. 'Anyway, you're all done. Pop up in ten minutes if you want feeding before you head out. And curfew is midnight so don't be late back.'

'Thank you.' He held out a hand and she shook it.

'D'you think you'll stay long?' she asked. 'In England, I mean.'

'I should think so,' he replied. 'Don't you read the paper? This is our home now.'

'Then welcome home,' she said.

13th March 1950

Dear Aggie,

I do hope all is well? I just got your letter and I have to say you've got me worried about you, darling sister.

If you want my advice, and your letter implied that you did, I think it's time to let Evie stand on her own two feet. She's eighteen after all. We weren't still living at home at her age, were we? And she won't have it half as bad as you did! She's got you and that young friend of hers – Delilah or whatever. That boy next door, when's he going to come good and get down on one knee? You should have a word with him, like Ginny Leyton's dad did to her young chap years ago. He was down that aisle faster than a whippet round the track at Wimbledon! Of course, nobody would be foolish enough to mess with old Leyton but I reckon you could give him a run for his money.

Besides Evie and all that, how are you? Is everything all right? We shouldn't leave it so long between visits, you and me. I did love seeing you so last year, both of you, and it does get a bit lonely out here on my own. Who'd have thought I, city girl through and through, would end up living alone at the bottom edge of a Devonshire village? You should come down this summer, stay as long as you want, there's plenty of room. Don Waters was asking after you when I saw him last. You remember him? Bought you a half a shandy that night we went to the pub?

Anyway, I look forward to hearing from you soon.

Gertie xx

4

Evie had left the kitchen door open so that she could feel the draught if her mother returned earlier than expected. Ma had run out to deliver a dress that she'd taken up for a woman over in Stockwell, so she wouldn't be long. It wasn't that Ma was against Lawrie as such; he was allowed to accompany Evie to the Astoria, and they were allowed to go out for a Sunday afternoon stroll in the park, but she'd never allow this, the pair of them huddled so close together that an ant would have struggled to find a path between their bodies.

Lawrie leaned on Evie's shoulder, his head lolling against hers more out of exhaustion than any amorous intention. She'd never seen him like this, quiet and staring into the distance. Nothing she'd said so far seemed adequate and she felt as though she was just repeating the same inanities over and again.

'They can't honestly believe you had anything to do with it. I mean, they don't have any evidence. Nothing links you to any baby, let alone that poor child. They're just desperate. They need to look as if they've done something. Taken some action.'

'He didn't want to let me go,' Lawrie reminded her. 'If that other fella hadn't come in, I reckon I'd still be there, sitting in one of those cells he told me about. It wasn't his decision, you know. He wasn't happy about it.'

Evie lit a cigarette and took a deep drag while she tried to think of something better to say.

'Bad habit.' Lawrie shook his head as she blew out smoke, though she was careful to angle her breath away from his face.

She grinned. 'I never had a dad before and I don't want one now, thank you very much.'

He put his arm around her shoulders and she leaned into him, pushing her nose into the wool of his coat. The wool held the scent of smoky bars and a faint hint of woody cologne that had belonged to a previous owner. He was a gentleman, was Lawrie Matthews. Too much so sometimes. He never made a move on her, was careful where he put his hands even when she could tell that he was holding himself back. 'Sorry I don't have much time tonight.'

'Don't worry about me. Only you shouldn't be going out, not when you've had such a shock. You look exhausted. Like you could fall asleep standing up.' She reached up and caressed his jawline; he hadn't even shaved, which was most unlike Lawrie.

His chuckle was frail, the ghost of a laugh. 'I wish I could tell Johnny that I'm staying home. If I could, I'd stay here with you. We never seem to get any time to ourselves these days.'

'What about tomorrow?' she asked hopefully. 'Delia and I were talking and it seems ridiculous that we've never had a night out at the Lyceum. I know you're playing, but you'll have breaks, won't you? I can come backstage and you can show me around.'

'Your mother will let you?'

'I don't see why not.' She sounded more confident than she felt.

'And you'll tell her that I'll be there too? I don't want her to think we're going behind her back or she'll not let you out again until we're married.'

Evie's heart almost stopped as he reached the end of his sentence. Was she reading too much into a single word? He squeezed her tighter and she threaded her fingers through his and tried not to show him what she was thinking.

'I think Ma's decided that she likes you, you know. She asked after you only this morning. I think she just likes to put on a show, making sure we don't get ahead of ourselves.'

'Conniving woman.'

'Just be glad she hasn't taken against you. If she had then she wouldn't leave this house without locking me in my bedroom first.' It was an exaggeration but not far off the truth. Evie had let her mother down before and it had taken months to earn back that trust.

'She's not so bad.'

'She has her moments.' Evie tilted her head towards his until he got the message and kissed her properly.

'You think the baby's mother is someone like yours?' Lawrie pulled away first, his mind elsewhere. 'I mean, a woman in a similar predicament, if you know what I mean.'

'Left holding the baby after some chap's done a runner? Only maybe she knew better than Ma did and got rid?'

'Evie, I'm sorry, I didn't mean...' His face was stricken with remorse.

'It's all right.' She waved his words away as if they didn't bother her. 'Everyone else will be thinking the same anyway. It makes sense.'

She'd picked up a *Standard* on the way home but Lawrie had been able to tell her more than the short, hurriedly filed report. The paper hadn't divulged that the baby was coloured but they had given an age. Evie had assumed on first hearing that the baby must be a newborn but apparently she – the baby girl – was almost a year old. Someone had cared for her for months before her death, had kept her fed and clothed and probably even loved her. Evie couldn't imagine what must have come over the person responsible, to suddenly do such a thing. A baby was a precious gift. Not everyone had a choice in the matter, Evie knew, but Ma had coped on her own. And, as Delia had pointed out, there were institutions for babies who couldn't be cared for at home. None of it made sense.

'Do you think it could have been an accident? We're assuming the worst but the baby could just have been ill. Maybe the mother panicked and didn't know what to do. You said the blanket looked hand-embroidered.'

'With flowers,' he confirmed.

'So somebody cared. Sometimes babies just die and it's not anybody's fault.' Evie's hand shook a little as she lifted the cigarette to her mouth.

'What if it was someone we know?'

For so long the only other coloured person Evie had ever known was an intensely serious engineering student from Nigeria who had lived on the next street over when she was fourteen. He'd spoken to her sometimes if they'd been waiting at the bus stop, just chit chat, but she could sense within him the same loneliness she felt, knowing that she didn't quite fit in. She'd never told him that her father had also been a student, just like he was. She worried that he'd ask her questions and she'd have to admit that her mother refused to talk about him at all.

'How dark was her skin?' Evie asked. 'Darker than mine?'

'I don't know. It's all mixed up in my head. If it weren't for that Rathbone fella telling me that she was coloured I'd think I'd imagined it. I can't believe that anyone we know would have done this, can you?'

''Course not.' Evie ground out her cigarette on the step. She'd have to remember to take that in later and hide it in the bin, else Ma would have words. 'You know, there are plenty of local women who've had a little secret flirtation. I mean, look at Aston. How many women have you seen leave on *his* arm at the end of a night?'

'*Aston?* That'd be even worse. An awful lot of fellas round here would not like the idea of one of their women being with one of us *darkies*.' His mouth twisted into a grimace as he spat out the slur.

And if anyone knew about that it was Lawrie, Evie thought, suddenly sour. 'You think there'd be trouble?'

'Let's just hope that it turns out like you said and the baby died of measles or some such illness.' His lips brushed her forehead and she knew he didn't want to talk about it any longer.

Evie's grandfather had been in the police, not that she'd ever known him. Ma had gone alone to his funeral and afterwards they'd moved into this house – his house – which had been the

Coleridge family home when Ma was a child, before she'd been thrown out for getting pregnant and bringing disgrace upon the family name. Evie had never really understood how a man could choose so easily to cut off his own flesh and blood, but she'd learned to give up asking questions after Ma had told her that if she brought the subject up again, she'd take her down to the graveyard and leave her there by his headstone until she got her answers. Ma did keep one photograph of the man on the mantelpiece, dressed in his full police uniform. His stern expression made her glad she'd not had to meet him. The thought of a man like that going after Lawrie made her feel sick.

She checked her watch. 'Ma'll be home soon. Are we just going to sit here talking?' She placed a hand on his thigh and felt him jump as though burned by her touch. 'You don't want to…?'

'I just – I don't want you to feel like you have to is all. Not on my account.'

'Will you ever stop thinking of me as a little girl?' she snapped, her tone sharper than she intended.

'I don't.'

She refused to look at him until he reached over and turned her head gently with his fingertips.

'I just want to do right by you, Evie, that's all.'

'Then stop treating me like I'm made of glass. I won't break if you touch me. Properly I mean, instead of all this careful patting and stroking. Why do you have to be such a gentleman all the time?'

He kissed her hand and laughed as she rolled her eyes. 'Why you want to rush everything?' She kept her mouth shut, forcing him to go on. 'I just don't want you to think that I'm only interested in one thing. I messed up before, I know that. I don't want to lose you again.' He paused for a moment. 'I love you, all right? And if we're going to be together for the rest of our lives then why do we need to hurry?'

'You love me?' Her first reaction was to smile, then to laugh. 'I love you too.'

'You do?' Now he was all smiles, leaning forward to kiss her.

There was enough light from next door to see Lawrie's eyes blacken as he came closer, the hand on her back pulling her into his body as his left hand slipped between the unbuttoned lapels of her wool coat. She opened her mouth to his as his palm brushed against her breast and she began to feel a little light-headed.

Was it wrong to want this? She knew what her mother would say: that she should know better, amongst other choice phrases. But Lawrie was different from other young men; different to anyone else she'd met. He wouldn't do anything she didn't want him to. He had asked permission to hold her hand the first time, for goodness' sake.

The front door banged suddenly, breaking them apart, Lawrie on his feet in seconds. Evie smiled as she watched him leap in one clean motion, his arms pushing him up easily as he vaulted the wall. He allowed a second's pause as he reached the summit and blew her a kiss. Then he was gone and she heard the creak of Mrs Ryan's kitchen door as it opened then closed.

'You been smoking again?'

Evie had to catch herself from falling backwards as her mother whipped the back door open.

'Sorry, Ma.' She picked up the butt and stood to throw it in the bin.

'You will be when you catch a cold. You shouldn't be sitting out there in this weather.'

A solid woman, thick through the middle and short enough to be called stout, Ma was the very definition of no nonsense. She never bothered with make-up these days and always sniffed whenever Evie wore a little herself, though she did hold her tongue now that Evie was bringing in her own wages. Ma had never married, which was Evie's fault. She called herself *Mrs Coleridge* to avoid receiving that look that people, especially women, liked to give her. Of course, once they found out about Evie she did still get that look, but there was nothing to be done about that. Back in their Camberwell days, when she occasionally stepped out with a chap who hadn't yet found out about her daughter, Agnes Coleridge's hair had been her crowning glory, thick and curly. Now she kept a shorter, more practical hairstyle, the locks falling no further than her second chin, the ebony losing its battle with the salt.

'I take it Lawrie was round?' Ma filled the kettle from the tap.

Evie stared at her mother's back, not sure if she was in trouble or not. 'Is that all right? We were only talking.'

'I do remember what it's like to be young, you know, and I wasn't born yesterday. He's not quite as quick as he thinks he is when it comes to jumping that wall. And you should take a look in the mirror.' Her mother raised her hand to her chin.

Evie mimicked her action, her cheeks flushing as she felt the irritated skin. Damn Lawrie for not shaving. 'Sorry, Ma,' she confessed.

'I'm sure you know better than to do anything foolish. Nóirín next door seems to think he's a sensible chap. Got his head screwed on right.'

'He wouldn't take advantage if that's what you mean,' Evie confirmed. 'In fact,' she said, taking a deep fortifying breath, 'I was wondering if you minded me going to see him play in his band tomorrow night. At the Lyceum. There'll be lots of people there, and Delia. She'll be my chaperone, if you like.'

Her mother snorted a laugh. 'If I was going to choose a chaperone for you then Delia Marson would be at the bottom of that list.'

'Please, Ma?'

'Do what you want. You're old enough. For pity's sake, Evie, take some responsibility for yourself, won't you, you're a grown woman.'

'Yes. Fine then, so that's where I'll be tomorrow night.'

'Good. Well, since you've nothing better to do you can help put away those dishes and then bring me a cup of tea. I'm off to put my feet up.'

Some things didn't change.

The Friday morning papers shouted of the macabre discovery in the pond, their articles more floridly written now that their intrepid journalists had had time to pry information from the local community – including Gladys Barnett, whose dog had made the initial find. Evie checked three different newspapers on her way to work but she was relieved to find that they hadn't printed Lawrie's name.

They had given the baby a name: Ophelia. It was mentioned

in more than one paper, as if there'd been a committee meeting held between all the journalists the night before and this was what had been agreed upon. The girl in the pond; the body in the rushes. Only it sounded wrong to Evie's ears. They must have taken the name from Millais' work. She'd seen the painting on a school outing to the Tate Gallery, but Hamlet's Ophelia had been a grown woman, making a choice. This was an innocent baby.

'You gonna pay for one of them?' The newsagent had spied her. She chose one at random and handed over the coins.

She was just on time for work, slipping off her coat and hanging it up quickly before grabbing her notepad and pencil and following Delia downstairs. Every morning they headed to the floor below to receive any special instructions from Mrs Jones, their supervisor.

They joined the other partners' secretaries at the back of the room, Evie noticing more than one of the typing pool girls look her way, whispering amongst themselves. They were talking about the baby – 'pond', 'Clapham Common', 'murder'. Did they know more than the papers had printed? Maybe the rumours had begun regardless. What would they be saying once they knew that Lawrie had found the baby? She'd have to tell Delia when they got back up to their own office, safe from the malicious gossipers.

'I don't know why anyone's surprised,' Mildred said, raising her voice. There was no doubting the target of her attack, not when she was looking right at Evie. 'My dad says this country's going to the dogs. If we let in all sorts then we've got to expect that things change, and not for the better.'

'You seem to know a lot about it, Mildred.' Evie's voice came out weak and she cleared her throat. Mildred must have been letting her views known before she'd arrived; that was why those girls were staring at her like that.

'I went to the church service last night and the woman who found her was there.' Mildred's face shone with glee. 'She was telling everyone that they'd arrested one of you lot. A darkie.'

Evie opened her mouth but she didn't know what she could say without giving Lawrie away. She gripped the edge of the table behind her as her body weakened, panic taking over.

'So what?' Delia butted in. 'They'd've questioned anyone who was there, whether they did it or not. It might not have anything to do with him.'

'Girls!' Mrs Jones marched in and everyone turned to face the front. 'Some hush, please.'

Delia put a hand on Evie's, squeezing it briefly.

Extract from the *Evening Standard* – Friday 17th March 1950

GRUESOME DISCOVERY ON CLAPHAM COMMON AS BABY FOUND DEAD

More details have emerged regarding the body of a baby that was found yesterday, hidden in the shallows of Eagle Pond, Clapham Common.

The discovery was made by a local woman, whilst walking her dog in the vicinity of the pond. Police have confirmed that the woman is unrelated to the case, and that they are already questioning a person of interest, a man who was discovered close to the scene.

The child has yet to be identified but we are able to disclose that the baby was female, 10-12 months old, and well cared for. It is still unknown whether her death was a consequence of foul play or accident. She was found wrapped in a white woollen blanket with a floral decoration so it is likely that she had a mother who cared for her.

Police ask that anyone who has any information call in at their local police station as soon as possible. If anyone knows of a baby of the right age who hasn't been seen in a while, or was in the area on the evening of Wednesday 15th March, or the early hours of Thursday 16th, please think carefully – you may have seen something which at the time seemed unimportant but may be vital to the police investigation.

There will be special prayers said for the deceased at both St Mary's and St Barnabas's churches again this evening for local parishioners who wish to pay their respects following a generous turn-out yesterday.

5

There were far better ways of spending a Friday evening than waiting on a cold station platform for an unreliable friend. But here he was, freezing his arse off at Waterloo as legions of buttoned-up office workers marched past him on their way home to the suburbs. They all looked the same: harassed and hunched over, their grey overcoats and hats giving the appearance of a national uniform. The shoes were the only clue; the most reliable way to tell boss from employee, the tenant from the landlord. Lawrie's own dress shoes were polished to a high shine but the soles were not original and the leather was cracked along the throat line.

Aston had rung him up on the telephone on Tuesday. A lifetime ago, it felt like. *Few more days and I'm a free man! Thing is, I need somewhere to stay...* And how could Lawrie say no? Aston had served in the RAF since 1942, side by side with Lawrie's brother until that last fatal mission, just weeks before the war ended. But of course, Aston was late. He hadn't been on the train he should have been on which meant that he'd missed it, probably 'cause he'd got chatting to some pretty girl on his way to the station, and they'd both have to wait for the next. As usual. Lawrie checked his watch; he still had time.

He felt a debt to Aston, not least because it was one of Aston's RAF contacts who had finally managed to get Lawrie his Post Office job. It had been Aston who had come down to Kingston two years earlier and talked Lawrie on to that boat, convinced Mrs Matthews that it was a wise idea to send her remaining son overseas where he could seek his fortune. She'd cried as she waved her surviving son off but she had a new husband to look after her now. Lawrie had only been in the way, Mr Herbert from the grocery store leaping at the chance to comfort the handsome widow as she grieved for her eldest son. *How well it all worked out in the end,* the new Mrs Herbert wrote to her son months later, taking his good news missives at their word.

The ship had been full of men seeking their fortunes, many of them having fought in the war just like Bennie and Aston, escaping the island life that was too quiet now that they'd experienced adventures across Europe and beyond. Why bother gambling with your life if all you did with your winnings was put it into the small farm that you could have had anyway, just by staying at home? Like Aston, they'd seen the advert in the *Gleaner* – cheap tickets back to the Motherland – and jumped at the chance to return. There was safety in accepting the embrace of the depleted British armed forces, crying out for men who'd already been trained up.

Walking the deck and breathing in air that was as salty as the unfathomable ocean beneath him, Lawrie had listened to tales of big houses, pretty girls, the wages even the most menial of jobs paid. He'd expected to arrive in the country of his schoolbooks, to walk the wide thoroughfares he'd seen on newsreels and have conversations, perhaps in a real English pub, with people who spoke like they did on the wireless. It would kill his mother if she ever found out how the English actually lived. Eating spam and shopping with coupons; living in bomb-damaged houses. It would destroy her if she could see her only living son now, if she knew that the police suspected him to be involved in the murder of a baby. She could never find out.

The next train pulled in and he watched the passengers pour out of the doors. He waited until the last old man hobbled off, no Aston in sight, and was about to give up when he felt a tap on his shoulder.

'Fancy seein' you here.' Aston looked smart in his demob suit, kitbag in hand, newspaper wedged under his arm and a smile on his face.

'What the...' Lawrie looked around him. 'What train you come on?'

'Came in over there.' Aston pointed vaguely to his right. 'We got time for a drink? I'm parched.' He put on a hoarse voice.

'Then you shoulda got here earlier. I got no time, not even for a quick one before you ask.'

'What's up with you?'

'Nothin'.' Worried that the police would come back and question him. Exhausted from not sleeping. 'I just got a lot to think about at the moment.'

'Lyceum, right?'

Lawrie nodded.

'Good-looking women there, I remember rightly.'

Aston was what Evie referred to as a ladies' man when she was in a good mood, an alley cat when he annoyed her, which was often.

'You was so drunk the last time you could barely stand. How you remember a thing?' Lawrie reminded him. Last time had been New Year's Eve and he'd had to throw himself off the stage mid-song to stop Aston from getting punched by some fella who'd taken against Aston dancing with his girl.

'Never forget a thing, boy. The women, they call me the elephant.'

Lawrie rolled his eyes and groaned.

'Get your mind out the gutter! It's 'cause I never forgot a pretty face.' Aston laughed and clapped his friend's shoulder hard so that Lawrie winced. 'Talking of which, how's your girl?'

'She got a name and I know you know it.'

'I apologise sincerely. How is Miss Evelyn Coleridge, might I ask?' Aston put on his best English accent and they both laughed as they negotiated their way across the concourse towards the exit, the crowds around them watching the departures board intently, waiting for it to announce their passage out of the city. A few commuters turned to see who these chaps were who dared to be so carefree and loud. 'We walkin'?'

''Less you feel flush enough for a taxi – 'cause I do not.'

They emerged from the station. Seven o'clock on a March evening and the skies over the city didn't even have the decency to turn black at night, the stars staying away in protest.

'Evie is well, thanks for asking. She's coming to the Lyceum tonight so behave yourself when you see her. She might even start to think better of you.'

'I doubt that.' Aston's words were mumbled as he tried to light a cigarette, his head bent to the match sheltered between his cupped palms.

'Well, you can at least try. You never know when a person gonna change their mind. I thought Evie's mother couldn't stand me but apparently she decided I'm not so bad.'

Aston snorted. 'That woman's a dragon, guarding she daughter like she's some fairy tale princess. Must be gettin' to realise no white fella'll marry the girl so she make do with a light skin boy like you.'

'Why you make everything an insult?' Lawrie elbowed his friend in the side.

'Just saying how things is,' Aston corrected him. 'Mrs Coleridge sees some dark skin bastard like me go near her daughter, she'd lock her away 'til the end of time. Man, she would never let me cross her threshold 'less she had a knife ready to cut me man parts off. You, on the other hand, are the educated son of a government man, or whatever your papa was. You got a steady job. Perfect son-in-law.'

'Steady job? Keeping hold of it's all I can manage these days.'

Aston acted like Lawrie had it so easy but, until now, he'd only ever known the RAF, had been safe in his barracks, insulated from real life. He'd not yet had to sit in those interviews with some shoddy-looking fella looking him up and down as he decided without even bothering with the CV, or asking a single question, that this nigger before him would not be working in his establishment.

'You work too hard, boy. You all right for money?'

69

'Fine. I been doin' some extra deliveries for Derek, you know?'
He knew that Aston felt a responsibility towards him, though he
wished sometimes that he didn't. Sometimes he just wanted to be
left alone, to get on with things his own way without Aston or
Mrs Ryan or anyone else feeling like they needed to intervene.

'All right. But you just say the word if you need anything.'

A light drizzle began to fall as the men crossed the road and
turned onto Belvedere Road. Lawrie pulled up his collar as they
walked the dingy damp street that ran parallel to the Thames,
the beginnings of the new Royal Festival Hall blocking the view
to the river. Each time he passed, he had to wonder at the vast
building site that was slowly transforming into a great beast of
a concert hall. It beggared belief that they would leave people
without proper houses to live in and spend a fortune on a so-
called festival, as if people could come and dance themselves out
of strife and not worry that they were still having to use ration
books and make do.

They climbed the steps up onto Waterloo Bridge as raindrops
landed on Lawrie's cheeks like saltless tears. Back home when it
rained he had liked to stand outside and let it baptise him, the
water cleansing, rejuvenating. English rain made him feel grubby,
falling from that filthy sky, its dank grime sinking into his skin
until he felt contaminated.

'You ever goin' tell me what is the matter?' Aston said, breaking
the silence.

Aston would find out soon enough. Lawrie wiped his face with
his hand and forced himself to speak, recounting the events of
the past two days to his dumbstruck friend.

The Lyceum was still fast asleep when they arrived via the stage door. Aston dumped his bag on a rickety wooden table in the green room and sat down with a sigh. They were the first to arrive, the other band members cutting it fine as usual. The Johnny Sands Band they were called. This was their regular Friday night slot and they usually had at least one booking on a Saturday as well. It had taken a while to build their reputation but Johnny had ambition, as well as an eldest son back in Jamaica who he wanted to bring over when funds allowed.

Telling Aston had lifted a weight, and while the shadow of his macabre discovery still loomed over him, Lawrie already felt better. He always enjoyed playing this dance hall. Although the audiences in the poky Soho clubs were more appreciative of his talent, he felt immersed in the history of this old theatre, part of something that had existed long before his time and would continue on long after. He could imagine the ghosts of Shakespearean thespians and beautiful opera sopranos who used to draw the crowds. Maybe one day people would recall hearing Lawrie Matthews at the Lyceum. He'd happily give up his job tramping the south London streets if he could make a decent living from music but chance would be a fine thing. Of all of them, only Johnny was getting by as a musician. His wife, Ursula, worked in a factory five days a week while Johnny looked after their two young offspring. She was home by four, and then off went Johnny. He could play the piano as well as sing – hotel bars paid his wages on the nights when the band wasn't playing. But there wasn't much call for a solo clarinettist and no one would pay to hear Lawrie sing. He could hold a tune all right, but Johnny had that rich tone to his voice that made people close their eyes as they listened, letting his voice sink into their souls like butter melting on toast. Lawrie would have been embarrassed to get up before an audience and be mediocre.

Aston reached into his bag. 'Got any glasses?' He pulled out a bottle of Scotch. 'I reckon we could both do with a little pick-me-up.'

At the back of the room was an ancient cast iron sink, five mismatched mugs drying on the side. Lawrie chose the two least tannin-stained, and handed them to Aston who poured two fingers of whisky into each.

'To a new life in London.' Aston raised his drink, Lawrie doing the same.

'Cheers.'

They clinked their mugs together and drank, the fumes burning the hairs in Lawrie's nostrils before the heat hit the back of his throat.

'So this all happen yesterday, right? You had any more trouble today?' Aston asked, not ready to change the subject. 'The cops, I mean.'

'Not a word. Nothing new in the papers either, I checked.' Lawrie's hands had trembled as he tried to turn the pages of the newspaper that morning, expecting any moment to see his name printed there in black, sweat lifting the ink from the paper onto his fingertips. 'It's strange, they still never mentioned that the baby was coloured.'

Aston shrugged and lit another cigarette. 'Maybe they're worried about vigilantes. Don't we know at least one fella would like an excuse to take matters into his own hands?'

'You think there'll be trouble? 'Cause it'll get out at some point. Can't see how it won't.'

'Almost certainly. You better watch your step. They get desperate to tie someone to this, you're the obvious choice, 'less they know a lot more than they're letting on.' Aston leaned over and refilled Lawrie's mug. 'Your boss know?'

Lawrie nodded. At work that morning he'd gone straight to Donovan and told him everything that had happened the day before. Arthur had suggested it was better to come clean, even though Lawrie hadn't technically been on duty at the time. He'd still been wearing his uniform and it wasn't out of the question that Rathbone might go sniffing around his place of work, asking after Lawrie. Donovan's lips had pressed so tightly together as he listened that they'd vanished entirely into his chubby face. None of it had happened during his shift but he could see in his boss's narrowed eyes that he had no room to mess up from now on.

'You think that Rose could—'

'No!' Lawrie snapped the syllable, surprising himself.

'I not sayin' you would—' Aston stopped talking as they heard voices echo along the corridor.

'You here already?' Johnny walked in first, taking his role as band leader seriously. He was a smooth talker, five years older than Lawrie.

'Just about.' Lawrie greeted Moses and Sonny as they came in, shaking hands with Aston.

They'd formed the band right after arriving in London, though they'd run through a few changes of personnel since. Moses and Sonny were always together; drums and a double bass required transportation and a portion of the band's earnings was always allocated to keeping Moses's rusty old van on the road. Al was the current fifth member, on trumpet.

'I should go. Head out front to where the action is.' Aston winked.

'See you later?'

'Perhaps, but if I disappear it only means I got lucky. 'Sides, it might be wiser to steer clear of Evie. You know I only put she in a temper.'

'What is it with you two?'

Aston walked off without answering.

Lawrie had never been able to fathom a reason for this enmity that existed between the two people closest to him. He guessed that something had happened between them at the party where he'd first introduced them. The party which had ended so badly. The one thing both of them had in common was a reluctance to talk about whatever had happened, and the last thing Lawrie wanted was to dredge up bad memories of that night.

Johnny was warming up his fingers at the piano in the corner and Lawrie began to assemble his clarinet, massaging grease lightly into the cork. It would need replacing soon, he noticed; it was wearing as thin as his nerves.

'They asked for upbeat tonight.' Moses unpacked the sheet music. 'Nothing slow 'til the end. Get everybody dancing and sweating.'

'I could use something upbeat meself,' Al said, eying up the bottle of whisky on the side. 'Anyone else have a knock on the door this morning?'

Johnny stopped playing. 'Police, you mean? Last night. I was already out but they scared the hell out of Ursula. Lucky she had the pickney right there when she answered the door so they leave her be. They still was acting sus though. Wanting to know when Joy was born, where she was born, all that. They went all along the street. Ursula know 'cause she stood out on the step and watched 'em.'

Al blew out a lungful of relief. 'I thought it was just me.'

'You never told me they come to the house.' Moses frowned. He and Sonny shared a room in the same house that Ursula and Johnny's family called home, the landlord making the most out of each inch of space.

'You was out at work, same as me,' Johnny shot back.

'Well, yes, but—'

'This is 'cause of the baby, right? Clapham Common?' Lawrie interrupted them.

Al sparked up a rollup as he spoke. 'They never come right out and say, but they was asking me where I was Wednesday night. Who I was with. And I asked around at work and seems like they only been asking those who are of the Negro persuasion. Not a single white fella knew what I was on about.'

'The baby was coloured,' Lawrie told them, his eyes trained on the floor between his feet, his chest growing tight as the men fell silent. Without looking he could feel their eyes, all of them staring at him.

'They tell you that?' Johnny finally broke the tension.

'They wouldn't answer a single question I asked them,' Al said, sounding put out. 'Why they tell you?'

Lawrie reached over and poured himself another measure of whisky. 'They didn't tell me; I saw her,' he said quietly. 'I was the person who found her in that pond.'

Johnny whistled, its arc descending; Moses's mouth fell open.

'They took me to the police station for questioning but they let me go,' he said, the words tumbling out now. 'It was a woman walking her dog who saw her first. She come running and I didn't realise what she'd seen until I was almost in the pond myself.'

'Just as well there was a witness,' Al said, laying a hand on Lawrie's shoulder. 'Else I reckon they'd have questioned you a damn sight longer. Way that copper spoke to me, I started to wonder if I did it after all, in a moment of madness, and I just forgot.'

'They think one of us did it though,' Moses pointed out. 'You think we know who did it? Could be someone we're acquainted with.'

It was a sobering thought. The baby had to have at least one black parent and there were only so many black people around, most of them men. Lawrie only knew a few women whose skin was dark enough: Evie; Ursula Sands; another woman whose name he couldn't remember but had travelled over on the boat with them and now lived at the far end of Somerleyton Road. More were starting to turn up each month, their husbands saving up enough to bring them over, but, barring the birth of Johnny's youngest, he couldn't think of anyone else who'd had a baby in England yet. It was as if this child, Ophelia, had been spirited to Clapham Common from somewhere else entirely.

Johnny made a show of checking his watch and stood, signalling that it was time to go even though Lawrie could see from the wall clock that they still had ten minutes. 'Come on, fellas. For now, we got to trust the police will catch the real culprit. We all are sensible upright citizens after all. None of we got anything to do with this.'

They followed their leader onstage, Lawrie feeling temporarily soothed but he wasn't sure if it was the effect of the whisky or the new knowledge that he wasn't alone. If the police were questioning everyone then it meant that they hadn't singled him out. He'd begun to wonder if Rathbone had only been biding his time, searching for scraps that could be woven into a chain to trap Lawrie. He knew there were people out there who'd be happy to help; at least one person, who he'd not seen or spoken to in months but who had every right to bear a grudge.

He shook off those dark thoughts, closing his mind to them, and it was just the usual adrenaline that kicked in as he reached his spot on the stage, sliding his feet along the solid wood until he found a comfortable stance. The nerves would pass soon enough, but those moments before they started playing, before the music took over, always made him feel like one of the tigers at London Zoo. He'd gone there with Evie the previous autumn. She had leaned against the railing and stared in awe at the big cats, lounging lazily in their compound, but all he could think was how sad they looked, these magnificent beasts now tamed and cowed by their conquerors. If anyone could understand the tigers it was him, trapped in a foreign land and reduced to parading himself before a paying audience. But then he'd raise his clarinet, the reed rough against his lips, and feel like a king.

They warmed up the crowd with a little calypso, Johnny

strumming a Lord Kitchener tune on his guitar before segueing into swing for the mainly white audience. The night had barely started but the place was already half full. The men had all slicked their hair back with pomade, the humid air heavy with the scent of Brylcreem. The girls were dolled up in their best dresses, coiffed and coy, every one of them with an eye on the entrance, watching for the next eligible gent. He couldn't see Evie but she'd be there somewhere, trawling the dancefloor as she'd said to him, trying to find Delia a lad to dance with so that she could abandon her friend for Lawrie later on. Aston would be sticking close to the bar, ready to fritter away his money on the first pretty girl who dared to dance with a coloured man; the sort of modern woman who had their own place, or shared with girls who wouldn't judge them for bringing home a man who they'd likely never see again.

It surprised Lawrie how many of these women existed in London. Back home such behaviour was unthinkable. An unmarried girl who spent the night with a fella back in Kingston would be ruined. Here it seemed like a badge of honour. What the men could do, the women could do just as well.

For the first time in a long time he found himself thinking of Rose. Maybe it was the opening bars of 'In the Mood', a song they hadn't touched in almost a year, after Sonny protested that he was hearing it in his dreams. It was a guaranteed crowd pleaser and Rose had been humming it that first day as he'd inched his way down that hated spiral staircase into the deep level shelter beneath Clapham Common.

He'd played those notes a thousand times or more, and his fingers moved of their own accord as his mind slipped back into the past. Rose Armstrong. She had looked so respectable, dressed neatly in her WVS uniform, the ring finger on her left hand banded in gold. Lawrie had admired her at first; had even been grateful for her help. He'd thought she was a friend.

That had been his first mistake.

1948

Evie watched them from across the street, concealing herself amongst the steady flow of commuters who rushed in and out of Clapham South tube station. The newcomers emerged, blinking into the bright sunshine, through a secret door that she'd never noticed before, hidden in plain sight. She'd only seen men so far, which was disappointing; she'd hoped for a girl, someone her own age who might need help settling in. Someone who would be grateful to learn how things worked in London, who might become a friend. Ma had told her that they'd have a shock in store, these newcomers who had travelled from so far away, that they would take a while to get used to the city. Maybe that was why Evie's father had left, unable to settle in and think of London as home. Ma said there was no point talking about him since Evie would never meet him; he didn't even know that Evie existed.

When she'd been younger, Evie had hoped he would come back to London, that one day there would be a knock on the door and he would be standing there with his suitcase and a brilliant white smile. When Ma punished her, often for something as slight as spilling a drink or grazing her knee in the school playground, banishing her to her bedroom to think on her mistakes, Evie made up stories about him. In her daydreams, her father was an African king and Ma was a wicked witch who had stolen Evie away from his kingdom. He had spent years searching for her and when he found her they would go back to his palace and she would eat all the food she wanted, wear only new dresses and all the people of the land would envy her.

These days she knew better. She would never meet him and that was for the best. Too much time had passed and she'd be embarrassed for him to see them now, her and Ma. He was clever, she knew that much. He'd been over on a mathematics scholarship from Sierra Leone according to Aunt Gertie who sometimes let go of tiny fragments of information after a third gin. No doubt he had made his fortune by now. An impressive man who would be disappointed to find his daughter with aspirations no higher than to become a qualified secretary; her mother a charlady who took in piecework to pay the bills.

A couple of large army tents had been set up on the grass close to the shelter entrance and a Union Jack had been raised to make it clear that this was an official operation. Government sanctioned. They weren't expecting trouble but Ma had told her to stay away just in case. She thought that Evie had gone to the pictures with Delia, a thrilling lie that had been stammered out over breakfast. Delia had been kept home from college for the last two days with a stomach virus so there was no risk of her running into Ma by accident. Anyway, how could she stay away? She didn't know anybody who looked like her and now here were a whole group of people whose skin was even darker than hers. An entire ship full of them!

She watched on but still she could see only men. Evie bit her lip, not sure what to do. *Men have needs,* Ma said. Evie had to be wary of being left alone with a man, even though she wasn't quite certain what would happen if she was. What would she say to a strange man from another country anyway? She had no idea, but she didn't want to walk away. Instead, she made a bet with herself. She'd walk up to the next female volunteer who came out. She could pretend that she had some questions about the WVS. She was sixteen now, old enough to join if she wanted.

She crossed her fingers and almost immediately a woman did appear. She wore the usual WVS uniform but this woman made it look glamorous, the lines fitting her body as if it had been tailored. Her hair was immaculately coiffed in neat red waves that sat below her standard issue hat. She led out her charges confidently, six men whose laughter floated out to Evie on the breeze. They all wore jackets despite the fine June day, the temperature having risen to well over seventy. One of them threw a ball into the air, casually, spinning it higher each time it left his hands. The jackets came off and were set down as markers to form a playing area. Evie found herself walking across the road before she knew she'd taken a step, like Karen in *The Red Shoes,* though her plain brown lace-ups were anything but fit for a princess.

The woman had set herself up with a fold-up chair, carried out from the nearest tent by one of the men. She sat and fanned herself with a slim pamphlet or magazine, her legs crossed. Her shoes were standard brogues but with a small heel and polished to a shine. She flicked her hair back as she watched the men remove their shoes and socks, piling them to one side. She was knowingly beautiful and Evie noticed more than one of the men throwing a glance or a comment her way, trying to attract her attention.

The game got underway and, with the men distracted, Evie moved closer. 'Excuse me?' The woman didn't hear her so she took another tentative pace forward as though playing Grandmother's Footsteps, wanting the woman to turn but uncertain what to say when she did.

'Rose?' A male voice called out from behind her, both Evie and the woman turning. 'Have you seen my notebook?'

'You left it lying about. Marge almost threw it away.' The woman, Rose, reached under her chair and retrieved a battered blue book, a pencil trapped within its pages.

The man looked at Evie and she felt her cheeks redden beneath his stare. He looked only a little older than her but he was different to the boys she'd gone to school with. Years of rationing and light deprivation had left them scrawny and pasty. This man was well-fed, tall, and the sun hit the angles of his cheekbones so that it seemed to her, in that moment, that he was the source of the light.

'Can we help you?' Rose walked over.

'Oh. I just…' What was wrong with her? She'd been standing across the street for half an hour, thinking of nothing but clever introductions, and now she couldn't formulate a simple sentence? 'Sorry, I…'

'You're from round here?' the man interrupted.

'Yes. I live over in Brixton.' She pointed in the general direction.

Rose handed him the notebook. 'Lawrie, stop pestering the poor girl. She only came to see what was going on, didn't you?'

Evie nodded, feeling foolish. The man called Lawrie smiled at her and for almost six seconds she forgot to breathe. She felt sweat gather in shallow pools under her arms, trapped by the restrictive white blouse that was prescribed as uniform for her secretarial college. She should have made more effort with her hair, not just scraped it back and forced it into a bun. Compared to Rose, she felt like a little girl.

'Why don't you come and watch?' Rose invited. 'This lot are mad about cricket and it'll be nice to have a girl to chat to.'

Lawrie fetched another chair for her, setting it beside Rose's before running off to join his friends. As Evie sat she caught the glint of Rose's gold wedding band and felt inexplicably relieved. Evie shielded her eyes from the sun with her left hand and watched the cricketers. Lawrie was fielding, the closest man to her, his notebook tucked into his back pocket. She noticed that the smile never left his face. She would know. She couldn't wrench her eyes from him.

Ten minutes into the match, the batsman hit the ball flying high into the air, Lawrie running backwards, his eyes tracking the arc of the spinning orb, raising his hands as it aimed towards him, answering his call. Cheers and groans erupted and Rose clapped, Evie following her lead. Lawrie looked over with a proud grin, winking at Evie as she smiled back and doubled her applause.

'Someone's got an admirer,' Rose commented. 'He's a handsome chap all right, our Lawrie.'

Evie blushed again but she was so captivated by Lawrie that she didn't think to read anything more into those words. She couldn't imagine that behind Rose's polite smile might lie a thin coil of jealousy.

6

Evie still got a thrill every time she saw him play, watching the other women stare up at him, admiring his good looks and his smart suit. She liked to stand far enough back that he wouldn't notice her, not wanting the spell to be broken.

The dancefloor was full now, men and women flirting as they spun around, shouting and laughing over the music as they shook off the working week. Friday night in London town; survivors of war. Who knew better how to live than those who had not so long ago wondered how short that life might be?

'Bloody boiling in here.' Delia fanned her face with a creased beermat. 'I'm sweating like a priest in a brothel, as my old Pa says.'

'Don't let my mother hear you talk like that. She says it's not ladylike to speak coarsely. Of course she also claims that only men sweat but women glow.' Evie ran a light fingertip across her upper lip to check for moisture. Any warmer and she'd be 'glowing' off the tiny amount of powder she'd carefully applied to her face, just enough to take away the shine, not so much that her skin looked ashen.

The pair of them were standing to one side of the dancefloor, Delia not yet having seen a man worthy of a whirl on the parquet. Evie hardly got asked to dance and, on the few occasions it had happened, at least half she reckoned had been for a dare. Still, it didn't matter now that she had Lawrie. She'd worn red because it was his favourite colour It was a new dress, spotted by Delia in the window of Arding and Hobbs during their lunchbreak. Its full skirt was an extravagance, Ma tutting over the wasteful amount of material when she saw it, but even she had to admit that it suited Evie. Especially after Evie had lied about the price. As Delia reminded her, it was her own money to do with as she liked. She paid enough of her wages to Ma for the rent, she knew that, but it didn't quite quell the wave of guilt that crashed over her as she handed the notes over the counter to the shop girl.

'What d'you think of him?' Delia nodded towards a young man standing alone in the corner.

'Bit greasy-looking. A charmer, I bet, the sort who'd try and have his way for the price of a drink. A small drink at that.' Evie cast her judgemental gaze upon him. He was good-looking, she'd give him that, but there was a predatory glint in his eye that put her off. Delia always went for the no-hoper types. Her last beau, Lennie, had been with more girls behind her back than Evie could count on her fingers, and those were just the ones that Delia had found out about. She'd been besotted though, and forgave him each time until one of his conquests had got herself in the family way and, unluckily for Lennie, had a father who had the brawn and

87

reputation to make sure she was married before the baby made an appearance.

Delia leaned closer to Evie and lowered her voice. 'Then what about this one just in front?'

He was only a few feet away. Fresh-faced and young.

'He's ginger,' Evie pointed out.

'What's wrong with that?'

'Isn't your cousin ginger? It runs in the family, see. What if you ended up married to him? I'd put money on you popping out a whole brood of ginger nuts.'

The girls giggled and the lad in question looked over as he heard their laughter, woven through a break in the music. Evie looked away quickly but Delia, more brazen, held his gaze.

'Shush! He's coming this way.' Evie tried to straighten her face as Delia smoothed her skirt.

'Evening, ladies.' His smile was wide, his teeth not quite white but straight enough.

'Evening,' they chimed.

'Gosh, you two are a pair, aren't you? Chalk and cheese.' He only had eyes for Delia.

It had always been the same, right since schooldays. Delia was the pretty blonde girl with perfect flaxen pigtails, taking the teacher's praise even though everyone knew Evie let her copy her work when she was stuck. Delia was made reading monitor while it was suggested to Mrs Coleridge that her daughter might be better off in a remedial class, even as Evie sat in the corner reading *The Twins at St Clare's* and wondering how she could talk her mother into letting her go away to boarding school. Their schooldays might be over, but instead of the teachers it was young men who now reminded her that she was different.

'D'you come here often?' Delia asked the young man.

'Every Friday. I'm Sid.' He stuck out his hand for Delia to shake. 'Nice to meet you.'

'I'll just be…' Evie pointed vaguely in the direction of the bar, excusing herself before the situation became awkward. She could do with a drink and Sid looked too wet to make any untoward advances on Delia.

The queue at the bar was dominated by men and Evie wasn't afraid to cough delicately but insistently, hoping that some chivalrous gent would let her go ahead.

'A nice little trick.'

Evie groaned as she recognised the voice in her ear. 'What d'you want?' She looked over her shoulder into Aston's grinning face.

'A drink, that's all. It is a bar is it not?'

'Don't you have some cheap tart to impress?' Evie spotted a gap and slipped through but he followed.

'No, but I am getting a drink for a lovely young woman I've been dancing with,' Aston said, raising his voice. 'She's a real lady. Don't go in for no fakery, acting all chaste and innocent when she's anything but.'

'I'm sure.' Evie tried to laugh but it faltered in her throat.

'Don't you look down your nose at me, Miss Coleridge. I never been less than a gentleman where you're concerned. I know when to keep my mouth shut.'

She bristled. 'It seems to me you're just doing what suits you best. You keep your mouth shut because you have to, so don't act like you're doing me any favours.'

She spat the words over her shoulder before ordering her drink from a hot and bothered barmaid. She paid but when she turned to leave Aston had vanished. Logic told her that he'd do as he said and continue to keep silent but that didn't stop her from feeling anxious. She was stupid to have reacted to him at all but she could never help herself when he taunted her.

Sid had managed to entice Delia onto the dancefloor so she made her way towards the stage. She caught sight of Aston but he was deep in conversation with his lucky lady, a tall brunette, both older and more stylish than Evie had imagined. They stood face to face but so close that their hip bones touched, their lips brushing as they talked. It didn't look likely that Aston would be coming back to Brixton with her and Lawrie at the end of the night.

The set came to an end, the crowd roaring their disapproval as Johnny placated them with promises of a return. Someone switched on a recording but the music sounded tinny after the luxury of a live band. Evie discarded her half-full glass on a table and pushed on past the last few revellers who stood in her way.

'You staying up there all night?' she called up to Lawrie, basking in the curious gaze of those around her.

He grinned and jumped down to the dancefloor, pulling her against him, kissing her. She relaxed into his hold and was disappointed when he soon released her.

'Let a fella catch his breath,' he joked, seeing the look on her face. He kissed her again. 'Where's Delia?'

'She met a chap. Seems like a decent sort.'

'So we don't need to worry about her?' He steered her towards the door that led backstage and the noise of the crowd faded as it closed behind them. 'You want a drink?'

'No, I'm all right. I suppose we've only got ten minutes or so.'

The band were in the green room, sharing out the rest of Aston's whisky and lighting their cigarettes. Evie poked her head in to say hello before Lawrie pulled her along to an empty dressing room. Kept for the few occasions that the Lyceum had a famous singer, the room was set up with dressing table, mirror and chair. He closed the door firmly behind them before sitting on the rickety wooden chair and pulling Evie onto his lap. He kissed her, hard, and she felt his hand on her thigh, working its way beneath her skirt.

'You feeling all right?' She pulled away and held the back of her hand against his forehead. 'You seem rather amorous this evening.'

'Well, if you will wear a dress like this...' He plucked at the hem with his fingers and smiled. 'You look beautiful. And it's not often we find ourselves alone somewhere your mother won't come bursting in. You did want me to be more forward, didn't you say?'

'I know, I shouldn't complain,' she said, 'only I do get the feeling I'm just a distraction.'

His smile faltered. 'I was talking to the boys earlier and they've all had visits from the police. To do with...'

'Ophelia,' Evie finished, even as she felt her throat constrict at the name. 'But isn't that good news?' she asked. 'It means they're not just looking at you.'

'I had to tell them,' he said. 'That it was me who found her. Somehow I can't help feeling it's all my fault. I know how ridiculous that is but I can't help it. I felt so relieved when I found out they'd been round to everyone, even though they scared Johnny's wife half to death.'

Someone, probably Johnny, started up a tune on the piano next door, the others lending their voices to the melody. They all seemed in good spirits, none the worse for wear. Surely the whole thing would blow over soon enough. Evie knew what desperation was but murder just didn't add up. She was convinced that when the inquest was finally held it would be written up as a tragic accident, the unfortunate disposal of the body the only unsavoury element. Funerals weren't cheap, everybody knew, and for a person already struggling to put food on the table...

'And now you're the one worrying,' Lawrie accused her, taking in the expression on her face.

She hung her head in mock shame and took hold of his hand, sliding it until it rested on her inner thigh. 'Sorry,' she whispered.

They didn't have long. She dared to unbutton his shirt, just halfway, and bent her head to kiss the soft skin, feeling his breath catch as his chest pushed out to meet her lips. Her boldness left her light-headed, exhilarated and triumphant. She had wanted this for so long, to know that he desired her. To pull away and hear a soft sigh of disappointment on his lips. To give him permission when he leaned forward and pursued her once more. She was in safe hands that pushed boundaries that he had set in his own mind, his fingers causing her heart to pound as they patrolled the area a strict inch below her knicker line, his kisses keeping to the cotton lines of her bra when his mouth strayed south. They made good use of the time they had, Lawrie cursing when Johnny rapped on the door.

'Give me a minute,' Lawrie called.

Johnny chuckled. 'You got two.'

Evie shook out her skirt and buttoned the bodice of her dress as she stood. She held out a hand to Lawrie but he shook his head: 'You go ahead.'

She opened her mouth in query but then saw his fluster and felt her own cheeks heat up as she realised his problem. 'I'll see you later? I have to be out of here by eleven else I'll be late home.'

'Should be done by half ten. I can't let my girl go home alone.'

'Prince Charming.' She kissed him and left, feeling lighter as she skipped back out to the ballroom.

Delia and Sid were sitting down at a table now and Sid had bought them all a drink.

'Delia tells me your chap's in the band.' Sid looked impressed.

'He's ever so nice,' Delia informed him. 'Treats Evie like gold, don't he?'

'As he should,' said Sid.

Evie sat down and took a sip of her gin and orange, wondering if the glow in her cheeks was visible in the dim light. Lawrie would be free in less than an hour. Three was a crowd but then it was also her job as best friend to look out for Delia and make sure Sid didn't get ahead of himself.

'So I was wondering, Evie,' Sid asked her, leaning forward as

Delia beamed at the interest he was showing to her friend. 'Where is it you're from? Originally, I mean.'

Best behaviour, she reminded herself, plastering a false smile across her face.

Extract from the *Daily Mirror* – Saturday 18th March 1950

OPHELIA KILLER STILL AT LARGE

Police in London confirmed that they have released the man they were questioning over the death of baby Ophelia, though they have stated that the investigation has thrown up several new leads – police believe they have a list of potential male suspects with a connection to the area. The identity of the mother is still unknown.

DS Kenneth Rathbone spoke to the press on Friday afternoon, making the following statement: 'We would like to remind the public that any information, any tiny detail or suspicion, could be vital. Please contact the police immediately if you think you may have seen or heard anything on the night of Wednesday 15th March, or since. Our investigation is of course centred on the Clapham Common area but enquiries have also led us to Brixton and Stockwell. We believe it likely that the perpetrator of this crime lives locally.'

A special service was held at St Mary's church on Thursday evening. In attendance was Mrs Gladys Barnett, the dog walker who made the gruesome discovery. She was reluctant to speak to the press but did make a short statement, to the effect that the police had asked her to keep certain details to herself, and that she was uncertain whether the man questioned by police on Thursday has a connection to Ophelia or not. Police have maintained that Mrs Barnett is not a suspect in this case.

Members of the public can contact their local police station with any information regarding Ophelia or if they were in the Clapham Common area on the evening of Wednesday 15th March or early hours of Thursday 16th. All information will be treated in the strictest confidence and anonymity is assured.

7

'I just don't see why we have to fit our lives around his.' Evie glared at him from the other side of the wall, both of them with a mug of tea in hand to help keep warm as they leaned against their respective front doors.

'We don't, but this is his first time living in London. Properly I mean, not just visiting. Having to find a job. Somewhere to live. Wouldn't you do the same for Delia?'

Lawrie was too tired for this. After getting home from the Lyceum he'd managed less than two hours sleep, tossing and turning as he wrapped himself up in blankets like a cocoon against the weather, needle-hard rain pelting the thin glass panes of his bedroom window. Then he'd been back out onto the dark pre-dawn streets that always felt less real on a Saturday, the usual early risers of the weekday safely tucked away in bed. His mood had worsened once he'd seen that morning's paper left out on the kitchen table. He was on that list of suspects the article talked about, that much was certain.

Last night he'd thought that she understood how confused and unsettled he felt, but today she'd pulled a face as soon as he said that he couldn't take her to the pictures. He wanted to wait for Aston to return and, no, he didn't know when that might be. Yes, usually they did go to the pictures on a Saturday afternoon, but to call it a tradition when they'd been doing it for a few months was ridiculous. Maybe he'd been asking for trouble to say it in that way but she had to understand that he wasn't going to change his mind.

'He's a grown man. And it's not like Mrs Ryan can't let him into the house if you're not here.' Now she was pouting.

'She would if she was home but she's not,' he pointed out, trying to keep his voice calm. Derek had gone out for the day, probably to the football or to the pub, Arthur was at work and Mrs Ryan had popped out to the shops which, on a Saturday, usually included catching up with her friends at one of the cafés on Atlantic Road. Those ladies could chat for hours. 'He's not got a key.'

'He could bear to wait outside for a little while. Might teach him a lesson. Teach him that he can't just treat Mrs Ryan's house like a free hotel,' Evie told him. 'He's the one who chose to stay out all night. Look at the time! It's the afternoon and he's still not shown his face. He'll be all cosy in some trollop's flat somewhere.'

'Trollop?' He knew it would end badly but the sound of the word made him chuckle.

'Oh, it's funny, is it?' Evie's expression was thunderous. 'You say you love me but you never put me first, not even ahead of Aston bloody Bayley. It's not fair, Lawrie, not when we only have the weekends together.'

'Come on, Evie.' His whole body felt heavy and try as he might, he just couldn't summon any words he thought might placate her.

'Fine. You've made your choice. I hope he stands you up.' She stood on the doorstep, one hand on the frame. She was giving him one last chance to change his mind even though they were far too late for the main programme at the cinema.

'I'm sorry.' His shrug was lacklustre. It was all he had the energy for.

The door slammed behind her and he was surprised to feel relieved. At least it put an end to the argument for now. He went back inside and headed towards the kitchen, leaving the front door off the latch just in case Evie came round. She was always quick to react but she usually calmed down just as rapidly and she wasn't one to hold a grudge, though Aston would probably say different.

He sagged into a kitchen chair and laid his crossed arms on the table, resting his head down upon them. Maybe they should have just gone to the pictures. Aston could have fended for himself and Evie was right, there was no guarantee he'd make an appearance. He'd done it before, arrived in town on a Friday and then disappeared until the Sunday, only tempted back by the prospect of a free roast dinner.

With time to kill he should write to his mother, but he didn't know what to tell her. She'd be appalled if she knew what had happened to him but he didn't feel he could lie. Not when there was every chance that Mrs Ryan would want to add a postscript of her own.

He heard the front door open. 'Evie?' Hope lifted his head.

'Sorry to disappoint,' Arthur called out and Lawrie could hear the scuffing sound of him wiping his feet on the doormat. A moment later he appeared having shed his heavy coat but not the cloud of cold air that followed him inside like an invisible shadow. 'I take it you're expecting Miss Coleridge.'

'Not really. We fell out.'

Arthur examined Lawrie's expression before laughing, throwing his head right back. 'Man, I don't miss this misery. The rest maybe but not this.' The older man carried a brown paper bag, cradling it like a child. Like a baby. Lawrie's gullet burned as bile rose up.

He took a gulp of his tea, now lukewarm, and winced. 'What you talkin' about?'

'Love!' Arthur laughed again. 'You think I'm too old for such craziness? Let me sit myself down. I must say, I take more pleasure these days in lifting the weight from my feet than you young fellas take in chasing the girls.'

'Arthur, you talk like you're old enough to be my grandfather.' Despite his bad mood he felt a smile flicker on his lips.

'No, boy, only old enough to be your father.' Arthur sighed as he sank slowly into the chair, savouring the feeling of each individual muscle as it relaxed, enjoying the lightness as his body weight lifted from swollen ankles that were finally done with his long shift.

'Cup of tea?' Lawrie offered.

'You read my mind, boy.' Arthur's eyes were closed now, his

head tilted back. 'What happened anyway? Just a lover's tiff, I hope?'

Lawrie filled the kettle in lieu of answering. There was only a dribble of milk left in the bottle on the windowsill but he knew Arthur preferred his brew dark. He struck one of the long kitchen matches and lit a ring on the stove, keeping his back turned as he tried to keep his voice light. 'Just Evie wanting everything her own way as usual.'

'Typical female. You may as well get used to it.'

Even with his back turned he knew that Arthur was watching him. Lawrie busied himself, straining the cold tea from the pot in order to reuse the leaves.

'She's got a bee in her bonnet over Aston. She wanted us to go to the pictures but I thought I should wait in, case he comes back. She thinks I put him first, ahead of her.'

'I see why she might think that but he's your only friend from back home. Your only connection to your old life,' Arthur pointed out. 'Besides, you let her walk all over you now, what happens when you get married? You can forget about seeing Aston then, especially once you got children to think of.' Arthur paused. 'He does treat this house like his own personal guesthouse, turning up when he likes. It might teach him a lesson if you did just get on with your own life 'stead of waiting around for him to turn up.'

'So are you saying that Evie is right or I'm right?'

'You can't both be?'

'And that helps me how?'

Arthur shrugged. 'Was I sent here to solve all your trivial problems, boy? Just saying things as I see them.'

The kettle began to whistle, giving Lawrie an excuse to keep his silence.

Arthur placed his hands against the tea-cosied sides of the teapot as Lawrie placed it down, warming his icy palms. 'I prayed for you last night, Lawrence. This just a trial, you know? You being tested is all. You stay strong.'

'You been listening too much to Mrs Ryan and her bible stories.' Lawrie saw the reproach in Arthur's eyes and regretted his harsh tone. 'Sorry. I know you just want to help. It's not just me suffering, though. The police have been knocking on doors.' He sat, exhaustion overtaking him once more.

'I hadn't heard that. They haven't spoke to me.'

'Then you're the only black man they haven't spoken to.' Lawrie pulled a face.

Arthur's sigh was heavy. 'They decided what the culprit looks like already then? Sounds about right.' He grinned suddenly. 'Maybe they think me too old for such a caper. No woman goin' look twice at an old fella like me, they think? More fool them!'

Lawrie couldn't smile. 'What about at work? Are people talking?'

'A little. I mean, some fellas was saying that it must be the mother did it. There's that home up on the other side of the Common, you know, for unmarried mothers. Some young girl in a moment of desperation. Maybe they tried to take the child away from her.'

Lawrie nodded slowly. Evie had been born in that home. She'd told Lawrie one day as they'd walked barefoot on the grass, not far from the home on Cedars Road, and he'd just built up the courage to take her hand, feeling the soft warmth of her palm against his.

'There is something quite strange about seeing a body when the life has gone from it,' Arthur said. 'When my wife died, I could see right away she had left me. Moved on as they say, nothing but flesh left behind. The child was a different matter. He barely lived a minute or two but I wanted to see him. Stupid, but I thought that if I held him I'd discover something about the man he should have become.'

Lawrie's throat was blocked, as though the stopper from a glass jar had been jammed down tight. He had no meaningful words to offer, just frivolous and empty placations.

'I suppose I'm telling you this because bad things happen. All the time. Not just to you but to everyone. I'm not trying to compete with you, you understand, but I can imagine a little of how you're feeling. Wondering, why you? When will things get back to the way they were? All of that is normal, you know. And if you need help then just ask. Myself and Mrs Ryan at least,' Arthur qualified. 'I cannot speak for Derek. God only knows what goes on in that boy's head.'

'Mrs Ryan's been good to me.'

Arthur nodded. 'She's worried 'bout you. You're too good at keeping your feelings to yourself and letting everyone take up the attention. Like Aston. And Evie.'

'I don't mind. I'm used to it. And I don't know what I'd do if I didn't have them.' Especially Evie, he was realising. He should have put his foot down, made her come inside with him. They could have spent the afternoon together indoors quite nicely and

Mrs Coleridge would have assumed they'd gone to the pictures as usual.

'I know something that will cheer you up.' Arthur reached with glee into his paper bag.

'What you got there?' Lawrie leaned forward to get a better look.

'It was going to be a surprise but you look so damned miserable! I said that I would cook for us all tomorrow. Sunday dinner. Make myself useful and cheer up the troops. Lord knows we all need it. Everyone is so glum at the moment, not just you. I blame the weather.' He brought out a bag of dried beans, then a glass jar filled with a reddish-brown powder.

Lawrie reached for the jar, twisting off the lid. The seasoning smelled of his mother's kitchen: warmth from the pepper, garlic kicking the back of his throat. 'Arthur, I could kiss you. Where you get this all from?'

'Derek told to me the other day that some wise fella opened up shop a few stalls down from him. He got a deal with his cousin back home to send stuff over. Only been there a couple days but him almost sold out already. The English was standing around. Watching as if we mad. The crowd! I surprised you didn't hear 'bout it. Ursula Sands got in there, haggling over the last of the beans until the fella ripped the bag and split it in two, like he King Solomon.'

'Pray for the day the English discover that food can actually taste of something before you tip a pound of salt onto it.' Lawrie brought the jar to his nose once more and breathed in deeply, the spice warming his soul. 'How much did all this cost?'

'More than it should, but the man promised me that he was sorting out regular shipments. Once a week, he hoping. A real genius, this fella is. He be buying his own house in no time. No more shift work for meagre pennies for that man.'

'We should have thought of this, you know. Set up our own stall and got Derek to help us,' Lawrie said. Forget working three jobs – this fella would be rolling in money in a matter of weeks so long as he could keep up with the demand.

He heard the front door close and Arthur stood up. 'Cup of tea, Nóirín?' He took a clean mug from the tree on the side.

Nóirín? Lawrie shot Arthur a look which was pointedly ignored.

'Yes, please, Arthur love.' Mrs Ryan struggled in, arms weighed down with shopping bags which Arthur leaped forward to take.

'I was just hearing about the feast this dark horse of a man is preparing for us tomorrow,' Lawrie told her.

'Bless his heart.' She smiled at Arthur, who Lawrie could swear blushed.

Suddenly, there was a knock on the front door, more of a thump, which seemed excessive when there was a perfectly good doorbell.

'Now who on God's green earth can that be?' Mrs Ryan looked peeved, tutting as there came another great thump. 'Are they trying to batter down the door?'

'I'll go.' Lawrie got up and made himself useful. Besides, Arthur and Mrs Ryan – *Nóirín* – were looking like they wanted a minute to themselves. God only knew what Derek would make of it if there was something going on between those two.

Whoever was at the door was impatient enough to give the door another great thump, rattling the letterbox for good measure. 'I'm coming!'

Lawrie opened the door. Two seconds later he wished he hadn't.

8

She had almost turned back immediately, regretting her haste before the door had clicked closed. Then she heard the Ryans' front door shut and it was too late. She couldn't bear the thought of having to ring the bell, waiting for him to answer, wondering if he would accept her begrudging apology. She needed to calm down first. Wait until her temper had cooled enough that her pride was no longer important. She already knew that she'd let Lawrie down. He'd only wanted someone to talk to, and she could admit to herself that she wasn't even that bothered about the pictures. It was Aston who had put her in such a foul mood. Just the mention of his name was enough to make her temper rise.

The hallway was thick with the miasma of boiling cabbage, and Evie's nose wrinkled in distaste. Any stranger who walked in would think the Coleridge house a little shabby, and they'd be right. The wallpaper was faded, and the woodwork begged for a lick of paint, but money was tight. But while there were higher priorities than decorating, no one could claim that the Coleridges kept anything other but a spotless home. Not a single speck of dust was allowed to settle, nor a single item left out of place.

'No pictures today?' Ma was crouched before the open oven door as her daughter entered. Two pans boiled violently on the stove, the kitchen window clouded over by steam which made Evie's face tingle.

'Long story.' She sat at the small wooden table which squatted along the wall opposite the back door, a chair either side. They'd only ever been two, every meal eaten facing one another through a silence that varied from companionable to glowering. 'Just as well, anyway. You got dinner started early. Need a hand?'

'No need, love, but I'm glad you're home.' Ma held her back, wincing as she moved from her crouch to a standing position. 'I thought we'd crack open that bottle of wine. You know, the fancy one I won at the church tombola. Might be all right, eh?'

Evie nodded warily. Her mother rarely drank and never at home unless they had a visitor. On those special occasions Ma would pull out the dusty bottle of Glenfiddich that lived at the back of the sideboard, first opened before Evie had started at school. She could recall each separate event: the vicar at Christmas; Aunt Gertie when she had visited them three years before (though she'd brought her own gin, and let Evie have the odd thimbleful); the time Mrs Hargrave from down the road had lost her marbles and mistaken Ma for Evie's grandmother who had died back in 1923. Evie had been sent out to find Mrs Hargrave's son who lived in a large semi-detached down in Herne Hill. The son had driven back up with Evie in the passenger seat of his flash two-seater, and she'd tried not to look terrified as he pressed his impatient foot to the floor, gathering up his senile old mother before whizzing her off to an old folk's home, never to be seen or heard of again.

'Are we celebrating something?' Evie asked now.

'You could say that.' Her mother plonked down the bottle of burgundy along with two of the crystal wine glasses that had lived up on the top shelf for decades, droplets of water still clinging to the cut edges where they had been rinsed out. Ma sat down. 'Evie, I know that the last couple of years haven't been easy, but things are looking up now, don't you think?'

'Never been better.' Evie smiled, thinking of Lawrie and trying to forget their stupid argument.

'I'm proud of you, you know?' Ma reached over the table and squeezed Evie's hand.

'Gosh, Ma, what's up with you today? You're not dying, are you?' The words flipped off her tongue and she bit it to stop from making things any worse. 'I'm sorry. I didn't mean it like that.'

'It's fine, love. I mean, we're both here, aren't we? Surviving? Won't be long before you're leaving me behind and starting a family of your own.' Ma wrestled the cork from the bottle and poured barely an inch into each glass. 'I know it won't make up for growing up without a father and—'

'Like you said,' Evie interrupted, 'sometimes things happen for the best. Cheers.' She clinked her glass against her mother's and drank. The wine was rich and she held it in her mouth while she decided if she liked it or not. It was different, not as bitter as gin or fiery as the Glenfiddich, which had set Evie's throat on fire when she'd sneaked a drop from the bottom of the vicar's glass after he'd left.

Ma took a suspicious sip of the wine and wrinkled her nose. 'Your aunt Gertie wrote to me. I was thinking maybe we should invite her to come and stay this summer for a week or two. What do you think?'

'It'd be nice to see her. It was very generous of her, having me to stay for all that time.' Evie had been glad that her aunt's house was on the outskirts of her small Devon town. It was easy to hide away from the locals who had stared at her without shame every time she went to the local shop. They'd clearly never seen a coloured person before, not in real life anyway.

'Least she could do,' her mother said. 'She didn't exactly do anything to help when you were born. I could have done with a little of her generosity back then.'

'I suppose she was afraid. Of my grandfather, I mean.' Evie took another gulp from her glass, for courage. 'That baby in the pond, d'you think, maybe, that she's like me? It would make sense, wouldn't it? And you still know people at the home on Cedars Road. Could she have come from there?'

Ma's reply was interrupted as they heard shouting through the wall from next door. Mrs Ryan was shrieking and Evie could make out a second, lower voice. A man with a Cockney accent, getting gradually louder. She jumped as the wall thudded, as if something heavy had been thrown against it, shaking the crockery on the shelves of the Coleridges' kitchen.

'What on earth…' Ma began to speak but Evie was already on her feet and rushing to the front door.

She didn't know how, but she knew that Lawrie was in trouble; her fears proven when she threw open the door and startled the uniformed police constable who stood at the end of the Ryans' path, his hand moving to his baton. 'Go back inside, Miss,' he ordered.

Evie ignored the policeman and walked outside, down the path. The Ryans' front door stood open and she could hear scuffling, a dragging sound, before three men appeared. Lawrie was in the middle, awkwardly supported by the other two men, plain-clothed but clearly coppers. They squeezed out of the door, almost falling onto the path, another man strolling out behind them. This man was older, with a thin moustache that reminded her of Errol Flynn, though this man was no movie star hero with his pasty pitted skin and receding hairline. He paused on the step as he noticed Evie, puffing a cloud of smoke around the cigarette that was glued to his bottom lip.

'Lawrie?' Evie reached out a hand towards him without thinking, the man closest to her knocking it away. 'What's going on? Where are you taking him?'

'Who are you?' The detective was eyeing her with interest and her stomach clenched, those few sips of wine now burning at the base of her gullet.

She took a deep breath and held onto the wall to steady herself. 'Evelyn Coleridge. I live here.'

'Well, Miss Coleridge, you should learn to mind your own business.' He blew out a stream of smoke and smiled. 'Unless you've got something of use to tell me?'

'You leave her alone!' Lawrie twisted in his captor's grip, his cuffed hands sending him off balance, stumbling, earning a sly punch in the head for his trouble. They held him so that Evie couldn't see his face properly but when the man who'd thrown the punch drew back his hand, the signet ring on his little finger was bloodied. Evie heard a sob and realised belatedly that it had come from her own lungs.

The pockmarked detective gave a signal and his men began to move once more, taking Lawrie towards the van they had parked up against the kerb. Mrs Ryan appeared in the doorway, her face blotchy and red, Arthur behind her and holding her back. Across the road Evie saw the net curtains twitch, and a few of their more brazen neighbours had actually come outside to get a better look. At the end of the road were a couple of children who'd stopped their game to watch the show. This was nothing but a street circus, the ringmaster surveying the scene with a thin smile on his face as he flicked ash from his cigarette. He looked like a man used to getting his own way; confident and satisfied in what he saw before him.

'You can't do this. You can't just force your way onto private property and haul a man away,' Mrs Ryan called. 'What d'you think you're playing at? I shall be making a complaint.'

'I'm perfectly within my rights, madam. This man is under arrest for murder.' The words landed amongst them like a doodle-bug, a terrible silence broken by the clamouring of four people talking at once, shouting over one another until order was brought – a piercing whistle blasting the air, stabbing through Evie's brain.

It was Ma, standing in the doorway with her father's old police whistle in hand. 'Let's sort this out in a sensible fashion, shall we? Now, who are you exactly?' She pointed at the detective, his jaw now clenched.

'Detective Sergeant Rathbone.' His lip curled as he stared at her, not used to being challenged.

'Well, DS Rathbone, I must warn you, my father was a DI for quite some years and he told me all your little tricks. James Coleridge?' Ma's tone still filled with pride when she spoke of the man who had come to despise his own daughter.

Rathbone clenched his jaw. 'I knew DI Coleridge. He was a great man, may he rest in peace.' His eyes slid from Ma and rested on Evie, the corner of his mouth turning up slightly. If he knew of her grandfather then he no doubt knew who Evie was. What she was.

'And I know this lad, Lawrie. There's no way he did what you're saying he did. I'd bet my life on it. He's a good lad. It'd be very embarrassing if you missed the real culprit after putting on this song and dance, with all these people watching.'

'He's already lied to me once, Mrs…?'

'It's still Coleridge.'

Evie held her breath.

Rathbone smirked. 'Of course it is. Well, *Mrs* Coleridge, I'm just doing my job, as I'm sure your old man would have appreciated. Your nigger friend here lied and I want to know why. That's all. Maybe it's a question your daughter can answer.'

'You leave Evie out of this and don't treat me like a fool, lad.' Ma's voice hardened as Evie took a step back, away from the detective's accusation. 'Your game won't wash with me. I'm perfectly capable of picking up the telephone to your superiors. I've known Jim Garvan since I was young enough to bounce on his knee.'

'Hold up, lads.' His men paused by the side of the van as Rathbone took hold of the cigarette in his mouth and blew smoke in Evie's direction. 'I used to look up to your father, Mrs Coleridge. He taught me a great deal. Even went to his funeral when he was taken too soon. Don't remember seeing you there, though. Or this one.' He gestured at Evie with his cigarette.

'I was there. Front pew with my sister.' Ma bristled with indignation.

The detective glanced over at his men, giving a nod. They shoved Lawrie into the van and slammed the door on him. Rathbone leaned forward. 'Jim Garvan? I know him well. Better than you, I'd say, 'cause if he was here he'd make sure you knew exactly what you are: a traitor. Way I hear it, you broke your father's heart running off with some darkie chap who didn't even stick around once he got what he wanted.' He turned and spat on Mrs Ryan's well-swept path. 'Jim Garvan wouldn't give you the time of day, *Miss* Coleridge.'

Ma was silent as Rathbone walked away to a red car which was parked up behind the van, her face pale in contrast to her flushed cheeks as she stared after him. Evie could hear the man whistling, as if the altercation had put him in a better mood, had buoyed him up as surely as it had deflated her mother.

'Derek'll sort it, Evie love. Soon as he gets home. He knows people. Lawyers and the like.' Mrs Ryan wiped her eyes on a lilac handkerchief. 'We'll get him out.'

Evie just nodded as her mother turned and went back into the house without another word.

'Evie?' Arthur looked over his shoulder as he pushed Mrs Ryan gently back inside. 'I'll pop round when we have news.'

'Thanks, Arthur.'

The door closed behind them and Evie watched as first the van, then Rathbone's car, drove off down the street. From the corner of her eye she sensed a cascade of curtains being dropped back into place, each house slightly out of time with the next.

Walking back into the house she was struck by the density of the silence, the only sound the shuffle of her slippered feet as she went to the kitchen in search of her mother. She found her there, looking out of the window, her hands resting on the cold hard steel of the sink. The rings on the stove had been turned off and she missed the regular sound that the boiling potatoes had made as they hit gently against the side of the pan.

'Ma?'

There was no reply, her mother's body as still as one of the waxworks at Madame Tussauds, as if she'd been posed to model as the perfect housewife. Evie knew this mood well, though it had been eighteen months or so since she'd last seen her mother like this. Her first instinct was to walk away but experience told her that would only make things worse.

'Ma, would you like another drink?' Wasn't that what people did in the novels Ma got from the library? Things went wrong and they had a brandy or a Scotch and felt better.

Her mother turned and leaned against the counter, staring at Evie with eyes that were red and swollen, though she wasn't crying. Evie sat down at the table and drained her own glass.

'You know what they'll do to him?'

Evie shook her head and poured more wine, holding the bottle with both hands to stop it from shaking. 'We might as well eat something. Arthur said he'll come and let us know as soon as they hear.' In her head she begged her mother to shut up. She didn't want to think about what Lawrie might be going through as she sat safe at home in a warm kitchen. He'd be cold in just that shirt and there was no one to tend to his wounds.

'He's already taken a bit of a beating from the looks of him,' Ma continued. 'If they've any sense they'll throw him in a cell and leave him for a bit. No food or water. And then later tonight, or maybe they'll let him stew until tomorrow, they'll drag him out for questioning. But they'll only be interested in a confession so they'll threaten him and he'll get a bit more of a beating, and maybe, eventually, he'll give in and tell them what they want to hear.'

'I'll mash the potatoes, if you want. I think there's a bit of marge left over, isn't there? Remember when we used to make them with cream and butter?' Evie went to the larder and brought out the dish but there was only a congealed sliver of bright yellow margarine left, embedded with toast crumbs. It turned her stomach and she put it back, wiping her hands on her skirt.

'Are you listening to me, Evie?'

'He didn't do it, Ma. Why would he confess to something that he didn't do?' She grabbed the masher and unhooked the colander from the wall.

'Will you leave those bloody potatoes Evie! Sit down and listen.'

She bit back a quick retort and sat back down at the table, her head turned away from her mother. 'Lawrie's innocent. He could never have done something like that. Like you said, they can't have any evidence so I just don't understand how they expect him to confess to anything.'

'Because. It's what they do. My father used to tell me all sorts of stories.'

'Well, maybe that's all they were.' Evie drank her wine but it wasn't working. Not with Ma going on and on. 'You don't know what they do these days. Like that detective said, you don't know anyone in the police, not like you thought you did, and I don't want to think about whatever horrible things they might be doing to Lawrie. I'll wait for Derek to come home – he might actually be able to help. He'll know someone. A solicitor or someone who knows what's what.'

'Derek Ryan? Don't make me laugh! If you're waiting for him to save Lawrie then you may as well resign yourself now to not seeing him again until they march him into court.'

'I bet that would suit you, wouldn't it?' She couldn't hold back any longer, trying not to scream. 'You hate to see me happy. I know you do. You want me to be as lonely as you, stuck in this miserable house for ever.'

'How bloody dare you!' Ma moved surprisingly quickly, Evie too shocked to do more than shrink back against the wall as her mother converged upon her at speed. 'I put a roof over your head, food on the table, saved you from ruining your own useless life.' She banged her hand on the table in time with her words. 'You're an ungrateful bitch.'

Evie watched the bottle of wine, mesmerised by its progress as it hopped closer to the edge of the table each time her mother's palm slapped the surface, eventually hurling itself to the floor in a blaze of red, her skin prickling as shards of glass struck her shins.

Ma stared down at the mess, a tear falling from her chin to mix with the spilled Burgundy on the floor. 'Clean that up.'

She left the room.

9

He shivered, the thin blanket doing nothing to keep out the cold. It stank of the many men who'd come before him, shoved into this small, mean room and given all the time in the world to wonder where it had all gone wrong. Lawrie curled into a ball on the cell's narrow cot, his head turned away from the bucket which he'd had to use to relieve himself.

They'd taken his watch from him and there was no clock hanging on the bare, yellow-stained walls. It was dark outside, he could see that much from the tiny high window, but the light had changed while he was being interviewed so he didn't know how long since night had fallen. His head pounded and he pushed it into the thin pillow on the cot, the pressure stilling the beat momentarily.

He hadn't been able to see Evie's face as they dragged him out of the house, though that was perhaps a good thing. He would have lost all hope if he'd looked into her eyes and seen disappointment, or worse, accusation. Was she scared for him? For herself? Scared that he might know more than he was letting on. She'd never think him a murderer, he was sure, but he wouldn't blame her for not quite trusting him.

Rathbone had conducted the interview, a constable sitting beside him and taking notes as his boss did all the talking. Everything was being done by the book. He wasn't charged yet, that would come later, they said, as if it were only a matter of time before he confessed.

You said you didn't leave the house until five, Rathbone had told him. *But you were walking the streets in the early hours. Right when the body was being dumped.*

I was coming home from work.

Rathbone had read back Lawrie's original statement, word for word, and Lawrie realised what he'd done. He'd started at the wrong moment. A stupid, simple mistake. He'd heard the word 'morning' and in his fatigue assumed that Rathbone meant from breakfast time, not all the way from midnight when he'd been onstage playing 'Light Up' and enjoying the limelight, pretending he was Buster Bailey, exhilarated at the applause that accompanied his flawless performance.

Was all they had on him, just a tiny stupid mistake? He talked them through his journey home from Soho, every detail from the conversation with the bouncer on the door to his minor daily run-in with Donovan at the sorting office, to clocking off after his shift and deciding to take a cycle across the Common.

You can check, he told them. *Ask the doorman what time it was that I left. Ask Mrs Ryan if the teapot was still warm when she got up. You'll see there was no time for me to do anything else.*

He remembered running for the bus and gave thanks that

he'd made it. If he'd had to wait half an hour for the next then his alibi would have been shattered. If they bothered to check it. Rathbone had just smiled and nodded, as though nothing Lawrie had told him was a surprise.

Mrs Barnett remembered something, he said, unable to hide his sly smile. *She saw you twice that day, ten minutes apart, she reckons. You cycled past her and she saw a parcel sticking out of the basket. That wasn't there by the time you got here now, was it? Which begs the question: what were you carrying, and where did it go?*

He hadn't known what to tell them without dropping Derek in it as well as himself.

You think that poor child… He'd struggled to compose himself. *I came from work, that's the honest truth. I never seen that child before. I live with three other people – you don't think one of them might notice if I bring a baby home one day?*

Not if the baby lived with your fancy woman. Who is she? Can't have been easy. You can't hide a baby that looks like that, can you? It's understandable. She was desperate. You were just helping her out.

Lawrie just shook his head and told them over and over that there was no fancy woman. The way Rathbone looked at him, he wondered what he knew. They'd been asking around. What had they been told? Not enough, it seemed, for after a couple of hours he watched as Rathbone checked his watch and made a decision. They'd sent him along to this cold cell so that they could go home to a warm fire and a hot meal.

He heard shouts echoing along the corridor. Swearing, the slurred tones of a drunk. It was Saturday night, he remembered, sitting up with a start that set off the pain in his head once more, like a child was bouncing a rubber ball against the inside of his skull. He was supposed to be playing with the band. Would Mrs Ryan have known to call Johnny? Did she even know his number? She had Lawrie's mother's address. Would she be writing to Lucille Herbert now, letting her know what a failure her surviving son had turned out to be? Mr Herbert's son was a bank manager now. He would tell his new wife to forget about Lawrie, to think of the family that remained on Jamaican soil. Lawrie's stomach folded in on itself, a one-second warning which gave him enough time to lean over the bucket before he threw up.

He lay there all night, barely sleeping for the noise, the smell of his own vomit and piss. He tried to distract himself with music, practicing scales in his head, then moving onto the songs he knew Johnny would have put on the set list. Usually it worked better than counting sheep but in the past few days it was a method that failed more often than it worked, especially now, when he knew he should be playing those notes on stage at that very moment.

Daylight brought new hope and he began to pace as the light turned from black to grey, stretching out his aching muscles, three steps in either direction. It was something to do. He could hear people arriving for work, shouting greetings down the corridor, warning who was a spitter and who might be violent. They didn't mention Lawrie and he had begun to worry that they'd forgotten about him when he heard the sound of a key in the lock. He sat down quickly, not wanting to look like trouble.

'Breakfast.' A uniformed policeman shoved a cup of water and a tin plate at him. 'Toast'll have to do you.'

'You know when I'll get out of here?' He took the plate,

suddenly starving even though he could see how dry the toast was, the margarine just sitting there in a thin anaemic slick on top.

'Who says you will?' The officer sneered, and with that the door slammed shut.

He swilled his mouth with water first, getting rid of the taste of bile and spitting into the hated bucket. He began to eat the toast, chewing each mouthful until it was mush, before swallowing. It passed the time. Someone down the hall began to scream, a high-pitched shriek that went up and down like a siren. Several boots ran past Lawrie's door and he heard the bang of a heavy cell door crashing into the wall, more shouts before the screaming was cut off mid-breath.

Maybe this was all part of it. Part of the torture. Knowing that he couldn't see what was happening, they were putting on some sort of act outside to terrify him into a confession. He stood, leaving the second round of toast untouched, beginning to pace once more. If he just knew what time it was… He gave up and lay down, finally falling asleep to be shaken awake what felt like a moment later.

'Up. Get up.' It was Rathbone glaring down at him. 'Your solicitor's here. Fancy that, eh?'

Lawrie blinked up at him. 'My solicitor?'

'You deaf?' Rathbone looked as though he'd slept as badly as Lawrie, his dry skin almost translucent. 'Come on then.'

His limbs had stiffened but Lawrie managed to shove himself to his feet and follow Rathbone back to the same old interview room. The detective didn't follow him in, just slammed the door, closing Lawrie in with his visitor. Reluctantly Lawrie sat down, wondering how the hell this man had found him.

The man on the opposite side of the table wore an expensive suit, likely from Savile Row. 'Mr Matthews? I hope you realise that I've got better things to do with my time than journey halfway across London on a Sunday morning.' He could have narrated a Pathé newsreel.

'I'm sorry, sir.' Lawrie picked at a rough hangnail. 'Only I'm not sure who you are or who called you.'

'That would be Derek Ryan. He's the one paying for my services, though this is the first time he's involved me in a murder.' The last word hung in the air.

Lawrie repeated. 'I didn't do it, you know, what they're saying.'

The solicitor sighed, his body relaxing a little as he leaned forward, becoming more human. 'Well, it doesn't much matter to me whether you did or didn't but that detective's like a dog with a bone. However, I can't see that they've got a good enough reason to hold you. They don't have enough to charge you with anyway.'

Lawrie felt his eyes prick with tears. 'You think so?'

'You weren't the first on the scene when the body was found. You've no connection to a baby, or any woman who has a child of the right age. No motive.' The solicitor removed his spectacles and rubbed his eyes with thumb and forefinger. 'The only thing I can't tell them is why you're refusing to answer a very simple question.'

The parcel. 'It's nothing. I was doing a favour, that's all.' Lawrie lowered his voice. 'For Derek, if you know what I mean.'

'Ah, yes. Understandable then. It makes no odds at this point, the judge would laugh them out of the courtroom if they tried to make a case against you right now. Come on, let's sort out whatever paperwork needs doing and I'll drive you home on my way.'

Lawrie followed the solicitor out of the police station, stumbling slightly as he saw Rathbone waiting out on the street, leaning against his red car, the usual cigarette in his mouth. He said nothing, just stared at Lawrie with narrowed eyes. They had to walk past him, Lawrie's hip scuffing the wall as he gave the detective a wide berth.

The solicitor handed Lawrie a card with a Chancery Lane address. 'Murder isn't exactly my specialty. If they try anything else, and I'm sure they will, this is a decent chap for you to call. He's not cheap, so if you can't afford him you need to ask the police to supply you with representation. They have a legal obligation to do that much.'

His car was a sensible grey four-door Vauxhall Ten, its interior as immaculately presented as its driver. Lawrie sank back into the seat and tried to enjoy being chauffeured home. He thanked the solicitor once more as they pulled up in front of the Ryans', shaking his hand stiffly when it was offered.

He'd barely put both feet on the pavement when Evie shot out of her house, throwing her arms around him. He held on to her tightly and closed his eyes, his head resting on hers. He could feel her trembling as behind him the car drove off.

'I thought...' Her voice broke off as she gasped back a sob.

'I'm all right, Evie, I'm all right.' He pulled back slightly so that he could look in her eyes. 'It was all a misunderstanding. I didn't lie to them, you know. At least, I didn't mean to. I forgot to tell them I'd been working in Soho is all.' He wiped the tears from her cheeks with his thumbs, cradling her face in his palms. 'You believe me, don't you?' He wouldn't tell her about Derek's deliveries unless he had to.

''Course I do,' she assured him. 'I was just worried that… Ma said that…'

'Your mother doesn't know everything.'

'No,' she agreed, her laugh bitter. 'I'm finding that out.'

'Cavorting in public? Evie, what would your mother say?'

He looked over Evie's shoulder to see Aston standing in the Ryans' doorway.

'Ignore him,' Lawrie whispered in her ear. To his friend: 'I take it she threw you out? Whoever she was.'

Aston grinned, showing off his chipped front tooth, a souvenir from the plane crash that had killed Lawrie's brother. 'Actually, I took my young lady out for lunch yesterday and then to the pictures. Only got back this morning so I missed the show you put on for the neighbours.'

Lawrie felt his temper rise but he swallowed it back down; he didn't want Evie to see him erupt. 'You know, if I'd taken Evie to the pictures instead of wasting my time sitting indoors waiting for you then maybe I'd not have ended up in a police cell overnight.'

'Did I ask you to sit in and wait for me?' Aston countered. 'I could have occupied meself plenty well enough 'til you got home.'

'I should tell you to go to hell.'

'Serious?' Aston held his arms out, widespread in disbelief. 'I said I'm sorry.'

'No, you never did.'

He could feel Evie's arms squeezing him, wanting him to leave Aston and pay her some attention.

'Fine then. I'm sorry. And Evie, I'm sorry Lawrie made you miss going to the pictures.'

She murmured an acceptance that Lawrie knew she didn't mean.

'Just go back inside,' he ordered. 'Let me talk to Evie.'

Aston winked and disappeared back inside the house.

'Evie? Come in for a bit?'

She shook her head. 'I told Ma I'd make the dinner. She missed church with a bad head.' She lowered her voice, checking over her shoulder to make sure Aston hadn't crept up on them once more. 'You ever think that the culprit might be close to home? The police haven't questioned him, have they? They probably don't know that he exists since he swans up here when he feels like and vanishes as soon as he gets bored.'

Lawrie stared at her, then laughed. 'My goodness, you really think Aston could do a thing like that? Besides, he's careful. I never seen him with a girl round here. I swear he checks they don't live anywhere round south London before he'll buy them a drink.'

'That doesn't mean anything,' she insisted. 'What if he forgot to be careful one time?'

'No.' He said it firmly, shaking his head. 'Even if he slipped up, he wouldn't do a thing like this, not even by accident. He's got his faults but he admits to them. He'd hold his hands up and take his punishment.'

Evie nodded but didn't look convinced. 'You know him best.' She kissed him. 'You'll come round later on?'

'Promise.' He kissed her back and gave her one last squeeze before letting her go.

The party had begun in the kitchen by the time he walked in, the entire household gathered. Aston and Derek were kindred spirits, both adept at chancing their luck, and they talked over one another, their laughter bellowing and contagious, only Lawrie immune. Arthur had Mrs Ryan's pinny on, the top half-folded down so it looked more like a chef's apron. With his spectacles perched on the end of his nose he looked part cook, part scientist, measuring out precise portions of rice. The chicken was laid out ready in a roasting tin, but the glossy rawness of the meat made Lawrie's stomach turn. Rathbone had even managed to steal this from him; the simple enjoyment of a home-cooked meal.

'Lawrie, love, sit down. I need to sort that eye of yours out.' Mrs Ryan fetched down her first aid box. 'This might sting a bit.'

Wasn't that what Rose had said to him, all those months ago? So much had changed since then. He bit his tongue and tried to breathe as she tended the cut below his eye as gently as she could, his foot tapping out the rhythm of his wound as it throbbed with pain.

'Well done, love. Now, it's not going to look pretty for a few days but it's not as bad as it could have been. And will you see what your pal's brought us?' She picked up a large bottle of Harvey's Bristol Cream. Aston always brought her favourite sherry, his method of payment for the roof over his head. 'Get us the glasses down, will you, Derek? The good ones. We should have a toast to Lawrie's safe return.'

'Thanks to Derek.' Lawrie dug out the card he'd been given. 'We're to call this person if anything else happens.' He drained his first glass in two gulps and accepted a second. He felt strange, his skin feverish and his bones less than solid, as though he were watching events unfold from a viewing point slightly outside of his actual body.

Mrs Ryan put the card up on the shelf. 'We were all in a tizz, weren't we, boys? Lucky Derek managed to get hold of his fella in the end.'

'Did they tell you anything else about the baby?' Aston asked, impatient to get to the facts.

'Shouldn't matter, I know, but don't you think it's worse that it was a girl?' Mrs Ryan crossed herself. 'Poor mite. Never had a chance in life.'

'They'll catch the bitch soon enough,' Derek said, bowing his head away from the sideswipe his mother gave him. 'I'd bet you any amount of money it's a woman.'

'Then they're questioning the wrong people,' Lawrie said. 'You never wonder why?'

'You know why. Think about it. Work out when that baby was conceived and you can see why they're looking at anyone who arrived in summer '48,' Aston pointed out. 'But what they're missing is that a lot of fellas moved on already. Those who had relatives up north and whatnot. Sam, for one.'

Lawrie nodded. Sam hadn't lasted long in London and they weren't on speaking terms when he left. He was just the kind of man to leave chaos behind.

'Exactly! Fine, some bloke got lucky one Saturday night, but who's to say he had anything to do with what happened to that baby girl? They should be looking at the women who were hanging around,' Derek said. 'Plenty of sluts turning up at parties, looking to spread their legs for the first spade who'd take them outside.'

'Derek Ryan, that is not the sort of language I expect to hear in my own house!' Mrs Ryan pointed to Jesus on the wall, who looked down at Derek disapprovingly, it seemed to Lawrie, as he drained his glass a third time.

'I'm goin' outside,' Aston announced, holding a rollup aloft. He nudged Lawrie hard. 'Comin'?'

Reluctantly he got up and followed him out into the yard, shivering slightly at the change in temperature. He leaned against the brick wall and waited.

Aston lit his cigarette first, putting off what he had to say. 'You're not goin' to like this but I meant what I said the other night.' He paused and took another drag. 'You should check in with Rose.'

'Why would I?' He knew why. He'd been trying to block out thoughts of Rose for days now.

'That whole entire conversation in there. That's why. You need to be certain.'

'What? You think she wouldn't have been straight round here?' Or her husband? He'd have loved a good excuse to come round and start a fight.

Aston shrugged. 'Is it not better to know either way?'

Lawrie turned and went back inside to where at least it was warm. He longed to run next door to Evie but her mother would tell him where to go. He wished he'd begged her to stay outside with him, just for a few minutes longer, just to hold him until he felt normal again. He'd have closed his eyes and pressed his nose against her skin, breathing in her sweet fragrance until he forgot the terror that had spread from his belly to every inch of his body as the policemen had grabbed his wrist, twisting his arms until his shoulders screamed. When he was with her, everything was right with the world. Damn what Aston said; he wasn't going anywhere near Rose Armstrong.

1948

'Ladies and gentlemen! Thank you kindly for your attention. We'd like to play you a little music. I hope you like it.'

Johnny stood before his audience as if it were the Royal Albert Hall and not a drab south London church hall. They'd been invited to play by the mayor himself, hoping to forge relations with the local community and hush the naysayers. Johnny didn't seem to notice the group of local men sniggering at the back, propping up the makeshift bar that was serving tea and lemonade – though Lawrie could see from his elevated position that more than one person had brought their own supply of liquor. The crowd looked like a humbug: the newcomers lining the wall to Lawrie's left, a clear separation between them and the natives.

The band had only snatched a few hours of practice. Lawrie had rented a room with Sam, on trumpet, but few of their fellow residents were music lovers and they'd been issued particular hours at which they could play, most of which coincided with the opening hours of the labour exchange. They were managing well considering, but every now and then their timing went off or

Johnny decided to skip a verse, sending the rest of them off into panicked improvisation. It was fun, though. He'd forgotten this buzz, the joy he got from riffing off other musicians. They were just playing simple tunes that everyone knew, nothing obscure for this crowd, but Lawrie was surprised at how good they sounded.

'Lemme introduce ourselves. We're all neighbours now and we'd like to thank you for the warm welcome.' Johnny gave each band member their moment in the spotlight and Lawrie stepped forward, bowing his head an inch as his name was called. The people below clapped politely as if they were at a council meeting rather than a dance. 'Now come on, folks. I want to see you have some fun. I want to see me some dancing. Who's brave enough to show the rest how it's done?'

Nobody moved, no matter what colour their skin. The girls whispered behind their hands, giggling and prodding each other. The men looked as if they'd rather be anywhere else. Lawrie and Moses exchanged a glance, the latter rolling his eyes.

Then a young girl stepped forward, bright blonde hair and an emerald green dress. She held out her hand. 'Any takers?' No one replied and she moved her hands to her hips. 'Really? No one? Christopher Marson, where the hell are you?'

One of the men at the bar was pushed forward by his friends, reluctantly joining the blonde in the middle of the dancefloor. They looked enough alike that Lawrie guessed that they were brother and sister rather than a couple.

'A one, two, three…' Johnny counted them in and they were off, the two dancers moving self-consciously as everyone watched.

By the end of the song, ten couples were dancing. Three songs later segregation had been outlawed, mixed partners talking and laughing like this was just the usual night out in Brixton.

'Good work,' Lawrie told Johnny as they took a break.

'I know what I'm doing,' he replied. 'Some persons just need a little prod is all. You coming out?' He flashed the inside of his jacket, revealing a slim bottle of whisky.

'I'll just grab a lemonade.' He wasn't as big a drinker as the others, despite Aston's best efforts to convert him. He'd left London the day before, heading back to his RAF base now that his leave was over.

There was a queue at the bar as thirsty dancers took a breather. Lawrie queued politely, listening to the strange accents surrounding him. He paid for his lemonade and was making his way towards the back door when she appeared.

'Fancy seeing you here!' Her smile was wide as she blocked his exit.

'Hello, Rose.' He took a step back, her proximity unnerving.

'You look surprised to see me.' Rose raised an eyebrow.

'Yes, though thinking about it I'm not sure why. You do live round here after all.'

They both laughed a little, the hollow sound of two people meeting outside of their usual circumstances and realising that they don't know each other as well as they thought.

'You sounded good. The band I mean. Proper professional,' she told him. 'You got sorted I assume? With somewhere to live?'

'A place over in Somerleyton Road, though I'm still looking for work. The only income I've got right now is the odd gig like this one.'

'Something'll come up soon. A strong young man like you should be in demand.'

Rose was different tonight. Down in the shelter she'd been motherly, making sure her charges were eating right, that they knew how to use the buses and the dreaded tube. Now she looked up at Lawrie through dark eyelashes that were spiked with mascara, a strange smile on her face.

'People are wary of us still. Maybe they think we won't last once winter comes.' He tried to make light of it, not wanting her to take offence.

It wasn't Rose's fault after all. The man who'd interviewed him that afternoon for a factory job had said it straight enough – *Nothing personal but we don't take niggers on here. The men don't like it.* He'd shrugged apologetically as if to say, *that's just the way of the world,* and Lawrie had walked out without another word. It had been too much of a shock.

Rose just nodded. 'Let me ask around. I can let you know if I hear of anything. I don't suppose there's a telephone where you are but I can pop round if you give me the address.'

'Thank you. That would be very kind.' He gave her the details before making his excuses and walking off to join the band. Something about her, which he couldn't put his finger on, was making him feel uneasy.

The others were outside, passing Johnny's bottle of whisky and smoking. Even though the hour was getting on, it was daylight still. It was disconcerting enough now but Aston had told him that in winter the nights were so long that there were days when the sun barely bothered to rise. Not something he was looking forward to. Lawrie was the only non-smoker, soon surrounded by a fug of grey as the rest puffed away. He didn't mind but neither did he feel any need to partake. His father had always endured ill health, had bad lungs after suffering from a severe bout of bronchitis while away at boarding school. There was no smoking in the Matthews household, no drinking, no vices of any kind. He could imagine what his mother would say if she could see him now and it wouldn't be good.

He wondered about Bennie, how he had ended up friends with Aston. That afternoon when Aston had showed up at the house in Kingston, unannounced but with the last photograph of Bennie Matthews in his pocket, Lawrie had been amazed. His older brother had always been the studious type, clever enough to be thinking about a career as an engineer when he answered the call to fight for the mother country. Lawrie had wanted to follow in his footsteps ever since they'd been children playing in the yard. He'd sat on the porch deep into the night with Aston, and a bottle of white rum that Lawrie's mother didn't know about, and listened wide-eyed as Aston regaled him with tales of two young men let off the leash in a faraway land. He'd never even been drunk before that night, never been so sick or felt so ill the next day. Aston had laughed and drank tea with Lawrie's mother while he convinced her that the best hope for her younger son was to try his luck on the other side of the ocean. It would be an adventure, Aston had said, and he hadn't been wrong so far. It was only that Lawrie was beginning to think that maybe he wasn't the adventurous type.

'We need a proper name for the band,' Johnny announced. 'People can't ask for us if we don't have a name. And we could all use the money, right?'

Only Moses and Sonny had jobs so far, both using old RAF contacts to get jobs on the railway. Sam had barely bothered to look and Johnny was determined to try his hand at music even though he had a wife and child who were hoping to join him in England sooner rather than later.

'Anyone have access to a telephone? Or know someone who does and might be willing to take messages for us?'

'I could ask Rose,' Lawrie said. 'I just saw her in the hall and she said she wanted to help.'

'Who?' Moses asked.

'You know, Rita Hayworth from the shelter.' Sonny nudged him.

'Oh, yes. But is she offering to help us or just you, Lawrie?' Moses grinned.

Lawrie's cheeks burned and he took a gulp of lemonade.

Johnny lit a cigarette. 'Same difference, ain't it? Lawrie, find her later and ask about the telephone.'

'You could offer her some sort of payment. In kind, since you're short of money.' Sam cackled as he passed the whisky bottle to Lawrie.

'She's a married woman, if you must know.' The liquor burned his throat as he tipped the bottle, trying to make it look like he was drinking back more than he was. 'Her husband will be here somewhere.'

'Just ask her.' Johnny ushered them all back inside where they were greeted by rapturous applause, the crowd eager to restart the festivities.

They were midway through their first song when he saw Rose again, dancing in the centre of the floor with a dark-haired man. Her husband, presumably, since his hand was fixed firmly to her behind. It was only as they turned so that the man faced him, spinning Rose around as she threw her head back and laughed, that he recognised him, missing two whole bars in his distraction. Rose's husband was Cary Grant, the drunk who'd punched him in the face not a week before, giving him the black eye that was only just healed enough that it wasn't the first thing people noticed about him. Did she know? Had she known all along? Maybe that was why she'd been so friendly, she'd just been making sure he wasn't going to cause trouble by going to the police or looking for revenge.

Frank, she'd called him. A good-looking fella, but then he'd have to be to catch Rose's eye. He was no longer catastrophically drunk, just dishevelled from the heat of the hall. His dark hair was slicked back and he'd loosened his tie, dancing with glee. As Lawrie watched him, Frank looked up and their eyes met, Lawrie's fingers freezing once more, but Frank looked away; he didn't know Lawrie from Adam. Rose, however, never looked up once.

She knew all along, Lawrie thought soberly. He'd put money on it.

Extract from the *Evening Standard* – Monday 20th March 1950

Local police released a shocking statement last night containing previously unreported information related to the tragic death of the baby known as 'Ophelia', whose body was discovered on Clapham Common last week. The police hope this new information will prompt new witnesses to come forward.

'The autopsy report confirms that the baby was deceased when she entered Eagle Pond,' Detective Sergeant Rathbone told the press conference. 'Cause of death is determined as an overdose of a common medication and therefore it is still unclear whether this death was due to murderous intent or accident.'

When questioned about possible suspects, DS Rathbone confirmed that the police are working on several strong leads, focusing on the recently formed Caribbean community in that part of London. For the first time the detective reported that Ophelia is thought to be of either coloured or half-caste background.

Current thinking is that an English woman has found herself in an unfortunate position. There were several public events held in the weeks following the arrival of the *HMT Empire Windrush* and the age of this child lends itself to the idea that she was the result of an encounter during this period.

If this new information prompts even the vaguest of memories then the police ask that you get in contact. Any information will be treated confidentially and DS Rathbone asked that we remind the public to consider that any person who could either commit infanticide, or even think to dispose of a body in such a callous way, denying her a Christian burial, is a danger to our community.

10

The rain was so heavy that those who might usually walk to work had decided to take the bus. Progress was slow. Evie had enough to worry about after reading the *Standard* article the night before. Ma had thrown it down on the table in front of her without a word and her heart had sunk as she read their call for information. All she needed now was to be late for work. Two women sat in front of Evie, one of them bouncing a baby in her lap. A boy, judging from the blue knitted bonnet. He was a happy little thing and Evie smiled as he dribbled around the sodden rusk he held in one tiny woollen-mitted hand. She wiggled her fingers at him and he blessed her with a gummy grin.

'It makes you shiver, don't it,' the mother was saying. 'I mean, nothing like this ever happened before. Not round here.'

Her friend agreed: 'My Norman said it was a mistake from the start. Soon as we heard. We should have been looking after our own, not bringing over more hungry mouths to feed. They're not like us, you know. I'm only surprised it's took this long for something to happen.'

'Exactly what I said! They should have rounded 'em all up, soon as it happened. Lock 'em up until they find out which one did it. They'd be falling over one another to come forward with information if there was something in it for 'em. Even if it were an accident, you can't just go dumping a baby in a pond like that.'

'So much for the missionaries! They should drag 'em all down to church, make them learn what it is to be a good Christian.'

Evie felt sick as it dawned on her that they were talking about Lawrie, about the other recent arrivals from the Caribbean. She pressed her back into the seat, hoping they wouldn't notice her. Would they want to lock her up as well, even though she'd been born within spitting distance of where they now were?

'You know what the real problem is? Those floozies who go out dancing with them. Some stupid girl's gone and got herself into trouble, you mark my words.'

'Well, you wouldn't want to get landed with a baby like that, would you? No decent man would be able to pass it off as his own!'

The baby gurgled at Evie and the rusk fell from his hand, landing on the floor by Evie's feet. He let out a shriek and the friend turned to see what the matter was, her smile freezing as her eyes fell on Evie.

Evie forced a smile. 'He's a beautiful baby.'

The women exchanged a glance and turned to face forward, the mother pulling her son down onto her lap so that he could no longer see Evie. Her actions were rewarded with an angry yelp as he lost his new-found friend.

Evie got off at the next stop despite the driving rain, her umbrella blowing inside out within seconds. She struggled to right it but it was a cheap, flimsy thing, not constructed for more than a light drizzle. She jammed it into a bin as she passed. At least the rain would hide her tears, she thought, marching along Battersea Rise, focusing on putting one foot in front of the other.

'What happened to you?' Delia asked, her forehead wrinkling as she saw her best friend walk in, drenched and miserable.

Evie just shook her head, scared to speak in case she started to cry again. She was ten minutes late and she was relieved to see through the glass panel of his office door that Mr Sullivan was occupied, busy in conversation with young Mr Vernon.

'Oh, Evie!' Delia stood and Evie fled, seeking sanctuary in the tiny cupboard that served as the ladies' WC, locking the door behind her.

The mirror above the sink showed the damage inflicted by rain and misery. Just as well she hadn't bothered with mascara that morning; it would have run all down her face and made her look even more of a sight. Her hair had formed wet curls, stuck across her forehead. She pulled the hand towel from the rail and held it to her face, hoping it was clean. At least it was dry.

Delia knocked on the door. 'Evie! Let me in, will you?'

She knew from experience that it would be easier to let her in quickly before she caused a scene. Delia locked them both in as Evie perched on the closed toilet lid.

'I've covered for you with Mrs Jones so you're welcome.' Despite her brusque tone, Delia looked concerned. 'Evie, has something happened? Lawrie's not in trouble again, is he?'

Evie shook her head. 'No, I just…' She couldn't hold back the tears any longer.

'Oh, Evie, then whatever it is, it doesn't matter.' Delia hugged her, crouching in the small space.

'I just, I feel like everyone's watching me. Have you read the papers? I mean, if anyone finds out that they arrested Lawrie...' Delia was the only person she'd told about Lawrie's arrest but enough people had seen it happen. Word could get around in no time. 'He won't be safe. He has to spend all day out on the streets and what if someone decides to take matters into their own hands. There were these women on the bus, the way they looked at me...'

'Evie, this will all blow over. Trust me. And Lawrie will be fine. People know him round our way. They see him every day, delivering their letters. Things might be horrid for a while but once they catch whoever did this, things will be back to normal in no time.'

Evie blew her nose on the rough loo paper and managed a weak smile. 'Thank you. You always make me feel better.'

'That's my job,' Delia pointed out. 'Best friend duties. Now come on. I told Sullivan you'd gone to fetch stationery but even he'll realise soon enough if you're not at your desk. Get out of that wet coat and we'll have a nice hot cup of tea.'

Evie nodded and let herself be led by the hand back into the office. The radiator was on full blast and she arranged her coat along it, feeling the steam rise. She warmed her hands on the mug of tea that Delia brought her along with two ginger snaps that were supposed to be for clients only. If Mr Sullivan noticed her odd behaviour then he didn't say a word, simply calling her in for dictation and issuing tasks as they arose. The tax year was drawing to a close and she supposed he had his hands too full to pay attention to a young secretary. Delia made up for Evie's uncharacteristic silence, talking endlessly about her evening assignation with Sid from the Lyceum.

'He must be keen,' Evie said as they packed up for the day. 'It's been less than a week.'

'I know. I really shouldn't let him think he's something special but I can't help myself.' Delia peered out of the window. 'There he is!' She waved frantically, tutting as Sid failed to notice her, and rushed off shouting goodbye over her shoulder.

Evie took her time going downstairs, waiting for a couple of buses to pass by below the window to make sure that Mildred and her cronies would have left. Famous last words, she thought, as she emerged onto the street and saw who was waiting for her at the bus stop.

Rose Armstrong hadn't changed in the two years or so since Evie had last seen her. Red hair, dark and sophisticated, a million miles from the carrot hue of Delia's new beau, perfectly set in waves that sat up on her shoulder. Her navy blue eyes were bravely outlined in deep black mascara despite the inclement weather, and Evie had never seen her without the bright red lipstick that she hoarded, fearful that the prolonged austerity might cause a shortage.

'Hello, Evie. Been a while.' The words came out smoothly but Evie saw her mouth twitch as she spoke.

They hadn't seen one another since the party almost two summers ago. Rose had written to her once, a couple of weeks afterwards, a pitiful page of excuses that just reminded Evie of her own foolishness. She'd held a match to the letter afterwards and burned it in the kitchen sink while Ma was out, rinsing the ashes away so that she could almost believe there never had been a letter at all.

'Can we talk?' Rose asked. 'I know it's the last thing you want but I promise you this is important. I read the papers like anyone else. I just need ten minutes of your time and then I'll not bother you again. I swear.'

Evie's bus pulled up and it would have been so easy to bypass Rose and skip on board. She chewed her lip as she watched the crowded bus stop empty and took a step towards the vehicle.

'Please? I'll buy you a cup of tea.' Rose forced a laugh. 'And a slice of cake as well if you're hungry.'

Underneath the make-up Rose looked tired, Evie thought. She didn't want to sit and drink tea with her but she could see that Rose would not have chosen to wait for her in the freezing cold for no reason. And she'd mentioned the newspaper. Rose might know something, something that could be useful for Lawrie to know.

'All right,' she said, injecting her tone with as much reluctance as two syllables could bear the weight of.

They went to the nearest café, the one that Evie usually went to with Delia. At this time of day it was almost empty.

'We close in twenty minutes.' The waitress didn't look best pleased to see them.

'We won't be long. Tea for two, please.' Evie took them to the table furthest from the window.

'I wanted to come and see you before. To explain properly,'

Rose said when they were settled in their seats, coats shed and unable to bear the silence that Evie forced upon her. 'Did you ever get my letter? I know it was ages ago now.'

Evie nodded.

'I did come round after that. Just before Christmas, not the one just gone, the one before. Your mother answered the door and said you'd gone to stay with a relative.'

'I had pneumonia. The doctor said the city air was bad for my lungs.' Evie's tone was flat as she recited the words her mother had told her to say after she'd sent her away.

Rose looked down at her hands. They sat in silence for a few pained minutes, Rose struggling to find the words she obviously needed to say; why else had she come? Evie enjoyed watching her torment.

'I'll get right to it then, shall I?' Rose asked eventually.

Evie nodded again.

'I know that it was Lawrie who found the baby.' Rose kept her voice low.

'The papers haven't mentioned his name. I checked,' Evie said, defensive even as she felt a tendril of anxiety stir deep inside. She'd examined all the papers she could think of, had visited different shops each day so that the owners didn't cotton on to her, but could she have missed one vital report?

'No, I know. But Frank saw the paper, asking for information, and he rang the police station. Out of spite. They came straight away when he gave them Lawrie's name,' Rose told her, her face twisted in apology.

'I suppose this was DS Rathbone?' Evie said, shaking her head in disbelief.

'Yes.' Rose fixed her gaze on her hands, sitting clenched before her on the table top. 'Turns out he knows Frank, sort of. They went to the same school, would you believe. Over the moon he was, Rathbone, once he started questioning me. And Frank was sitting there smirking at me the whole time, the jealous fool, too stupid to realise what that copper would be thinking about him, let alone me. It took ages. Rathbone wouldn't leave me alone even though I told him it was all ages ago and I hadn't seen Lawrie in well over a year.' She stopped talking and pressed her lips together so firmly that they all but vanished.

Evie bit her lip. 'And?'

Rose looked up. 'And what?'

'And what did you tell him?' Evie's voice rose as she leaned forward over the table.

'I just… I… Hang on.'

Rose rummaged in her handbag and found a packet of Craven 'A', her hands shaking slightly as she flipped open the lid and took out a cigarette before offering the packet to Evie. She paused before accepting. They took a moment to light them as the tea was delivered, the waitress watching them warily as Evie's fingers shook with barely controlled anger, the match flame wavering.

'God, that's better.' Rose blew out a lungful of smoke, angling it towards the ceiling. 'Look, I told him nothing new. Just what I knew Frank would tell him anyway.'

'Which was?'

'That I…' Rose sniffed and at least had the decency to look ashamed. 'I told him that I had entertained the thought – that I—'

She took a deep breath and let it out, her body sagging. 'You're really going to make me say it?'

'You weren't this embarrassed about telling everyone once upon a time,' Evie pointed out.

'I was living in a dream world back then, thinking that Lawrie could save me! Crazy, isn't it?' She laughed bitterly. 'Rathbone told me that you and Lawrie are still together, by the way. I think he was trying to make me jealous but I'm happy for you. I really am.'

'Rose, you need to tell me what you said to him,' Evie told her, leaning forward. 'They arrested Lawrie at the weekend, did he tell you that?' Rose nodded, blinking her damp eyes, her face pale. 'You need to tell me now if you've said *anything* that can be used against him.'

'I kept to the facts. Nothing incriminating. I said that I knew Lawrie from being a volunteer. I'm still in the WVS so I told him to check with them. And that we'd had a... flirtation, but that I hadn't seen him since.' The rouge on her cheeks couldn't disguise her guilty blush.

Evie leaned back as she sipped her tea, hoping to remove the bitter taste from her mouth.

'Did Rathbone ask you anything else?'

'He wanted to know if I'd ever had a baby, or got myself in the family way,' Rose admitted, dropping her gaze from Evie's cold stare. 'If I'd ever left Frank. If I made a habit of running around with other men behind my husband's back.' She laughed softly. 'That was when Frank finally stood up and told him he'd asked enough.'

'And?'

'And that's it. I told him I'd been careful, that I'd never got myself in the family way, not even with Frank. And I did leave him for a while, but not long enough to cover up something like that.'

'You actually left Frank?' Evie couldn't help but raise an eyebrow. 'So why go back? Why not get a divorce? The way you read it in the papers, everyone's doing it these days.'

Rose had bitten away most of her lipstick by now. 'I stayed in Putney with my sister, Stella, for a while, but she'd just remarried. Her new husband didn't want me there and Frank kept coming round drunk and making a scene. I tried to get my own place. I still had some savings, enough to rent a flat for a few months, but it was disgusting. Miserable but it was all I could afford.' She smiled wryly. 'I've not had a proper job since the war, and the jobs I did then aren't open to women any longer. Apart from anything else, I couldn't afford a solicitor.'

'No choice but to go back to being a bored housewife,' Evie sneered, feeling her lip curl in disgust. What was it about Rose that made her feel like this? This sick hatred that was swirling up now and threatening to overcome her.

'You don't understand, Evie!' Rose slapped her hand on the table, before whipping it back, startled as Evie by her outburst. The waitress glanced over anxiously as she fussed with the sign by the door, flipping it to read CLOSED. Rose leaned forward again, her voice low and fierce, quiet tears flowing in twin mascaraed streams down her face. 'I hate Frank. I can't stand to be near him so don't you dare sit there and think that my life is easy. I did my best to make it clear to that copper that Lawrie could never have done what they're accusing him of. I certainly didn't make it any worse than it already is.'

'Are you really that dense?' Evie hissed. 'Can't you do simple maths? That baby was probably born eight or nine months after you first met Lawrie. Rathbone has proof now that Lawrie knew a local woman at exactly the right time. Even if he believes you, it's not too far to leap to the conclusion that you weren't the only woman who made eyes at Lawrie. You've made things ten times worse than they already were.'

'But I came here to warn you!'

'You came here because you felt guilty, because you know you've landed Lawrie right in it. Rathbone only has your word that you didn't leave your husband to cover up a pregnancy. And Frank's no good – he'd hardly admit to his wife giving birth to another man's child, would he? You've just given Lawrie a motive, you absolute fool.'

Evie slammed back her chair, twisting her arm as Rose leaned out to grab her. She heard Rose call her name, begging her to come back, but she couldn't breathe. She flew out of the café, almost crashing into a passer-by on the pavement. It had just started to rain again but, for once, she was grateful, the cold water cooling her down as she managed to catch her breath. She walked fast, heading towards home on foot. She could catch the bus further down, when she knew she was safe from Rose Armstrong.

She jumped on the bus halfway along Battersea Rise and sat down, soaked through now and shivering, her day ending as miserably as it had begun. Now that she could think rationally she could kick herself. She should have questioned Rose, as thoroughly as Rathbone had done. Because she didn't know how long Rose had been away from her husband. Long enough to bear a child? Evie had been out in Devon for months, had had no contact with anyone in London bar her mother and Delia while she was gone. She had no idea whether Lawrie had seen Rose in that time. She'd never asked him because she was too scared of what his answer might be. And now, as hard as she tried, she couldn't shake the thought that perhaps Rathbone might just be right about Lawrie.

11

Tuesday had not begun in any better fashion for Lawrie.

'There was a bloke round here yesterday after you'd left,' Bert told him as they packed their bags at the start of their shift at the sorting office. 'Asking questions about you.'

He could guess who easily enough. 'About me? Who? What'd he look like?' He tried to keep his tone level but the words came out in a fast staccato.

'Skinny chap with a 'tache. Walked in here like he owned the place and asked if you were in. There was only me and Dave out here. He asked to speak to the boss.'

'He spoke to Donovan? You hear what he was asking?'

'Nah. He showed him something, a card, and then Donovan took him into the office.' Bert frowned. 'I'd put money on him being a copper, though. You're not in trouble, are you?'

Lawrie glanced over at the closed office door and, as if psychic, Eric Donovan threw it open, glaring at him. 'Matthews! In here.'

'Sir.' He took his bag with him in case proof were needed that he was just trying to get on with his job.

Donovan was squeezing back behind his desk when Lawrie entered, every square inch of it covered: paperwork, tea-stained mugs, manila folders. Lawrie thought he even spied the ripped cover of a paperback novel amongst the litter. Funny, he'd not thought of Donovan as a bookworm. He preferred to keep his rather less flattering perception of his boss as an unkempt jobs-worth, with no skill meriting the promotion to his current role save his ability to lick the boots of his own boss.

'Don't bother sitting,' Donovan warned.

Where would he have sat anyway? There were four large personnel folders stacked up on the chair opposite Donovan, one of which was Lawrie's own, he could see. He stood behind this tower, his bag slung over his shoulder, hands crossed before him respectfully.

'You know why you're here?'

Lawrie shook his head. 'No, sir.'

'The police have been round, Mr Matthews. Asking questions about you. D'you know what about?'

'You know I spoke to them after what happened. That I was there when they found that poor baby. I would guess it was about that.' He tried to keep his gaze steady as he addressed Donovan.

'Trust me, son, I've no problem letting you go if I find out you've lied, either to me or to DS Rathbone.'

'Sir, I promise. I told you exactly what happened. Everything I know.' Thank God he'd been straight with Donovan from the beginning. 'I don't know what sort of monster could even think of doing such a thing but it's got nothing to do with me. It was just my bad luck that I happened to be passing.'

'If there's any more trouble then—'

'There won't be,' Lawrie interrupted.

'I won't protect you, you know. Just 'cause we've got an arrangement on the side, don't think I'll risk my neck for you.'

The idea almost made Lawrie laugh. As if he'd ever imagined that Donovan would go an inch out of his way to help him!

'I know, sir. I'll make sure it doesn't happen again.'

'Donovan sighed. 'Last chance. Now, you've got something for me?'

Lawrie pulled a brown paper bag from his coat pocket. 'Here you go, sir.' An off-ration pound of sugar procured by Derek. 'Mr Ryan says that you might want to stock up while he has availability.'

'Tell him I'll be in touch.' Donovan secreted the package away in a drawer. 'Back to work then.'

Lawrie made good his escape. The newspaper article had been a blow and he'd been half expecting Rathbone to make an appearance. He'd have to watch his step. Rathbone hadn't leaked his name yet but there was still time. And if he was caught delivering black market goods then that was it. A criminal record for sure and after that, no one would be able to help him. Two years of hard work wasted – no job, no freedom. Evie wouldn't even stick by him if she had any sense.

He wasn't sure if people were looking at him suspiciously or if he'd lost that layer of thick skin that he'd grown since arriving, learning to ignore the occasional under-the-breath comments and pointed stares that were part of walking these London streets. Things were different now. He was a suspect, even if no one knew that he'd been arrested. Just by being a black man in Brixton he was a person of interest. He kept a wide berth when passing anyone on the street and fixed a smile to his face that he hoped appeared good-natured.

The houses were as familiar to him now as the drizzling grey rain, the odd jagged gaps in the terraces where children played and built forts amongst the rubble no longer shocking, but the dark skies and damp air gave them an ominous feel, as though behind the net curtains lurked accusers. Was it just him or was Mrs Harwood less friendly this morning as he handed over the parcel that had come from her daughter in Leeds? And when he passed Mr Thomson on Kellett Road, didn't they usually exchange a nod and a smile that today was one-sided?

It was a relief to get home after the working day, to close the door behind him and shut out the world. He could hear Mrs Ryan humming away in the kitchen but he wasn't in the mood to face her cheeriness. He slunk upstairs to his room and sat down heavily on the bed. He was tired, that was all. Aston had left half a bottle of whisky on the windowsill and Lawrie took a swig straight from the bottle, hoping to dampen the prodding anxiety that had trailed at his heels all day.

It was Tuesday he remembered suddenly, Agnes Coleridge's bridge night. He and Evie always took advantage of her mother's absence. Sometimes they just stayed in the backyard and talked, but with the weather as grey and cold as it was, he'd suggest going to the pictures. It would make up for them not going on Saturday.

He swallowed another mouthful of whisky and lay down on the bed. He only closed his eyes for a second, hoping to clear his mind, but the slam of the front door startled him awake. Checking his watch he found he'd been dead to the world for over an hour. The whisky had left a stale residue on his tongue and he winced as he swallowed, his throat dry and rasping. Rain was pelting against the window and the sky outside was oppressively dark.

He swilled his mouth with water from the bathroom tap and splashed his face until he felt normal. Evie would notice if something was wrong and he was a terrible liar. She was late. That hadn't been her at the door else he'd have been shouted for. She usually called round on her way home, just to say hello.

He ran downstairs and found Mrs Ryan in the kitchen peeling potatoes.

'Did you go out?' he asked.

'No, love.' She looked confused. 'Oh, you heard the door. Just a fella selling tea towels.'

'Evie's not been round? I fell asleep, must have missed her.'

'No, she's not called round. I've not been out since you got home.'

'Maybe she got held up at work,' he said. She should have been back well before now.

'She'll be round soon enough,' Mrs Ryan told him. 'Cup of tea?'

He shook his head. 'I'll go and see if she's home yet.'

He felt nervous knocking on the Colcridges' door, even though he did it every morning. It was different when he had the uniform on. He was doing his job. Now his anxiety was growing again, worrying that Evie was having second thoughts. Maybe she'd decided that Rathbone was right and Lawrie must have had something to do with the baby's death.

Then the door opened and there she was, looking a little sheepish.

'Hello,' he said.

'Hello,' she replied.

She kept her eyes lowered, not quite meeting his, and she looked pale.

'Is everything all right?' he asked, his heart in his mouth. 'You didn't call round.'

'No. I was late getting home from work.' She met his gaze and he saw that her eyes were a little red. 'But Ma's gone out. Why don't you come in?'

He nodded, unsure. He'd never been inside the Coleridges' house before. Agnes had made it a strict rule, despite turning a blind eye to him climbing the back wall; the doorstep was as far as he was allowed. Evie stepped back to let him in, surprising him with a kiss as she shut the door.

'Are you sure this is allowed?' he asked, pulling back slightly.

She frowned. 'I wouldn't have invited you in if it wasn't. Ma won't be home for hours and it's tipping buckets down out there.'

She took him by the hand and he followed her into the front room, still unsure as to what Agnes Coleridge would say if she walked in and found him there.

'Why don't you light the fire and I'll fetch us something to drink.' She handed him a box of matches and disappeared.

He could hear her in the kitchen, the gentle bang of cupboard doors. He struck a match and crouched before the fire, studying it. He'd never lit a coal fire before; never had to. There were twists of paper woven between the lumps of coal, and he held the match to one. The paper flared and he watched it burn but nothing else happened. Sighing at his failure, he straightened up, looking down at the framed photographs on the mantelpiece as he did so. One was a portrait of a stern-looking man; Evie's grandfather, he guessed. On the other side of an ornamental clock sat a happier picture. A little girl, a younger Evie, stood between Agnes and a woman who must have been Agnes's sister. The aunt Evie had stayed with in Devon.

He turned as he heard her soft footsteps behind him. 'This photograph,' he said. 'You and Agnes look so happy.'

She carried two glasses of lemonade, putting them down carefully on the coffee table, on coasters, before walking over to look. 'Gosh, that was taken about ten years ago. Aunt Gertie came to visit us just after the war had started. She wanted Ma and me to go down and live with her until it was over. I think she was lonely. Her husband had died not long before and they'd not had children. I went, once the evacuations started, but Ma refused to leave. She was in a terrible mood that day. She didn't want to go sightseeing and she kept reminding us, but she cheered up eventually. It was a lovely day, the sun was out, and Gertie decided she wanted a souvenir so she got a policeman to take our photo. She had one of those fancy little cameras.'

'I don't think I've ever seen your mother smile before,' Lawrie joked.

'No,' Evie agreed. She looked down at the cold hearth. 'Haven't you lit a fire before?'

'Ah, see, I tried but I think there must be a trick to it.' He shrugged apologetically.

She got down on her hands and knees and reached up, tugging his hand until he dropped down beside her. She took the matches from him. 'Let me show you.' She struck a match and held it to the twists of paper dotted amongst the coal and kindling, her hand dancing as she moved it quickly between them.

'As easy as that?' Lawrie put his arm around her waist as they both stared like proud parents at the immature flames, growing in confidence and stature before their eyes.

'With a bit of luck.' Evie blew gently on the edges, encouraging them to take hold.

His grip tightened and she leaned into his kiss. He pulled her to her feet, their lips barely parting as they moved to the sofa. What harm were a few kisses after all? Just a temporary reprieve.

It felt like hardly a moment passed but when he did finally come to his senses it had been almost half an hour. She reached over and passed him a glass of lemonade. He drank half of it down in one go.

'You must be thirsty,' she said.

'Like a man in a desert,' he told her, smiling.

She looked away and took a sip of her own drink.

'Is something wrong?'

'No.' She spoke quickly, then sighed. 'You'll think I'm being daft but I had started to wonder. I mean, I thought that maybe your heart wasn't in it. In me.' Her attempt at a smile failed. 'If maybe you'd rather be with someone else.'

He put down his glass, carefully, right in the centre of the coaster. 'What's all this? Evie, I would never even look at another woman. Why would I when I have you?'

Her smile didn't quite reach her eyes. 'Rose came to see me. That's the real reason I was late home. Frank's spoken to Rathbone, told him the whole story, but there's nothing to worry about. He'd have found out eventually and this way we know what he knows.'

There it was again, the panic rising up from the pit of his stomach. 'When was this? After Rathbone let me go? Or before?'

'I'm not sure,' she admitted. 'I should have asked her but I was so angry I could barely think. She seemed different. Like she was actually sorry. I don't think she said much, it was more Frank, trying to get revenge.'

'The man already put me in hospital once. How much revenge does one person need?' He smiled but he could feel his lips tremble.

'This will blow over. They'll catch the real culprit and everything will go back to normal.'

'You don't want to throw me out and wash your hands of me?'

'What? Now? When Ma'll be gone for at least another hour? No chance!' She took hold of his face, gently rubbing her hands against the coarseness of his chin, the stubble having grown since his morning shave. 'Come here.'

He was so grateful for her. Whatever was going on with Rathbone or Rose or Frank Armstrong, he had Evie, and Evie had forgiven him for his mistakes. He kissed her back and decided he'd speak to Agnes when he got a chance. He'd ask for Evie's hand, get her mother's blessing. Everything had to be perfect. Evie deserved that.

21st March 1950

Dear Gertie,
How are you, darling sister?

I can imagine you must be rolling your eyes as you read this and I'm sorry. I know I promised to write more often but you know how things get. And it's not like I've been buried under the mounds of your correspondence. With that said, I told Evie I'd write back so here we are.

We're both fine. Better than fine, in fact. Evie has bounced back as if nothing happened and is stepping out with the young lad from next door that I told you about, the postman. Lawrie's his name. I must have mentioned that he's Jamaican. There are loads of them round here now, you'd be shocked. Even since last year I'd swear there are more of them. Lawrie's all right, though. He's a well-brought up lad, very polite. I wouldn't be surprised if he got down on one knee before the end of the summer, at least that's what I'm hoping.

I haven't forgotten what you told me and I think that maybe now is the time to cut the apron strings, as they say. There is one fly in the ointment. I don't know if you've read in the papers down where you are but there was a baby found dead up on Clapham Common. I know it made it into the bigger papers but I don't suppose people in Devon care that much about what goes on up here day to day. Anyway, I thought I'd better let you know since it was Lawrie who found the body. He's had a bit of trouble with the police over it, as you can imagine. I don't know what will happen so I suppose I just wanted to warn you, in case someone down your way mentions it. I know for certain that Lawrie's not involved but we know from Dad that it doesn't always matter.

Saying all that, I wondered if you fancied a trip to the big smoke this summer? Evie keeps telling me that she'd be happy to see you. I get the impression that you two grew quite close during her stay with you and it would give us a proper chance to catch up. Chat about the future and all that.

Let me know. We'll go to a theatre show and go for a posh dinner at that restaurant on the Strand again. What do you say?

Love from your little sister,

Aggie xx

1948

Evie knocked on the door and waited. The curtains at the front window were shut tight and there was no sign of life. Was this the right house? It looked as if no one was home.

She knocked again, less tentatively, and put her ear to the scuffed wood of the door, taking a swift step backwards as she heard footsteps from inside. Strange, it sounded like the tapping of high heels but Lawrie had warned her that there were only men living here. He'd told her because he was a gentleman, making sure it was all right with her to spend her Sunday afternoon in such company. She'd nodded and shrugged as if it was nothing new. She hadn't been worried at the time, only now beginning to feel a little nervous.

The door swung open. 'Fancy seeing you here! Edie, isn't it?' It was the woman from the shelter, Rose. 'Sorry to keep you waiting, we're all out in the backyard what with it being such a glorious day – you're lucky Sonny has sharp ears and heard you knocking.'

Evie followed her to the back of the house, knowing she'd

missed the natural opportunity to correct Rose over her name. She wasn't good at making a fuss. Besides, why was Rose even here? She wasn't wearing her WVS uniform today. She wore a navy floral dress and heels that weren't practical for everyday use. Ma would have tutted at the sight.

The house was larger than Evie's, a whole storey taller, but the ground floor was laid out similarly with the kitchen leading out to the backyard. Unlike her mother's this kitchen floor was cluttered with several mouse traps, along with the droppings of the wily creatures who'd avoided them. She could see immediately the cause of the infestation: breadcrumbs were trailed willy-nilly across counters and there was an open container of porridge oats lying abandoned. Inviting the enemy to tea quite literally. She followed Rose's lead and they tiptoed across the filth to the yard.

The backyard had been converted into a living room of sorts. Stacked wooden beer crates formed a circle of seats around a long tea-chest-cum-coffee-table. Lawrie sat between two other men who Evie recognised from church that morning. Across his lap was a musical instrument, though Evie couldn't put a name to it, a long black tube with silver keys. This was why she had come: he'd invited her round to listen to the band practice. Ma thought she'd gone round to Delia's. Another lie. She'd have kittens if she knew where her daughter actually was.

'Would you care for a drink, Evie?' Lawrie stood to greet her. 'It's safe. Rose brought some ginger beer and some clean glasses that won't give us typhoid.'

She watched him pour and took the glass from him, almost dropping it as his hand brushed hers. She tried to smile but one of the other men was watching her, as though he were trying to puzzle her out. She shouldn't have come. Except that there was something compelling about spending time with these people with whom she had nothing in common and yet, just by being here she felt suddenly less alone. Less of an oddity and more at home.

'Where are my manners?' Lawrie looked flustered now. 'Boys, this is Evie. Evie, Sonny over there is our drummer, and this is Johnny, our glorious band leader.'

'Glorious? I like that, man. Welcome, Evie. And thank you, Rose, for the refreshments.' Johnny lifted his full glass. 'You fancy moving in here and looking after us permanently?'

'I'm just here representing the WVS. Making sure you chaps are settling in. Now, Evie, fancy making yourself useful?'

Evie nodded, feeling four sets of eyes watching her.

'Then let's get stuck into that disgusting kitchen. I've brought some food that was left over from the shelter but it'll be a feast for the vermin. Good thing I know what men are like and thought to bring some cleaning supplies.'

'You can say no,' Lawrie told Evie. 'I didn't invite you here to clean up after us.'

'Might as well make myself useful.' It wasn't as if she could sit there like the Queen of Sheba while Rose scoured the kitchen and swept out mouse poo. What would he think of her?

She took the spare scarf that Rose handed her and tied back her hair before picking up the broom. As she began to sweep, music started to play, deep velvety tones that made her want to stop and listen. Looking out of the window she saw that it was

Lawrie's instrument that made that wonderful sound. Johnny began to sing along and the third man, Sonny, beat out a rhythm on the tea chest. She recognised the tune: 'Wonder When My Baby's Coming Home'.

'Good, aren't they?' Rose said.

'Very,' Evie agreed, forcing her eyes away from Lawrie before Rose could notice. 'Do you do this for all the men? Make sure they've got food and somewhere decent to live?'

'Good Lord, no!' Rose lowered her voice. 'To be honest, I'm not sure the powers that be would be thrilled to find out that I'm here at all.'

Evie looked at her. 'You're here as a friend then?'

'Yes, I suppose you could say that. And what brings you here? No homework to get done before school tomorrow?'

'I'm not at school. I'm at secretarial college.' Evie picked up the smaller dustpan and brush, turning her back on Rose as she swept shit and crumbs and stray oats into the dustpan.

'Oh well, that's different,' she laughed.

'Yes, it is,' Evie corrected her, finally finding some courage. 'It's not the same at all. You can't be a secretary anywhere these days without a qualification.'

Rose held up a placatory hand. 'That's me told then.'

'Lawrie invited me over and I said yes.'

'You've seen much of him?'

Evie shrugged. 'We bumped into each other at the Astoria yesterday.' And went to a café afterwards, Lawrie and Sam, Evie and Delia. 'I saw him again at church this morning and he said to come over if I wanted to hear them play.'

'And so here you are.'

Rose didn't ask her any more questions but talked for ages about the dance the week before that Evie had been forbidden to attend even though Delia had been allowed. Apparently Lawrie had been ever such a love and, when Rose's husband had abandoned her to meet his pals in the pub afterwards, it was Lawrie who walked her to the bus stop and made sure she got on safely.

The music stopped and was replaced by a chorus of greetings and laughter. Evie looked up to see Sam walking in through the back gate. He'd made her laugh the day before, teasing Lawrie and making fun of the film they'd just seen. He and Lawrie shared a room, up on the top floor he'd told her. Evie was just glad to see another friendly face. A fifth man followed him in carrying a huge instrument case on his back.

'This'll have to do.' Rose released Evie from her servitude. 'It's not perfect but it's a hundred times better than it was.'

There was an empty crate beside Lawrie but Rose was too quick, even in heels. Evie found herself perching between Sam and the latecomer, introduced as Moses.

'So, we still need a name,' Johnny reminded them. 'You know, most bands name themselves after the band leader.'

'And since that's you…' Sam laughed. 'Although we never did make a decision on that either, did we?'

'I stand at the front. That good enough? And was it not I who put us all together in the first place, Sam Miller?'

'C'mon fellas, we just need a simple name,' Lawrie reminded them.

'How 'bout Johnny's Jokers?' Sam suggested.

'How 'bout you watch your mouth—'

'The Johnny Sands Band will do for now,' Lawrie raised his voice over the squabbling. 'We just getting started out after all. We can come up with something else later.'

Johnny nodded in appreciation while Sam kissed his teeth but let go of his argument.

'I like it,' Rose said. 'It has a ring to it.' She put a hand on Lawrie's shoulder and Evie saw Sam choke back a snigger as he clocked it, exchanging a gleeful glance with Moses.

What a fool she'd been. She'd come round because she'd dared believe that Lawrie liked her. Only here he was, smiling at Rose as she leaned against him. How naïve of Evie to assume that just because Rose was married, she wasn't a rival. Ma said all the time that morals that had loosened during the war hadn't been tightened since. Even on their own street things went on behind closed doors. Everyone knew that Mrs Foster's youngest daughter wasn't Mr Foster's. He'd been a prisoner of war, kept captive in France for over a year before Flo was born.

'You work, Evie?' Johnny drew her back into a conversation she hadn't been paying attention to.

'Evie's at secretarial college, aren't you, Evie?' Rose smiled at her. 'I wish I was still a young whipper-snapper like you. No worries, living at home, not having to pay bills.'

Evie felt them all staring at her, very aware suddenly that she was still wearing the dress her mother had approved for church: blue and white checked, knee length and buttoned to a Peter Pan collar that now felt tight around her neck. Her ankle socks were white cotton. She was dressed like a schoolgirl. Rose was right.

'I should go.' She stood up before she could feel more of a fool. 'I promised Ma I'd wouldn't be long. Thank you for having me, though. I liked hearing you play.'

'But you didn't get to hear my bass!' Moses protested.

Lawrie jumped up. 'I can walk you home if you like.'

'Thank you. That would be kind.' She smiled, hoping that Lawrie didn't fathom the real reason for her premature departure. Rose was what Delia would call a tart, she decided. It would serve her right if her husband found out what she was up to. And if Evie was too young for Lawrie then Rose was definitely too old. She was twenty-five, if she was a day.

'This supposed to be band practice,' Johnny told Lawrie.

'Five minutes, man.' Lawrie jammed his hat on his head and led Evie back through the house. They crossed the street, heading towards the main road.

'I'm sorry about all that. The cleaning, I mean. I didn't even know Rose was coming round. She means well but she can be a little forceful!'

'At least there weren't any live mice running around!' she said.

'Reckon I would have been the one screaming loudest if there was,' he joked. 'Honestly, I hate that place. Soon as I can afford something better I'm out of there.'

'You know, my next-door neighbour takes in lodgers. I can ask if you like. She's just let the front room but she has a box room as well.'

He slowed his gait and she felt the back of his hand brush hers, the tingle spreading the length of her arm. 'You wouldn't mind having me as a neighbour?'

''Course not.' She looked up and smiled.

'Then I'd be very grateful. And I was wondering… would you like to come to the Astoria with me on Tuesday?'

Tuesday was Ma's bridge night. As long as she was home before ten she'd never know. 'I'd love to.'

'Perfect. I'll meet you out the front? Six o'clock?'

She made him leave her at the corner, just in case Ma happened to be out the front of the house for some reason. Halfway down the street she dared to turn back and there he was, watching. He tipped his hat to her before vanishing back the way they'd come.

12

'What's that long face for?' Ma asked.

They were eating breakfast, or at least Ma was. For a few days after her confrontation with Rathbone, her mother had been in one of her dark moods and was only just coming out of it. Evie was reluctant to tell her what she'd seen in case it caused a regression.

'I saw that detective again. Across the street, just now.'

She'd gone to the window for the daylight, to pluck her eyebrows. A movement had caught her eye as she clicked the compact shut: Rathbone climbing out of his car. He leaned against the vehicle as he lit his cigarette, his eyes on the Ryan house. Evie hadn't moved a muscle but he'd sensed her presence anyway, looking up and offering a salute. He looked happy with himself as he walked off down the road.

'You stay away from that man,' Ma told her.

'I was hardly going to walk up to him and wish him a good morning,' Evie pointed out. 'Should I tell Lawrie, d'you think?'

'Why? Just cause that man's loitering around here doesn't

mean that it's anything to do with Lawrie.' Her mother looked as unsure as Evie felt.

She hurried out to catch the bus to work and was lucky, a 37 showing up just as she reached the stop. She climbed to the upper deck and sat down as they pulled away. Even travelling the same route every day, she loved to look down and spot changes to the urban scenery: the bomb sites that were slowly beginning to disappear, the new buildings that stuck out like a book put back in the wrong place on the shelf. It was all so untidy but she could barely remember what it had all looked like before the war. Before the air raid sirens had started sounding on a regular basis and she'd been shipped off to Devon for the first time. Unless the bus was packed she was usually left alone in her reverie so she looked up in surprise when she felt a weight press down on the double seat.

'Fancy bumping into you here, Miss Coleridge.'

She turned away from the houses of Acre Lane and stared straight into the face of DS Rathbone, his skinny lips turned up in the smile of a villain from a B movie.

'Didn't mean to startle you.' Mock concern was etched across his face. 'Only I thought it was time me and you had a little chat.'

'I don't have anything to say to you.' Her heart began to race. 'Except that you're looking at the wrong man. Lawrie's a good person.'

'You may very well be correct.' He leaned closer and she was repulsed to feel the tickle of his moustache against the shell of her ear. He was wearing too much cologne and the stink caught in her throat. 'I did a little investigating, see, and it seems I had my eye on the wrong house all along.'

She felt her mouth drop slightly as if she were his marionette, helpless to resist. 'What do you mean?'

'I mean that we've had a lot of people coming forward with information. Lot of concerned citizens round this neck of the woods. Most of them don't know anything at all but we had one very interesting telephone call with a person who gave us your name.'

Evie's chest tightened. She felt like she was wearing a corset, barely able to breathe. It wasn't warm out but she felt the tingle on her skin as her forehead broke into a sweat. 'My name?'

'Don't play the innocent, Miss Coleridge. I know why you disappeared off to Devon for all those months. The truth, I mean, not the story you told everyone.'

'I was ill.' Her voice was barely louder than a whisper. 'I went to my aunt's to recuperate.'

'For six months?' He pulled out his notebook. 'You left London in early November 1948 according to your previous employer, after only a few weeks in the job. And Vernon & Sons have you starting with them in late May of 1949.'

'I had bronchitis,' she whispered, scared to look behind and see if anyone else could hear their conversation. 'I needed to leave the city because of the air.'

'Bronchitis, eh? Or was it pneumonia? It's easy to get confused, isn't it, Miss Coleridge? I mean, six months is quite a while.' He lowered his voice. 'Long enough to vanish before anyone realises there's anything going on. Long enough to give birth to a baby girl and then – well, that's where I get stuck. I was hoping you could tell me what happened next. My mystery caller couldn't tell me so I wonder what you did with your baby, Miss Coleridge. Would you like to tell me now so we can save time?'

Evie closed her eyes, hardly able to believe what was happening. Only two people in the world knew: Ma and Aunt Gertie. Neither of them would have called the police.

'I'm a reasonable chap, Miss Coleridge. Or can I call you Evelyn?'

'I'm sorry, I don't know what you're talking about.' She wiped treacherous tears from her cheeks.

'Then maybe I should talk to Mr Matthews. Find out what he knows.'

'No!' She began to sob. 'Please. Please don't. Lawrie doesn't know.'

In front of them was an older woman, her head turning slightly as she heard Evie hiccupping back the tears. Evie willed her not to turn around; she couldn't bear it. She'd thought that nothing could be as shameful as her mother discovering what she'd done, but this was far worse, being forced to admit her mistake to this vile man. And here, where anyone could be listening in.

'You're not leaving me an awful lot of choice.' He sighed as if she'd disappointed him. 'Is it the bus? We can go down to the station if you'd prefer. Would that be better, Evelyn? Have a nice chat over a cup of tea?'

She knew that he was playing a game with her but that didn't mean it wasn't effective. He wouldn't leave her alone until she talked. They were beside Clapham Common now, the north side, the trees beginning to show their blossom. On the other side of the bus she knew they were passing Cedars Road, the imposing building where Evie had been born standing halfway along.

'It's got nothing to do with Lawrie. He doesn't know.' She spoke in a whisper, her eyes on the middle-aged woman in front.

'He's not the father? Then who?' Rathbone's pencil was poised. 'I'll need a full name, Evelyn.'

Evie paused. 'I never knew his name. There was a party. That was where it happened. I never saw him again, he left London the week after. Went to stay with his brother up north somewhere, I heard. Birmingham or Manchester, somewhere like that.' She found her handkerchief in her bag and blew her nose.

'But it was a girl. I found the birth certificate. Registered in Exmouth last April.'

She'd shut out the memories for so long that they felt like someone else's, like a movie she'd seen. 'She's not Ophelia, I promise. My aunt, she used to be a nurse, she said there was nothing to be done. She was born... well, she never...' Her voice sounded crackly in her ears, like listening to the news on the wireless during a rainstorm. 'I was supposed to give her up anyway.'

'Right.' Rathbone seemed less certain now. 'So she died?'

Evie nodded and gulped back tears.

'Idiot yokels down in Devon, they could have bloody told me.'

She felt the seat raise slightly as Rathbone got up and pulled the cord to request the next stop.

'Thank you for your time, Miss Coleridge,' he said, as if he hadn't just ripped her life apart along the seam she'd tried so hard to stitch together, and vanished down the stairs.

This was her own stop, she realised, but she was paralysed, the shame an overwhelming weight keeping her body pressed into the seat. Could it have been Rose? Hadn't Rose tried to grab onto her as she'd left the café, as if she had something more to say? She was capable of anything, Evie knew that; and she'd known that Evie had been in Devon.

She forced herself to take slow breaths and the panic began to dissipate, her senses returning fully as the bus stopped opposite the Town Hall in Wandsworth. She stumbled down the stairs and checked her watch. She was already late for work. There was a telephone box and she rummaged in her purse for the right coins, the operator efficiently connecting her to Mrs Jones.

'I'm ever so sorry,' she said, her voice naturally hoarse. 'I was on my way to work and I was sick. I think I ate some bad fish last night.'

She closed her eyes and rested her forehead against the cool of the glass panel as Mrs Jones gave her a stern talking to for letting Mr Sullivan down, biting her lip as she heard that Mildred would take her place for the day.

At least Ma wouldn't be home until later. She did for two families on a Wednesday, the Rodgers whose house overlooked the Common, and the Proctors over in Balham. When she got home Evie ran upstairs to her bedroom and reached under her bed, her fingertips grazing the item she sought. It had been pushed right to the back, against the wall, and she had to lie on her belly and stretch out with her arm to grab it.

The music box had been a Christmas present when she was eight years old, a lost treasure found by Ma in a junk shop. The japanned wood was smooth under Evie's fingertips, inlaid with a painted woodland scene. She sat cross-legged on the floor, her back against the bedframe and undid the catch, the tiny dancer within springing upright. She wound the key and watched the ballerina twirl as the steel comb teased out the theme to *Swan Lake*. The box had been made to hold something small and precious, jewellery perhaps, but Evie had none. Instead she had kept the one reminder that, for a very short time, she had had a daughter, even if she had only ever lived in Evie's own thoughts. She lifted out the hand-crocheted booties, a spur-of-the-moment purchase from a market stall in the Devonshire village where her Aunt Gertie lived.

Until she'd handed over the coins, watching over her shoulder to make sure Gertie was still busy at the fishmonger's, she hadn't realised how badly she wanted to keep her baby.

1948

'Hello there!'

He turned on the doorstep, his key in the lock, surprised to see Rose. In one hand she swung a string shopping bag though she looked far more glamorous than the everyday housewife off to the shops.

'I was hoping to catch you,' she said. 'It's such a lovely day and I wondered if you fancied taking a dip.'

'A dip?' He shook his head in confusion.

'Brockwell Lido's only ten minutes from here.' She laughed as she realised he hadn't a clue what she was talking about. 'It's an open-air swimming pool. It's the perfect day for a swim, don't you think?'

Lawrie glanced up at the sky. It was still blue enough but were Londoners really so crazy they'd bother to build themselves a swimming pool that was open to the whims of the British weather?

'I don't have a bathing suit,' he told her.

'Aha!' She reached into the bag and, with a magician's flourish, produced a pair of navy swimming trunks. 'I swiped Frank's for you. And I've another pair if one of your friends fancies coming along.'

He wasn't really in the mood for company, but the thought of floating in cool water overcame his doubts. He was meeting Evie later on and he didn't want to be in this foul mood, caused by yet another wasted day of job hunting. Jobs miraculously filled by the time he arrived for an interview; not qualified; too qualified; 'If it were up to me… but…' At the last place the excuse had been 'no foreigners', silence greeting the sight of Lawrie's passport as he waved it under the man's nose. But for the gold letters spelling 'Jamaica' beneath the coat of arms it looked just like any other British passport. Not good enough apparently. It made Lawrie wonder if anything ever would be.

Leaving Rose on the doorstep he ran upstairs to find Sam. It was a simple matter of uttering the words 'swimming pool' to entice Sam into the escapade.

Rose led them down Railton Road, her chatter filling the silence. Sam kept looking across at Lawrie and grinning. *Barely in the country three weeks and you already got two girls after you*, he'd said back at the house. Perhaps it would have been more sensible to turn Rose down but she was just being nice. He didn't want to hurt her feelings. And it wasn't as if her invitation had been just for him.

'You haven't asked me yet,' Rose reminded him.

'Asked you what?'

'If I've had any luck. With the band. Getting you work.'

He hadn't even given it a thought. It wasn't as if the band was ever going to pay his way. If he didn't get a job soon he'd have to talk to Aston, see if there was a chance of anything with the RAF.

'You got good news?' Sam asked.

'I should tell Johnny first really, since he's the bandleader.' She shot Lawrie a sly glance. 'But since you're here… I've got you a slot at the Lyceum next Friday night. Early on, before the crowds get there, but if they like what they hear then they'll have you back. It's a foot in the door, as they say.'

'The Lyceum? Sounds quite grand.' Grander than a church hall at least.

'It's not as fancy as it was. It was a theatre back in the olden days but now it's a ballroom. Gets packed in there on a weekend.'

'Thank you, Rose,' he told her. 'We're very grateful.'

Rose paid their entry into the lido before Lawrie could say or do anything, her magical bag holding towels as well as a picnic of paste sandwiches and lemonade. She disappeared to get changed as he and Sam did the same. Frank Armstrong's trunks were a disconcertingly good fit on him, slightly tight on Sam. The lido was packed on the warmest day of the summer so far, the water chock full of splashing toddlers and pre-school age children, their mothers taking the opportunity to exchange gossip as their offspring paddled and played.

'Lord have mercy,' Sam muttered, and Lawrie turned to see what he was looking at.

Rose had emerged from the changing rooms. She wore a two-piece swimsuit in emerald green, similar in cut to that worn by several of the young mothers, nothing obscene in itself. It was Rose who turned an innocent swathe of material into a garment that drew admiring and envious eyes. Lawrie had found it easy to ignore the swing of her hips when they were encased in her knee-length skirt but now he couldn't look away, his eyes drawn upwards to her chest as his skin flushed with blood.

'You should maybe hold that towel in front,' Sam said, chuckling as he shoved Lawrie's arm so that the towel in his hand covered his crotch.

'This way, boys!' If Rose knew what was going through Lawrie's mind then she didn't show it, pointing towards a space big enough for the three of them.

She spread her towel on the ground and Lawrie quickly moved so that Sam was between them, ignoring the bemused glance from his friend. He threw his towel down and sat quickly, his legs pulled up so that the bulge at his crotch was hidden by the baggy material.

'Now isn't this civilised?' Rose unpacked sandwiches and passed them out. 'Sorry, it's just fish paste. I prefer cheese myself but it's a bit thin on the ground still. I don't suppose you're used to the rationing yet.'

Lawrie chewed and stayed silent. The bread tasted of nothing and luckily there was only a thin pink line of the paste which tasted like week-old fish chewed up and spat back out. He ate it because it meant he could save the eggs he'd bought for the next day. Eventually Rose got bored of speaking to Sam and lay back, closing her eyes against the sun.

'Hey,' Sam whispered. 'You think she'd come to the pictures with me tomorrow night?'

'She's married.' Though she wasn't acting like it.

Sam shrugged. 'So what's she doing here then, with us?'

'Maybe she's lonely.'

'But you don' care if I ask her?'

'Why would I care? I'm seeing Evie tonight.' Lawrie lay back and tried to ignore Sam.

'You playin' a long game there, boy.' Sam laughed. 'She just a kid. You got to marry a girl like that just to get a hand in her underwear.'

'Maybe I don' think like you.' Lawrie squinted up. 'Maybe I want a nice girl.'

'Girl next door,' Sam teased.

'She might be just that soon enough.' He realised once he'd spoken that he'd not told Sam of his intentions, that Evie's neighbour might become his new landlady.

'What you mean?'

Lawrie sighed. 'I came here for quiet and relaxation, not to listen to you talkin'.'

'I just want to know what you mean, that you might be livin' next door to Evie. You not walkin' out on me?'

He could see that Rose was listening in now, Sam's raised voice having stirred her awake, and he wasn't in the mood for an argument. He stood and walked to the edge of the pool, feeling the gaze of every person he passed land upon his dark skin. Should he climb up to the high board and dive off like he used to when he and Bennie visited their cousins over in Westmoreland? They would dare one another to climb higher and higher, jumping off the cliff into the clear salty sea, the sun glinting off blue waves as they swam and explored the dark caves beneath. The pool was too busy, he decided. The last thing he needed was to draw the ire of a clan of local mothers.

He dived in from the pool edge instead, a graceful and understated effort that left little splash. The water was cold and his senses sharpened as his arms and legs fought through the resistance, propelling him towards the other end. Up and down he swam, worries and concerns slowly draining out of his body, as if they were being funnelled out through his kicking feet, every damned job interview, Sam and Rose, all left in his wake until he felt weightless. After fifty or so laps he turned and floated on his back, staring up at that blue sky that reminded him of home. He bumped against the wall and put out his arms to anchor himself as he caught his breath.

'I thought you'd never stop.' Rose appeared beside him, her hair caught beneath a green swimming cap that matched her costume. 'You're ever so fast. I couldn't keep up.'

'I'm used to swimming in the sea,' he told her. 'No waves here so it's easier. Less effort.'

'I'll bet.' She looked impressed. 'Are you glad you came then?'

He nodded. 'I feel clean for the first time in days. We don't even have a decent bathroom in that place, you know. The bath is rusty so I just been using the sink in the bedroom to wash in.'

'Gosh, that's…' She looked up at the sky, thinking. 'Do you have any plans tomorrow afternoon?'

Lawrie laughed. 'Getting a job, I hope. I shouldn't even be here really. I can't afford to be lazing around, having fun.'

'I can help,' she insisted. 'Come round to mine tomorrow, around one o'clock. Bring your smart clothes, whatever you've been wearing for interviews, and I'll wash them for you. Press them. Not to be rude but if what you were wearing earlier is anything to go by, your clothes haven't seen an iron since you left Jamaica.'

'They've not,' he confessed.

'There you go then. You need to look clean and presentable. You can have a bath while I sort out your clothes and when you leave you'll be in perfect order to go out and get that job. What d'you say?'

No. He knew that's what he should say. Going round to the house of a married woman while her husband was out at work? His mother would have slapped the back of his head and told him she was just knocking sense into him. And Evie, what would she think of him? But neither of them would understand. A bath! Warm soapy water to clean off the sticky film of stale sweat that even now, lying back in the cool water of the pool, just didn't want to shift.

'If you're sure it's all right,' he said.

22nd March 1950

Dearest Aggie,
About time! I'd begun to think I'd never hear from you again, apart
from the usual Christmas and birthday cards. I'm glad all is well
up in your neck of the woods.

So Evie has learned her lesson and is doing things the right way
round this time. Glad to hear it. The quicker she gets that ring on
her finger the better. Perhaps it is just as well they brought over
those folk from the Caribbean, for all the trouble they cause, else
you'd have been growing old together in that house, I'm sure. I
can't imagine any decent young British man wanting to throw his
lot in with her, I'm afraid to say. Don't take offence, you've said
it yourself, several times. I love Evie, you know I do, but it's time
for you to think about yourself for once.

On the subject of Evie's new chap, I hope the police have got
someone for that awful Clapham Common murder. If you're sure
that he's got nothing to do with it then you could do worse than
putting in a good word. See if you can speak to one of Pa's old
friends. Jim Garvan maybe? He and Pa used to be thick as thieves
and I'm sure he'd look into it for you. The quicker they cross him
off their list, the better for all of you.

How would June suit you for a visit? Then, thinking longer term,
I've got a cunning plan for when Evie's finally left home. There'll
be nothing holding you back then. Time for a new start for you,
perhaps down here in Devon? I'll sell the Brixton house and you
can come and live with me for a bit, see if you like it. Then we
can either get you a little cottage here or we can just get on together

and live off the savings until we grow old, two little old ladies! I know you say it's too quiet here but we're not that far from Exeter after all and I know you never go out anywhere. When was the last time you went out dancing or to a West End show? You can't miss what you don't know, can you? And Mr Francis from the local shop was asking after you the other day. He's not a bad sort and his wife died a few years ago. You could do a lot worse, Aggie. Just think about it.

Let me know about June and I'll check at work to make sure I can get the leave. The first two weeks suit?

Love you lots,

Gertie xx

13

Mrs Coleridge was standing on her front doorstep sweeping out the dirt, her broom banging against the hallway skirting boards as she steered the dust towards the open door. Her presence seemed serendipitous.

'Good afternoon, Mrs Coleridge,' he called out, missing out his own gate and walking up the Coleridges' path. He took off his cap.

'Afternoon.' She paused, wary. 'Did you want something, Lawrie?'

'Yes. If you have a moment I'd like to thank you for what you did for me. On Saturday, I mean. You put yourself in a difficult position for me and I am grateful.' He couldn't tell from her face if he was making things better or worse.

'I'm not sure I helped but you're most welcome. Just finished work, have you?'

'Yes.' He swallowed and tried to summon his courage. 'I was hoping to talk to you about something. About Evie.'

'Right now?' She glanced back inside the house, though Evie was surely still at work.

'Yes? Or I can come back another time.'

She laughed then, at his expression. 'Bless you, Lawrie, do I scare you so badly?'

He thought it safest to stay silent.

She sighed. 'Come inside and we'll talk. I've got a pot on already.'

He followed Mrs Coleridge into the house, stopping to take off his boots in the hallway. He padded to the kitchen in socks that he only now remembered needed darning on both big toes. Please God let her not look down at his feet. The kitchen was familiar from another angle, looking in from the backyard. Now, from the inside, he could see the neatly stacked plates on the shelf, the door which concealed the pantry, the calendar on the wall, the picture a child's drawing of a house. He moved closer to get a better look. On the bright green lawn stood a pink woman and a brown child, both in blue dresses. Beside the girl sat a black cat on one side, on the other what looked like a sheep, grey and woolly.

'That's Evie's artistic masterpiece,' Agnes said, pulling out a chair for him. 'From when she was in primary school. It embarrasses her now but I like it. I just buy one of those little books with all the dates in each year.'

'Doesn't look too much like Brixton,' he joked, glad to hide his feet under the table as he sat.

'No. I think it's supposed to be Devon. That's where my sister lives. Evie used to wish we could live there instead of London.' Agnes' face went dark. 'I told her not to be so daft. Bad enough round here with people staring at her.'

'That must have been difficult,' he said. 'Still, things must be better now. Eighteen years is long enough for people to get used to you, isn't it?'

Agnes snorted as she unwrapped a slab of cake from greaseproof paper. 'Fat chance. If you haven't realised by now then you will soon enough. People need someone to look down on. Makes 'em feel better. If it weren't us it'd be someone else. That strange young man who lives the next street over. Or the Cohens across the road. Anyone different. There'll always be someone a bit different to point the finger at. Fruit cake?'

He nodded. 'Very kind of you, Mrs Coleridge.'

'My pleasure.' She brought over a china plate with a slice of cake. The teapot was already sitting on the table and she poured out two cups before sitting down. 'You know, you should probably start calling me Agnes if you're here for the reason I think.'

'Oh. Yes. Agnes. Well, with everything that's going on, maybe it's the wrong time, but I wanted to talk about my intentions towards Evie.'

She nodded, her mouth full of cake, washing it down with tea. 'About time. It's been long enough now. I see the two of you together, I'm not blind. She cares for you very much and I think you feel the same.'

'Very much so.' He stirred a spoonful of sugar into his tea, avoiding the intensity of her gaze.

'You'd not let her down?'

'Goodness no,' he said, the teaspoon falling to the table with a clatter. 'I would never do that.'

'And you won't be upping sticks any time soon? Heading back to Jamaica, for example?'

'I'm staying put.' He broke off a chunk of the dense cake and stuffed it into his mouth, to stop himself from saying anything incriminating. Under Agnes' unwavering gaze, he felt the same rising anxiety as when he had been interrogated by DS Rathbone. Should he reassure her that he had nothing to do with that whole business, or was it better to not bring it up at all?

'Excellent.' Agnes beamed and clapped her hands together. 'So we should be planning a wedding then.'

The cake was like concrete, bonding to the roof of his mouth even as tiny crumbs broke off and lodged in his throat. He gulped back tea but couldn't completely shift it.

'Of course, there's a lot going on at the moment. Wait until everything's settled down a bit with this baby business. Although maybe it would be better to show Rathbone that you're a respectable family man.'

Lawrie frowned. 'I want to marry Evie because I love her, not because I'm scared of Rathbone.' Indignation finally dislodged the cake, setting off a coughing fit.

'Goodness.' Agnes jumped up to fetch him a glass of water. 'I'm glad you feel so strongly.'

'Thank you,' he croaked, draining the glass. 'And I do. Feel strongly. About Evie, I mean.'

Agnes looked down at him thoughtfully. 'Wait there,' she said eventually.

She went out into the hallway and he heard her in the front room, rummaging around in a drawer from the sounds of it. She reappeared and placed a small black box in front of him. He looked up at her and she sighed heavily, opening it up.

The ring looked like an antique, a family heirloom, perhaps; gold with a large, gleaming sapphire embedded within it. Lawrie blinked, confused.

'Take it then.' She pushed the box towards him.

'This is…' he began.

'Just hold it, will you?' She pushed it again, harder, and he had to shoot out his hand to catch it before it fell off the edge of the table. 'Quick hands,' she said. 'All that cricket, I suppose.'

'Agnes, this is too much. I can get a ring. I've got savings. I don't need charity.'

But he couldn't take his eyes from the sapphire as he found himself picturing it on Evie's finger. He could never afford anything like it.

'That was my grandmother's ring,' Agnes told him, her voice soft with memory. 'She married down, more's the pity for me, but it got passed down to my sister. She never wore it so she gave it to me for Evie.'

The ring box felt comfortable in his palm. With any luck he'd be able to take some leave from work, maybe in September at the very end of summer. That gave him a few months to save up for the honeymoon. He'd need a new suit. His pay-out from the pardner would cover the suit and a small reception, the deposit on a room for him and Evie while they saved up for a house deposit.

Agnes caught his smile. 'Keep that safe and take her out for dinner. You can afford to take her out for a decent meal, can't you? I'm sure you know by now that Tuesdays are my usual bridge night over in Camberwell. Next week?'

Lawrie nodded.

'Now, you'll need to make a reservation. I know you've got a fancy telephone next door but go in person. Avoid any nasty surprises on the day. And take some money in case they want a deposit.'

He stood to leave, his grip tight on the ring box. 'Thank you, Mrs Coleridge. Agnes, I mean. I promise I won't let you or Evie down.'

'I know that, you daft boy. I wouldn't let you anywhere near her otherwise.' She looked away and he wondered what she was really thinking.

For once he was glad that he didn't have time to see Evie that evening. He was bursting with excitement and scared he'd give the game away. Everything was looking up: Rathbone had been nowhere to be seen for days and the band were playing for a wedding party at Wandsworth Town Hall that evening. He could use it as a research opportunity, work out what sort of cost to expect for such an event. He'd been going to catch the bus but took Moses up on his offer of a lift in the van, his arse feeling every bump in the road as he, Johnny and Al travelled in the back with the instruments.

'You think I can get my hands on some money in the next month or so?' he asked Johnny, who managed the pardner that all the band members and some other Brixton residents paid into. Opening bank accounts had proved tricky for most of them when they'd first arrived in London and it seemed easier to organise themselves into a scheme where they all paid in each month and took turns to withdraw the proceeds.

'Reckon it's your turn,' Johnny replied. 'What you need it for?'

'Oh, I just thought to maybe have a week by the sea,' Lawrie told him, for he'd considered that Brighton might do for a honeymoon.

'Hey man, watch you'self!' Johnny slapped the wall of the van as Moses hit yet another bump in the road and Lawrie felt his spine shudder.

It was a relief to pile out of the van into the driveway, Moses running round to let them out. The breeze was up, pushing the smell of hops and yeast into his lungs as he breathed in; the brewery where Arthur worked was less than a two-minute walk away. Rising three storeys, the upper level of the building in front of them was lined with relief sculptures, altogether more impressive than the Lambeth Town Hall that Lawrie was most familiar with.

'Hey! Hey, you there.'

Lawrie turned to see a portly middle-aged man coming their way point a finger at Moses who had just begun to unload his bass. Impatiently, he ran down the steps and hurried over to the van.

'What are you doing?' he demanded. 'You can't just park here, you know. This is private property. I shall call the police.'

'Excuse me, sir, but we are the Johnny Sands Band.' Even after almost two years Lawrie could see Johnny's chest swell with pride as he introduced them. 'We have been booked to play this evening.'

'You're…' The man paused, his cheeks reddening. 'Oh. I mean, perhaps there's been some mistake. I thought that I had booked a normal dance band. I was very clear with the lady I spoke to that this was a wedding.'

'You spoke to my wife,' Johnny explained, rummaging in his jacket pocket. 'And you have no need to worry, sir. This isn't our first wedding. Why don't you have a read over the set list? You let me know if any changes need to be made.'

The man took the paper and, out of his sight, Johnny nodded at Moses who resumed unloading the van. Lawrie watched on, deciding that this was not going to be the easiest of evenings.

'Damn Ursula and her posh telephone voice,' Sonny muttered. 'That man knew before what we looked like, no way we would be standing here right now.'

'Hush your mouth.' Johnny overheard him. 'You rich now? You can afford to turn down a job?'

'Well, I think this all looks fine.' The red-faced man came to a decision. 'Stick to this list, please. And I will need you to move that van round the back. Here, I'll show you. You'll feel more comfortable there I'm sure.'

'Yes, massa,' Sonny muttered, grunting as Johnny elbowed him in the ribs.

Not for the first time, Lawrie was happy that he played an instrument that could be carried quite easily, Moses struggling along with his bass as they followed the man to a side entrance. Inside was as grand as the exterior, all marbled floors and quiet corridors.

They had been provided with a spot at the front of a large room, a dancefloor right in front. The tables were circular, all of them seating eight people and covered over with white tablecloths. Polished cutlery was laid out along with empty plates and a fleet of waiting staff were lined up at the back of the room, all of them staring as the band walked in. Most of them looked younger than Lawrie, only just out of school if they were at all.

'All right, boys.' Johnny grabbed their attention once they were all set up. 'We stick to the set list else our host is likely to have a heart attack. He wants us to play quiet, until all the guests are seated, then we can take it up a notch for the dancing.'

Sonny sighed loudly, putting his whole body into the effort. 'Ever feel like we might not be welcome?'

Johnny turned on him. 'Serious? What you want me to do? They are paying us to play, not the other way round. We mess up and all these person goin' tell their friends that this band nuh good. You want that?'

'Let's play.' Sonny twirled his drumsticks and threw them down, picking up his brushes. 'Quietly.'

None of them were looking at each other when they began to play, barely seconds before the first two couples walked in, laughing and joking, staring curiously at the band as they took their seats on the far side of the room. The waiting staff started into motion, their white-gloved hands ferrying water jugs and wine bottles as the seats began to fill and the bride and groom entered to applause and cheering.

Johnny was a huge fan of Gershwin for these formal occasions that they played occasionally, and Lawrie began to relax as they hit the opening bars of 'Summertime'. The people seemed to be enjoying it too. The sense of foreboding he'd felt from the second they pulled up outside began to fade.

They took a break as the desserts were going out, some sort of treacle pudding covered in thick custard that made Lawrie's mouth water. He'd grown to like the stodgy suet-based puddings that Mrs Ryan served up with her Sunday dinner, usually fighting Derek for seconds.

'See?' Johnny accused Sonny as they sat on the kitchen step. 'No trouble. Just a bit of refinement is all they wanted. You want to prove them right, that we can't behave just as well as they can?'

'When I say different?' Sonny threw his arm out, Lawrie swerving out of the way to avoid getting smacked in the face.

'You got attitude,' Johnny told him. 'You just got to learn to hush your damn mouth in front of a paying customer.'

'You know, I don't have to be here,' Sonny told him. 'I already a got a job that pays the rent. I play music 'cause I love it, not so I can bow and scrape to some—'

'Sonny!' Moses interrupted. 'Come on now. Everything here's just fine.'

'Thank you, Moses,' Johnny slapped the younger man's back. 'See? Common sense!'

Sonny muttered something under his breath that Lawrie couldn't catch. Johnny shook his head and walked away a few feet. It was clear from the way he held his back that he was angry and trying not to let it show. Lawrie took the hip flask that Al passed him and took a swig. He wasn't sure that Sonny needed any rum in his veins but it was easier to keep the flask moving than rile the man up any further. It was a relief when Johnny returned and ordered them back inside.

The second set was for dancing, the music getting louder and faster as the guests, now fairly inebriated, hit the patch of carpet designated as the dancefloor. Sonny took his mood out on his drums and Johnny began to dance a little now, the crowd enjoying his moves.

It all went wrong so fast that there was no way that anyone could have prevented it.

She was a young woman, mid-twenties with dark brown hair that she'd carefully waved before coming out that night, though in the heat of the dancefloor it had gone limp, her face shiny with gin. In slow motion, Lawrie saw her stumble, then trip, her coordination lacking so that she fell to the ground right at Johnny's feet. Even if Johnny had given it a second thought, any person's first impulse would have been to reach down and help. So Johnny did just that. He bent down and put out his hands, the woman gratefully accepting his assistance. Maybe it all would have been fine except that her heel had snapped in the fall and, as Johnny had dragged her upright, her weight sent her stumbling once more, this time into Johnny's arms.

Sonny stopped playing first, then Lawrie as he noticed the missing beat. Johnny was just standing there, the drunk giggling girl with her arms locked around his neck; he couldn't have shaken her off easily if he'd wanted to. Which was when the husband had come charging over, the mortified guests parting like the Red Sea to let him through.

'Gerroff my wife!'

'Ah shit.' Moses began to back away, moving his precious bass behind him.

'Sir,' Johnny said, holding his hands outstretched, his palms like a shield. 'I think that your wife needs some assistance.'

'What you sayin' about my wife, eh?' The husband pushed his

wife aside now, one of her friends darting forward to grab her away as he jabbed a finger at Johnny's chest. 'Who the fuckin' hell d'you think you are?'

'Come on, Peter.' The best man, still on duty, walked across as the crowd gathered. 'No harm done.'

'No harm? Did you book this… this nig-nog band?' Lawrie could see the man turning red in the face. 'Don't you read the papers? Fuck's sake, they kill their own kids and we're supposed to welcome them in with open arms?'

There were gasps from the audience and Lawrie saw their expressions change. The same people who a few moments ago had been whirling around, laughing and singing, a couple of the girls daring to wink up at Lawrie, were now regarding them all with hostile faces. Frowns replaced smiles. A low hum of murmurs started up. Lawrie copied Moses and took a step back.

'How the hell am I meant to get this drum kit outta here?' Sonny whispered. 'They goin' to kill us.'

'Sir, I'm sorry, this is just a simple misunderstanding.' Johnny addressed the husband, his voice strong but Lawrie could see his hands shake a little. 'I only meant to help your wife get up off the floor. I'm a married man myself. Two blessed children at home. Honestly, I never meant to cause offence.'

'There we go, Peter.' The best man breathed out in relief. 'All just a mistake.'

Johnny had turned back to look as he heard Sonny, having already decided where the altercation was going, beginning to pack away his kit, and so he didn't see the punch coming. He hit the floor hard, the air rushing out of him in one short groan.

No one else had been involved but then suddenly everyone was, fists flying. Lawrie ducked down to grab his case, crouching over it protectively as he packed away his clarinet, wincing as a kick caught him in the back.

He heard Sonny howl as his cymbals went flying, the women either screaming in fear or egging their men on, the bride in tears, her bridesmaids arranged about her like petals on a flower. Johnny had risen to his hands and knees and Lawrie ducked down to help him up, using the clarinet case as a shield and hoping to God it was strong enough to protect both him and his precious instrument. They ran out through the kitchen, surprising the chef and the few waiting staff who remained and were tucking into the leftovers, slowing down only to give Moses a hand with his bass.

'Get in the van,' Johnny ordered them. 'Keep your heads down, I'll go fetch the others.'

Lawrie hesitated, not wanting Johnny to think him a coward, but then he heard the sirens out on the street and nodded, crawling into the back of the van with Moses and letting Johnny close them in.

Waiting there in the darkness, time slowed right down. Lawrie could hear the police vehicles draw up close by, the slam of car doors and the distinctive timbre of the local London coppers as they went into the building. It seemed an age before he heard Sonny calling out, begging to be let back in to get his drums, his voice fading away as he was dragged past the van. The first car drove off and Lawrie dared to crack the van door, sticking his head out to see Johnny and Al being shut into the second.

'You think it's safe to go out?' Moses peered round the door. 'We need to get Sonny's drums.'

Lawrie watched the second police car drive off before he and Moses sloped back into the building. Staff had already moved the band's equipment, the drums, blessedly undamaged, Lawrie's sheet music and stand, all of it cluttered at the end of the corridor. It made a pitiful sight but Lawrie was just glad not to have to step back into that room with the guests. He crouched to gather up the music, kissing his teeth as he saw footprints, several pages ripped almost in half. His recent fear filtered away to be replaced with anger. He itched to push that door open, see if that fella was still there. Guest of honour, probably, for getting rid of the undesirables.

He kept his head and took his fury out on the kerb outside instead, kicking it viciously as they closed the van doors and prepared to head back to Brixton. His entire body was buzzing now with rage at the injustice. That some fella could start a fight and then call the police, knowing that his victim would be the one arrested.

He'd been a fool to think things were looking up. Sonny was right; they weren't and never would be welcome here. It didn't matter what his passport said. A man with black skin could never be considered British.

1948

The Armstrongs lived in a prefab house just off Clapham Common, one of a row of identical houses that looked as though they'd come straight off a toy factory conveyor belt. They'd been thrown up in a hurry to house those who'd been bombed out of their homes and had a temporary appearance, lacking in sturdiness; the sort of house the least lucky of the three pigs might have lived in before the wolf came calling. They were far from the usual English terraced homes that Lawrie was having to get used to. Those long rows lacked privacy but their bricks and mortar made him feel safe; they had survived not only the passage of decades, but a long and costly war.

Lawrie double-checked the house number she'd scribbled down for him the day before and knocked on the door, gently, as if he were afraid of putting his fist through the cheap wood. The net curtain at the window twitched as Rose peered out, smiling.

'Come in!' She opened the door with a flourish, beckoning for him to come inside quickly.

Perhaps she was worried about what her neighbours would

think. He wondered if anyone had seen her let Lawrie in, and if they would say anything to her husband. Did he care if they did? It was amusing to imagine the look on Frank Armstrong's face upon finding out that his wife had invited a *nigger* into his own home. For a bath, no less. Frank would have to bathe knowing that the dark skin of a Jamaican man had sat in the same place, his buttocks resting in the precise spot where Lawrie's own had. He should make sure to wipe his arse along the bottom of that tub.

'What are you smiling at?' Rose laughed.

'Nothing.' He snapped the grin off his face. 'Just happy at the thought of being clean.' He followed her into the kitchen. 'I suppose there are the public baths but I can't afford to go down there every day.'

Rose shuddered. 'I never feel clean, using public facilities. You never know who's used them before you. I even had a bath after I got home from the lido the other day. Would you like a drink? Tea? Water?'

'Water, please.'

She took his bag from him and shook out the creased shirt and trousers, draping them over the back of a chair, ready for laundering. He'd called one of Aston's contacts and fixed an interview for the following morning. Right after that he'd arranged to go round and meet Mrs Ryan, Evie's next-door neighbour. The room was tiny, Evie had warned, but it would be clean. And close to Evie. They'd gone to the pictures the evening before, just the two of them, and been able to talk freely for the first time. He'd never really talked to a girl like that before. A girl who made him feel at ease whilst simultaneously exciting him more that any person he'd known before. He paid attention to every word she said, storing away fragments of information. Her favourite flavour of ice cream; the way she sat on cinema seat, her body tilted forward so that she didn't miss a second of the programme; the way she blushed when he complimented her.

'I bet you haven't got one of these in that dump of a house of yours.' Rose interrupted his thoughts to show off her refrigerator, a huge metal contraption that hummed loudly in the corner of the kitchen. She made him watch while she showed off a small box which made ice, fighting to extract cubes from a tray and dropping them into the water before handing him the glass. The water was too cold and set his teeth on edge but he felt he should drink it all.

'Very – cold.' He smiled, his lips numb, handing back the empty glass.

'Come on, then. Let's get you cleaned up ready for that job interview.'

He let her take him by the hand and drag him upright, leading him back along to the bathroom. It was small but functional, with the luxury of an inside toilet. No outdoor privy for the Armstrongs. The bath was sparkling white. His mother would have been impressed. Rose bent to turn on the taps, her skirt stretching across her backside as she did, and he looked away.

He still wasn't sure what to make of this attention Rose was showing him. It was motherly for the most part. If she'd been twenty years older then he'd not have thought it strange at all, this attempt to take a young man under wing but Sam had taunted him all night long. *She after you,* he'd said. *She got that look in she eye when she see you, like a dog when its owner drop a piece o' meat on the floor. She just waiting for the right moment. Then she pounce!*

Sam was just being Sam. Rose was a nice woman, it was just a shame about the husband being such a bastard. No wonder she was lonely. His mother had always said that girls like Rose, flirting with the boys and spending all their time on their looks and their clothes, they'd end up with the sort of men who fell for such deceptions – and a foolish man was never a good husband. She'd approve of Evie, though. Evie was a nice girl, innocent-looking but with a slow beauty that struck him a little more each time he saw her. She was still shy around him but he'd seen her with that blonde friend of hers, laughing and full of life. Once she got to know him maybe he'd be able to make her laugh like that.

'Bubble bath?' Rose interrupted.

'No, thank you.' He just wanted her to hurry up and leave. He'd wash quickly and then make an excuse to come back round later to collect his clean clothes.

'I'll fetch a towel. Soap is there.' She pointed to the dish on the side, a thick block of carbolic soap sitting on it, barely touched. 'That's what Frank uses. Unless you'd prefer a softer fragrance? I do have some nice lavender-scented.'

'No.' He smiled. 'This is fine.' He could well imagine Sam's taunts if he arrived home smelling like a woman.

'Go on, get yourself in there and I'll pass in a towel.' She closed the door behind her and he began to unbutton his shirt.

The bath filled up quickly. Lawrie undressed quickly and carefully placed his clothes on the closed lid of the toilet, resting his underwear on top to make a pyramid. He stepped gingerly into the water, hopping a little as the tender soles of his feet protested against the heat. It took him a good minute to adjust to the temperature before he dared to squat, then to sit, water splashing about him as his body displaced it. He sank down and lay back, his knees bent so that his head could rest against the back of the bath. He closed his eyes.

'Here you are. Oh, you are tidy! Frank always just throws his clothes on the floor.'

Lawrie's eyes flew open as Rose walked in on him, breezy as you like, as if it were perfectly normal to walk in on a naked man you barely knew. She held two fluffy cream towels in her arms, hugged against her chest as she looked down at him. Thank God his knees had sprung up automatically, concealing the worst.

'Rose, I...' He tried to look casual as his hands moved to cover himself.

'You're not embarrassed, are you?' Rose laughed. 'Oh, you are!' She pushed his neat pile of clothes to one side and perched on the lid of the loo. 'I've seen it all before, love. I could see almost as much of you at the lido yesterday.'

'It's not the same.' The words croaked out.

'Why? Because everyone's half-undressed? Is that what makes it more acceptable?'

'Yes. I suppose that's it.' He waited, expecting her to get up and leave. 'And I'm more than half undressed.'

She stood up and he breathed out in relief. 'You make a good point.' She smiled and he only blinked but her blouse was on the floor before he realised she'd unbuttoned it. 'It's only fair, I suppose.'

'Rose, that's not...' The words dried up on his tongue as she unzipped her skirt, his body betraying him as she kicked it off and stood before him in just her black lace brassiere and knickers.

'You're a grown man, aren't you? I thought you liked me.'

'Yes, but, I mean—'

'And you're doing nothing wrong if that's what you're worried about. It's not as if *you're* married.'

'You are,' he said, in case she'd forgotten. Every inch of his skin was tingling, only partly from the steam which, much to his shame, was not the only thing rising.

'Frank doesn't deserve me.' She reached across him to pick up the bar of soap. 'He barely even notices me these days as long as there's food on the table when he gets in from work. Then he's straight out to the pub and by the time he gets home... Well, let's just say that even when he's in the mood he can't always do much about it. Can't even get me knocked up! Probably just as well under the circumstances.'

He watched, fascinated as her hands began to work the soap into a lather. Once satisfied, she placed her palms against his chest and massaged the soap into his skin. He gave up any pretence of wanting to run away and let her lift each arm in turn, her hands slipping across and under. She was thorough, watching him as he tried to remember how to breathe normally.

'Did you have a girl back in Jamaica?' she asked, pushing him forward so that she could do his back.

He shook his head. 'I kissed a few but usually they were more interested in my brother. They all liked a man in uniform, you know, and I was just a boy next to him.'

'You're a virgin?'

His face burned and he turned his head away.

She rinsed the suds from his skin and pushed him back. 'How old are you again?'

'Nineteen.' His breath choked off the last syllable as her hand reached lower, stroking the soap along his inner thigh. 'I'm just waiting. For the right girl.'

'And am I the right girl?' She took hold of his cock in her hand. 'Don't answer that.' She released him and he let go of the breath he'd been holding. 'You're clean enough. Chop chop!' She held out the towel for him.

He clambered, ungainly, from the bath and let her wrap him up tucking the towel tail in at his waist before putting her arms around his neck to kiss him. She tasted flowery, like scent. Her tongue was pointed and insistent and he felt helpless as she took his hand once more, leading him this time to the bedroom.

This then was the marital bed, clearly still in use even if just for sleeping as she claimed. On one side the table held an eye mask and a bottle of fancy-looking lotion; the other was scattered with loose change and a folded copy of the *Daily Express*.

Rose pushed him down onto the bed and kissed him again, moving his hands to her breasts. He did as he was told, struggling with the fastening of her bra and grateful she finally reached back and unclipped it with one hand. She didn't seem bothered by his incompetence, rather she seemed to enjoy issuing instruction and he followed each one with growing enthusiasm. He'd not even thought that he should be more careful, that if Rose were to fall pregnant then everyone would find out what he'd done, not just Frank.

As soon as it was over he felt his ecstasy wash away in a wave of shame. What on earth had he been thinking? He should have left as soon as he realised her intentions. Hell, he should have listened to Sam and never come round. He'd ended up on Frank's side of the bed, his head on a pillow that smelled of men's cologne and hair pomade. Guilt twisted his gut like a corkscrew.

'Was it that bad?' Rose asked. She lay on her side, watching him.

'It was incredible.' The words fell flat but he didn't know what else to say.

She didn't respond and when he looked at her she had turned on to her back and closed her eyes. He lay himself back and stared at the ceiling for a while until he felt his heart rate return to normal. She still hadn't moved and so, unsure whether she was actually asleep or just pretending, he stole out of the bedroom in search of his clothes.

14

Evie woke just after two that Friday morning, unable to fall back asleep no matter how many times she turned, or how many sheep she counted. She read a chapter of her book but that didn't help. All she could think about was Lawrie. And how she still hadn't told him the truth.

Just before five she gave up and crawled out of bed, padding across to the window and pulling back the curtain. The street was silent, the street lights casting their amber glow. It was a cold night, not spring like at all. She heard a click from below, from the house next door as Lawrie left for work, and slunk back behind the curtain so that he wouldn't see her.

She felt like a traitor. A spy and a liar. Guilt burned acidic flames deep in her gut, a constant pain that she only now realised she had been managing ever since the night of the party. Rathbone's discovery, the lying to Lawrie, all of it was fuel to the fire, Evie's grand hopes for the future turning black and charred the longer she kept her silence.

'Your aunt wrote,' Ma told her at breakfast. 'She's definitely keen to come up this summer. That'll be nice, won't it?'

'Lovely.' Evie pulled the crust off her dry toast even though she knew her mother would berate her for not eating it.

'Well, don't get too excited. I thought you said the other day that you wanted to see Gertie. Between you and me, I did mention that with a bit of luck there might be wedding bells sometime soon. Don't you think?' Her mother's laugh grated on Evie's fraught nerves.

'I don't know, do I?' Evie was too tired to care if Ma took offence. Sod's law that right now she felt like if she laid her head down she'd be fast asleep in seconds.

'Well, I wouldn't be surprised. I mean, it's been almost a year, Evie. Ellie down the street married her young chap after only six months!'

'If you mean Ellie Walker then she was in the family way and she had no choice,' Evie reminded her. 'And I've learned my lesson, remember?'

'I wasn't implying any different. Just, you know, maybe it's time you put some pressure on. Told him to get a move on.'

'Ma, can you just leave it! Lawrie will ask me to marry him if and when he's ready.' She wanted to get up and leave the room but she'd only be making trouble for herself. Better to wait it out and let Ma get the last word in.

The silence stretched out until Evie began to think that maybe, for once, her mother had decided to pay attention to her daughter's words. She was about to excuse herself from the table when her mother spoke once more.

'Something's wrong. What is it?'

'Nothing.' She looked away.

'Evie, don't lie to me. You look like you haven't slept in a week. Nothing's happened with Lawrie, has it?'

Evie stared at her mother in surprise. Since when had Ma cared so much about Lawrie anyway? 'No, Ma. Only what with everything that's happened the last week... I've been thinking that I should tell him the truth. About why I really went to Devon.'

'Absolutely not.' Ma put her mug of tea down heavily on the table. 'Why would you do such a stupid thing? It was nothing to do with Lawrie then and it's got nothing to do with him now. You made one little mistake, that's all.'

'It wasn't a little mistake, Ma, that's the point.' Evie gave up on her toast, the bread a day past its best anyway. 'I had a baby. If she'd lived—'

'But she didn't. Evie, you can't destroy your one chance at happiness because of this.'

'But it's not fair to Lawrie. And who's to say that he'd break it off? He might forgive me.' *Might.* If only she could be certain; she would have told him everything months before.

Ma laughed, a dark, guttural sound without mirth. 'Evie, have I not taught you better than that? A man will never look past a woman's indiscretions, no matter how long ago. D'you want to end up like me? Alone and unwanted?'

'You're not alone,' Evie muttered. 'You've got me.'

'Yes. I have you.' Her mother pressed her lips together as if trying to stop the flow of words, knowing they would wound, but to no avail. 'Don't you understand? You're my darling girl but you're also the reason why I'm on my own. Why no man worth his salt will come anywhere near me. And if that baby had lived then you would have ended up just like me.'

Evie's chest tightened. 'Her name was Annabel,' she said.

'You were lucky,' her mother said, her voice hard as granite. 'I know you were upset at the time but if you'd kept her then you wouldn't be sitting there arguing with me about whether a boy might want to marry you. You'd be resigned to life as a pariah. Trust me, you've had a lucky escape.'

'Didn't you do exactly the same? You were supposed to give me up and you didn't. You kept me. I only wanted the same as you!'

They'd had this same argument in the last days of Evie's pregnancy, shouting over a different kitchen table in Devon. Ma had stormed out in the end, staying away for hours before coming back home and kissing Evie's forehead as she lay on the couch listening to Aunt Gertie's favourite radio programme. She'd never guessed that it could have been so easy to talk her mother around, but in the end it hadn't even mattered.

Ma stared at her with pity. 'You weren't thinking straight. You couldn't help it, Evie. I know what it's like. All those months with a life growing inside you, you're supposed to feel protective, like you could never be without the child you give birth to. It's God's way of helping us become mothers.'

'If God made us that way, why is it so bad?' Evie whispered. 'Do you wish you hadn't kept me?'

Her mother looked her straight in the eye. 'Sometimes, yes. I do. That doesn't mean that I don't love you. I do. But if I'd known back then how things would turn out then I would have handed you over to Sister Mary in a heartbeat. I'd have run straight home and begged my father to forgive me. I'd have met someone else in time. Got married and had a nice house somewhere. Had children who looked like me, Evie. You just remind me of a man I haven't seen in almost twenty years.'

Evie bit down hard on the inside of her cheek to stop the tears from falling. 'So you'd have been happier without me.' Evie didn't wait for her mother to answer. 'I've always known it. Maybe that's what happened to that baby in the pond. Her mother was someone like you, someone who decided she'd made the wrong decision.'

'I shouldn't have said what I did.' Her mother stood up and began to collect up the breakfast plates. 'Evie, I do love you and that's why I can't bear to watch you ruin your own life. Nothing good can come of telling Lawrie and he'll never find out as long as you keep your mouth shut.'

'Rathbone knows.' She braced herself for the explosion but her mother remained silent, still standing with her back to her. 'Ma? Did you hear me?'

She could see the tension stiffen her mother's body as she threw crockery into the sink, crusts and all, turning the taps on full.

'How?' She turned and leaned against the sink, arms folded. 'You didn't bloody tell him, did you?'

''Course not! I'm not a complete idiot. He found out that I'd been away. There was an anonymous phone call, he said. He did some digging and found the birth certificate.' Evie could feel the sting of tears, her head aching with the effort of holding them back.

Her mother closed her eyes, her hands gripping the counter

behind her now. Evie stood up slowly, ready to make her escape. She wanted to kick herself for being so silly, for getting so worked up over a few words. Hadn't she always known that her mother blamed her for everything that had gone wrong in her life? It shouldn't have been a surprise to hear her say it finally but just because you knew that a blade was sharp didn't stop it from hurting when it sliced through skin.

'Did you tell him anything else?'

'I told Rathbone that she died,' Evie said. 'I told him what happened. I mean, he'll have to leave me alone now, won't he?'

'Yes, love. You did well.' Ma opened her eyes and smiled briefly, barely a flicker, but enough to soothe Evie's concern. 'Now don't ruin it by doing something stupid. You do love Lawrie?'

'Of course,' Evie said. 'And I trust him. More than anyone in the world.'

'Never trust a man. Not with something like this, not even Lawrie. He does love you Evie, I know he does, but if he thinks for a second that you're not the woman he thought you were…' Ma shook her head. 'He'll be gone before you can blink.'

She walked over then, her arms outstretched, and Evie let her mother comfort her though every inch of her skin itched to run away, to leave this house and never come back. Lawrie loved her. And if she wanted him to carry on loving her then she'd do as she was told and keep her mouth shut. He was her only chance of escape.

'Lyceum tonight?' Delia asked, the second Evie walked in to the office.

'Why? So you can meet Sid and ditch me as soon as we get there?' She'd meant it to sound jokey but her voice didn't cooperate, the words emerging harshly from her throat. 'Sorry,' she muttered, taking her seat, 'I didn't mean it like that.'

'You sure you're all right?' Delia tilted her head, staring intently at her friend. 'You shouldn't be here if you're not feeling well still.'

'I'm fine. Just tired, that's all.' And not in the mood for talking. She looked away, hoping that Delia would get the message. 'Shall we go down?'

Mrs Jones was giving out the day's tasks to the typing pool when they got downstairs.

'Nice of you to join us.' Mildred smirked at the pair of them, even though they weren't the last to arrive. 'We were just saying, Evie, how sorry we felt for you.'

'For me?' Evie frowned. 'Why?'

'All this business about the dead baby. My dad's got friends in the police. He said they've been knocking on all the doors where you lot live. Have they questioned you yet?'

They had all turned to stare, Evie's face blazing with heat as she stammered out her reply: 'It's got nothing to do with me and, no, the police haven't been round to *my* house.'

'Well, that's good to know.' Mildred smiled once more, her eyes narrowed. 'It would be awful if they got the wrong idea.'

'What do you mean, wrong idea?' Delia demanded.

'Oh, nothing really. I was just thinking about that time when Evie was ill. None of us saw her for months! Paper says they suspect a man but I think maybe they should be looking for a woman instead.' Mildred turned round as Mrs Jones reappeared at the front of the room.

Delia linked her arm through Evie's. 'She's full of rubbish,' she whispered.

'Yes,' Evie agreed, but her heart raced. Surely if someone as naturally stupid as Mildred Thompson could guess Evie's secret, then anyone could work it out.

15

Lawrie and Arthur arrived early at the Atlantic pub, but they weren't the first there. Lawrie recognised quite a number of fellas already standing at the bar or seated around the table in the back room where Sonny had set himself up as chairman of whatever this was. Sonny's face was set rigid, the most serious Lawrie had ever seen him. Before him was a notepad and pencil, and the drink that Moses passed to him looked like lemonade. Lawrie had never seen Sonny drink anything apart from beer, rum or whisky.

He felt a nudge against his arm as he waited at the bar, looking over to see Johnny: 'Glad you got home safely.'

'Thanks to you.' Lawrie winced. 'Man, that must hurt.'

'Ah.' Johnny touched his face gingerly. His mouth was swollen, his cheek marred by a green and purple bruise. 'Yes, Ursula was not impressed. I hope to God that bastard's hand hurts as bad.'

Arthur's laugh was arid. 'That devil is probably out there right now, telling anyone who will listen how he taught some monkey a lesson. I hear what they say 'bout me at work, and they don' bother to check if I can hear or not. They don' care. You think that's the end of it? This is just the start, I tellin' you.'

'This was one drunk man with his drunker wife,' Lawrie argued. 'We learned a lesson: that we should stick to places we know, but there's no reason to expect any more trouble. Nothing else has happened anywhere else.'

'Exactly.' Johnny slapped a hand against his thigh in agreement. 'Things will settle down. Soon as they sort out this baby business. You hear what that fella say last night? I blame the newspapers, they the ones pointing the finger at us. They find the culprit and this all goes away. And I got my money on a woman. My Ursula, she loves herself a detective novel and she say to me that poisoning's women's business. That baby was fed something bad, the papers say. Not beaten or strangled which would be a man's business.' Johnny took a swig from the flask 'That's what Poirot says.'

'Who?'

'This detective in Ursula's books.'

'Well, I for one would rather have a discussion with fellas like us than listen to some detective fella in a book.' Arthur took his pint and they followed him to the head table, Moses waving them over.

'Aston comin' tonight?' Sonny asked. 'He knows 'bout this sort of thing.'

Lawrie shook his head. 'He went away for a few days. Said he was going down to somewhere on the coast. Bournemouth maybe? Then he wanted to head over to France. They go every year, the fellas he used to fly with. They like to go back and say thank you to the folk who helped them out during the war. Though from the sounds of it they just sit around drinking wine and eating cheese.'

'You didn't want to go?' Moses asked.

'No. Means nothing to me, to visit a place I've never been. I'd rather remember my brother the way he was back home, not think about him dying in a field in France.' Lawrie took a drink from the flask as it came round. 'Anyhow, last thing I need right now is that copper thinking I've done a runner.'

'True,' Sonny agreed. 'Ain't nothing they like more than an excuse to lock any one of us up.' Johnny sighed and opened his mouth to speak but Sonny held his arm up, calling for silence.

'Everyone here?' Sonny addressed the room, the men around him murmuring their assent. Lawrie counted thirty or so men and a couple of women, an impressive number for a meeting that he had only heard about that afternoon. 'All right then. I want to thank you all for comin' at short notice. Perhaps a few of you think there isn't a point to this.'

Lawrie stared down into the swirling centre of his beer. It wasn't that he didn't agree with Sonny, it was more that he didn't want to attract any more attention.

'Point is, these people think we beneath them. They ignore the fact that we all got passports that say we are British. That we got a right to be here. This entire city is still half fallen down and they think *we* are what's ruinin' things for them? Hitler, he the one who bombed this place to smithereens, not I. Not any of us. I mean, can you imagine someone less likely to be a murderer than Moses?'

Moses grinned innocently and everyone laughed. He was the same age as Lawrie but his round face made him look younger than his twenty-one years. Chubby and soft, he was the most good-natured fella Lawrie knew.

Emboldened, Sonny stood, his voice gaining volume. 'See, I not lookin' to solve all our problems right here tonight. I just want to propose that we look after one another. They think we all the same so let us be just that. Let us join together and have a weekly meeting right here. A place where we can come and discuss what is goin' on. We locked in a system that is too difficult to change one by one but, if we act together, maybe we can do something about this.'

Lawrie looked around at the crowd, every man transfixed by Sonny, no longer the surly pessimist that Lawrie had thought him, now a man of sensible action that anyone could agree with. Lawrie put his hands together, leading the applause as Sonny looked bashful and sat back down.

The thought occurred as the clapping died down and Sonny began to talk once more, of collating problems and forming a regular committee, that one of these men could be the father of Ophelia. If he was, did he even know it? Lawrie looked around, noting which of the faces were most familiar, discounting those he knew had arrived more recently. He considered the women: one was with her husband, the other he knew was sweet on Sonny which was probably the main reason she'd come along. He couldn't see how either of them could have kept a baby quiet, not when everyone he knew lived practically on top of one another, sharing houses to keep the rent low. No, he kept coming back to Derek's idea: that it was a local woman trying to hide her mistake.

Could it be that someone in this very room was Ophelia's father and had no idea?

He'd made the reservation at a restaurant that he hoped would feel special without being intimidating. As Agnes had suggested, he went there in person to make sure that they, and he, knew who they were dealing with. They asked for a deposit which he paid, though he heard the maître d' take a reservation over the telephone with no mention of pre-payment. There were battles worth fighting and this wasn't one.

He told Evie a tiny white lie: that he'd meet her after work on Tuesday and they'd go for something to eat before the pictures. 'Why don't you wear that red dress I like?' he suggested.

'To sit in the dark?'

'I just like that dress, but you wear what you want,' he'd replied with a smile.

He waited outside Vernon & Sons as the girls filed out in chattering pairs and trios, the men carrying their briefcases. Evie was one of the last out and he smiled when he saw the red hem of her dress peeking out from below her buttoned up coat. She'd put on make-up as well, he noticed. She might not know where they were going but she'd worked out that this wasn't the usual night out at the movies. Perhaps Agnes had said something. He embraced her but kept his kiss to her cheek, knowing that curious eyes watched them. Taking her arm, they walked in the opposite direction from the usual café, up St John's Road towards the Junction.

'Where're we going?' she asked, looking over her shoulder in confusion.

'I want to treat you for once.' He ushered her through the entrance of Arding and Hobbs.

They crossed the ground floor, passing the multi-coloured linens of the drapery department and the subtle glances of the over made-up shop girls. The lifts were at the back of the shop, the quickest way to reach the fifth-floor restaurant. He hoped the food was decent. He'd looked at the prices on the menu to make sure he could afford them and checked the venue with Agnes who'd nodded approvingly. The ring box was in his jacket pocket, growing heavier the longer it sat there. He was amazed that Evie hadn't asked him what on earth that gigantic lump was sticking out of his chest. The lift operator pressed the button and he felt his knees weaken slightly. All he could hear was his own heart, pumping blood at a wild pace as if he'd just run a mile. How was it that no one else could hear it?

They entered the restaurant past the grand piano, the pianist booked for later on when the restaurant was at its busiest. The maître d' recognised Lawrie immediately, greeting the couple and taking them to the table by the window that Lawrie had requested. Lawrie's palms were sweating as they walked, his eyes drawn to the stunning stained-glass cupola that dominated the ceiling. Evie gave a shy smile as her chair was pulled out for her. Through the glass onto Lavender Hill they could see the tiny office workers below as they swarmed across the road towards the station, heading home. Evie looked as enchanted by the view as Lawrie was with her.

The restaurant was almost empty, only a handful of early diners dotted throughout. Everyone looked very serious, talking in low, civilised tones. Lawrie and Evie were the youngest by a decade, if not more, and everyone else looked comfortable. The men moved easily in their jackets, tailored second skins. Lawrie fidgeted, raising his shoulders to try and loosen the fit of his suit, bought for him by his mother a year before he'd left Kingston. He'd thought that, at eighteen, he wouldn't grow any more. Now, at twenty-one, his once-skinny frame had broadened, strengthened, partly thanks to his job. He'd gone from a deskbound student who rode his bicycle to class, to a working man who thought nothing of walking miles every day on foot. If she said yes, and please God, she would, he'd have to buy a new suit for the wedding. A man couldn't get married in clothes belonging to a child. Lawrie ran a finger between his neck and the stiff collar, adjusting his tie self-consciously.

'So what's the occasion?' Evie had finished gorging herself on the view and was watching him now.

'What d'you mean?' Even his watch felt tight on his wrist and he tugged at the band.

He had made a plan in his head: order the food and some wine, make a toast to Evie (to be improvised after his attempts to put words on paper had failed, every effort sounding stilted and false when he read them aloud). Then his great hope was that the wine gave him the courage he needed to get down on one knee.

'Why are we really here?' She reached out and put her hand on his, stopping him from shuffling the cutlery. 'Is something going on?'

The waiter saved him, arriving with a jug of water. 'Have you had a chance to peruse the wine list, sir?'

'Yes, thank you.' Lawrie pointed to the one he wanted, making sure the waiter took note and didn't accidentally bring a more expensive bottle. 'Are you ready to order, Evie?'

She nodded and ordered tomato soup followed by lamb cutlets.

'I'll have the same.' Lawrie handed over his menu and the waiter vanished.

'So?' Her right eyebrow rose.

'What? I can't treat you for once?' His laugh sounded fake. His palms were clammy. 'Would you rather have just gone to the pictures?'

'No, of course not. I'm sorry. I didn't mean to sound ungrateful.' She looked away. This wasn't going the way he had hoped.

The waiter saved him. 'Your wine, sir.' He opened the bottle in front of them with ease, Lawrie watching his technique for future reference, then poured barely a splash into Lawrie's wine glass, waiting.

He was supposed to try it, he knew, and determine if the wine was decent. He lifted the glass to his nose as he'd seen in movies, inhaling the strong aroma of fruit and something spicy. He held a small drop on his tongue and let the taste fill his mouth, nodding to the waiter.

'I hope I passed the test,' he said once the waiter was out of earshot. 'I don't have a clue when it comes to wine.'

Evie took a tentative sip and smiled. 'Tastes very nice, actually.'

'In that case I'd like to make a toast.' He raised his glass. 'To you, Evie. I've not always enjoyed my time in London. I was homesick, I suppose, for a long time. And things weren't as I had expected. I was foolish. Like Dick Whittington.' Someone had said that to him before, he couldn't remember who. 'I thought life would be easier here. That I'd walk into a good job and make my fortune.'

'It's not foolish to have dreams,' Evie told him. 'Life just doesn't turn out as you imagine, that's all.'

'You don't need to tell me that. I thought I'd walk straight off that boat into a perfect life. Hasn't worked out that way exactly but then I never dreamed of meeting you, so…' He paused to collect his thoughts. 'I was so angry with myself when I messed things up. And then you went away for all those months and all I could think was that it was my fault.'

Her smile didn't reach her eyes. 'I was ill. You couldn't have prevented that.'

'No, but I thought – I worried that it was because of what happened, you know, at the party. That Agnes sent you away so I couldn't hurt you again. I was so happy when you came back. When you forgave me.'

'I forgave you before I even left London,' she admitted.

'Really? I wish I'd known.' He pulled a face and was glad to hear her laugh. 'But I want to promise you that I'll never do anything like that again. I won't lose you again.'

'I know. I trust you.' Evie clinked her glass against his and they drank. 'We should be toasting you though, Lawrie. Don't you see how well you've done? You arrived with nothing and now you've got a good job. And you get to play music and be paid for it. Wasn't that your dream once upon a time?'

'It'll never make me rich.'

'There's more to life than money,' she reminded him. 'Johnny manages.'

'Only 'cause Ursula works six days a week. It's selfish of him, with two children to feed, and another child left back home with Ursula's mother. When I have a family, I want to be able to support them. Sometimes you've got to leave one dream behind to follow another.'

He reached into his jacket pocket, trying to retrieve the ring box which was now refusing to come out. He tugged, ignoring the rip of the stitching. Evie watched him, her hands flying up to her mouth as he dropped to one knee before her.

'Evelyn Coleridge, will you do me the honour of becoming my wife?'

His heart stopped as she made him wait the briefest of seconds before nodding, her cheeks glistening with the tears that quickly began to stream from her eyes as he slipped the ring onto her finger. It was a perfect fit, as Agnes had assured him it would be.

The soup arrived and Lawrie clambered back onto his chair, the waiter smiling his congratulations. The sky outside was now pitch black, rain speckling the window. The low-lit restaurant felt cosy now, a waft of warm scented steam rising from the soup.

'Are you happy?' He picked up his spoon.

Evie laughed as she blew her nose. 'Of course. These are happy tears, I promise.' She held up her left hand and looked closer. 'Isn't this...'

'Your grandmother's ring,' he confirmed. 'Your mother gave it to me.'

Evie's eyebrows shot up. 'Ma knows?'

'You think I'd dare ask you to marry me without getting her blessing first?'

She blew on a spoonful of soup. 'You must have really won her over.'

It certainly seemed that way. Perhaps it was like Aston had said and Agnes had realised that it was best for Evie to marry a man with the same colour skin as her own. Which was crazy, really. He'd seen the girls Evie worked with and not one of them was better looking, not even Delia who he secretly thought was quite plain once you looked past the blonde hair.

'What are you staring at?' she asked, a twinkle in her eye.

He grinned back. 'How can I not stare when I'm sitting opposite the most beautiful girl in this lovely city?' It was the sort of line Aston would have come up with, but Lawrie meant it.

It was a charmed evening where nothing could go wrong. They had coffee afterwards, real coffee like he drank in the Italian cafés in Soho. Evie pulled a face at the bitter taste but once he'd added sugar she liked it, though she still couldn't see why a person would choose it over tea. He watched her drink, wondering why it had taken him so long to realise that all that mattered was Evie: being with her, marrying her, spending the rest of his life with her.

Finally he had some good news to send home.

1948

She finally knew why they said that love was like walking on air. At least, perhaps it was a little early to say that she loved him, but she'd certainly never met a person who made her feel as strange and giddy and special as Lawrie Matthews did. On Wednesday evening they'd met at the Astoria and she told him as they took their seats that Mrs Ryan next door would rent him her box room for less than what he was paying to share with Sam.

'You serious?' The joy on his face was infectious.

'You should see the room first. It's tiny! Barely room for the bed, but it's clean and she'll provide breakfast and dinner in the rate. She says you can go round tomorrow and have a look.'

He let out a low whistle. 'Evie, you just saved my life. I'll take it. I just got to make sure I can pay first. Can she wait a day? I got a job interview Friday morning and I could go round after that?'

He'd be living next door, so close. And her mother wouldn't even know until it was too late. They'd talked about movies and about the band before the programme started and afterwards, as he left her at the end of her street, he'd kissed her on the cheek and told her that she was the prettiest girl he'd seen in London.

'I don't suppose your mother will let you come out on Saturday night? There's a party at our house,' he told her.

'I'll see what I can do.'

She was too embarrassed to admit to him that there was no way Ma would let her go. But then luck seemed to fall on her side. When she got home from college on Friday evening, Ma told her that she'd been called on as a replacement for a bridge game in Camberwell that weekend. She'd be out of the house on Saturday evening.

It was worth the risk, she finally decided. What other boy had ever told her that he liked her? Ma said that boys liked what they knew, that they all ended up married to their mothers. None of them had mothers who looked like Evie; that was her point. Evie wasn't stupid and she wasn't going to let her opportunity pass her by. What if some other girl turned Lawrie's head in her absence?

Delia talked her through the tricks her sisters had used in their day and it was too easy for Evie to draw her bedroom curtains and pile a few clothes under the bedsheets to form a human-shaped lump. If her mother glanced in the doorway late at night she wouldn't notice that it wasn't Evie. She hoped. Then, when she did creep home, Ma would be snoring her head off, her sleeping tablets ensuring nothing short of a bombing raid would wake her.

To be on the safe side she waited until Ma had left before grabbing her packed bag and running round to Delia's to get ready, Delia jumping at the chance to try out her older sister's make-up using Evie as a guinea pig.

'I don't look like me,' Evie said, turning her face this way and that and wrinkling her nose at her mirror image. She rubbed at the rouged cheeks, trying to soften them. She felt like she was wearing a mask, her skin tingling like mad after the amount of blending that Delia had had to do. The powder had lightened her complexion and she wasn't sure she liked it.

'Leave it!' Delia smacked her hand down. 'You look lovely. Lawrie won't know his luck.'

The girls swapped places before the glass, Delia taking care of her own make-up since Evie didn't have a clue.

'Thanks for coming with me,' Evie said as they finally set off. 'I don't think I'd have the nerve otherwise.'

'Not like I've anything better to do.' Delia sniffed. ''Sides, I need to meet this Lawrie, don't I? Make sure he's not a wrong 'un.'

It had been two weeks since Delia's brother had caught Lennie, her previous chap, down an alleyway just off their road, with a girl who wasn't Delia. Lennie had ended up with a black eye and the girl, some tart from over Stockwell way, had run off so fast she'd left her knickers on the fence. At least that was what Chris Marson was telling everyone.

'You made it.' Lawrie was sitting on the front wall of his house as the girls tottered up in their heels, Evie's borrowed from Delia – wandering around the streets in high heels was another item on Ma's list of unapproved activities.

'Thanks for inviting us,' Delia beamed.

'You want a drink?' Lawrie looked at Evie.

She nodded and followed him into the house. Bunting had

been strung up all along the garden fence, continuing into the hallway. 'It looks very festive round here.'

'Ha! That's one word for it.' He tweaked one of the triangles. 'I s'pose it's better than the bare walls.'

They'd managed to keep the kitchen clean though it still had a look of condemnation about it. On the table were laid out a mismatched array of mugs and chipped glasses along with three bottles of gin and a bottle of orange cordial. Beneath she could see a couple of crates full of pale ale. Lawrie fixed her and Delia both a gin and orange and she took a polite sip, hoping her grimace came out as a smile. As long as she only drank a tiny bit she'd be fine.

Sam, Johnny and Moses were out in the backyard already, setting up for the band to perform, Sam wolf whistling when he saw Delia, who blushed, flattered.

'If I might be so bold, I reckon I already spotted the finest-lookin' girl of the night,' he said.

Lawrie kissed his teeth softly. 'Come on now, is that any way to talk? Be a gentleman.'

'Nothin' more gentlemanly than showing appreciation for a lady,' Sam argued.

'You don't mind him.' Moses spoke softly but moved swiftly to Delia's side. 'He got no manners but I can show you round.'

Evie took another sip of her drink and watched as Delia and Moses walked off together to the other side of the yard, Sam looking mildly perturbed. He caught Evie watching him and winked. He seemed a nice chap, funny.

'I thought this was s'posed to be a party?'

Evie turned to see a stranger walk into the yard from the kitchen.

'I thought you were s'posed to get here three hours ago,' Lawrie shot back, his eyebrow raised high as he smiled broadly at the newcomer who had cast such aspersions on their festivities.

Shorter than Lawrie by a couple of inches, this man wore a Forces uniform and carried a bag over his shoulder. He met her curious gaze and smiled.

'I don't believe we've met. Aston Bayley.' He held his hand out.

So this was Lawrie's best friend. A ladykiller, he'd called him. She could see that was true already.

'Evie Coleridge.' She shook his hand. 'Lawrie's told me all about you.'

'Oh really?' Aston raised an eyebrow in Lawrie's direction.

'He told me you've been like an older brother to him,' she clarified.

'I do my best.' Aston took off his cap and wiped his forehead with the back of his hand. 'Pleased to meet you, Evie. Now, I been hours on a hot an' crowded train to get here. Anything to drink?'

They told her they were just warming up but Evie was mesmerised by the performance the band put on – just for her, Delia and Aston until a few guests began to arrive. Delia had been asking questions about Moses but Evie really had only met him the once before. Anyone would be better than Lennie, though, she pointed out. Delia had almost smiled at that. A few more men wandered into the yard, most of them looking at the girls with interest but Evie just smiled politely and sipped her drink. Delia got up when a good-looking stranger came up and asked her to dance but Evie shook her head whenever an offer came her way. She was there for Lawrie. What would he think if he looked up and saw her dancing with some other chap? When Aston asked if she wanted a second, then a third drink, she said yes. The taste was growing on her and she didn't want him to think she wasn't used to drinking. They sat on the old crates and talked a little but mainly listened to the music. Evie leaned against the brick wall, her back soaking up the last of the day's warmth. She felt relaxed and happy.

'So when you meet Lawrie?' Aston asked.

'I met him on Clapham Common,' she told him. 'And then we ran into each other by accident at the pictures. We'll be next-door neighbours as of tomorrow.'

'Is that so?' Aston offered her a cigarette and Evie hesitated before taking one. 'You a good girl, Evie?'

She frowned. 'I have smoked before.' One cigarette, stolen from Delia's sister Susie's handbag.

He pulled out an engraved silver lighter, flicking it into life and holding it out for her. 'What age are you?'

'Sixteen.'

He raised an eyebrow. 'Your mother knows you're out? Drinkin' and smokin'? You do this every weekend?'

'No!' Now she was caught between the truth, which made her seem too young, and a lie, that would make her look loose. 'Actually, my mother doesn't know I'm here. She's gone out though so as long as I'm home before she is…'

'You lied to your mother?' She couldn't tell if he was impressed or disapproving.

'I never have before but I wanted to see Lawrie.' She stared into her glass, the gin acting like truth serum. She shouldn't drink any more.

Lawrie came over then and rescued her. 'I see you two are getting along.'

'Evie was just tellin' me you goin' be her new next-door neighbour,' Aston said. 'I never knew you was movin'.'

'It only happen' yesterday,' Lawrie explained. 'Don't worry. My new landlady says you can stay on the floor of my room if you get stuck for somewhere to stay. As long as it's not for too long.'

'Mrs Ryan is ever so kind,' Evie said. 'And her house is a lot nicer than this one.'

'Any house is nicer than this one.'

They all turned as Rose pushed through the growing crowd. She looked out of place, far too glamorous for the backyard of an almost derelict house. She made Evie feel dowdy, even as dressed up as she was. Perfect porcelain skin, blemish free, lips drawn red in a perfect bow.

'You weren't expecting me,' she said, looking at Lawrie.

Aston's laugh broke the awkward silence. 'Come on, let's fetch these ladies a drink.' He took Evie's glass and pushed Lawrie towards the house.

'I didn't know you'd be here, Evie.' Rose took the spot vacated by Aston. 'Are you here with Sam?'

'No. Lawrie invited me.'

'Did he now?' Evie could have sworn that Rose's eyes narrowed. 'I don't suppose you've another ciggie?'

'Sorry. Aston gave me this one.' Evie offered the cigarette but Rose shook her head and laughed.

'Oh no, darling, I don't share. Not with anyone.'

Evie didn't know what to say.

'So you've been spending time with Lawrie, have you?' Rose asked.

'A little. We went to the pictures on Wednesday.' She hated how young she sounded. Children went to the pictures. Adults like Rose went out for dinner and drinks. Rose was probably too sophisticated to be impressed with an ice at the interval the way Evie had been.

'He's a busy boy, isn't he? He came round to mine only the day after that.'

To her house? He must have popped round on band business. 'I know the band appreciate you taking their messages.'

'Messages?' Rose laughed. 'Amongst other things. I mean, why else does a young man call on a woman during the day when her husband's out at work.' She lowered her voice and leaned closer to Evie. 'I shouldn't be saying this out loud but it's best you know now. I can see that you've got a crush on him but you're too young, Evie. Barely out of school. And it's like they say, all blokes want one thing. Lawrie certainly didn't say no.'

Evie just stared, not ready to believe what Rose was telling her.

'Oh, goodness, I've shocked you, haven't I?' Rose's hand flew to her mouth, stifling another mean laugh. 'I know, I'm a married woman. 'Til death do us part and all that. I just couldn't help myself. One day you might understand.'

'You and Lawrie…?' Evie couldn't say it, looked across to the kitchen door where the man in question was emerging with Aston, deep in conversation.

He'd kissed her. Only on the cheek, but she'd taken it as a sign of his intent towards her. That he respected her and wanted to do things the right way. But all the time he'd been playing with her. He didn't need Evie when he had Rose.

'I'm sorry, Evie, I didn't think you'd be this upset.' Rose reached across and brushed a tear from Evie's cheek.

Evie flinched. 'Get off me.'

Had they lain there afterwards and laughed as they wondered how to let her down gently? Had Lawrie only been kind to her because she'd offered to find him somewhere better to live? Once his feet were under the table at Mrs Ryan's might he have told her that he was sorry, that she wasn't for him?

Her head was spinning, her body swaying as she stood up and the gin made its effect known. The back gate was blocked now, people crowded into the yard waiting for the band to start playing once more. Delia was nowhere to be seen. She'd have to go out the front. She stumbled towards the house, walking straight into Lawrie as he came out of the back door.

'Evie?' His face changed as he saw the tears streaming down her face. 'Wait up.'

'Leave me alone,' she shouted over her shoulder.

She elbowed her way through the kitchen and into the hall-way only to find another knot of guests blocking the front door. Alcohol clouding her judgement, she made for the stairs, not stopping until she reached the top of the house, nowhere else to run.

She backed into a corner as Lawrie walked up the last few steps slowly. 'Whatever she said to you, I can explain.'

'Too late for that.' Sam was her unexpected hero, appearing from behind Lawrie. 'I warned you. You should never have gone near that whore's house.' He shoved Lawrie into the wall, hard, taking him by surprise. Taking Evie by the hand he pulled her into the bedroom to her left. 'Come on.'

He slammed the door and turned the key, Lawrie's body smashing against it as he did so. They stood there in silence as Lawrie raged against Sam, Evie not able to pick out all the words, though Sam did. He had a huge grin on his face. Anger turned to pleading on the other side of the door and then Evie heard Aston's voice, calming his friend.

There was one last bang on the door. 'I'll come back,' Lawrie promised. 'I can explain, Evie. I promise I can.'

Once he was gone she felt easier, able to survey her surroundings. This was a room of two halves, two narrow beds taking up most of the room. One was neatly made and the other was not, its sheets untucked and twisted. She sat on the made bed.

'Is this your bedroom?' she asked.

Sam nodded. 'And Lawrie's.'

She could guess that it was Lawrie's bed she had sat on, but she didn't want to offend Sam by saying anything.

'I thought you two were friends?'

'Not any more. Not since he decided to leave me in the lurch. He tell you that? I can' afford to pay for this room on my own but he don't care. He don't care 'bout no one but himself.' He sat next to her on the bed.

236

The room was stuffy despite the open window and it smelled rancid, like unwashed clothes and gone-off milk. Evie tried to take shallow breaths.

'I should go.' She made to stand.

'Wait a while,' he said, shooting out a hand to stay her. 'He might be tryin' to trick you. Waitin' out there on the stairs all quiet.' She nodded and settled back down. 'Besides, you can do better than him.'

'I don't know. Rose is so beautiful. I can't blame him for liking her.' He was just like every other boy she'd liked. Not interested in her. Interested in the girl who looked normal. Like the women in adverts and in magazines.

'I tell you a secret? It was I who invited Rose, not Lawrie. He ditched her once he got what he wanted and he would do the same to you, if he got the chance.' Sam took her hand in his. 'Better you see him for what he is. You want a fella can treat you right.'

Evie smiled. 'Thanks for making me feel better. I'll be all right. I just thought he was different is all.'

'You too good for that fool.'

Sam's body was pressed against her now and a sober Evie might have moved away, but there was something comforting in his closeness. In his soothing words.

He put his arm around her. 'How you feel? Better?'

'I suppose.' She felt numb. She'd lost her grip on time, couldn't work out if they'd been hiding away in the bedroom for five minutes or fifty. She could hear music from the yard but couldn't concentrate to listen for a clarinet. For Lawrie.

She turned her head, meaning to ask Sam to help her sneak out, but instead she felt his lips press against hers, his tongue forcing its way into her mouth. She tried to push him away but he pulled her tight, her arms pinned. As her body froze, she found herself reasoning that surely her lack of enthusiasm would alert him to the fact that his attentions were unwanted. But somehow she ended up lying down on her back instead, her head spinning. She managed to turn her head, Sam's kisses finding her neck as she heard laughter from outside, a dirty joke being shared two storeys below. Her body felt flat beneath Sam's weight, flimsy like a blade of grass, easily bent by his heavier tread. Evie closed her eyes as she felt rough fingers pushing up her skirt, grabbing at her underwear. She tried to move, to free her hands and push him away, but she couldn't. She cried out as he shoved forward, the pain shocking her out of her numb state. He just hushed her, his mouth pressing down on hers as he began to move, rhythmically, the bedstead squeaking as it knocked gently against the wall.

The second his weight lifted, she was violently sick. All over Sam, all over herself, all over Lawrie's bed. Sam cursed and jumped away, tripping on the trousers round his ankles. He looked down at her, a curl of distaste on his lips.

'Let us not tell Lawrie about this,' he said, 'else we'll both be in trouble.'

✳ APRIL 1950 ✳

'Alligator lay egg, but him nu fowl'
JAMAICAN PROVERB

1st April 1950

Dear Gertie,

I can't tell you how happy your last letter made me. The relief! I don't think I ever realised just how miserable I've become. The idea of leaving this place for ever – I have to say it sounds too good to be true. Did you really mean it? I do hope so, I don't think I could bear it if you told me you were only joking, especially now that it's actually happening. Evie's young man finally got up the courage and asked her to marry him so that's it. She'll be gone soon enough, though September is the month they're talking about which seems a long way off. I suppose at least it's proof they've not been getting up to no good. No rush, it seems.

For now, a June visit would be perfect. Come for a couple of weeks and we can get our plans set. I was a bit cheeky and already went down to the agent on the high street. He reckons that there's a housing shortage in London, due to all the bombing, and we'll get rid of this place in no time. There's nothing left here for me now. Even the bridge lot only put up with me because I'm reliable. I'm sure they'll be just as happy to get shut of me.

There is one thing. You remember the baby in the pond? Well, that detective seems to be leaving Lawrie alone and now he's been after Evie. He knows, Gertie, about the baby. Not all of it, thank goodness, but enough that now she's talking daft, that she should tell Lawrie about it in case he finds out! I've tried to nip it in the bud but she won't listen to me. I know you had said to try Jim Garvan, only I had a bit of an incident with the detective and he seems to think that Jim wouldn't help. Because of Dad and me falling out, you know. It was all a bit embarrassing, actually, he said all this stuff about how I'd broken Dad's heart. Called me a traitor, if you can believe it. In front of that nosy Irish woman next door as well. So there's no point in me asking Jim. But maybe you could? For old time's sake, you know? It's not as though you did anything wrong after all so he can't say anything to you and I'm worried that if I get involved it'll make things worse. Just write him a letter is all. I'd be very grateful.

Anyway, I'll get up off my old knees now and let you get on. June it is, and again in September for the wedding? Take a photograph of Devon in the sunshine, if you've still got that natty little camera, and post it up for me, won't you? Give me something to look forward to.

Love always,

Aggie xx

16

Evie was on the way back from the shops, her arms pulled to their full length by the weight of two bags full of as many groceries as the Coleridges' ration books would allow. Not far to go, she reminded her screaming limbs, trying to force her feet to pick up the pace as she drew closer to home, the front door barely eight feet away when the car door opened and Rathbone's head appeared over the roof of his Morris Minor. He was parked right outside her house.

'Evelyn, a word.'

As usual he had a cigarette poking out the side of his mouth.

Her body sagged. It had been over a week and she'd dared to hope that he'd crossed her off his list. She glanced around but thankfully no one else was out on the street.

'We can do it here if you like but you might prefer to come down to the station.' He took a step towards her, rising up onto the pavement. 'Just to clear a few things up, that's all.'

'Now? I need to put away the shopping.' She summoned up the last vestiges of her strength and made it to the gate, pushing it open with her knee, trying not to panic.

'I'd hate to have to make more of a fuss about it. After all, you don't want the neighbours to talk. Let's not make this into a rigmarole.' He rolled the 'r' and smiled.

She knew he'd do just that, and enjoy himself while he was at it.

'Can I just drop this in to my mother and tell her where I'm going?' She had no intention of telling her mother. The last thing she wanted was for Ma to come marching out and make a dirty great scene in the middle of the street.

He nodded and she struggled up the path, letting herself in and shutting Rathbone out. She dropped the bags in the hallway and leaned back against the solid wood of the door, closing her eyes as she tried to breathe normally and quash the giddy sensation of terror that was beginning to turn her stomach.

'Ma!' she called. A muffled reply came from upstairs, her mother still busy in the boxroom where she did her sewing. She'd no idea then that Rathbone had been creeping about outside. 'I've got to go out. I'll leave the shopping on the kitchen table.'

She did as she'd promised and ran out of the house before her mother could come down and scold her for not putting the food away. Her heart was racing as she let him hold the car door open for her. Thank goodness Lawrie was still out at work.

When they got to the police station Rathbone led her inside without making any sort of fuss, showing her into a small room with a table and two chairs, facing one another. He left her there and vanished while she sat and waited. She wondered if this was the same room in which Lawrie had been kept.

She watched the clock tick past the minutes, rubbing her arms vigorously: the room was freezing. There was a radiator along one wall but it was cold when she put her hand to the painted iron. She'd only thrown on a cardigan to run to the shops, the day bright, but now she wished she'd thought to put on her coat.

Forty-five minutes later Rathbone walked back in, two steaming mugs in one hand and a folder held in the other. He handed one of the mugs to Evie. He slurped tea out of the other as he sat, dropping the heavy folder on the table between them.

'Thank you for coming in without a fuss, Evelyn. I'm in a much better mood for it.'

She hated the way he said her name but at least he didn't call her Evie. She could pretend that Evelyn was someone else; a silly little girl who'd made a terrible mistake. Evie had a bright future that this horrid man couldn't ruin. She just had to be sensible and play along.

'All I'm asking for is the truth,' he told her. 'No tricks.'

She nodded, warming her hands on the mug.

'Good. All I want is for you to tell me what happened to your child. Your daughter.'

She looked up at him in surprise. 'I told you already. She died. I mean, she was… stillborn.' She always stumbled over that word.

'I thought we were going to be honest with one another.' He sounded disappointed in her, as if she'd done badly on a test.

'We are. I am, I mean, that is what happened. Just like I told you before.' She lifted the cup to her lips, pretending to drink as she cast her eyes down. She couldn't bear to look at him but she worried that if she looked away he'd think she was trying to hide something.

'All right. In that case, let's go back to how this all started.'

He pulled out a sharp HB and his notebook. 'July 1948, I'd say. According to the records, a baby girl was born near Exmouth, Devon in April of 1949 so if you count back… Are you certain Mr Matthews isn't the father?'

'No. I mean yes, I'm sure.' She hung her head and stared into the tea. If only. 'He's got nothing to do with this. Even now we've not… we've never…' she coughed, embarrassed. 'We're waiting until we're married.'

'Waiting until you're married?' He chuckled to himself, unkindly. 'Forgive me, Evelyn, if I struggle to believe that. Bearing in mind that the evidence so far shows that neither of you have been particularly self-restrained in your conduct up 'til now. Who was the lucky chap then? Tell me the truth now.'

She took a breath. 'His name was Sam. I never knew his surname, I swear. He used to share a room with Lawrie when he lived on Somerleyton Road.' She blinked away a sudden flash of memory, a blurred image of that bedroom as she remembered it. 'Lawrie invited me to a party at the house. That was where it all happened. I've not seen Sam since and I don't think Lawrie has either. He moved into the Ryans' house the next day.'

'So there was a to-do at this party and you decided to go to bed with your chap's friend. In his own bedroom, no less! Meanwhile Mr Matthews was chasing after Mrs Armstrong at the same time according to her.' Rathbone was scribbling notes but she couldn't make out his scrawl upside down. 'Honestly, I begin to wonder if you lot have any control over yourselves.'

Evie bit the inside of her cheek and stayed silent. He wanted a reaction but she wouldn't give it. A lifetime of Mildreds had prepared her for this.

Rathbone ordered her to tell him the names of everyone who'd been at the party that night. She hesitated before listing the names she knew, her voice breaking a little as she gave up Lawrie's friends. 'I'm sorry,' she said eventually, 'I know there were a lot more people there but I don't know who they were. I never met them properly.' At least, she reasoned, she knew that all the people she'd named had already been questioned. It wasn't as though she was giving Rathbone new information. With one exception.

'Aston Bayley?' He scanned the list, before flipping quickly through the pages of his notebook. 'He's not been interviewed. Who's this chap then? Is he another ghost like your Sam whateverisnameis?'

'He was in the RAF but he turns up in London every now and again.'

Evie felt a twinge of guilt as Aston's name went down in the book. He might not have anything to do with what had happened to her, she reminded herself, but that didn't mean he wasn't involved with this case. If the police started looking at him then they'd leave Lawrie alone. She took a gulp of oversweet tea.

Rathbone closed the notebook and smiled. 'At least we're moving in the right direction.' He reached for the folder that still lay between them. 'Let's carry on, shall we? Can you explain this to me?'

He whipped a sheet of paper out and laid his trump card before her with a flourish. It was an official document, Evie's eyebrows raising as she realised what it was. The record of birth was for Annabel Coleridge, born 26th April 1949. Evie shivered and pulled her cardigan tighter. Her eyes fell upon the middle column: *Name and Maiden Name of Mother.* Scrawled below was not her own name as she'd expected but that of *Agnes Elizabeth Coleridge.* The father was left as *Unknown.*

'Evelyn?'

She didn't reply, the words swimming before her eyes.

Rathbone sighed and pulled a packet of cigarettes from his jacket pocket. She tried to take one when she was offered but her hand was shaking so much that in the end he lit one for her and placed it between her trembling fingers.

'I don't understand.' She inhaled deeply, closing her eyes against the smoke.

'It is an odd one, isn't it,' he agreed. 'You've not seen this before then?'

She shook her head, unable to take her eyes from that damning sheet of paper, her fingers tracing the child's name.

'Agnes Coleridge is not the mother of this child. You are.'

'Was,' she said softly.

'Are,' he repeated. 'She didn't die, did she?'

Her head snapped up. 'What? No, you're wrong. She's... You – you're wrong.'

Rathbone shifted in his seat. 'Read the date on that bit of paper.'

She did. The date of registration was 29th April. Three days after the birth.

'You tell me that your baby was born dead. So why not register it as a stillbirth? Why register it as a birth three days later? And there's no death certificate for an Annabel Coleridge born on this date.' He leaned forward, Evie sitting back. 'All I can conclude is that Annabel Coleridge did not die. At least not then. Not in April 1949.'

For some reason, she'd always thought she was having a girl. Fifty-fifty, her aunt had said, laughing when she told her. She'd wondered if she should name her for her aunt, a reward for her kindness in putting her up for the long winter as she hid away from the world, but Aunt Gertie had shaken her head and said it would be cruel to saddle a baby with such a hideous name as Gertrude. Besides, it wasn't likely she'd ever meet her great aunt. Evie didn't say anything. She'd already decided to keep her daughter but she knew that if she said anything too soon then Ma would be on the next train out of Paddington, determined to change her mind.

The labour had been long, worse than Evie had anticipated even after all her mother's gleeful warnings. Ma had enjoyed recounting in great detail the pain, the lack of dignity involved. Evie was just getting her comeuppance as far as her mother was concerned. Evie had given birth in the upstairs bedroom that had been hers for five months. Gertie had worked as a district nurse for two decades and Ma was keen to keep prying eyes away from their business. *Just be glad you're not stuck in a cold dorm room with nobody to help you but a pair of disapproving nuns.* She wished Ma's timing hadn't been so perfect, arriving only the day before.

For days she'd been praying, keeping her fingers crossed that the baby would hurry up and come early, desperately uncomfortable and finding it impossible to sleep without her swollen belly getting in the way. She wondered how on earth that huge lump could possibly find a way out of her, especially *through there* but Gertie had assured her that it would be fine. Her calm manner balanced out Ma's agitation.

Breathe, Evie, deep breaths, Gertie had instructed, Evie raging back. How the hell could her aunt know anything when she'd never given birth herself? Her body felt as though it would rip apart, the moments of respite growing fewer and farther between. Gertie ignored her and told her when to push. Somehow she found the strength, feeling a rush that panicked her, before she heard Ma cry out that it was a baby girl. She thought she heard a sound, a whimper, but Ma told her later that she'd imagined it. Evie had tried to sit up but Gertie held her down while she cut the cord, then Ma disappeared out of the room with the baby. Gertie wiped her brow with a warm damp flannel and checked her over. She'd need a stitch or two but she'd done a fine job, she was told, as if she'd just handed over a satisfactory school report.

And then she'd waited for Ma to bring her daughter to her. Gertie busied herself sweeping the soiled towels into a heap and left the room, promising to come back with a change of bedclothes. Evie thought she heard a cry through the wall and smiled. Ma would be back soon with her daughter all cleaned up and ready to be held. Then she would show Ma that it wasn't so ridiculous to want to keep her. She was ready to be a mother.

After a while she called out but there was no reply. The house had fallen silent. She swung her legs over the side of the bed and was testing her weight on gelatine legs when Gertie rushed back in and told her to lie down, tucking the sheets around her so tightly that she could barely move her arms. There was a manic look in her aunt's eyes but she still didn't realise that something was wrong until Ma came back in, wiping her eyes, and she'd known that something awful had happened.

Take it as a blessing, Ma had said. *God knew that this child came from a bad place and He saved you both.*

'What happened to my daughter?' she asked Rathbone, her voice barely a whisper.

'You tell me,' he replied.

But Evie just stared back at him, daring to let hope sprout from the seed he had planted.

'You need to talk to my mother,' she repeated, several times over the next hour. 'Please. I swear I've told you all I know. She's the one who registered the birth after all, not me. And how could I have hidden a baby for almost an entire year without anybody noticing?'

'Somebody did,' he pointed out.

'I wouldn't have hidden her. I wanted to keep Annabel but Ma wanted me to give her up for adoption.' Evie wiped her eyes. 'She'd never have let me live under her roof, not with a baby. Not so I could shame her a second time.'

'Do you think she might have put her own name on the birth certificate so she could go ahead with the adoption?' Rathbone asked.

Evie shrugged and Rathbone sighed and declared the interview terminated. She heard his stomach growl. It was after one.

'You can go. For now.' He pocketed his notebook and stood up. 'Come on then, I've not got all day.'

She didn't have any choice but to follow him back outside to the red Morris Minor. She wondered if Lawrie would still be at work. If he saw her get out of Rathbone's car what would she say to him? She wouldn't lie to him again, she couldn't. But it was too soon to tell him the truth. Too much was now unknown. She needed to talk to Ma and find out if it was true, if Annabel was really still alive. And if she was then Evie needed to find out who had taken her away.

Ma whipped open the front door as soon as Rathbone's car pulled up outside the front of the house, her face pale and worried. Evie saw her swallow hard as she saw the detective coming towards her.

'Afternoon, Mrs Coleridge.' Rathbone took off his hat as she stood back to let him in, Evie trailing behind. 'We need to have a word. Evelyn, why don't you go and put on a pot of tea for us, eh? Make it strong. Milk and two for me.'

Ma showed him into the front room, trying to catch Evie's eye but her daughter ignored her, staring at the floor. It was so quiet that she could hear her mother's breathing, and the catch in the back of the throat as she went to speak but didn't know what to say.

'Mrs Coleridge?' Rathbone's voice demanded an audience.

'We'll talk later, Evie. Once I sort this out.' Ma's words came out in a rush as she closed the door in her face.

Evie waited outside for a moment, pressing her ear close to the door, but although she could hear their voices, she couldn't make out the words. Boiling the kettle was a distraction at least and while the tea brewed she stood on the back doorstep and smoked two cigarettes in a row. She felt feverish, sick to her stomach, her head pounding like it had been the day after the party. Ma had had no sympathy, angry at her for sneaking out and coming home in such a state. It took a few more months before she discovered just how serious a state Evie was in.

She took down two cups and saucers, part of the good tea set, and put them on a tray along with the milk jug and the sugar bowl that barely held enough grains for Rathbone's taste. She went to grab the teapot and, on impulse, lifted the lid and spat. For a moment she froze, horrified by her own behaviour, then she replaced the lid and added the pot to the tray. The china rattled in time to the shaking of her hands as she picked it up.

'Ah! Lovely.' Rathbone greeted her as she walked in and put the tray down on the side, pouring out the two cups and adding milk and sugar to his as requested.

Rathbone took the cup she gave him and swilled back the hot tea in one. 'I'll say this for you, Evelyn, you do know how to make a good cuppa.'

Ma looked stunned as Evie passed her the other cup and saucer, not looking up. Afraid to look her in the eye, Evie thought.

'Well, I think I've got what I came for. For now.' Rathbone checked his reflection in the mirror, smoothing down his skinny moustache with thumb and forefinger and replacing his hat.

Then he was gone, Evie still standing like a statue, staring at the door.

'So what did you tell him?'

'You're better off not knowing. Trust me.' Her mother looked up and Evie saw that she'd been crying.

'You did it, didn't you?' she said, her skin prickling with horror. 'You took her from me and put her up for adoption behind my back.' She stepped forward as her mother looked away. 'I've seen the birth certificate, Ma. It's got your name on it instead of mine. You wanted to be able to sign the paperwork without getting my permission. Am I wrong?'

Ma shook her head, silent rivulets running down her cheeks.

'Jesus Christ.' Evie turned away, unable to think of any words to convey the depth of her anger, her betrayal. 'And if this other poor baby hadn't died, if Lawrie hadn't been in the wrong place at the wrong time, I'd have never found out.'

She wrenched open the door of the sideboard. The old bottle of Glenfiddich still had a good inch left in it. She poured it into a dusty glass from the back of the cupboard and swallowed it down in one, the fumes almost choking her. She coughed and wiped her mouth with the back of her hand.

'Evie, what are you doing?' Ma stood but Evie took a step away, evading her.

'How did you do it?' Evie demanded. 'You weren't gone for long. Where did you take her?' The words came like bullets.

'Does it matter?' Her mother combed her fingers through her hair, a nervous tic that she rarely showed.

'Yes!' Her voice cracked and she tried to swallow, coughing as her throat burned from the whisky. 'You stole my daughter from me. I want to know how you did it. *How* you could do that to me?'

She tried to remember exactly what had happened. Ma had

come back to the bedroom and hugged her as Evie cried and begged to see her baby. She remembered being brought a mug of hot milk to help her sleep, Ma holding it to her lips until she'd drunk it all down. That was all she'd known until the next day. Her mother had admitted later that she'd ground up a couple of her sleeping tablets into the milk, just to help her settle. By the time she was up to asking questions, Ma just told her to hush, that it was all sorted. And to her shame she'd found it easier to just go along with it.

She narrowed her eyes as a slow dawn of realisation crept through her. 'You waited until I was asleep, didn't you? You drugged me so that you had time to get rid of her.'

Ma simply nodded. 'I tucked her up in a basket and left her in your aunt's car until you were asleep. I'd already made arrangements with Sister Mary from Cedars Road. She helped me all those years ago, when you were born there, and I trusted her to find a good family for the baby. She told me to take the child to a mother-and-baby home in Exmouth, to make it easier for you. Gertie drove me over there and we left her in their care. I said I'd go back a few days later with the birth certificate. I knew how upset you'd be and I didn't want to leave you right away.'

'How thoughtful.' Evie spat the words out, her mother flinching. 'So that's where she is? And Rathbone's heading back down to Devon?'

'Not exactly.' Her mother sat back down, her hands twisting in her lap. 'When I went back a few days later they told me they'd struggle to find someone who'd take her. They had a list of childless parents as long as your arm but not one would consider taking a coloured child. They thought it might be a good idea to bring her up to London. Big city, less small-town gossip, they said. As if I don't know better than anyone!'

'So where is she now?' Evie cried. 'Tell me!'

'I took her to Sister Mary. I left you in Devon for a week or two to recuperate, remember?' She picked at a cuticle, her gaze entirely focused on her hands. 'I came back on the train with the baby and I took her to Cedars Road. I knew I could check in on them and make sure she found a home. I didn't want her growing up in one of those places for abandoned children. I'm not a complete monster.'

Evie felt compelled to laugh at the absurdity of her mother's words but she knew if she started she might not be able to stop. What else was she if not a monster?

'When I spoke to Sister Mary again last June she told me that the adoption had all gone through. She went to a family in Hammersmith, a vicar and his wife, God bless them. Just returned from missionary work in Zaire and wanted to give an unwanted child a good home.'

Annabel was alive. That was what she had to remember. Hammersmith wasn't that far away. She might have walked past this vicar and his wife, maybe even as they pushed a pram along the street.

'I only went ahead with what we'd already agreed,' Ma pleaded. 'You were the one who changed your mind at the last minute.'

'It all makes sense now. You were so angry when I told you I'd decided to keep her. I ruined your life and you wanted me gone, not stuck in your home with a screaming brat.' Evie cast her head back towards the ceiling. 'I'm a fool. How did I never suspect?'

Ma flinched at the accusation. 'You can't understand, Evie. I lost my chance at a normal life. I didn't want you to make the same mistake and I knew that with Lawrie you had a golden opportunity. He was always asking after you, all those months that you were away. Aren't you happier now, without that burden? With that ring on your finger?'

Bile rose up and Evie dashed to the kitchen, hand across her mouth, only just making it to the sink before she vomited up whisky, her oesophagus on fire from the corrosive liquid.

'Evie, love, are you all right?' Her mother came up and put her arms around her from behind.

'Get off me!' She pushed her away, hard enough to make her stumble.

Evie's throat tightened as images flicked through her mind like a movie. A baby girl being handed to two smiling parents. Sleeping in a cot, tucked in amongst fluffy blankets. Her first smile shared with a woman who wasn't Evie, calling that woman Mama for the first time, laughing as she was congratulated for her first steps. A first birthday party, any day now, with a cake and a candle that her father blew out for her. Would they have changed her name or was she still Annabel to them?

'I never wanted you to find out like this.'

'You didn't want me to find out at all,' Evie clarified.

Agnes Coleridge had always been formidable, had done her best to hide any weakness even from her own daughter. Now she looked small and tired but Evie couldn't feel pity, only the heat of her anger and the cold steel of the sink, grounding her as she clutched it with both hands. She couldn't stay here.

'Where are you going?' Ma tried to grab her hand as she pushed past. 'Evie?'

Evie walked out into the warm April sunshine. She didn't know where she was going but she had to get as far away as possible from her mother. This wasn't her home any more.

Extract from the *Evening Standard* – Wednesday 5th April 1950

Police have announced the arrest of a Putney woman in the Ophelia case, almost a month after the body of a baby was discovered in the shallows of Eagle Pond, Clapham Common.

DS Kenneth Rathbone spoke at today's press conference, naming the suspect as Annette Dudley, age 29, of Lacy Road, Putney. Previously known as Mrs Sanderson, Mrs Dudley had recently remarried and moved to her new husband's address. It was apparently a concerned neighbour from her prior address in Southfields who came forward with the information that led to Mrs Dudley's arrest on Sunday.

Mrs Sanderson, as she was, had been well known amongst her neighbours as she was often spotted coming and going to various dances and parties following the death of her first husband during the war. More than once she was observed returning home accompanied by gentlemen who stayed overnight at her address. The witness could not swear to it but has mentioned the possibility that one or more of these men was of a duskier persuasion than is usually seen in the vicinity.

In April of last year a pram appeared outside Mrs Sanderson's house and she was seen with a baby, presumably her own.

'She kept herself to herself,' one local man told us. 'She always kept a blanket over the baby so you couldn't tell if it was normal or one of them. I wouldn't have been surprised either way.'

Mr Dudley claims that the child was not his and that he was in fact rushed into marrying his new wife just six weeks ago when she told him she was pregnant once more. The police tell us that they have no reason to doubt his account. No eyewitnesses place Mr Dudley at the Southfields house and he is thought to be the victim of a duplicitous woman, eager to escape her miserable life as an unmarried mother.

17

Evie sat like a statue, her back pressed into the hard wood of the pew. Lawrie could feel the apprehension in the air as she kept her head turned to the front, well aware that her mother was only a few feet away. It had been over a week now and Evie still refused to talk about whatever had gone on between her and her mother.

He stood with the rest of the congregation, fumbling for the hymn book.

'What's she doing?' Evie whispered to him, one verse in.

He looked across. Agnes was singing but without her usual gusto, her head down in her book. She was alone now. She and Evie had always sat together on the left back pew, Mrs Ryan and her charges on the right pew, but now Evie had changed sides. She hadn't been back home once. Instead, she had sent Lawrie round with a list of what she needed and he had drunk tea in the kitchen while Agnes packed a small blue suitcase for him to take to Delia's. She'd been just as reticent as her daughter when he'd dared to ask what had happened between them.

'She's just singing the hymn,' he replied.

He was glad that Agnes slipped out of the church the instant the service was over, allowing Evie to relax as they strolled back to Mrs Ryan's. Evie had been invited over, Mrs Ryan wanting to have a special dinner in honour of the Easter holiday.

'I was thinking,' Evie said. 'Is it too soon to get married next month?'

'People will think there's a reason for us rushing into it,' he joked.

'Is it rushing? We've been together almost a year after all, and we love one another, don't we?' She looked up and he saw in her clear gaze that she was serious.

'But we've only been engaged a couple weeks,' he said, surprised. 'Why not September like we said? That's when I got my leave. So we can go away on honeymoon afterwards. Didn't you tell your boss?'

He'd got it all planned out in his head already. Get married in the church here, the reception in the hall next door with the band providing the music. Then they'd catch the evening train down to Brighton and spend a week by the sea. He'd worked out costings with Mrs Ryan's help (the idea of flowers hadn't even crossed his mind). Agnes had been going to make the dress. They couldn't marry without the dress, so Evie would just have to forgive her mother for whatever it was she'd done.

'It's just that I can't stay at Delia's for ever. And I won't go back to Ma's before you say anything. I could try and find a room to let but it seems such a waste of money when we could be living together.' She squeezed his arm. 'September seems so far away!'

'Let me see if I can get some overtime,' he found himself saying. He could always speak to Derek about extra deliveries.

'Things are back to normal now. I reckon we could use a celebration.'

'You're right there.' He'd been shocked at how the news had affected him, hearing of the arrest of the Putney woman. People spoke of a weight lifting when they had such news but he had never understood it until that moment. Annette Dudley's arrest had felt like a sack of rocks falling from his back. Ever since he'd felt as though he were skipping instead of walking. 'There's something else you should know.' He braced himself. 'Aston's at home.'

'He's back, is he?'

'Turned up last night,' Lawrie told her. 'No advance warning, of course.'

He'd just been sitting there, feet firmly under the table as Mrs Ryan brought him a sandwich made with the last of the bread. Lawrie got the impression he'd been expecting to spend the weekend elsewhere but had suddenly been left with nowhere else to go. He'd slept in while Lawrie had dressed for church, saying one Sunday's attendance wouldn't save his soul, even if it was for Easter. He was probably right.

'Now, Evie, I've got a nice piece of beef in, thanks to Derek. You do eat beef, don't you?' Mrs Ryan caught them up, dragging Arthur behind.

'It's my favourite, Mrs Ryan.'

'And after dinner, Lawrie, I'll sit down and write to Lucille. Your poor mother! It's been weeks since we last wrote.'

Lawrie had to stifle a smile. He'd made up for his silence with a six-page letter back home, full of his good news and with not one mention of any baby or the police. He knew Mrs Ryan well enough to know she wouldn't land him in trouble.

Aston had made himself useful for once and laid the table. The best tablecloth, last seen at Christmas, cutlery laid out properly, napkins, even two candles as a centrepiece. Mrs Ryan oohed and aahed and Aston smiled bashfully as Evie rolled her eyes. Lawrie nudged her, hoping they'd both behave, but the smell of the beef was making his mouth water and all he cared about was how long it would be before he could eat.

'Sit yourself down, Evie,' Mrs Ryan invited.

She sat, Lawrie taking the seat beside her as he saw Aston make a move. No way was Aston going to be allowed to wind Evie up today. It was supposed to be a celebration, not only of their engagement but of Lawrie's freedom. Rathbone's car had not been seen in a week. Lawrie would have enjoyed seeing that twisted smile wiped off the detective's face when he found out the truth.

Derek appeared carrying a heavy cardboard box. 'Some wine came in from France the other day. Supposed to be decent.' He unpacked a few bottles and went in search of a corkscrew.

Arthur put on his glasses and inspected the label of one of the bottles. 'Looks drinkable.'

They all sat down, Arthur tugging at Mrs Ryan's apron until she joined them and stopped fussing with the potatoes that needed to go in the oven. Six of them round the table. Arthur sat at the head, Derek at the bottom, the two men of the house. Wine was poured, and Arthur led the congratulations. Mrs Ryan even took a suspicious sip. Sherry and the odd Snowball at Christmas were her usual tipples.

'Are we almost ready to eat, Ma, I'm starving?' Derek rubbed his belly.

'Less than an hour. You'll last,' his mother told him. 'Evie, love, you can smoke out in the yard, if you'd like. The boys can show you.'

Lawrie let her go without him. He'd told Aston to play nicely with her and this was his chance to show that he could be civil. Derek was there as chaperone so hopefully they could manage five minutes together without fighting.

'You find out yet what happened with her next door?' Arthur asked once the trio had closed the door behind them.

'Evie won't tell me. You think I should be worried?' Stupid question; he was already worried.

'They'll sort it out by the wedding, surely.' Mrs Ryan slammed the oven door on the potatoes and sat back down. 'A girl needs her mother on her wedding day. And whatever else you say about Agnes, she's a cracking seamstress. She'll send Evie up the aisle looking a million dollars.'

'I don't know. Evie wants to move the wedding up to next month. She says that the sooner we move in together the better.' He could tell from Mrs Ryan's expression what she thought of that idea. 'I mean, it makes sense the way she puts it but it won't be the wedding we wanted. No honeymoon for a start, I can't change my leave.'

'I thought she was staying with her friend, whatshername?'

'Delia. She is. I think she feels a bit awkward about it, though. Like she's imposing.'

'And yet we get the privilege of young Aston for days at a time without any rent money,' Arthur commented. 'How long did you say he's staying for this time?'

'God only knows,' Lawrie replied. 'I'm sorry. If he's taking advantage I can talk to him. Get him to put his hand in his pocket at least.'

'No, Lawrie, this is still my house and I make the rules.' Mrs Ryan patted Arthur's hand. 'I said he was welcome to stay any time and that stands. He brings us presents every now and again, doesn't he?'

'Well, that's another thing. If me and Evie get our own flat then I doubt she'll want him staying with us. September was perfect. Time to save up, time for Aston to get a job and find himself somewhere to live…' Lawrie sighed and drank some more wine. He'd just have to put his foot down with Evie. She could make it up with Agnes if she was so unhappy staying with Delia.

The back door opened but only Derek came in, his face telling its own story as he closed it behind him. 'It might be sunny out but with them two it feels more like the bleeding Arctic.'

Arthur looked over at Lawrie and shrugged. Wasn't it typical? Just when he thought everything was sorted. Getting back to normal. Things going his way. Lawrie stormed outside, but the pair of them were just standing there in silence, a few feet apart.

'Everything all right?' He felt a little deflated, denied the opportunity to let out his own frustration.

'Fine,' Evie said, her smile looking a little too forced.

He looked at Aston who just shrugged and threw his cigarette butt into the flowerpot ashtray before walking back inside. Evie looked away and, just for a moment, she seemed like a stranger. Not his girl.

'What's going on with you?' He walked closer and she let him fold her into his arms.

'Nothing.'

He rested his head upon hers and breathed in. She smelled like Evie. And she fitted beneath his chin as though she had been made for him, their height as complementary as their minds.

'Why you won't talk to me?' he asked. 'You don't trust me?'

'I do. Of course I do. It's just... sometimes there are secrets that aren't just mine, you know?' Her smile was sad as she looked up at him. 'What if I promise that I'll tell you everything before we get married?'

'In September? And do it properly, like we talked about?'

She nodded. 'Yes. I was just having a panic before. We'll do it properly.'

'Good.'

He gave in though he knew he should try harder. What was so terrible that she couldn't tell him? Something that Agnes had done, he guessed, else why would she leave home the way she had, with no warning? And with this bull-headed determination not to go back.

They went back inside when Mrs Ryan called out that dinner was ready. Aston kept his manners but didn't say a word to Evie directly all through the meal. He was just his usual raucous self.

Lawrie drank a little too much wine, his head fuzzy by the time Mrs Ryan started to clear the empty plates from the table.

'I should go,' Evie said suddenly. 'I told Mrs Marson I wouldn't be late home.'

'It's still early, Evie,' Mrs Ryan protested.

'I can walk you back,' Lawrie offered, not trying to talk her into staying.

The fresh air did him some good, even though the silence between them grew oppressive the closer they got to the Marsons'. She'd said that she would tell him everything, he just had to be patient. She'd backed down over rushing the wedding already, it wouldn't be long before she sorted things out with her mother. This was between Agnes and Evie, nothing to do with him.

They kissed briefly at the end of the street and he watched until she was safely inside the house. It was all going to be just fine, he told himself.

On a whim, partly because he felt like another drink, partly because he didn't want to go home and have Aston tell him what a coward he was for not demanding the truth from Evie, he detoured to Johnny's house.

Johnny's place was on Somerleyton Road, just up from where Lawrie had spent his first few weeks in London. The imposing Victorian façades had survived the war for the most part but these former family dwellings had been carved up into rooms, Johnny's family occupying two such rooms at the top of a building at the Coldharbour Lane end of the street. Sonny and Moses shared another room on the ground floor of the same house. Another family of three, and a room whose occupants seemed to have changed every time Lawrie went over, made up the rest of the household.

He went round the back, hearing voices and laughter over the wall. Unless it was raining or freezing cold, they always sat out back, jumpers and jackets on even in the height of summer.

'Ah, look who grace us with his presence!' Johnny stood closest, reaching out to greet his friend.

'You fell out with Evie?' Moses always seemed to know when something was going on.

'Nah, man.' It wasn't quite a lie after all. 'I just walked her home and since you were sort of on me way...'

Johnny passed him a bottle of beer. 'Good to see you.'

The sun was low in the sky but there was still almost an hour before it would set, and Lawrie gladly took a seat next to Moses on one of the crates. It was just the four of them. The Originals as Johnny called them when Al wasn't around.

'We just sayin', who you think they gonna pin this baby death on now?' Sonny asked.

Lawrie choked a little as his beer went the wrong way. 'What you mean? They got that woman. They gonna leave us alone now.'

Moses chuckled. 'Nah, man. I tellin' you, at work all the talk now is what a whore that woman is, she let some blackie sleep with her. They sayin' if they find that nigger they make sure he won' touch no other white woman. As in, he won't be physically able to.'

'They gon' break his hands?' Sonny asked.

'Worse.' Johnny made an arrow with his own hands, pointing to his crotch. 'You watch out, Sonny.'

Lawrie shuddered. He'd thought it was over, the spotlight off him at last. He'd not considered that there was still a fella out there who'd fathered the child.

'It wasn't you, was it, Lawrie?'

Moses was teasing, he knew, but he still had to stop himself from reacting.

'I'm not sure I've ever been to Putney,' he fired back. 'Besides, I'll be a married man in a few months. First of us to tie the knot on English soil.'

'English, Jamaican, don't matter what soil it is, boy. Your life will never be your own again,' Johnny warned. 'You marry the wrong woman and your life be over.'

'Don't you listen! Evie's not the wrong woman and Johnny done well himself with Ursula,' Sonny said. ''Sides, the other alternative is ending up like Aston. That boy! How he keep up with all these different women every week?'

'Even Aston is lookin' to settle down now,' Moses said.

Lawrie looked at him in surprise. 'Aston? You know something I don't?'

'He never told you 'bout Elaine?'

Lawrie looked around but the rest of the band seemed as mystified as he was. 'Elaine?'

'You don't know? I met her one time when I ran into Aston on Oxford Street. Few weeks back it was and they been shopping. Holding hands and everything,' Moses recalled. 'Him carrying a lot of shopping bags, fancy ones, like from one of them high class shops on Regent Street.'

'Must be true love then,' Johnny said. 'Only a crazy person goes shopping with their woman.'

'When was this?' Lawrie asked.

This Elaine, whoever she was, her name had never come out of Aston's mouth, not in Lawrie's presence, at least. Evie had mentioned that she'd seen Aston with a brunette woman at the Lyceum but he'd thought nothing of it. Why wouldn't he have told Lawrie, of all people, if he was getting serious about a woman?

'Not too long. Month or so ago. Before this trouble all started though, I can tell you that much.' Moses clicked his fingers. 'I got it! It was the weekend before the baby was found. I was up in Soho 'cause me tailgut snapped, you remember, that Friday night at the Lyceum? And then I decided I may as well have a stroll along and check out the price of a new shirt 'cause mine was all gettin' yellow. Definitely it was the week before 'cause I saw him the next Friday evening and he never said nothin' 'bout her. Seemed like he was avoiding me and I did wonder what was up.'

Johnny lit a cigarette. 'Think he been seeing this girl long? She white?'

'Yes, and they seemed very familiar. Hadn't just met that day or anything. She wasn't English, though. Had an accent, like French or German, one of those. And she was definitely in charge. Wasn't keen to stand there on the street making chit-chat. She said they had an appointment for something or other.'

'So Aston has a foreign girlfriend, who he's been seeing for a while and isn't keen to associate with his friends. And even *I* never heard of her. His best friend.' Lawrie shook his head. 'What he up to?'

'You think maybe he's got a reason?' Sonny asked. 'Like maybe Elaine had a baby and he don't want to get her in trouble?'

'You think he got something to do with the murder?' Moses

asked, looking worried. 'See, I forgot about her until just now. I didn't think it was important.'

'Aston?' Johnny laughed. 'No way, man. He not a babykiller. This girl sounds like she got money – you said they been out shopping in fancy places. Strange sort of thing to do if they plannin' to commit a murder, don't you think? Anyway, they arrested that Putney woman.'

'Then why not tell us about her. Not even Lawrie. And he must have been in London that week, right? When the baby was found.' Sonny disagreed.

Lawrie leaned back, conflicted; feeling betrayed that Aston hadn't wanted to introduce him to his woman; feeling like a Judas for thinking even for second that Aston could do something so awful. Unless he'd been given no choice.

'We could let the police know to interview him. Get them off our backs for a while,' Moses suggested.

'No.' Sonny waved that notion away like a mosquito. 'You weren't at the meeting the other day? We spoke about this. We don't do that to our own. Besides, do that and you put them back onto Lawrie.'

'Why you think that?' Moses asked.

''Cause I found the body, Moses. You forgot? You tell Rathbone that a friend of mine, until recently thought to be in another part of the country at the time, was actually gallivanting around London the week that baby died, you know what he'll think? That we were in it together.' Lawrie laughed harshly. 'You would land me right in it.'

'Then where the hell was Aston when all this took place?' Moses asked.

'I dunno, but he wasn't out on Clapham Common killing a baby.' Lawrie was adamant. Aston was a lot of things but he wasn't a bad man. If he'd hidden this woman from everyone then there was a good reason. 'Anyway, this woman they got, her name is not "Elaine". Elaine got nothin' to do with this so therefore neither does Aston.'

'Yes, but—'

'Hush you mouth, Moses.' Johnny interrupted. 'Besides, things won't go on like this. We'll get a few more bookings once things have calmed down.'

'No more weddings.' Sonny stared at Johnny darkly. 'And what you mean a few more? We struggling?'

'Well, the book is looking a little empty,' Johnny admitted. 'We just got the Lyceum and a couple gigs round Soho coming up.'

'I thought there was a church dance soon?' Lawrie tried to think back a couple of weeks.

'They cancelled,' Johnny said quietly. 'But just as well. I mean, we don't want to be playing church halls, do we? Jazz and calypso and proper dance music, that's what we want, none of this sedate dull English stuff.'

'Just as well none of us rely on the band to pay rent.' Sonny looked hard at Johnny, the only one of them who did.

Moses changed the subject to cricket and Lawrie drank another two beers as the light faded into darkness, the men now illuminated by the light from an upstairs window. Lawrie was just thinking that he should get going when he'd finished his beer when they heard the smash.

'Johnny!' It was Ursula's voice, panicked.

A third-floor window scraped open and Johnny's wife pushed her head out, calling for him once more.

'What the hell go on?' he shouted up.

There was another crash and Lawrie could hear the screams of the women and children upstairs, the wail of the baby. Johnny didn't wait for a reply but ran into the house, Lawrie slower to react, the alcohol dulling his senses. He followed Moses and Sonny inside, more out of curiosity than fear. Even after what they'd spoken about that afternoon, he wasn't expecting what confronted them as they arrived in the hallway.

Ursula pounded down the stairs. 'Don' you open that door, Johnny! They out there. They got weapon and all sort.'

'Who?'

'I don' know, Johnny. Men. White men.' Her voice lowered now to a hiss. 'You hear them?'

They stood there in the dark hallway, their faces barely visible in the twilight. Lawrie listened and could make out the voices on the other side of the solid front door. Two sounded like they were right there, laughing as they stood close enough to ring the doorbell if they'd wanted to. He sniffed suddenly. Something was burning.

Johnny nudged Moses and pointed to the door that led from the hallway to the room Moses and Sonny shared. 'You smell that?'

'Shit, man!' Moses threw open the door and they peered round the frame as he ran inside and turned on the light.

The cause of the smash had been the window to this room, a brick lying in the centre of the carpet with glass spread every-where like confetti, all over the beds. Their attackers weren't the smartest, at least. Their second shot had been a poor attempt at a Molotov cocktail, the glass bottle still intact. It was the burnt wick that had made the rancid smell as the threadbare carpet beneath it smouldered. Moses picked the bottle up gingerly, placing it in the steel sink in the corner of the room while Sonny stamped on the floor until the smoke desisted, a black scorch mark left behind.

From outside came the sound of whooping, pounding footsteps moving away along the pavement.

Ursula came down then, her nightgown tied tight and her hair under a scarf. 'They gone, thank the Lord. I jus' seen them run off round the corner.'

'All right.' Johnny kissed her cheek. 'You go up and check on the pickney, I go out and make sure they gone.'

They went together to the front door, Johnny gingerly releasing the lock before throwing it open, perhaps hoping to surprise any foolish man who'd stayed behind. There was no one there when they went outside. Lawrie smelt the urine before he saw the faint streams that ran down off what was left of the front window, at least six skinny waterfalls that pooled on the weed-strewn slabs beneath.

He turned back towards the front door to see Johnny staring at the words that had been daubed in red paint against the chipped black of the front door: NIGGERS GO HOME.

For a full minute, nobody said a single word.

9th April 1950

Dear Gertie,
You must be wondering what on earth you've done to deserve another letter from me so soon. I wish I had better news or didn't have to bother you with my problems, but I have no one else to talk to.

Evie has left. Walked out on me. I told you that detective was hanging about. Well, he carried on with his digging and found me out. And of course he told Evie, thinking that her baby must be the baby in the pond. I had to tell her the truth then. She'd have worked it out soon enough. The way she looked at me! I thought that now, with her engaged to Lawrie finally, she'd understand. I thought she'd be grateful that she's got a bright future ahead of her. Anyway, she just walked out. She sent Lawrie round a few days ago to collect a suitcase of her clothes and things. Thank goodness, he knows none of this else I'm sure he'd be reconsidering marrying her. If anyone knows what men think of an unmarried mother, it's me after all.

I wish we could talk. A lot's gone on since I last saw you and I feel like I'm about to burst with it all but I daren't write it all down. I can hear you now, saying 'I told you so'. And I knew at the time it was a risk but I felt it was worth taking. There's still a chance Evie will come around. If only because Lawrie's already suspicious. I could see him looking at me, the questions on the tip of his tongue, but he was too afraid to ask. He is a lovely lad. Totally in love with Evie. I do sometimes think she might get away with telling him the truth, the way I've seen him look at her.

I don't know if I can bear to wait for your reply. You have a telephone, after all. I'm going to call you on Tuesday afternoon. I do for the Rodgers on a Tuesday and she's never home. I'm sure they won't notice one tiny telephone call. I'll ring you at three o'clock so please be in. I need your help, big sis. Yes, yet again. Please be in.

Love,

Aggie xx

18

It was odd sleeping in a room with Delia, listening to the sound of another person breathing. Evie hadn't slept through the night since she'd ended up at the Marsons'. She should be more grateful, she knew. After all, she'd had nowhere else to go. This bed, with the spring sticking up just where she would have been most comfortable, was a blessing. But this wasn't her home. The room was messy, clothes strewn everywhere and the dressing table covered in the paraphernalia of young women: make-up and hair brushes, half empty jars of all sorts of creams, and that wasn't the worst of it. There were men living in this house who left strange smells in the bathroom and edged nervously around Evie as if she might break if they came too close. She couldn't remember feeling so awkward and out of place.

But she couldn't go home. She couldn't bear the thought of facing her mother again. Ma must be glad that she'd left. She knew where Evie was but she'd not made any attempt to come round. Ma wasn't all that old, after all. She could still have a life, away from Evie. It used to be all she talked about, selling up as soon as Evie was out from under her feet, moving away to a place where nobody knew her story.

The morning of her day off, she waved Delia off to work before getting dressed, leaving the house half an hour later. It was a lovely warm April day and the few of the Marsons' neighbours who bothered to plant anything at the front of their houses were seeing the benefit now that spring was in full bloom. Stone pots and planters of brightly coloured flowers gave Evie an idea and she made a detour to the high street florist, asking the woman behind the counter for advice. She'd never bought flowers before. Ma said that they died within days so what was the point in wasting money on them. An old poster was stuck up on the wall, asking for information on the Clapham Common baby. They must have forgotten to take it down after that Sanderson woman had been arrested. The florist saw her looking at it and, despite knowing she should keep her mouth shut, Evie told her that she wanted to lay some flowers at the pond. For baby Ophelia. The woman looked at her strangely but didn't say anything. But Annette Dudley had not cared about her daughter and no child deserved that. A child deserved love; that was why Evie had decided she had to find Annabel. Just to be sure that her mother was now telling the truth and she'd gone to a good home. Then she would leave her be. She paid too much for a bouquet of white carnations and caught the 37 to Clapham Common.

No one would know that Eagle Pond had been the site of such a macabre tableau only a few weeks prior. It was a peaceful spot, serene, a pair of ducks breaking up its mirrored surface. A little boy, barely out the pram himself, his mother gossiping with an older woman on the path, was tugging at the long grass, laughing as it came free from the soil and tumbled him backwards into its soft lawn. Evie cut off the path onto the grass, smiling as she watched him, her eyes widening as he took off suddenly, toddling at pace towards the water's edge.

'Hey!' she cried out as she picked up her speed, waving in the direction of the mother who was a good ten feet away, barely glancing round at Evie's shout. 'Excuse me? Hello!'

Evie hooked her hand into the boy's duffel coat hood just as he stumbled over the edge, screaming as the cold water shocked him. Throwing her flowers to the ground, she managed to grab him under his armpits and lifted him onto dry land as he cried out for Mummy.

The mother had finally awoken to the danger and rushed over, pulling her son from Evie's grasp. 'What did I tell you? You don't go near the water!' She smacked his bottom and Evie bit back a retort, seeing that it was pointless. The boy's sobs intensified as he was dragged away without a thank you to his rescuer.

'Don't mind her, love, it's just the shock. Makes people forget their manners.' The older woman walked over to Evie, whose ears were still ringing from the high pitch of the boy's shrieks. 'Shame about your flowers. Were they for someone special?'

'Sort of.' Evie stared down at the crushed petals, dark with pond mud where the mother and child had trampled the heads into the ground. 'They're where they're supposed to be, at least.'

The woman's expression slid into the same wariness that she'd seen on the florist's face and she smiled vacantly before walking away. Evie's shoes were caked in mud. There was a bench set back from the pond and she sat down gratefully. There was no rush, she reminded herself, no appointment to keep. Once she'd stopped shaking, she took off her shoes one by one, wiping them clean on the grass as best she could. They'd have to do; it wasn't as though she could just go home and change. She'd cross Lawrie's route and if he caught sight of her, she didn't know what she would say. Her shins were speckled with dirt and she waited for it to dry before brushing off the worst of it. Doubts were creeping in but she did her best to push them away. Not knowing was worse than knowing the truth, she reminded herself.

It had taken days to build up the courage to get this far. Even Delia didn't know the real reason she'd taken the day off work. She'd said that she wanted to make a start on the wedding plans, Mr Sullivan reluctantly granting her the leave. Not because she wasn't owed or deserved it, he told her, but that he didn't want to lose her. She'd never given it much thought before but there were no married women working at Vernon & Sons. Wives, with a bit of luck, soon became mothers. Would it feel different to carry Lawrie's baby, a wanted child? She had prayed every day with Annabel, wishing hopelessly that it was all just a bad dream.

Now that she was only a few minutes' walk away from her destination she felt paralysed, her encounter with the toddler having knocked the courage from her. She was hollowed out, staring at the sad brown remnants of those innocent carnations. She couldn't bear to pick them up and dispose of them properly. They would rot eventually, fade away into the soil beneath soon enough. What sort of tribute was a poor cheap bunch of flowers anyway?

Ma had always said that it was the thought of leaving Evie to rot away in a children's home that had made up her mind in the end. That the idea of her growing up without love was too cruel to bear. Evie couldn't help but think that if her own mother had her time again, maybe it would have been Evie found tangled up in the shallows of Eagle Pond, eighteen years before. But Agnes Coleridge had kept her daughter and suffered, never letting Evie forget how lucky she was. Evie pushed herself to her feet with effort. If she meant to go through with her plan then best to get it over with.

Cedars Road was only a stone's throw from the north side of the Common, a wide thoroughfare lined with Victorian villas that remembered the war well. Many of the buildings still stood, though they showed their wounds clearly. Like everywhere else in London, progress was slow. Evie turned into the driveway of one of the houses, about halfway along. Only a small sign screwed into the brickwork beside the porch gave away its precise use: Cedars Road Home for Women and Babies. The place of Evie's birth. The place where her mother had taken Annabel.

She rang the bell by the door and waited, her weight shifting from one foot to the other. Glancing down she noticed a splash of mud that she'd missed, right in the centre of her skirt. Too late. She heard clipped footsteps echoing towards her, the click of the locking mechanism.

The woman who opened the door was dressed in a plain navy blue and white uniform, a nurse's watch pinned to her sagging bosom. Her sparse greying hair was severely pinned back into a greasy bun. She looked Evie up and down, finding her wanting.

'Can I help you?' she asked, folding her arms across her chest.

'I'm not sure.' Evie panicked, suddenly unprepared even though it was all she'd thought about for days. 'I wondered what it is you do here exactly. I mean, I know what the home is for, sort of, only I know someone who—'

'Relative, is it?' The woman was impatient, the fingers of one hand playing with the set of keys hooked onto her belt.

'Yes.' She felt relief at answering even so simple a question correctly.

'Come in then.' The woman walked off, leaving the door hanging open. 'Close that behind you.'

Evie followed her into a reception room, presumably one they kept for show because Ma had told her what it was like living here as an inmate and this room seemed far too welcoming. The woman gestured towards a sofa and Evie sat down, smoothing a hand over the soft brown leather. This was where they brought the distraught parents then, allowing them to convince themselves that their daughters would be left in safe hands. The room was bright and airy with high ceilings. Framed artwork decorated the walks and Evie saw that some of it was amateurish: bright coloured abstract landscapes that reminded her of childhood.

'We let the girls paint every now and again. Keeps their minds occupied,' the woman said. 'Mrs Devonport. I'm the matron here. I didn't catch your name.'

'Miss… Bayley.' She grabbed at a name. She couldn't give Coleridge in case this woman remembered her mother; she looked old enough to have been working here when Evie was born. She didn't want to taint Matthews before the name was even hers.

'I'm here on behalf of my parents. My sister, she's in need of a place to stay. She's only fifteen. You must know how it is. My father doesn't want anyone to know.'

Mrs Devonport sniffed. 'How far gone is she?'

'She's just begun to show. That's how my mother realised what she'd done. She reckons four months or so.'

Mrs Devonport said nothing, just looked at Evie, her eyes narrowed. With a jolt Evie remembered that she wasn't exactly inconspicuous. With her dark skin, this woman was trying to work out what sort of family she was from. Where they were from.

'My father is furious,' she said quickly. 'We don't live round here. He wants to make sure no one we know accidentally bumps into my sister while she's away.'

'We're full at the moment,' Mrs Devonport told her. 'Can I ask you, was the father also…' She waved a hand in Evie's general direction.

'No. He is white. Very pale, in fact.' Too much, she thought. She'd made him sound vampiric; had the oddest image of this imaginary white-skinned ne'er-do-well in her mind and had to bite her lip to stop the incongruous giggle that bubbled up in her throat.

'I don't mean to cause offence,' Mrs Devonport continued, her face contradictory. 'Reason I ask is that I'm assuming she won't be keeping the child.'

'No. We had heard that you could help with that. That you place babies with families that can care for them when their mothers can't. Or won't.' Evie's chest tightened.

'We do, only when they look – foreign – it's difficult. Most adoptive parents want a child what looks like it could be theirs, even if they know that it isn't.'

'So you're saying that if this baby was born with dark skin – like mine, for example – then it might be tricky to find an adoptive family? You've had experience with this sort of thing?' Evie held her breath as she waited for the answer. It had been less than a year. Surely this woman had would remember Annabel.

'Once.' Mrs Devonport stretched out the word as if reluctant to let her admission out. 'But it was a very specific situation. One of the nuns arranged a private adoption that went through our books but it wasn't really to do with us. The mother wasn't one of our girls, you see, and the child was only here for a few days before the new family came to take her.'

Evie exhaled. Her mother had told her the truth then. Annabel was safe, hopefully in a happier home than Evie could have provided. She'd expected to feel something more but the numbness prevailed, as if her body was trying to protect her, not convinced by the evidence before her.

Mrs Devonport stood. 'If you want to leave your details I can have someone contact you if a place does come available. It is unlikely though so I would advise you to look elsewhere.'

When Evie reached the pavement outside, she glanced up as she saw a movement at one of the second-storey windows. A girl stood there, younger than Evie and pale as a ghost. She was motionless, her slight body only visible from the torso upwards. In her arms she held a blanketed bundle. Her baby. To anyone else she would have made a pathetic figure, hopeless and vulnerable. But all Evie felt was envy.

Extract from the *Evening Standard* – Wednesday 19th April 1950

SHOCK TWIST IN BABY OPHELIA CASE – WOMAN RELEASED

Annette Dudley, 39, of Putney, was today released without charge following the production of new evidence. Sanderson was charged last week with the murder of the baby girl known as Ophelia, whose body was discovered in Eagle Pond, Clapham Common, last month. It was thought that Mrs Dudley was the mother of that baby girl, but her one-year-old son has now been found.

Police say that it was Mrs Dudley's sister who came forward with the baby boy who had been in her care since December, following her engagement and subsequent marriage to local bank manager George Dudley.

'We all wish that Mrs Dudley had found fit to disclose the truth when first questioned,' DS Kenneth Rathbone told this reporter. 'We are yet to decide whether to charge her with wasting police time and holding up what is a very sensitive investigation.'

The police were keen to reassure the public that they are already picking up the investigative strands that were dropped in light of the Dudley arrest. DS Rathbone stressed that any information, no matter how trivial, should be reported to the police.

'We fought a war and sacrificed so many good men in order to preserve the great British values that have been undermined in such a brutal way through this child's death,' DS Rathbone told the press conference. 'I urge the local community to help us bring her killer to justice.'

19

The news hit Lawrie like a punch in the stomach. Aston slapped the paper down onto the kitchen table.

'You watch, there'll be trouble now,' he warned.

As if there hadn't already been trouble. Word was that Johnny's house wasn't the only victim of a violent attack. Ursula had insisted on getting the police round, for all the use they'd been. One constable had appeared, younger than Lawrie and less sure of himself. He'd only taken notes when Ursula stood over him and offered to write them for him if he wasn't able. In the darkness, she'd not got a good look at any of the five or six men, only able to confirm that they'd been white. They'd all worn hats so that from above, as she peered out of the window from behind the curtain, they looked much alike.

The band played a club in Soho that night, one of a handful of safe venues, and Lawrie was glad to see that it wasn't just him who was worried.

'They as good as sayin' it's one of us,' Sonny ranted. 'May as well be all of us the way they talk, the way they look at me. How dare they say such things? Like we all criminals when we the ones getting attacked in our own homes, vandalising us, trying to intimidate us into leaving.'

'You been here long enough to know this nothing new,' Moses pointed out. 'This murder business just making 'em feel better. Proof that they was right all along. We just got to ride it out. 'Less you want to do what they say and get on that boat home.'

Sonny kissed his teeth and stared down at the floor, shaking his head. 'So we just get on with things? You give up or you go on. That's it? Two options?'

'Two options.' Moses grinned. He'd always been quiet but since the wedding, and the attack at Johnny's, he'd begun to stand taller and speak before he was spoken to. 'Who here can afford to go home anyway?'

Not Johnny, with a family to support. Sonny, maybe, but nobody else. They'd made that trip from Kingston banking on settling in England for the foreseeable future. The mother country had sent out its mayday message and her plea had been answered, but memories seemed short.

Soho, at least, was a sanctuary. Just walking from home to the bus stop these days Lawrie felt as though he was being watched; sized up and considered, his paranoia growing daily. Might it be him? Was he the father? Had he done the deed? The unspoken questions echoed continuously in his ears when he was out on the terraced streets of Brixton but the Soho crowd were loose, eager for music and jazz and cigarettes and whisky. They saw a musician when they looked at him in his new sharp suit (for his wedding, a justifiable expense), not a criminal.

'You think you can give us all a lift home tonight, Sonny? Be on the safe side?' Johnny asked.

Sonny nodded. 'It'll be a rough trip but you'll get home in one piece.'

Afterwards, riding each bump in the road, his arse turning numb on the hard floor of the van, Lawrie wondered whether he might not have been better taking his chances on the bus. It reminded him of the last time he'd made such a trip, the night of the Wandsworth wedding.

'You got plans tonight?' Aston asked at breakfast the next day. 'I thought we should call another meeting. See who knows what.'

'I'm taking Evie out.' Lawrie stirred his porridge, avoiding Aston's stare and wishing his friend had stayed in bed rather than deciding to rise according to Lawrie's pre-dawn alarm.

'This is more important. You even read the paper? Pickin' up old strands, they say. That's you, Lawrie, if you forgot.'

'Forgot? How could I?' He struggled not to raise his voice. 'But until they come callin', my life is goin' on as normal. I'm not hiding, Aston. I'm not changing my life just in case Rathbone comes back knockin'.'

'Sensible boy.' Arthur sucked at his tea. 'Lighten up, Aston. My money's still on the mother, whoever she is.'

'Well, I agree with you on that,' Aston told him. 'See, I been thinkin—'

Lawrie groaned.

'Least I don't just stick me head in the ground, pretendin' like none of this happen.' Aston threw his spoon down on the table with a clatter.

'I'm going to work.' It was easier to walk away from Aston than concede that he might have a point.

He was first in as usual and got on with sorting, head down, not giving Donovan a chance to come in and find him at rest. No doubt he'd read the *Standard* and was ready to remind Lawrie how lucky he was to have this job.

'Matthews!' The bellow came later than expected, the office bustling and Lawrie about to head out into the beginnings of a glorious spring day.

Bert shared a smile of commiseration with him as he slunk off to see the boss. Bert was a decent fella. He'd have liked to get to know him better. Perhaps if he'd made more effort to get to know the people he worked with, he wouldn't feel so alone now. Maybe when this was finally all over.

Donovan was sitting behind his desk when Lawrie walked into the office, fingers steepled as he leaned his elbows on the surface.

'Close the door.'

Lawrie did as he was told and was surprised when Donovan gestured to him to sit. The folders had been cleared from the chair and the whole place looked more organised than on his last visit.

'You promised me that you had nothing to do with that baby,' Donovan said.

'And that's true, sir. Hand on heart.' He placed his hand on his chest, feeling the quickening beat of the organ he swore upon.

'So why have I got this detective hanging around? Asking about you, insinuating that I'm receiving stolen goods, threatening me?' Donovan was sweating, Lawrie noticed.

'He's desperate. You heard they had to let that woman go? You know it's got nothing to do with me.'

'I don't know, Matthews, that's why you're here. Have you been talking? How does he know about the sugar?' Donovan dabbed a handkerchief delicately against his forehead. 'What've you been saying?'

Lawrie tried to think but his head was fuzzy. 'I didn't tell him anything. Why would I get myself in more trouble?'

'Well, when a policeman comes to my house and asks me, in front of my wife, why our sugar bowl is full to the brim, I don't appreciate it, Mr Matthews. I don't care if you did it or not, I'm going to have to let you go.'

Lawrie's head snapped up, Donovan refusing to look him in the eye. 'Sir, you can't! I've done nothing wrong, you know that. Just over a few bags of sugar?'

'It's not up to me now, Matthews. Rathbone could report both of us and if it comes down to my job or yours then I've made my decision.'

'That's what he said? That if you didn't fire me he'd come after you?'

It wasn't a question. Lawrie knew quite well by now what Rathbone was like. If his boss had any sort of backbone then maybe it wouldn't have worked but it didn't take a genius to suss Donovan out. He'd cave in an instant, only the tiniest amount of pressure needed to reduce him to this wreck.

'Sir, I promise you I never said a word.' Lawrie swallowed

down his distaste at the words he was about to say. 'But you let me go like this, then I might have to.'

His boss stared at him, the threat unexpected. Lawrie just hoped the man didn't look down and see how his hands trembled in his lap.

Finally Donovan spoke: 'How about we come to an arrangement? We both keep our mouths shut and you hand in your notice instead of me firing you. I'll sort it out so that you get a month's pay and a reference. You're to leave immediately and stay off the premises. I'll drop your wages in at Derek's stall.'

'What if this were all to sort itself out before the month's up?' Lawrie asked. 'If they arrest someone, the real culprit I mean, then Rathbone will leave us both alone.'

There had to be some hope. He couldn't see how he could fund his new life with Evie just by playing his clarinet a few nights a week and cycling round south London delivering bags of sugar and the odd pair of stockings.

'I'll think about it,' Donovan said eventually. He pushed a pad of paper and a pen across the desk. 'Keep it brief.'

His hand shook as he dashed off a note, little more than a line, and signed his name below. He walked out of the office in a daze, glad that most of the men had already headed out on their walks. Only Bert lagged behind.

'Everything all right?' he asked Lawrie.

'Not really.' His laugh was brittle. 'Donovan's let me go.'

'What? Fired, you mean? What for?'

'Long story.'

Lawrie tried to walk around him, needing to get out of the

building before he lost control, his head pounding with the effort it took to hold back the tears.

'What about the union? He can't do this, you know. Had it in for you since day one, even I've noticed and I'm not the most observant bloke around.' Bert put a hand on Lawrie's arm. 'You want me to talk to Gary for you? He's the shop steward.'

Lawrie shook his head, not trusting himself to speak without his voice wavering. He put his hand out, shaking Bert's before leaving the building.

He didn't want to go straight home and his feet carried him towards the market. Mrs Ryan would make such a fuss and he didn't think he could bear it. He passed through the Art Deco archway into Reliance Arcade. The market reminded him of home even though the offerings were often pitiful in comparison. The vegetable stalls were muted in colour; no bright green bananas or yellow-brown plantain. The carrots looked stunted and the only food in abundance seemed to be cabbage. He stopped off to buy a bag of apples, the red-tinged variety that was Derek's favourite.

He could see Derek up ahead, putting on a grandstand performance for a crowd of housewives who'd gathered more for the entertainment than because they had a need for the oven gloves that Derek was trying to sell them. Lawrie stood at the back and watched the show.

'Now, ladies and gentleman.' Derek looked up and winked at Lawrie, grinning. 'See this baking tin?' He held it aloft. 'I'm sure you all have one of these at home. You're making the Sunday dinner and you want to make sure you put the perfect roast potatoes out on the table. The sort of roasties your husband talks about down the pub they're so good.'

A knob of lard went in and Derek laid the tin on a lit camping stove, dangerously balanced on a slab of wood. The patter continued as the pan heated up, the women laughing as Derek poked gentle fun at members of the crowd. He possessed a level of confidence that only Aston could rival. If only Lawrie had a similar gift then maybe he wouldn't be in such a mess.

'Now look, ladies, when I drop this egg into the fat.'

Derek cracked an egg more expertly than his mother would have believed, dropping it from a height into the tin. There was an audible sizzle as the liquid egg hit the hot spitting fat.

'You can see and hear how hot this tin must be and yet...' Derek pulled on his oven gloves and lifted the tin aloft, tilting it so that the frying egg could easily be seen, its white no longer translucent. 'I can hold onto this as long as I want, my precious hands protected from the heat. This is a quality product, ladies, a must-have for any kitchen and on special today only! Come on, ladies, who'll give me three bob and save their fair hands from the heat of the oven?'

Most of the crowd dissipated quickly, uninterested now that the spectacle was over. Derek didn't look concerned. He shifted eight pairs of the oven gloves immediately, Lawrie waiting until the last transaction had been conducted before walking up.

'Fancy a cuppa?' Derek produced a flask from under the counter and Lawrie ducked under.

Derek folded out two camping stools and poured tea into the

flask's cup. He added one sugar cube and milk from a metal jug. 'You all right? Not to be rude but you look like hell.'

'I could do with something stronger, truth be told.' He did drink from the cup, though. He wasn't as evangelical about the healing properties of tea as Mrs Ryan but the sweetness was soothing. He laid out the bag of apples in exchange.

'You're not at work?' Derek took a hefty bite from a Cox.

'Been let go.' He drained the cup and passed it back to Derek. 'Rathbone found out about the sugar I've been passing to Donovan. Threatened him, said if he didn't fire me then he'd make it common knowledge.'

'Ah.' Derek laid a commiserating hand on Lawrie's shoulder.

'I don't know how he found out. I was careful. He was never anywhere near me when I made deliveries, and Donovan's stuff I always gave him at work.'

Derek laughed. 'Probably just a good guess. I could tell you the names of at least five coppers down his station who are on my books. Didn't I say he was a chancer, that Rathbone? He didn't know for sure until Donovan spilled his guts, bet you.'

It made sense what Derek was saying but it didn't exactly help Lawrie, knowing that Donovan was an idiot.

'You're worried about money?' Derek lit a cigarette. 'I can give you more deliveries, but this is another level. Booze and fags that need shifting. Some other stuff as well, the sort of stuff that if Rathbone catches you it'll mean big trouble. And I mean serious big trouble.'

Lawrie could see that Derek was offering him a lifeline but it was like being thrown a rope laced with glass shards. He could choose to tread water and hope not to drown, or catch hold of Derek's offer and risk worse. What would he say to Evie? She didn't know he'd been doing deliveries for Derek in the first place but she'd wonder where the money was coming from when he wasn't working for the Post Office. Unless he didn't tell her about that, either.

'Can I think about it?'

'Sure.' Derek rummaged around under the counter and brought out a bottle of Bell's, cracking the seal with one hand. 'Here, get some of this down your neck.'

Lawrie took a slug of whisky, wincing as it went down. 'Christ!'

'Take it easy young fella.' Derek laughed and topped it up. 'Especially this weekend.'

Lawrie's ears pricked up. 'You hear something?'

'Some fellas were letting it be known at the pub last night that it was their doing, the attack on Johnny's and those other houses. They wanted to know if anyone else was interested in getting involved.'

'You knew them?'

'Nah. They weren't regulars. Reckon they were coming round to stir up trouble off their own patch.'

Lawrie drank back the rest of the booze. 'You think you could find out a name? They tried to set fire to Johnny's place, you know? Someone could get hurt. And don't forget that includes your own house as long as me and Arthur are living there.'

Derek looked troubled. 'Aye, I suppose it does. I've got to get back to work but I'll see what I can find out. But you're not to do anything daft, right?'

Lawrie just nodded and ducked back under the counter, a little wobblier than when he'd arrived.

20

It was a relief to see Lawrie and Sid getting on. Lawrie had pulled a face at the idea of a night out with another couple, but the two men quickly discovered a mutual love of cricket. Lawrie had even gone so far as to suggest that Sid might want to go to Lord's with him and Aston that summer when the West Indies team came over.

The club was busy, the atmosphere buzzing with music and conversation. The women drank gin gimlets, the men stuck to bourbon and, as Evie watched their reflection in the mirror beside the table, she thought they looked like movie stars. They'd had supper at an Italian café on Charing Cross Road, the manager Tony welcoming them as if they were royalty. Lawrie was a regular there, apparently; she loved seeing this part of Lawrie's life, meeting the people he knew so well. They'd gorged on pasta and heaped bowls of ice cream, delivered to the table along with Tony's warm hospitality and conversation. He'd even offered to let them use the café for their wedding reception. For a second she wondered if her mother would consent to eating 'foreign muck' before she remembered that it didn't matter. She had no intention of inviting Ma to the wedding.

Afterwards they'd followed Lawrie through the labyrinthine Soho streets, Evie holding tight to his hand so as not to get lost. They were shown to a coveted table near the front of the cosy basement, Sid clearly in awe of his new friend's influence. Even Delia looked impressed. The dim lighting and haze of cigarette smoke veiled the club with a magical aura. Or perhaps that was the gin. The cocktails were strong; Evie felt a little giddy after the second.

'You're in a better mood tonight.' Delia leaned forward to let Sid light her cigarette, feeding the nicotine fog with her exhalation. 'You've had a face like a wet weekend for days now. You know I'll listen, if you want to talk about it.'

'It's complicated.' Evie glanced across at Lawrie but he was deep in conversation with Sid.

'It must be if you won't even talk to me. Even old Sullivan asked after you the other day.'

'Mr Sullivan did?'

Her boss wasn't the most observant when it came to women. To people in general. Give him a ledger full of numbers and he could unravel the most tangled of accounts but he still often called Delia by the wrong name, Betty, who had been secretary to the old Mr Vernon before the war.

'He says you don't sing any more,' Delia said. 'And you know, I knew I was missing something but I didn't realise what it was until he came out and said it.'

'What? He misses me humming away? I thought people found it annoying.'

'Who? And if you dare say Mildred I'll pinch you. You know she'd say anything to upset you.'

It had of course been Mildred, but Mildred wasn't the reason she'd stopped singing. She sang when she was happy and she hadn't been happy, not completely, since the whole business with Ophelia began.

'There's just been a lot going on,' she replied. 'What with the police and Lawrie and then the argument with Ma.'

'It wasn't just any old argument, was it?' There was a clarity in Delia's eyes that scared Evie, even though she couldn't possibly know the truth.

'I've told you already, I'm fine.' She tried to laugh it off. 'Can't we talk about this later when we're at home?'

'I tried to talk to you the other day when we were at home,' Delia reminded her. 'You make excuses every time. We're living under the same roof but we talk less than we did before.'

'Exactly! We spend all day together. I don't have anything new to tell you because you already know it,' Evie said triumphantly.

'But what about your mother?' Delia said quietly. 'You've never told me what happened. I'm happy having you to stay but don't you think I'm owed some sort of explanation? Mum's asking me questions and I don't know what to say to her, do I?'

'I just… look, I can't talk about it now, not here. I need the loo.' Evie fled.

What passed for the club's ladies' was a dank, pungent room with two skinny cubicles and a sink that hadn't been given a good scrub since before the Blitz. Its saving grace was that it was empty. Evie locked herself into the cubicle furthest from the door. The only light in the room was over the sink and she realised she'd closed herself into a grim cell, her nose telling her that the underlying stench that permeated the entire bathroom had its source in the porcelain bowl that she now stepped back from. She was about to slip back the lock and escape when she heard Delia walk in.

'Evie?'

She stayed quiet though Delia knew she was there.

'Evie, come on out!' Delia snapped. 'If you can't talk to me then who on earth *can* you talk to? And don't say Lawrie 'cause I reckon he knows even less than I do. How long have we been friends for now?' She paused and Evie knew she would be doing the maths, counting out the years on her fingers. 'Almost fourteen years. And you still don't trust me?'

'Fine.' She unlocked the door and walked out, met with a hug from her best friend.

The brick bathroom walls, once white, were now nicotine-stained, and Evie and Delia followed in the footsteps of hundreds of girls before them – lighting their cigarettes in preparation for the soul bearing to come.

'I swear, Evie, you can tell me anything and I'll take it to the grave if I need to,' Delia assured her. 'I'm only thinking the worst because, well, for you not to tell me what's going on it has to be pretty bad, doesn't it?'

Delia had no idea. The months of lying to everyone, the discovery of her mother's betrayal. It was hard enough to admit that she hadn't trusted her friend enough to tell her about the baby in the first place, but how could she explain what Agnes had done without making her mother sound a monster? Evie checked her face in the mirror: under the harsh bulb that hung above the sink her skin looked grey, her cheeks sunken under the strain of holding the truth inside.

She told Delia everything; she had to. Beginning with the first lie: that she had never suffered from pneumonia, that she had gone to Devon to hide the mistake she'd made. Brave enough to look her friend in the eye, she saw guilt rather than horror or disgust.

'Did you know?' she accused.

'I guessed,' Delia admitted. 'I wasn't sure but you were acting so strangely. You wouldn't talk about Lawrie and then one day you were just gone. I always thought it was *his* baby. I had no idea. I should have said something when you came back only—'

'Only I didn't want to talk about it,' Evie said. 'I thought she was dead, Dee.'

The rest of the story came tumbling out, so easy now that she knew Delia was on her side.

'Tell you what, I'd like to go round and give your mother a piece of my mind.' Delia's eyes shone with anger. 'I'd say she deserves a slap only it doesn't seem enough, not for what she's done.'

'She thinks she was doing what was best for me,' Evie admitted. 'But I don't know if I can ever forgive her and I don't know how to tell Lawrie. He doesn't know any of it and I feel so guilty. Tonight's the first time I've felt normal around him, and I know it's because you and Sid are here. I'm not worrying that he's going to ask me what's wrong, or get that sad look on his face because he thinks I don't trust him. And really it's the other way round. How will he ever trust me again when he finds out I've lied for so long?'

'You need to tell him,' Delia said quietly. 'You can't risk him finding out another way.'

'But how do I tell him now, after all this time? He'll call off the wedding, I know it.'

'Perhaps you need to have a little more faith in him. If I can understand, can't he? We all keep secrets, it's just that yours is a little – bigger – than most.'

Evie nodded, scattering more tears. 'I should feel lucky. Best friend in the world and a wonderful man who wants to marry me.' She ran the tap and dampened her handkerchief, rubbing away the salt tracks on her face, the slight blotting of mascara beneath her eyes. 'I can't help but feel that I don't deserve any of it.'

Delia punched her lightly in the arm. 'Come on, none of that nonsense. A horrid thing happened to you and it wasn't your fault. You just need to be brave for a little bit longer, that's all. Tell Lawrie. Tonight if you can bear it.'

Back at the table, Lawrie's eyes were glazing over as Sid talked motor vehicles. A mechanic by trade, Delia had already warned Evie about his obsession with all things car related. Happy relief washed over Lawrie's face as Evie retook her seat and reached out for his hand.

'Ready to go?' she asked. She was going to have to tell him now, before courage deserted her.

He nodded, leaning over to whisper: 'I don't think I can fake an interest in carburettors much longer.'

The house band began their next set as they stood to go, a tall American woman singing 'Crazy He Calls Me', the light sparkling off her jewelled necklace. Evie looked over her shoulder with regret. She'd have loved to stay and listen but this was more important.

Outside, the pavement was still crowded. It wasn't that late after all, only just after eleven.

'I thought we might grab a coffee back at Tony's before we go home,' Evie spoke quickly, forcing the words out before she could change her mind. 'There's something – ow!'

She cried out as Lawrie's grip on her hand tightened sharply. She followed his gaze and fell silent as her gaze alighted upon Rose Armstrong standing on the opposite corner of Shaftesbury Avenue, looking impatient as she smoked from a long cigarette holder. Around her shoulders was slung a man's jacket, its black formality incongruous against the pale green of her dress. Her heels were reliably impractical. Evie watched as the jacket's owner joined her, tucking a billfold into a trouser pocket. Frank Armstrong, she guessed. He was more handsome than she'd imagined, though his features were slightly blurred, like a matinee idol who had enjoyed his success a little too enthusiastically. He liked a drink, she remembered Rose saying.

Rose looked straight at them and froze, Frank's curiosity aroused as she failed to catch hold of his arm. Recognition washed over his face as he clocked Lawrie, Rose now grabbing at his hand as he started towards the road, clearly meaning to cross.

'Shit!' Lawrie swore under his breath. 'Come on.' He tugged

303

her back along the avenue in the opposite direction, checking over his shoulder.

'Lawrie, slow down!' Evie had to run to match his pace.

He looked down at her and she realised he was embarrassed to be running away. She looked back and saw that Rose and Frank were still on that street corner, arguing. Frank was throwing an angry arm in their direction as Rose grabbed on to his other hand, stopping him from going anywhere.

'Come on.' Evie spied a cab with its light on and stepped off the pavement, forcing it to stop. 'What? Are you going to stand about and wait for him to catch us up?'

She dove into the back of the cab, relieved when Lawrie followed her and gave the Marson's address to the driver.

'I'm sorry,' Lawrie told her. 'I just—'

'Hush. I know. No point in having an altercation in the middle of the street.'

'It was cowardly of me to run away like that.'

'No,' she corrected him, 'you were thinking of me. God knows, the last thing either of us needs right now is drawing attention to ourselves. Especially over Rose, of all people, though I do feel sorry for her.'

'Really?' His eyebrows shot up.

'Of course. I mean, I've got what she wanted: you. And she's stuck with that thug of a husband who's so hell-bent on revenge that he shopped his own wife to the police. I mean, that's not normal, is it? Married couples are supposed to stand by one another.' At least she hoped so, though whether that was a loyalty that extended to engaged couples she wasn't so sure. 'She waltzes around in her fancy clothes expecting us all to want to be like her, but what's Rose Armstrong got that I haven't?'

Lawrie thought for a moment. 'She does have one of those fancy refrigerators.'

'*Really?*'

Lawrie was grinning now, his bad mood swiftly evaporating. 'You're too good for me.' He leaned over and kissed her, gently, aware of the driver up front. 'And I'll pay for the cab.'

'Too right,' she laughed, and leaned her head on his shoulder.

When she closed her eyes, the rhythm of the taxi's wheels bumping along the road reminded her of the song that had been playing as they'd left the club. The singer had been no Billie Holiday but it was the lyrics that stuck in her head, making her feel even worse. How could she dare to say that she loved Lawrie? She couldn't even tell him the truth, never mind move the mountains for him.

There was only one coward in that cab, she knew, but how could she talk to Lawrie now, with a nosy cab driver listening in? The weekend, she swore to herself. They'd go for a walk on Saturday afternoon and she would tell him everything. Until then she'd keep praying that Lawrie loved her enough to forgive her.

1948

He'd known the moment he saw the look on Evie's face, the twisted smile on Rose's. He froze, just long enough for Evie to run past him into the house.

'Evie.' He gave chase. 'Wait up!'

He thought at first that she'd gone out through the front door but the fellas there just shrugged. Her footsteps on the bare wooden stairs gave her away as she ran and he went up after her, following to the very top of the house. Evie had backed herself into a corner, as if she feared him.

He reached out a placating hand. 'Whatever she said to you, I can explain.'

'Too late for that.' Sam appeared out of nowhere and pushed him into the wall, Lawrie too surprised to do anything but put out a hand to break his fall.

In a split second Sam had spirited Evie into the bedroom he shared with Lawrie, the key turning in the lock. Lawrie thumped the door in frustration. That two-faced bastard!

'Lemme guess...' Aston wandered up casually, drink in one

hand and a smoke in the other. 'You finally took my advice and decided to enjoy the delights of the beautiful Rose.'

'I don't need you giving me a hard time as well,' Lawrie snapped. 'You got any pearls of wisdom now, Mr Man of the World?'

Aston chuckled and sipped his drink. 'I never was quite in the same predicament as you find yourself in currently, Lawrie my boy. You can't just walk in there?'

'Sam locked the door, that no good…' Lawrie shook his head.

'Sam? Hmmm. You like this girl then?'

'Yes.' Lawrie lowered his voice, unsure how far it would carry. 'The thing with Rose, it was just, it was a mistake, you understand? I never meant for it to happen.'

'I understand completely. You know, you just slip over and land upon her and next thing you know.' Aston cackled as he mimed what he imagined Lawrie and Rose had been up to.

'All right, laugh at me all you want but help me get out of this,' Lawrie begged. 'It's Evie I like, not Rose. I'd happily never see Rose Armstrong again.'

'Well, isn't that nice to know!'

The woman in question appeared, as if things weren't going badly enough already. The only person left to turn up who could make Lawrie's predicament any worse was Rose's husband.

'Rose, I'm sorry. I—'

'Why you apologising?' Aston interrupted. 'Is she not the one got you into this mess?'

'I only meant to let Evie down gently.' Rose stepped around Aston as if he weren't there 'She holds such a candle for you, darling, and it seemed kinder to put her out of her misery.'

Darling? 'Rose, maybe this is all my fault…'

'Most likely,' Aston muttered.

'. . . but I never meant for what happened to – happen. I didn't turn up at your house for that. It just – things got out of hand. You understand?'

Rose stared at him, the smile fixed to her face like it had been welded on.

'I'm sorry,' he repeated. 'But, you know, you are married.'

She laughed and looked down at the floor. 'You know, you are right about that. Imagine if my husband were to find out what you did. That I invited you round in good faith, to help you out. And you took advantage.' The words were brittle, the shine in her eyes giving her away.

Aston cursed. 'Woman, you crazy? You want him to come over here lookin' for murder?'

'My husband is a very jealous man. You found that out already.' She shot Lawrie a look so sharp that he felt wounded. It was the first time she'd admitted to knowing that it was Frank who'd given him the black eye on that very first night in London.

'Come on, Rose, please!'

She turned back the way she came, her heels hammering against each step as if she wanted to cause damage.

'I never shoulda listened to you!' Lawrie hit the wall. 'What now?'

'Boy, you better run after her. She gets her husband 'round here, all hell's like to break loose,' Aston warned.

'What about Evie?'

'I'll wait right here and if she come out I'll tell her that you're sorry and that you're an idiot.'

Lawrie paused. 'You can't tell her where I've gone. Don't mention Rose's name at all.'

'The bitch's name will never cross my lips. Cross my heart.'

He left Aston there watching guard as he sped downstairs and out of the house just in time to see Rose turn the corner. He sprinted after her.

'You stay away from me or I'll scream.' She didn't look up when he drew level, just quickened her pace.

'Why, Rose? I'm sorry, I really am, but did you think we could just carry on behind your husband's back?' He waited but she didn't say anything. 'If you weren't married, things would be different,' he lied, crossing his fingers behind his back. 'Then we'd both be free.'

'And Evie is free. Is that it?' She looked up and he saw that she was only just holding back tears. 'Is that all it is? 'Cause I could leave Frank. I'd leave him tomorrow if I could but I've nowhere to go.'

'Then you picked the wrong fella in me.' He forced a laugh. 'I got nothin', Rose. No money, renting a tiny room in a house, just a single bed. I can't look after you, Rose, not as well as Frank does.'

'Money isn't everything. He's never at home. Just eats the food I put in front of him and goes out to the pub. All them years worrying that he might not come back and now I wonder if I'd not have been better off if he hadn't.' She gasped and covered her mouth with her hand. 'Oh God. I never dared say it out loud before.'

'You just say that because you think he doesn't care about you.

Maybe you do still love him.' Lawrie was grasping at straws, he knew, but if he could just calm her down and send her home wanting to save her marriage instead of end it then he might be safe. 'And maybe he does still love you, just doesn't know how to show it.'

'He thinks we have a normal marriage. We have a nice holiday every summer. He sees me in my fancy clothes and thinks I'm having a ball.' Rose laughed. 'He hasn't a clue!'

'Where does he think you are tonight?'

'Dunno. We were supposed to be going out for dinner in town. He'd promised and he ditched me to play golf in Wimbledon. He says he needs to hobnob with the bosses if he wants to get ahead at work.'

They reached the bus stop and Lawrie shifted his weight awkwardly from foot to foot. He wanted to run back to the house and go to Evie but he wasn't convinced that it was safe to leave Rose.

'What you said before,' he began, interrupted as the bus pulled up. Typical, the one time it came straight away was when he just needed another few minutes. Rose didn't seem to have heard him, jumping on board. He went after her, following her upstairs. He had to be absolutely sure that she wasn't going to have another change of heart.

'What are you doing?' she asked as he sat in front of her. 'I don't need you to escort me home, you know.'

'Sorry, I just – I need to make sure that you're not going to say anything. To Frank.'

'Ah.' She bit her lip and looked him in the eye. 'You think you get off that easy?'

'What do you mean?' Lawrie shook his head. 'I never meant for you to think…'

'You never think!' She was almost shouting now. 'What is it with men? Do you think this was just a bit of fun for me? I brought you to my home. To the bed I share with my husband. You thought that meant nothing?'

'I didn't know,' he protested, his voice low in compensation for hers. 'I never expected what — happened. I didn't go to your house expecting anything other than a bath and a clean shirt. I promise you.'

He looked around but the upper deck was blessedly empty. They were almost at Clapham Common already. He checked his watch carefully, not wanting her to notice. It had been fifteen minutes since he'd left the party.

'Go away, Lawrie.' She shook her head in disgust and turned away from him. 'I can't bear to have you near me.'

She looked smaller now, young, her cheeks smeared grey where she'd wiped mascaraed tears away. She'd keep quiet, he was almost sure of that. With his thoughts already turning back to Evie, he stood and rang the bell. 'I am sorry, Rose,' he said over his shoulder.

He trudged down the stairs, glad they'd made it no further than the stop opposite the tube station. He could run across the road and with luck a bus would come in the next few minutes to carry him back home.

The bus came to a halt and, as he put his foot out expecting to strike the ground, he felt a shove in his back, stumbling off the back of the bus.

'What the hell?' He turned to see Rose's furious face as she followed him onto the pavement.

She lifted her hand and he watched it happen, her hand moving slowly through the air as it made its way to his cheek, the palm slapping him, quite hard for a woman, he thought.

'Rose?'

It was more a bark than a shout and at first Lawrie thought that the sound had issued from his own mouth. But no. Rose turned to look and Lawrie was horrified to see that Frank Armstrong was right across the road, red-faced and furious. A bus pulled up on the other side of the road, Lawrie's bus back home, blocking him from view.

'Oh God.' The colour had drained from Rose's face. 'Lawrie, get out of here. I'll sort this out.'

'I can't just leave you.' The words came out of his mouth but his brain told him to run away as fast as his feet would move. 'What if he…'

'Just bloody go, would you?' She shoved him, hard. 'Stop trying to be a hero. He won't lay a finger on me, he won't dare.' She pushed him again.

Lawrie looked over his shoulder but when he turned back it was too late. Frank was right in front of him, his fist pulled back. Lawrie managed to lift an arm in front of his face, bracing for impact.

'Stop it, Frank!'

He heard the thud of the connection and fell backwards, his head bouncing off the metal of the bus stop sign. It was the last thing he remembered until waking up in hospital the following morning.

21

Lawrie woke up early, even though he hadn't set his alarm clock – or had a job to go to, the realisation weighing heavy upon him once the memory swam back into his sluggish brain. It took more than the usual effort to will his body upright, treading on Aston's hand as he swung his legs out of bed.

'The hell?' Aston sounded as if he'd only been half asleep himself.

'Sorry. Forgot you were there.' Lawrie lay back down, his head spinning. He'd drunk too much the night before and every thought took an effort to catch hold of, like trying to spear slippery pickled onions from a jar of vinegar.

Aston had been drinking with Derek in the kitchen when he got home just after midnight, still dwelling on his near encounter with Frank Armstrong. Everything was against him at the moment apart from Evie. The way she'd taken control of the situation, stopping that cab when he had been paralysed with indecision. He was sick and tired of Frank Armstrong getting the best of him.

'You know this can't go on, you comin' and goin' as you please.' Lawrie reached for the whisky bottle. 'I get married soon and then what? You think Evie's goin' make up the sofa for you to sleep on? I tell you now that she won't.'

'Look, I just need somewhere for a few days. I had a place sorted but it fell through temporarily is all. You know how grateful I am.' There was that Bayley grin, Aston's calling card. The way he'd escaped trouble his whole damned life. Now it just turned Lawrie's mood sourer.

Derek yawned. 'Christ, you two are like an old married couple. I hear my bed calling. Lawrie, let me know tomorrow if you want to take me up on that offer. I got a delivery coming in the morning.'

'What offer?' Aston asked, as soon as Derek had closed the door behind him.

'I lost my job,' Lawrie told him. 'Derek offered me some extra deliveries.'

'What?' Aston sat up. 'What happen?'

'Guess.' Lawrie's laugh was bitter as he poured whisky into Derek's dirty glass and drank.

'That copper?' Aston kissed his teeth. 'Man, that is not good. What Evie say?'

'Nothing. I ain't told her yet.'

Another cowardly action. He'd paid for dinner, for an extra round of drinks, even though he knew that he should be being careful. Sid had been impressed by him, he could tell, and that didn't happen all that often. It was a nice feeling and he'd been happy to open his wallet to prolong it and worry about the consequences later. Besides, it was still so easy to tell himself that it wasn't permanent. Donovan had said so, that if they caught the real killer then Lawrie would be in with a chance of getting his job back.

'This delivery of Derek's. Legit?'

Lawrie laughed again. 'What d'you think? I got no choice. Weddings don't pay for themselves and since Evie fell out with her mother I can't exactly ask old Agnes for help.'

'She tell you why they fell out?' Aston poured another two fingers into each of their glasses.

'No. I think she was goin' to tell me tonight but we ran into the Armstrongs, of all people. Ended up runnin' away like a little boy.'

Aston bent down, looking under the table.

'What's wrong?' Lawrie pushed back his chair to see.

'Just checkin' is all. Makin sure you still got two feet 'cause it seems to me like you don't want to put even one of them down where that girl is concerned.' Aston burst into cackling laughter. He was drunk, Lawrie realised, not that he was sober himself.

'You don't like her, that's fine, but it don't change what I feel about her. She'll tell me in her own time.' He slung back the rest of the whisky and stood. 'I goin' to bed.'

'You make sure she do tell you,' Aston called after him. 'That girl's got a secret and I would bet good money that you won't like it when you find out what it is.'

That morning, as Lawrie lay there, looking up at the ceiling with its web of cracks, the yellowing paint which hadn't been touched up in a decade or more, he suddenly remembered Moses's revelation, the girl on Oxford Street. He'd meant to throw it in Aston's face the moment he saw him but after the attack on Johnny's house, with everything else going on, he'd completely forgotten.

'Who's Elaine?' he asked now, rolling onto his side.

'What?' Aston's eyes opened but he didn't move. 'I don't know any Elaine.'

'Fine, maybe Moses got her name wrong. Pretty woman you was seen with on Oxford Street lookin' all cosy. You remember now?'

'Oh.' Aston sat up, looking shameful. 'I been meanin' to tell you 'bout that.'

'So you got secrets of your own? Go round pointing fingers but you just as bad.'

'No, man. It's not like that. I'll tell you it all now, how's that.' He reached out and poked Lawrie's arm, like it was all a game.

Lawrie said nothing, waiting.

Aston sighed. 'Her name's Helene. I known her five years or so, on and off. She's French. Came here during the war with her family. They're Jewish. She married a fella she knew for years, old family friend, but he treat her bad. 'Bout a year or so ago I met her for a nice lunch. She's well off, eats in those fancy restaurants that wouldn't let me in if I weren't with her. I had a little too much champagne to drink – I swear those bubbles make your head go funny – and I end up tellin' her that I love her.'

'You did what?' Lawrie couldn't imagine it. 'She's married, though?'

'See that's why I had to keep quiet. Her husband beat her and

I convinced her to go to the police, get him arrested. She went to a solicitor and between that and some other things he did, she gettin' a divorce. That's where we are. Waitin' for that to all be finalised. The husband, he showed up a few days ago, knocking on her door and beggin' for her to reconsider. That's why I ended up here on your floor 'stead of Helene's warm bed.' He lay back down and closed his eyes. 'See, if he finds out about me he'll make trouble. She gets to keep the house and some money. He finds out she been cheatin' then he'll try and take all that back.'

'You were in London then, that week when I found the baby.' *Just say that you weren't there*, Lawrie begged his friend silently. *Just don't have been anywhere near here.*

'I was in Notting Hill with Helene,' Aston confirmed. 'Ask her if you like. I want you to meet her anyway. Come over next weekend. Bring Evie.'

'Christ, you must be desperate if you're inviting Evie.' His effort at levity sank. 'Look, I do believe you. I just wish you'd told me it all at the beginning. Too much lying. We supposed to be friends.'

'I know. But Lawrie, I ain't never felt like this before. She is the one for me.'

Lawrie had to laugh then. Aston Bayley head over heels in love? If it wasn't before, the world was now completely topsy-turvy.

'We good?' Aston sat up. 'What time is it? I got me a job interview at nine. Best not be late.'

Lawrie laid back down and closed his eyes. How had this happened, that Aston was now settling down, getting a proper job, just as everything was going wrong for Lawrie? He embraced the cold despair that was becoming far too familiar to him and fell back asleep in its arms.

Aston was gone when he woke again just after ten, his head a little clearer than before. He'd meant to go down to the labour exchange but it was Friday after all. He'd not had a day of leave in months. Maybe he should walk down to the market and find out exactly how illegal this work that Derek was offering him was.

He dressed and went out, cursing under his breath as he saw the red Morris Minor had returned. He quickened his pace as he saw Rathbone getting out.

'Mr Matthews!'

He should have stopped but he was almost at the corner. Damned if he was going to put himself out for this man after what he'd done. He heard the sound of running footsteps and speeded up but Rathbone caught him as he turned onto Brixton Hill.

'Did you not hear me, Mr Matthews?' Rathbone laid a hand on his shoulder and it took all of Lawrie's willpower not to shake it off.

'Sorry, DS Rathbone. Didn't realise that was you.' He stopped walking then, knowing the game was lost.

'You're not at work today?'

Lawrie shoved his clenched fists into his jacket pockets and tried not to think about punching away Rathbone's gloating smile. 'I'm out of work at the moment. Thought you would know that.'

'No hard feelings, eh? Donovan's a weasel of a man anyway. Didn't take much to rattle him.'

He had to marvel at this man. No matter how much Rathbone

tried to ruin his life, he always managed to make it sound like he was just doing Lawrie a favour.

'I didn't know you cared.' He kicked his heel at the wall. 'So why are you making my life miserable, eh? 'Cause you think I'll confess just to have a roof over my head once the rent money runs out?'

'Not exactly.' Rathbone's expression turned calculating. 'See, I'm actually trying to help you out, son.' There was that favour again. 'If you've got no job then you can't pay for a wedding, right? I noticed your girl's left home. Staying with a friend, is she? I bet she can't wait for you to get that ring on her finger.'

Lawrie kept quiet. How the hell did Rathbone know so much about Evie all of a sudden?

'Honestly, I don't think you had anything to do with the Ophelia case, Mr Matthews, but I think you know someone who does.' Rathbone reached into his pocket and produced a sheet of paper which he handed to Lawrie. 'That's for you. Call it an early wedding present.'

'What is it?' Lawrie took the paper.

'Take a look.'

Rathbone shot him a cruel smile, then walked back the way he'd come, leaving Lawrie staring down at the folded piece of paper in confusion.

He waited outside Vernon & Sons for Evie to leave work. She was laughing at something Delia had said as they walked out together, her grin widening as she saw him. His chest hurt, like she had his heart in her hand and was squeezing, that grip growing tighter the longer he watched her. She walked up and kissed him on the lips, bold as brass for once, and he let her because there was still a chance that he'd got it wrong. That there was a perfectly good explanation and that she hadn't been lying to his face the entire time.

'I'll leave you two alone. I'm sure you've got a lot to talk about.' Delia squeezed Evie's arm as she left them. There was something odd in the look she gave him as she walked away, as if she knew something he didn't. Did Delia know already? Did everyone know but him?

Evie had been so shy when he first met her, barely said a word to him until the day he'd run into her at the Astoria on a Saturday afternoon. Delia had ditched her for some fool of a man who Lawrie could tell right away was no good; while she only had eyes for him, he was looking over her shoulder at some other girl. Lawrie had asked Evie if she wanted to sit with them, telling Sam to shift up so there was a seat for her. He'd been surprised when he felt the back of her hand accidentally brush against his. It sent a shock up his left arm, a pleasant bolt of fizzing joy that he'd never experienced before. The lights came down, hiding his shock, and he was sure that she didn't know what she'd done. He'd thought her young then, even for sixteen, and felt wary of her innocence. Maybe he'd been wrong all along.

They caught the bus, Evie talking about her day, not noticing that he hadn't said a word. She looked up in surprise when Lawrie stood and rang the bell for Forthbridge Road, only halfway home.

'Let's go for walk,' was all he said.

'It's lovely that you came to meet me,' she said as they crossed the road on to Clapham Common, 'but what's the occasion?'

'I'll tell you in a minute.' He couldn't even look at her.

He let her link arms with his and to any casual observer they would have looked like a normal courting couple, out for a stroll on a beautiful spring evening. There was a light breeze rustling the fresh green leaves in the trees. Fading sunlight dappled the path before them, blinking through the plane tree canopy that sheltered them.

'Rathbone came to see me this morning.'

He thought he felt a tremor in her arm, her grip tightening.

'Really? What did he want?' She looked up at him, her brow creased.

'He wanted to give me something, something that I think might belong to you.'

They had reached the bandstand. He steered her towards a wooden bench and removed his arm from hers, reaching into his pocket. Evie sat down, holding her hands in her lap and looking very young all of a sudden. He stood in front of her and passed down the sheet of paper.

'You know what this is?'

She gasped as she unfolded it, the paper shaking as she recognised the birth certificate. She nodded, her eyes fixed to evidence against her. 'He told you then.'

'I worked it out. Even I can do that. Even a foolish man like me can put two and two together. I know that Agnes never had a child last year. This is why you left, isn't it? To have a baby?'

She nodded again, wouldn't look at him.

'And I know that I'm not the father, though I'm trying to think who could be.' He shook his head and bit back a moan. This was so much harder even than he had imagined, even after practising the words in his head all afternoon. He took a deep breath. 'I don't know what to say, Evie. I just wanted us to be perfect. A proper married couple. Do everything the right way and damn what everyone round here thinks of us! That's all I wanted, Evie. I thought—' He paused to clear his throat. 'I thought you wanted the same.'

'I do.' It was barely a whisper, slipping away on the breeze. 'Lawrie, I never meant to lie to you. I'm so sorry, I wanted to tell you only Ma said—'

'Ma said? You blaming this on Agnes now? Seems to me you can stand up to her when you feel like it. So why not trust me? You lied to me for a year now almost and you'd've kept on lying if Rathbone hadn't come crawling round.'

'Lawrie, please, I'm so sorry. I tried to tell you last night. That's why we left early. I wanted to sit down and tell you myself only…'

She grabbed hold of his hands and he threw her off. She started crying, huge sobs that wracked her entire body, and he felt ripped in two. He wanted to put his arms around her and comfort her. He wanted to run away from her, as fast as he could. What a fool he'd been! Aston had been right about her the whole time. Somehow he'd known what Lawrie hadn't been able to see.

'It wasn't Aston?' he asked suddenly. 'Please, Evie, tell me it wasn't him.'

'No.' She shook her head violently, trying to catch her breath. 'It was Sam. At that party.'

That damned party. He groaned and threw his head back, staring up at the perfect blue sky, only now beginning to darken slightly as late afternoon merged into early evening. It made total sense, much more so than the story Sam had fed him about her leaving once she knew the coast was clear. Lawrie's bed had been stripped when he finally got home from the hospital the next day, still concussed, and Sam had claimed to have drunk too much and been sick. The truth was that he'd slept with Evie. They'd done it there, right on his own bed, teaching him a lesson.

'I thought the baby died, Lawrie.' The words stuttered out and he flinched at the pain in her voice. 'Stillborn, they call it. But Rathbone did some digging and found out that she — the baby — she's still alive. Ma had her adopted behind my back, that's why it's her name on the birth certificate.' She blew her nose.

'She took your baby? And now Rathbone thinks she's Ophelia?'

'No!' The shock on her face was a relief. All he had left was to hope that this was as bad as it got, that there was no further horrifying revelation left in store. 'When did he say that? Why does he still think that? I went to Cedars Road on Monday. I checked. She was adopted, that's what they told me.'

'Do you even hear what you're saying?' he cried out. 'You were running around behind my back trying to find a child that you hid from me! Were you ever going to tell me the truth?'

'I thought you'd leave me, call off the wedding. I know I did the wrong thing but it was only because I love you!'

He'd heard enough. 'I think it's for the best if we don't see each other for a few days. A week or so maybe.' He shoved his hands in his pockets and looked away, blinking as he did so. 'I just — I need...' The lump in his throat was choking him. 'I need time to think.'

'A week?' She stood and he took a step backwards, moving away from her outstretched arms. 'Lawrie, please! I'll do anything. Go and speak to Ma, she'll tell you it's the truth. I was just scared, can't you understand?'

'How can I trust you now when you lied to me for so long? Can you honestly tell me that you'd have come clean if you hadn't been caught out?'

She looked down at the ground, just for a split second, but it answered his question. He walked away quickly before she could see that he too was crying. Rathbone had meant to poison him against her but he couldn't blame the detective for how wretched he felt. That was Evie's fault. She'd lied to him, continually, and so the question became: could Lawrie marry a woman who couldn't tell the truth?

22

'It'll all work itself out.' Delia broke the silence, the darkness amplifying her whisper.

Evie didn't reply. How would Delia know anyway? Everything was going swimmingly with Sid and it wasn't as though Delia had ever had an illegitimate child and then lied about it. Delia had never had a mother who hated her enough to give away her own granddaughter.

'Evie?'

She thought about feigning sleep but Delia had practice in such deception. She'd shared this bedroom with her sister Kathy for sixteen years before she'd gone off and got married. The room might be pitch black, the curtains at the window dating back to the age of blackouts, but Evie was no match for a woman who knew what genuine sleep sounded like.

'Will it?' she said, turning onto her back. 'You didn't see him. He was so angry. So disappointed in me.'

'But he didn't break it off. He just asked for time. That's a good sign, surely.'

Was it? Or was it just dragging out the inevitable, making Evie suffer while she held onto hope? It was the not knowing that she was struggling with the most.

'Maybe you could go and talk to him for me?' Evie suggested. 'Just so that I know one way or the other.'

In the dark, Evie heard Delia weighing up her choices. When she spoke her voice was resigned.

'All right, but not too soon. If you've heard nothing by Thursday then I'll go round. You don't want him to make a quick decision, Evie, not about something so important.'

'Thank you.' It was surprising to find the saying true; she was already feeling better just sharing her worries. 'I don't know what I'd do without you sometimes.'

Delia gave a low chuckle. 'That's what friends are for.'

'Maybe one day I'll be able to repay the favour,' Evie said. 'Though you're so sensible, I can't imagine you getting into trouble.'

The silence stretched out between them, the air growing thick with tension until finally Delia sighed. 'I suppose I should tell you now, else it's not fair.'

'Tell me what?' Evie turned onto her side now, although she couldn't hope to see Delia's face in the darkness.

'That I'm not a virgin either. I mean,' she went on in a rush, 'I never got pregnant or anything, but I'm not perfect by any stretch. And I haven't told Sid. You'd think I'd have learned something from watching what you're going through but, well, it's not that easy. I understand that now.'

Evie breathed out, only just aware that she'd been holding it in. 'Not Lennie?'

'God, no!' Delia's voice rose too loudly and they both giggled, the tension bursting like a balloon at a children's party. 'Though maybe he had something to do with it. It was after I found out about that trollop he'd been with.'

Evie tried to think but Sid was the only other man she could remember seeing Delia with.

'Who was it then?'

'Promise you won't be mad? It was one of Lawrie's friends.'

'Not Aston?' *Please don't let it be Aston.*

She heard Delia take an intake of breath. 'It was Moses.'

'Moses!?' Of all the people it could have been, Moses was the last person she'd imagined. 'Are you sure?'

''Course I'm bloody sure,' Delia hissed. 'We met at that party. The same one where, you know... I couldn't find you. I heard that there'd been a bit of a kerfuffle and I thought you'd left. I got talking to Moses and we arranged to go to the pictures together. He was being so nice, the complete opposite of Lennie, so I said yes when he asked me.'

'You were stepping out with *Moses*?' And Evie had never known, had been too wrapped up in her own worries. 'Nobody said anything.'

'Nobody knew. I didn't tell anyone. I suppose I felt a bit embarrassed about it, if I'm honest. People were starting to say things, about the girls who went out with... well, you know, and I went round to the house the next day to call it off, only it turned out that he didn't live there.'

'He lives further down the street,' Evie murmured.

'I know that now. The chap who answered the door directed

me. And then by the time I found Moses, it seemed a bit cold to just turn him down like that. He was so easy to talk to as well. We had a few drinks and his roommate was out. I suppose I wanted to get back at Lennie, show him that he wasn't the only man who liked me. Daft, really, but there we are.'

'Moses, though!' Evie was full of wonder. 'Why keep it a secret? From me, I mean?'

'Like you didn't have enough problems! And I was too ashamed to tell you why I'd gone round there in the first place. I felt so stupid. I really did like Moses but it would have been pointless. I couldn't marry Moses. Imagine what my dad would say!'

Evie knew that Delia was waiting for her to agree, to tell her that she'd made the right decision, but her tongue couldn't form the words. She knew that the corrosive sensation in the pit of her stomach was disappointment. For all these years Delia had been telling her to stand up to Mildred and those other girls who had judged Evie, to ignore them and to think of herself as being as good as anyone else. But Delia herself had never believed this.

'Thank you for telling me.'

It was all she could think of to say.

She shuffled down into the bedclothes and turned to face the wall, relieved that Delia too fell silent.

She awoke early to a Saturday with no work and no Lawrie to occupy her time. Delia was still asleep but she could hear Mrs Marson in the kitchen downstairs, the low rumble of Delia's brother Chris talking to his mother. She dressed quietly and went downstairs.

In the front room Mr Marson was in his armchair as usual, pipe in mouth and his slippered feet raised up as he fiddled with the wireless. Evie had never felt the need for a father, and she had barely spoken to Mr Marson, even after living in his house for two weeks, but she saw now how a family could be. Delia and her mum had a right giggle together; Evie had never exchanged gossip with Ma.

No watching what you said in case it was the wrong thing. Running home from the pictures to peel potatoes before her mother decided it was time to put the tea on. No being made to feel guilty whenever Ma was in a bad mood and decided to treat Evie like a human whetstone, her tongue kept sharp by grinding down Evie's resolve to stand up for herself.

'Any plans for today, Evie?' Mrs Marson asked, pushing the teapot within reach as Evie sat at the table.

'Not really. I thought I might go for a walk since it's so nice out.'

'That sounds nice. Clear the old head.'

Evie ate a slice of toast quickly and pulled on her coat, heading out with a list of items Mrs Marson needed from the shops. She was paying rent money but she knew that she was hovering on the edge of imposition and the more errands she could run, the less awkward she felt. The air was sweet from the hyacinths in next door's garden, their pink and purple flowers swaying in the breeze. The Marsons lived on the other side of the railway station, almost in Stockwell but only a few minutes' walk from the shops. It was almost a shame they were so close but she didn't want to walk too far. She didn't want to risk running into Lawrie.

In the window of Bon Marché was a lovely dark navy dress. It would have been perfect for the honeymoon, for strolling along the seafront at Brighton or Bournemouth. Mrs Ryan had let slip that Lawrie had been saving up but she couldn't remember exactly which destination he'd been planning on.

She turned away and crossed the road, heading into the market, glad for once of the hustle and bustle of the crowds. As she stopped for vegetables she could see Ursula Sands a few stalls down, talking to another Jamaican woman, both of them wrapped up tight with scarves and gloves on even though Evie could feel the promise of spring in the air. Every week she saw new arrivals. She could imagine that one day people would stop staring; that in a few years it would be expected to see people with dark skin walking the streets. That the children she hoped to have – *would have* – with Lawrie would just be like anybody else. They wouldn't stick out like a sore thumb at school or be treated like they were thick. Ursula saw her and waved, Evie smiling back as she raised her own hand in greeting.

'Here you go, love,' the greengrocer said, handing over the brown paper bags, and Evie had to rummage for her purse, Ursula having vanished into the crowds when she next looked up.

She'd bought most of the items on Mrs Marson's list when she had the fright of her life, turning the corner and almost running straight into Aston.

Evie shrieked in shock and took a step backwards, her free hand flying up to her chest.

'The hell's wrong with you, girl?' Aston looked put out.

'You scared me.' It felt like her heart was trying to punch its way out through her ribcage. 'Why are you sneaking around like that?'

'I'm not sneaking. I was conducting business with Derek,' he informed her.

'Business? You?' She laughed a little, more out of habit than genuine mirth.

'You don't get to look at me like that no more,' he told her. 'All superior. I know what you are, *Miss* Coleridge.'

'You don't know me,' she spat back. 'Besides, why should I care what you think?'

'Because I'm Lawrie's friend. You went and broke that poor boy's heart and I don't like that one bit.'

'Neither do I,' she retorted. 'And I bet you've not told him that you knew all this time and didn't say a word.'

'I knew nothing,' he claimed, though his eyes seemed less sure.

'Maybe you didn't know everything but you knew *something*. You hinted at it enough times.'

It felt good to finally call him out on his behaviour, acting so supercilious all this time when he was no better than she was. After all, what did she have to lose now? For it had been Aston who cleared up the mess. Sam had thrown open the bedroom door, ready to abandon her, but Aston had been waiting. He'd pushed in, shoving Sam against the bedroom wall and looking down at Evie with a strange look on his face. Disgust, she'd thought. She'd heard him and Sam argue, her vision hazy and unreliable. The memory was vague but the one thing she was sure of was that Aston knew what had happened. She'd never understood why he hadn't told Lawrie straight away.

Now he looked contrite. 'I was supposed to look after you. Make sure nothing happened to you. I shoulda bashed that door down if I'd known you were going to do something stupid.'

'Something stupid?' She gasped. Had he thought she'd done *that* just to get back at Lawrie? That she'd wanted it to happen? 'I would have been happy for you to have bashed the door in.'

'Come on, Evie.' He pulled his tobacco tin out of his pocket and began to roll a cigarette, leaning up against the sunny wall. 'If you just told Lawrie in the first place, he'd have gotten over it. I mean, what with that messy business with Rose, he couldn't exactly climb up on his high horse. A lot of girls do what you did most weekends. Things aren't like they used to be.'

It was his wink that infuriated her the most.

'You can't compare me to those girls! If I'd wanted to do it then that would be different but I never... I *never*—'

The look on his face shut her up, his usual good-natured expression slowly melting away. 'What you sayin'? You sayin' that Sam...?'

But Evie stayed silent, her tongue heavy like lead against the roof of her mouth. She found she couldn't look him in the eye, couldn't look at him at all, her gaze falling to the pavement.

'Did he?' His voice was so small that she could hardly hear him.

Finally, she nodded and leaned against the wall next to him. 'I didn't think anyone would believe me. He told me to keep my mouth shut and I didn't want anyone to know. I thought people would think me a – well, you know what people would have thought. Besides, he was gone soon after.'

They stood there next to each other in silence – nothing between them, but the rise and fall of their breaths. Eventually his hand crossed her vision, a cigarette balanced between his fingers. She took it gratefully, as he held out his lighter before rolling another for himself. As she stole a glance at him, she found she was surprised by how shaken he looked.

'I'm sorry, Evie, I didn't know,' he said sombrely. 'I mean, I met lots of English girls who don't take much persuading. But I knew that you were drunk and that you weren't used to it. I suppose I shoulda said something, done something but...' He trailed off helplessly.

She took a drag from the rollup and felt almost two years' worth of guilt slip from her shoulders in the exhalation. They smoked in silence, the past years' animosity dissipating into the warm city air with each puff.

'You need to tell Lawrie the truth,' Aston said suddenly. 'He thinks you did this to teach him a lesson. To get back at him. You tell him what Sam did, he'll forgive you like that.' He clicked his fingers.

'It sounds easy but I don't know how.' Evie smiled sadly.

'You got nothin' to lose,' he pointed out.

Evie shook her head. 'You didn't see him. I don't know why he'd ever believe me now. He'd think I was just making excuses.'

'Nah,' Aston decided. 'He just needs a bit of time is all, though I don't know how he's going to take it.' Aston took a deep pull on the cigarette, throwing the butt to the floor as he made to walk off. 'Look, go home and stop fretting. I'll get this all straightened out. Lawrie'll listen to me.'

She peeled herself from the wall and nodded at him soberly before walking away.

'Evie?' She turned as he called after her. 'Don't go out tonight. Derek says there's goin' be trouble. Stay home and stay safe.'

23

The music was too loud, the room too hot, and Lawrie too unsteady on his feet. He rocked his way to the door of the small bar, the floor swaying as if he were onboard a ship, and felt his lungs sigh as he breathed air that wasn't full of cigarette smoke. He'd drunk far too much and his feet slid off the pavement into the gutter as he misjudged the distance. He sat down hard on the kerb, grunting as his behind hit the paving slab from an unexpected height.

Somehow he'd managed to keep his glass upright with most of the contents still swirling inside rather than spilled over the ground. He took a triumphant gulp of the cheap whisky, no longer wincing from its heat.

'What you doin' out here, man?' Aston landed next to him, more used to managing his booze.

'It's too hot in there,' Lawrie mumbled. 'Where's Helene?'

'She's with Guylaine.' Aston lit a cigarette and Lawrie put his hand out for one. 'What? Since when do you smoke?'

'Reckon I smoke a pack each night I play with the band

anyway so I may as well start.' He grabbed at the cigarette and put it between his lips. Aston struck a match and he leaned into the flame as he'd watched Evie do a hundred times, jerking back from the stinging phosphorus fumes and coughing as the harsh smoke filled his throat. Why did people think this was pleasurable?

'You need to get over this, you know,' Aston told him. 'Go and talk to Evie.'

'I'm just supposed to forget about what she did? Just accept that she been punished enough? Get over all the lies?'

Aston took a swig of beer, the label scratched off the bottle. 'I thought you were in love with her.'

'I am.' He lifted the glass to his mouth, then lowered it without drinking. 'I was. No, I am. That's the damn problem. I should just forget her. Haven't you been sayin' the same to me for months now? Besides, when are you such a sudden admirer of Evie Coleridge.' He tried another drag from the cigarette but it was just as nasty the second time and he threw it into the road with disgust.

Aston took another mouthful of beer, taking his time. 'I just think there might be more to it, you know? Was it not just the other week that you were worrying that Rose Armstrong might have had herself a little halfie baby with eyes like yours?'

Lawrie chewed his lip mutinously. 'It's not the same.'

'You keep tellin' yourself that.' Aston took a last swig. 'Come on, I'll fetch Helene and we can get out of here.'

Aston got up and disappeared back into the bar, leaving Lawrie in the gutter. He wanted to crawl back home to Brixton but he knew it wasn't safe. They'd come out west after Derek confirmed that there was trouble planned round Brixton: any coloured fella out after nightfall would be in for a kicking, that's how he'd put it. Lawrie had agreed to stay at Helene's house with Aston and given up his own bedroom to the Sands family, Ursula and the children, Johnny nervous that his house had already been marked for attack. Johnny himself was staying put with Moses and Sonny, armed with cricket bats, just in case.

Helene was a tall Frenchwoman, nothing like Lawrie had expected. That afternoon she'd opened the door to them barefoot and wearing a white shirt and men's trousers, her dark hair pulled back into a rough ponytail. She didn't look like any of the women Lawrie knew. In her late twenties, a year or so older than Aston, she owned a house in Holland Park, within stumbling distance of the bar. It had an airy attic space where she painted and she ran a gallery in Kensington Church Street. She had embraced Lawrie like an old friend, brushing each cheek with her lips.

Helene and Aston tumbled out of the bar, in the midst of a hushed, fast-paced argument in French. Lawrie hadn't even known that Aston spoke French until that afternoon. Recently he was wondering if he knew anyone as well as he'd thought. He felt like a stranger to himself these days.

'Come on, old friend.' Aston slid his arm under Lawrie's shoulders to support him. 'Back to Helene's before you lose your guts across the pavement.'

'I ain't gonna be sick,' Lawrie claimed, then felt his stomach flip in an effort to prove him wrong. He managed to hold himself together by concentrating on putting one foot in front of the other and leaning on Aston.

'You put on weight,' Aston complained. 'That's what happens when you get complacent. Too settled.'

'I won't worry about you ever getting fat then,' Helene said.

Lawrie barely knew the woman but he was beginning to understand how she'd managed to keep Aston's interest. He liked a challenge and she seemed to enjoy giving him one. Aston had boasted that he'd spent many a night at Helene's, all those times he'd gone AWOL at the end of a night, but Lawrie had heard him ask permission before switching the wireless on earlier to hear the news bulletin, and before using the last of the milk for tea. Sod's law that Aston found love just as Lawrie lost Evie.

Helene got bored and strode off ahead, her heels clicking away into the distance. By the time they knocked on her door, she had changed into a silk robe, a glass of cloudy green liqueur in her hand. Lawrie smelled the sweet spice of the pastis, reminding him of humbugs and liquorice sweets.

'You've had enough.' Aston saw him looking at the glass.

Using the wall to steady himself, Lawrie negotiated the wide hallway, following Helene and Aston down the narrow stairs that led off through a door, down into the basement. Until a decade or so ago this would have been the domain of the cook and the maid, hidden from sight behind the sturdy door. Helene had a woman come in, but she knew her way around her own kitchen. It was the room they'd spent the most time in, the most homely compared to the more formal reception rooms above.

The size of the house astounded him. Lawrie had been given a guest bedroom on the first floor which was light and spacious, the linen so soft that he'd wanted to lie down and sleep as soon as he'd arrived that afternoon. The ceilings were high, the windows wide, letting in great swathes of sunlight that glistened against the polished floorboards. Bright Turkish rugs were thick and comforting against his bare feet when he skidded across them like a child, his soles tickled by the luxurious fibres.

Helene pulled out a silver coffee pot and lit the stove. 'This will wake you up just in time to go to bed!'

'I'm all right,' he protested. 'I just want a pastis and a glass of water and I'll be fine.'

Helene and Aston exchanged a look and she moved the pot off the stove.

'One drink, then bed,' Aston warned.

He was sure they were sick of him. At five o'clock, Aston had sent him out to a restaurant along Kensington High Street to buy a few bottles of the red wine that Helene preferred. Lawrie might not speak French but he could read enough in their body language to know that he was being sent away so that Aston could take Helene to bed. When he got back he was careful not to disturb them, just left the wine in the kitchen and went back out to explore the area. He didn't know this part of London, another world from Brixton. He went into Holland Park and walked its paths for over an hour, but he didn't find the peace that he felt when he went to Clapham Common. The Common was bound to him so tightly now that it understood him. His worst experiences, his happiest moments since arriving in London, all of them were linked to it. Holland Park was beautiful but there was something stiff and ordered about the place. People stuck to

the paths, they minded their manners. Pretty to look at but not
for him.

He woke early the next day, sunlight pouring through the windows and stabbing his eyelids. His eyes felt as though they'd been
pickled overnight, stinging and sore. When he tried to sit up
he felt a hot needle of pain slip through his brain and fell back.
Christ, he'd never felt as bad as this. He tried to swallow but his
throat was lined with gravel.

On the table by the bedside sat a glass of water and he grabbed
for it, gulping it back. His stomach churned and he only just made
it to the bathroom next door in time to speckle the gleaming
porcelain of the toilet bowl. Just as well Helene and Aston slept
on the floor above. Between each convulsion he rested in a prayer
position, his head pressed against the cool china until he was sure
there was nothing left in his stomach and his brain no longer felt
like it might explode if he made a sudden movement. He had
barely eaten the day before. Or the day before that. For all Aston's
protestations, Lawrie's clothes were looser than they should be.

He sat up and used the edge of the sink to pull himself into a
standing position. He brushed his teeth until the vomit taste had
gone from his mouth and he was left with just the faint burn at
the back of his throat. He pressed his nose close to his armpit and
gagged. He reeked of stale sweat and whisky. Helene had laid out
thick cotton towels on the radiator for him to use so she must have
meant for him to have a bath. He ran the taps, water gushing out
in a torrent, unlike the trickle he usually got at home. There was
a round tub of bath salts on the side and he used the small scoop

inside to sprinkle a thin line across the water's surface, stirring it with his hand until the bathwater smelled of summer blooms and long days.

He soaked and drowsed, his headache gradually dissipating as though the healing waters were permeating his body and cleansing out the poison. The downside to this renewal was that the fog cleared and he remembered why he'd wanted to drink so much: to block out all thoughts of Evie. It hadn't worked. All of these secrets and lies, only uncovered because he'd decided to cut through Clapham Common one March morning. If he'd not been there then Rathbone wouldn't know who Lawrie Matthews was. He might have sent round one of his minions to talk to Lawrie and Arthur but that would be all. Ophelia would have been another sad story in the newspaper but nothing more. He and Evie would be getting on with their lives, planning a wedding and looking for somewhere to live afterwards. Would his life have been so terrible if he'd not found out the truth?

He lay there until the bathwater was cold before getting out and drying off with one of the luxurious white towels so soft that he felt like he was wrapped in cotton wool. He could smell fresh coffee now and hear Aston's laughter echoing up from the basement. He felt envious, that Aston could just pick himself back up, dust himself off as though there was nothing wrong.

'How you feelin'?' Aston used his foot to push out the chair opposite him as Lawrie appeared at the kitchen door.

'Better than I was an hour or so ago,' Lawrie admitted.

Helene placed a small cup of strong coffee before him, along with the pot. 'Help yourself.'

Someone had been out to the bakery already. There were croissants laid out, half a baguette and even a little brie. Lawrie was ravenous, devouring a croissant in less than a minute, barely savouring its buttery flakes before it was gone.

'I'll leave you two to talk while I have a bath.' Helene got up and kissed Aston on the forehead. 'We made arrangements to go to lunch with Guylaine. You remember her from last night Lawrie? You're welcome to come.'

Lawrie nodded even though he couldn't imagine anything worse than having to go and be polite around a stranger. He drank his coffee in the silent kitchen, the caffeine working its magic. He could feel it flowing in a stream around his body, waking up his limbs and sharpening his thoughts.

Aston's voice cracked the silence open. 'Look, I got something to tell you.'

'What? Don't tell me you're marrying Helene.' Lawrie poured more coffee. 'I wouldn't be so surprised. The whole world's turned upside down at the moment.'

'No, that's not it. I didn't say anything last night because, well, I needed to be sure you wouldn't do anything foolish. Like catch a cab back to Brixton.' Aston pulled a croissant onto his plate and began to pick it apart, flaking the pastry onto the expensive china. 'I talked to Evie. I think you should do the same.'

'*You* talked to her?' Lawrie laughed in confusion. 'You two never been able to stand one another.'

'I ran into her is all. I suppose I should tell you first of all that I had my suspicions about that night. The party. I knew something had happened, I just wasn't sure what.' The croissant was in shreds

342

and Aston brushed crumbs from his now greasy fingertips. 'It was – I think—' He took a gulp of coffee, grimacing. 'Boy, I don't even know how to say this.'

'Just spit it out.' Lawrie braced his hands against the table, fearing the worst.

'That thing with Sam – it isn't what you think.' Aston looked up at him, as Lawrie felt his brows knit in confusion.

'He forced himself on her. I never knew it at the time but as soon as she said it to me I knew she was tellin' the truth. It wasn't her fault.'

Lawrie stared at his friend, the brutality of his words hitting him like cinder blocks to the chest. His voice was a strangled cry when he next spoke. 'She just came out and told you? So why she didn't say it to me?'

'She was ashamed. And you already thought she was a liar so she reckoned you wouldn' believe her.' Aston leaned back in his chair, his face reflecting the misery that had turned Lawrie's body cold. 'Maybe I should have said something at the time, that I thought somethin' happen, but I never knew it for certain. I let you down. You left me at the house to make sure nothing happen to Evie and I failed. I know that.' He pulled his hands to his face and stared down at his lap. 'I'm sorry,' he whispered.

Lawrie stood up and pushed back his chair, letting it fall to the floor. 'How many times I ask you why you and Evie always at each other's throats, huh? How many? And you just say she *look down on you*. That she *got a problem*.' He sighed, too exhausted to be as angry as he wanted to be. 'You tellin' me that Sam hurt her. And instead of helpin' her I been too busy getting angry at her for something that wasn't her fault. And you're tellin' me that you knew! This whole time and you never said a word.'

Aston didn't look up but Lawrie could see the tears as they fell, forming a puddle on the polished pine of the kitchen table. He felt ninety years old as he dragged himself upstairs to collect his few belongings: his jacket and tie, his wallet with a few shillings and pence, his clarinet which he'd brought along just in case. Everything he had left in the world.

24

On Sunday Evie slept in, sleepily saying goodbye to Delia and waiting for the slam of the front door. The Marsons attended a different church to her mother and Lawrie but she didn't want to go. She didn't want to kneel and pray for others, and she was sick of praying for her own forgiveness. God wouldn't decide if Lawrie was going to take her back; that was up to him. She wondered what Ma would think when she saw Lawrie sitting alone. Would she guess what had happened? Would she care?

She took her breakfast – a round of toast and a cup of tea – back up to Delia's bedroom and watched out of the window as she ate, perched on the low windowsill. The street outside looked very much like her own but there were subtle differences. Delia's mother was often chatting to one or other of the next-door neighbours as she hung out her laundry or sat outside in the morning with her cup of tea. Mrs Marson was on speaking terms even with the family at the very end of the road. Ma never spoke to any of their neighbours, not even Mrs Ryan if she could help it. When they'd first moved in, a few of the women had been come round to the house and knocked on the door. The welcoming committee. Ma had offered them tea and they'd brought homemade cake. Coffee and walnut, Evie remembered. She'd been given a sliver on a saucer and told to stay upstairs out of the way while the grown-ups talked but she hadn't been able to resist peering through the bannisters, waving to Mrs Foster who, with her husband, ran the clothing stall on the market where Ma bought Evie's school uniform. Mrs Foster had looked confused and Ma had been in foul mood afterwards. There was no repeat visit and Ma had said good riddance. Without Evie she had no one. Just her cleaning jobs and her sewing work on the side. She must be lonely. She always had been; wasn't that why she'd tried to save Evie from the same fate? Suddenly she understood why she'd felt so out of sorts since leaving home: she knew exactly why her mother had done what she'd done. It didn't make it right, but she could at least listen. Maybe even forgive.

She knew it was a terrible idea even as she put on her coat and headed out into the light grey drizzle. Ma would turn everything until it was all Evie's fault and she'd end up feeling ten times worse than she did already. But there was also the tantalising chance that she might bump into Lawrie. He'd asked for time alone but she wasn't exactly defying him. He'd told her several times that she would feel better if she sat down with her mother and talked. He couldn't very well go back on that now.

She checked her watch: church services would be coming to a close and Ma should be home by the time she got there. Walking briskly until she reached the station, she dawdled the rest of the way. Turning the corner onto her street she saw Rathbone's car and felt a jolt of fear, like an electric shock. She could see him in the car. Doing a crossword from what it looked like, as if that were a normal way to spend a Sunday. Was he waiting for Lawrie? Catching her breath, she looked back as she knocked on her own front door; it didn't feel right to let herself in.

'Evie?' Her mother stood in the open doorway, her mouth trembling as she tried to dampen her wide smile. 'Come in, love. Please.' She stepped out of the way.

'Hello, Ma.'

Her mother led her into the front room, as if Evie were an important guest and not her own daughter. The room was freezing and Evie kept her coat on as she sat.

Her mother stood, her hands wound up in her apron. 'I'll stick the kettle on, shall I? Did you want to stay to eat? I've not got a proper meal, I'm afraid, just a bit of ham and some cold potatoes left over from yesterday, but it'll stretch for both of us. If you like.' She was nervous.

Her mother bustled out as Evie perched on the edge of the sofa feeling a decade older than she had the last time she'd been in this room. She stood and walked to the mantelpiece, picking up the same photograph that had so fascinated Lawrie, of that long-ago summer's day in Trafalgar Square. She remembered how excited she'd been about that day. Walking around London like tourists, something she and her mother never did. Eating in a restaurant for the first time, Aunt Gertie showing her how to tuck in a napkin so that she didn't spill gravy down her best frock. She'd fallen asleep on the bus on the way home and it had felt like a dream when she woke the next morning. The photograph was proof that it had really happened, arriving in a stiff, cardboard-backed envelope with its Devon postmark two weeks later.

'That was a lovely day, wasn't it?' Ma came back in with the tea tray. She'd even opened a packet of biscuits to mark the occasion.

'We don't have many photos, do we?' Evie put the frame back. 'Not much to remember us by.'

'What do you mean?'

'I don't know.' Evie turned to look at her mother, standing there bewildered, a hand pressed into her aching back. 'It's just that Delia's family, they go to the seaside every year and get a family picture taken. You can walk into their front room and see their lives all lined up in chronological order. And I'm not saying that I wish we could have gone to the seaside or anything like that. I know we couldn't afford it. But all these other photos are older than I am.'

'You think it's because I was ashamed of you. You think I never wanted to have our picture taken because I didn't want to be reminded.'

'You shoved all my school photographs away in a drawer, Ma. What else am I supposed to think?'

'Wait there.' Ma left the room and Evie heard her heavy tread on the stairs.

Evie sat and nibbled on one of the ginger biscuits her mother had laid out, trying to remember why she'd come. This was already awful, just raking up all the noxious feelings she'd pushed down over the years. She stood again, reaching out for her hand-bag, hoping to sneak out before her mother reappeared.

Too late. Ma walked back in, an old shoebox in her hand. She placed it reverentially in Evie's lap. 'There you go.'

Evie touched the box, her finger making a print in the dust that tickled her nose, making her want to sneeze. The cardboard felt soft and flimsy beneath her fingertips, time and neglect having depleted its strength.

'What's in here?' she asked.

'Old photographs. Just because I don't keep these things on display, it doesn't mean I don't care. I do, Evie, else I'd have binned them all. See?'

Ma hovered over her like a parent watching their child open Christmas presents but Evie felt like she was holding Pandora's box in her lap.

'Family photographs?' She dared to lift the lid and pull out a fistful of aged photos. On top were three copies of the same image, a posed family portrait taken in a studio. A young smiling man with his arm around a woman the spit of Evie's own mother. In her arms was a baby wrapped in a woollen blanket.

'My parents,' Ma said, perching on the arm of the sofa. 'And your aunt when she was a baby.'

Beneath was an almost identical photo but this one pictured Gertie as a little girl of two or three wearing a gingham dress with a large bow in her hair. A new baby lay in her mother's arms.

'This is you?' Evie pointed and Ma nodded.

The man, Evie's grandfather, didn't look how she'd imagined. In her head he'd become a Dickensian character, a Thomas Gradgrind type of man who had cared only for his own reputation and nothing for his daughter's happiness. The man whose image she held in her hand looked as though he'd only just managed to stop laughing, probably at his eldest daughter who stood there

349

with her arms folded. He looked a friendly sort of a chap. Just a normal father and husband who was evidently proud of his three girls. There was her own mother as a baby. The blanket was embroidered, large flowers adorning it. Even in black and white Evie recognised it.

'I kept that blanket. I wrapped you in it when you were a baby.' Ma watched Evie trace the pattern with her finger. Yes, she remembered, the blanket had been white, the daisies still bright yellow. She had taken it to Devon, for Annabel. She hadn't seen it since. She didn't trust herself to be able to ask without unleashing the pain that she was fighting to ignore, but she was sure that Ma had taken the blanket along with Annabel. It was some comfort to imagine that her daughter had something of hers to remember her by.

'He doesn't look anything like I imagined, your father,' Evie said, trying to take her mind away from thoughts of Annabel. 'I pictured him as a bitter and twisted old man but he looks… ordinary. Quite handsome, in fact. Friendly.' Not the sort of man who throws out his own daughter and refuses to meet his own granddaughter.

'He *was* friendly. And funny. Gosh, we used to laugh. But he also held some despicable views on anyone he saw as an outsider. He was a complicated man. I loved him very much and he told me that I broke his heart when I chose to keep you. I told him that he'd already broken my heart by forcing me to make that decision.'

'You chose me? Over him?' Evie had never heard this before. She'd always assumed that he'd thrown Ma out and that was that.

'He arranged for me to go the home on Cedars Road and told everyone that I'd gone to stay with a relative. That was what gave me the idea of sending you to Devon. I'd never have let you go in one of those homes Evie, never. Once the baby – you – had been handed over for adoption I was supposed come back and get on with my life as if nothing had happened. But I still hoped that David might somehow find out and come back for us. Stupid, really. He had no idea about you and I'd told him I didn't love him, to get rid of him. I had to make sure he left London because of your grandfather. He'd already had him beaten up and I knew he could arrange far worse. He knew some bad people through his job. And you were a part of David. I wanted to keep you with me.'

'David?' Evie had never even heard his name before. 'What happened exactly?'

Ma got up and walked over to the sideboard where she'd left the tray. She poured the tea but Evie could see her hands shake.

'Ma, leave it. I don't want any tea.'

'Something stronger?' She opened the sideboard door. 'I bought a new bottle of Scotch.'

'Ma, will you just sit down and talk to me. Tell me what happened with my father. You can manage that, can't you?'

A small nod and her mother came and sat beside her, facing her.

'I met him at a dance. It wasn't my sort of thing really but your aunt talked me into it. This was when she shared a flat in Balham with one of her girlfriends. She said that Pa was treating me like an old housewife, cooking and cleaning for him for little thanks. I was to stay the weekend with her and she'd take me out. And that's when I met David. I was nineteen so only a little older than you. Gertie was thrilled. She and this other girl, I can't remember her name now, they were headed to France for the Easter holidays with some boys they'd met. She gave me the key to their flat and we used to go round, me and David. It was innocent at first, just talking and I'd sometimes cook a meal. It was just somewhere we could be together 'cause I knew Pa would kill me if he saw David.'

'He found out, though.'

'Yes.' Ma shook her head, staring at the wall, her mind lost in the past. 'I met him at the tube station one day and he kissed me out on the street. It was the only time since the dance that we'd been so obvious. And someone saw. Next time I saw David he had two black eyes and a busted lip. He'd ended up in hospital thanks to your grandfather, not that he did it himself, you understand. He was at home eating a pie that I'd cooked for him, knowing all the while that my David was getting beaten half to death.' She rummaged in the apron pocket then gave up and blew her nose on the apron itself, pulling it from around her waist. 'I knew it was no good. Neither of us had any money and he didn't even have a job. He was a student, you see. I told him that I didn't love him, that there was no point in us going on if it meant risking his life. Last time I saw him he said he'd booked passage to go home and he waited for me to tell him not to go but I didn't. It was only a month or so after he'd left that I realised you were on the way.'

Evie had always assumed she was the product of a one-time mistake, her own father just as unknown to her mother as Sam had been to her. Ma had let her believe that for eighteen years rather than tell her the truth.

'Why keep this such a secret?' she asked. 'You loved one another. Why is that shameful? I thought that you must have hated my father, that he was no good.'

'Gosh no, he was the best man I've ever met, Evie. I never meant for you to think badly of him. I just didn't want to remember him, or remember that I was the one who sent him away. I thought you'd be angry, that you'd think it was my fault.' Ma reached from the shoebox and rifled through it, picking out a new photograph. 'This is him.'

The photograph had been taken by the seaside. Brighton Pier, Evie read, her breath quickening as she saw her younger mother standing hand in hand, smiling, with an equally young man. Her father. They looked so happy, gazing into each other's eyes instead of the camera lens, the same age, near enough, as Evie and Lawrie were now.

'We went to Brighton one Saturday. David was always complaining that he missed the sea and I thought it would be fun to have a real English seaside day out.'

He stood tall, much darker than Lawrie, smart in his white shirt and his jacket done up with one button. It must have been a warm day as her mother wore a short-sleeved dress, her cardigan slung over an arm. Her dark curly hair was pinned up and her smile was so wide that Evie realised she'd never seen her mother this happy. Behind them was clear sky and the railings of the famous pier.

'I almost lost this. They post them to you afterwards, you see, after they've developed them, and like a fool I gave this address. Well, of course your grandfather opened the envelope even though it had my name on.' She smiled. 'He threw it in the bin but I managed to sneak back and rescue it. I hid it in amongst the family photos 'cause I knew no one would throw them out but my father didn't like to look at them after Mother died. He didn't want to dwell on the past, he said.'

'David loved you very much,' Evie said, unable to tear her eyes from her father's face. 'And you loved him.'

'You're very like him, you know. He was very clever. And very stubborn.'

Evie laughed. 'I always thought I got that from you.'

Her mother didn't reply. Evie looked up and saw that she was crying.

'Oh, Ma!' It felt natural to open her arms and pull her mother close. All they had left was one another. 'Don't cry. It's going to be all right.'

'You're right to hate me.' Ma pulled back and blew her nose once more. 'I should have told you everything years ago. I don't know why I didn't. Maybe if you'd known the truth, we wouldn't be in this mess now.'

'It's not too late. We can start again, can't we?'

'Evie, I took your child from you.' She wiped her eyes with the back of her hand. 'I promise you, honestly, I thought I was protecting you but I realise now… it was selfish of me. I was thinking of myself and I had no right to make that decision for you.'

'No. You didn't. I won't forget what you did but I know why you did it.' Evie patted the box. 'I could have grown up in one of those awful children's homes but you gave me a proper home.

You made sure that Annabel had a proper home. I can't promise anything, but I don't want to cut you out of my life. I don't want us to end up like you and your father.'

Her mother smiled. 'Evie, you don't know how happy I am to hear you say that. Now come on, let's have something to eat and then I'll show you the patterns I was looking at for your wedding dress.'

Evie's heart sank. She hadn't told her mother that Lawrie had found out about Annabel. That there might not be a wedding. She just smiled and followed Ma next door to the kitchen, sitting as her mother brought out the leftovers and two plates. There were dirty dishes in the sink and there were stale crumbs on the table top, multiple mug rings when before Ma had never let a single one settle.

'There's something else you should know,' Ma told her as they began to eat. 'I'm leaving London.'

'What? When?' Evie paused, her fork halfway to her mouth.

'Soon. I'm not sure when exactly. Gertie invited me to Devon. She'll sell this place and we'll live off the money, I suppose.' Ma shrugged. 'There isn't anything keeping me here, is there? I've no real friends. What am I going to do with myself once you're married?'

Evie was still deciding whether or not to tell her about Lawrie when the doorbell chimed.

Ma frowned. 'Who on earth's that at this time on a Sunday?' She got up and Evie hoped that whoever it was didn't frighten easily. Her mother wouldn't shy away from giving them a piece of her mind.

'Evie!'

She heard her mother shout and had just pushed her chair back when they arrived, two policemen, grabbing her arms as she tried to stand. They took no consideration over the fact that she was a woman, barely five feet four and hardly a threat to them, wrenching her upright so quickly that she thought her arms might come free from their sockets. This, then, was what they'd done to Lawrie only a few weeks earlier.

Rathbone appeared in the doorway, cigarette in his mouth as always. 'Evelyn Coleridge,' he said, 'I am arresting you for the murder of Annabel Coleridge. You are not obliged to say anything but anything you do say will be taken down in writing and may be given in evidence.'

'Ma!' Evie shouted out as they handcuffed her and pushed her before them, heading out towards the street. 'Ma, what do I do?'

'It'll be all right. I'll sort it.' Her mother called out. She was trapped on the bottom stair, one of the men holding her back as they took her daughter away. 'Don't worry, Evie. Just do what they say.'

'Sensible woman, your mother,' she heard Rathbone chuckle behind her.

There were two police cars outside, sirens off but their lights flashing, enough to draw a crowd. There was nowhere to hide. Evie's vision blurred with tears of shame as they shoved her into the back of one of the cars. Everyone had seen them take her away. Everyone would find out what she'd done.

25

He knew that something had happened from the number of people standing out on the street. Early afternoon on a Sunday – everyone should have been indoors, the women sweating over a hot oven as they prepared the best roast dinner that coupons could provide, their husbands putting their feet up and smoking a pipe. As Lawrie walked past, they turned to look, something in their pointed gaze sending a shiver through his body.

Mrs Ryan waved as soon as she saw him. 'Lawrie, thank God!'

'What is going on?' he asked, turning back to look over his shoulder. Was it just him or were they all still watching him, as if they'd been waiting for him to arrive.

'It's Evie, love.' She wrung her hands, her forehead creased with anxiety. 'She's been arrested.'

'What?' He shook his head, not understanding. 'Evie? You sure?'

'She came to see Agnes and that dirty copper was waiting for her. Made a right scene. All the lights flashing, two cars and four fellas, just to take that poor wee girl away.' She shook her head. 'I sent Derek off to see if he can find out what's going on.'

He'd been a complete idiot. Rathbone had as good as told him that Evie was a suspect but Lawrie had been too caught up in his own concerns, too hurt at being lied to, to think that perhaps he should be warning her.

'When was this?' he asked.

'Not long ago. Maybe half an hour?'

He ran into the house passing Arthur in the hallway, arguing with someone on the telephone.

'Agnes isn't answering the door so I made Arthur call the police station but they won't tell him anything.' Mrs Ryan followed him inside.

'You know where Derek went?'

'Not exactly.' Mrs Ryan looked shifty. 'Well, probably he's gone to the Atlantic. But only 'cause some ex-coppers drink there. He'll have thought they might have had an ear out for this, what with it being in the papers and all.'

'Then when Arthur gives up with the police tell him to call there. There's a telephone behind the bar. I need Derek to give me a lift to the police station.' Lawrie opened the back door. 'You said Agnes definitely isn't answering? She didn't just go out?'

'I've been knocking on since they took Evie. I suppose she could have slipped out when I went to put the kettle on…'

He needed Agnes. She was the only person other than him and Rathbone who knew about Evie's baby and yet she was hiding away at home. He went out into the backyard and peered over the wall. He couldn't see well enough into the kitchen to make sure it was empty but he decided to chance it and swung his leg over the wall.

'Lawrie!' Mrs Ryan hissed up at him. 'Are you going in the back way?'

He nodded. 'I mean, if she is in there we can say we thought she might have had an accident.'

'Go on then. I'll go round the front.'

He dropped into the Coleridges' yard, light on his feet, peering through the kitchen window to check that no one was sitting there. He could see two plates left out on the table at the back, the cutlery left drunkenly askew amidst the remnants of a meal. They'd been eating when the police had called. The door was unlocked and he let himself inside just as he heard Mrs Ryan begin to knock once more on the front door.

He trod careful footsteps across the battered lino, his eye drawn to the plates of half-finished food, the chairs left askew in the chaos that must have unfolded earlier. Forcing himself on into the hallway he saw that on the low table by the door, next to the bowl of keys, was an envelope addressed to DS Kenneth Rathbone. Grabbing the letter he ignored Mrs Ryan while he checked in the front room but there was no one there, just a battered cardboard shoebox lying on the settee.

'Agnes,' he called up the stairs. There was no reply.

'She's not here?' Mrs Ryan looked perplexed when finally he let her in.

'Not downstairs,' he said. 'Can you go up and check? I don't want to walk in on her if she's up there.'

He went back into the front room while she went up, his heart clenching as he recognised Evie's coat and handbag laid over the arm of the sofa. The shoebox was full of photographs and he

359

picked up the top one, a family portrait. He looked closer and immediately recognised the blanket the baby was wrapped in.

White, with daisies that he would bet had been yellow.

Derek offered him a lift as soon as he asked, parking up on Windmill Drive and pulling out a newspaper, propping it up against the steering wheel. 'You take your time,' he said, as if Lawrie was headed off on a Sunday stroll.

Lawrie had told Derek as little as possible. It was better that way. There was no way of knowing how Derek would react if he knew the truth of the matter. He just hoped he was right and Agnes was close by. He didn't trust Rathbone with the letter, not without Agnes herself to verify her story.

Lawrie slowed his pace as he drew near Eagle Pond and saw Agnes sitting on the bench, a suitcase by her feet. Seeking forgiveness for her sins, as she'd written it. He'd guessed that meant the place where she'd last seen her granddaughter, before she'd laid her down amongst the reeds. She must have cursed Lawrie for being in the wrong place at the wrong time – almost as hard as he'd cursed his own bad luck.

'Agnes?' he called, close enough that she had no chance to run, keeping his voice light so that she didn't take fright. 'I've been looking for you.'

She whirled round. 'Lawrie? What are you doing here?'

He held up the letter. 'I'm sorry. You left the back door open. I wanted to make sure you were all right.'

'You've read it, haven't you? You must have known I'd be here. Did you call the police?'

He took a seat next to her on the bench and shook his head. 'I came here to see how you were. To see if you might change your mind and stay.'

'I won't.' Her voice wavered. 'I'm not just leaving Evie in the lurch, you can see that. I was going to call the police station once I was out of London, tell them to go to the house. You've read the letter; you know that I've written it all down.'

'And then what? You can't hide in Devon. They'll find you inside of a day,' Lawrie pointed out.

'I know that. I'm not going to Devon,' she said. 'I've got my own money, you know. I've been saving money for years, for Evie. It was for you, to help you buy a house.' She patted the suitcase by her side. 'I withdrew it from the bank the other week, just in case. With me gone, you can have my father's house. I telephoned Gertie and told her I'd been offered a housekeeping job abroad, that it was better pay and I needed a fresh start. It's all arranged.'

'Forget the house, Agnes. What about Evie? She'll be devastated,' he told her. 'You can't just leave her to find out the truth from Rathbone. I believe you, Agnes, that it was an accident. So will Evie.'

'It *was* an accident,' she protested, even though he wasn't contradicting her. 'I only meant for Annabel to go to sleep for a few hours.'

'Of course. Why would you take a healthy child from her parents if you meant to harm her?' He tried to keep his voice from trembling as he spoke.

'They were going to give her back, Lawrie. They said it was too difficult. People were saying horrid things about them, because she was coloured.' Agnes snorted her derision. 'As if I don't know what that's like! But I managed, didn't I? They wanted to dump her in a children's home and wash their hands of her. And him a man of God!'

'You spoke to them?'

'I tried to. I ran into Sister Mary down at the market the week before. She was a bit off with me and so I came out and asked her, was it to do with Evie's baby? She wouldn't say much but I already knew that it was a vicar and his wife had taken Annabel. She just said that they were having a bit of trouble. She hadn't given up hope but she'd let me know if they decided to give her back.' She looked back at the pond, caught up in memory.

'So how did you find them?' Lawrie tried to keep her talking.

'Easy. People talk, especially those who should know better. I went over to Hammersmith and went round the churches until I heard the rumours. A few coloured folk had joined the church and the popular gossip was that the vicar had been quite taken with one of the women. The wife could barely look at Annabel. Blamed her husband for forcing her to take her in the first place. When I knocked on the door she thought I'd come to take her away. Practically threw her at me! I couldn't just leave the poor thing there. I made up some story about the baby's mother wanting her back and the stupid woman, she was so happy! I could have smacked her.'

Lawrie already knew the rest from the letter. Agnes was a charlady for a house on the north side of Clapham Common. The family had gone off skiing for a week so it was the perfect place to take the child. Not knowing how to come clean to Evie, petrified that a neighbour would hear the baby cry, Agnes had crushed some of her own sleeping pills into the baby formula that the vicar's wife, Mrs Westland, had given her and fed it to Annabel. It was only the next day when she returned before sunrise that she'd realised the dose was far too strong for an infant.

He cleared his throat and hoped he sounded convincing. 'The Westlands will back your story. They'll confirm that they handed Annabel over to you. You just needed time, to talk to Evie. To explain it all.'

'That's it exactly.' She looked up at Lawrie, hope in her eyes for the first time. 'D'you really think they'll believe me? That it was an accident, I mean?'

'Only if you hand yourself in. If you run away then you'll lose everything. You'll look guilty in the eyes of the police, of Evie. Everyone will assume that you meant to kill her, and it'll only be a matter of time before the police find you.'

Agnes stared straight ahead for a long time before speaking again. 'I used to come here when I was living at the home, just before Evie was born,' she said, not really talking to Lawrie, her eyes fixed on the bulrushes in the pond. 'It was the only place where I felt at peace, that's why I brought her here. I couldn't think where else to take her. I just wanted a new start. Is that so bad? I couldn't do it all again, that's all it was.'

She closed her eyes in pain and in the silence, Lawrie held his breath, watching the wave of conflicting emotions crash through her face in a violent wave. Finally, she moved and undid the catch on her suitcase and slid her hand in, pulling out a bulging envelope which she handed to him. 'Take this then. For the wedding. Evie will need a new dressmaker.' She fastened the case back up and stood, smoothing down her skirt. 'Come on. Let's get it over with.'

26

There was no tea on offer this time, just the manila folder, much thicker now than she remembered. Rathbone took a seat opposite and slid the cigarette packet across the table towards her. She hesitated before taking one.

'I want a solicitor,' she said once it was lit. That was what Derek had told Lawrie to say if they arrested him again. She knew she was in trouble.

'I've sent for a solicitor but it might take some time, Evelyn. What with it being a Sunday and all.' He grinned, his teeth bright yellow under the fluorescent light. 'I thought we could have us a little chat before then. If there's a simple explanation that excuses the evidence I've got before me then you'll get home all that much quicker.'

She knew it was a trap. She also knew she wasn't guilty. 'What evidence?'

'The baby. Ophelia, or whatever they called it. It was your baby all along.'

She sat up in the chair, her body turning cold. 'You're lying. I checked. She was adopted.'

'Yes. By the good Reverend Westland and his wife.' Rathbone shuffled his papers and put one in front of Evie. 'From a home for mothers and babies on Cedars Road.'

The words on the page swam before her eyes. 'They killed her?'

He chuckled. 'A man of God killing a child? We're not living in biblical times, Evelyn. No. But they wanted to give her back. Spoke to the wife yesterday when she came in. She'd read all the newspaper reports but she didn't realise that Ophelia was her Sarah. That's what they'd named her. So many names for one tiny baby!' He held up a typewritten document, several pages long. 'She had an awful lot to tell me, Evelyn.'

'I don't know her.' Evie tried to keep the tremble from her voice. 'I never met them. I didn't lie to you, I didn't even know that Annabel was alive. You spoke to my mother, you know it's true.'

'I know what she told me,' he replied.

'And it's the truth,' she insisted.

Rathbone turned the page of Mrs Westland's statement. 'The 15th of March. Two days before your fiancé found a baby in Eagle Pond. A woman came to the Westlands' door, saying that she was from Cedars Road.' He looked up at Evie. 'She wasn't, though. I think she was probably your mother. The description fits.'

'Then why am I here? You left Ma back at home. you need to speak to her.' Her voice was hoarse now, barely a whisper as she tried to fit pieces of the puzzle together.

'Oh, I will. I'm just giving her some time to stew. When I look at your mother I see a woman who has given up her whole life for a daughter who doesn't give a toss. A girl who didn't want a baby messing up her life, not when things were finally starting to look up.'

'No, that's not—'

'Shut up!' He slammed his hand down on the table, Evie's words stopping dead in her throat. 'Your mother has been cleaning up after you this whole time. I'll deal with her in due course, don't you worry, but first I want to hear it from your own lips. You killed your daughter because she was in the way. You knew that Mr Matthews was close to proposing marriage and you thought that he'd call it off if he knew the truth. As indeed he has.'

Evie looked down at her bare finger, the engagement ring sitting in a pocket of her handbag where she taken it off, hating the feeling of desperation that descended upon her each time she glanced down at it.

'Sarah Westland was wearing a pink dress on that day, and Mrs Westland handed back the blanket that had arrived with the baby. A white blanket with yellow daisies on it. Sound familiar?'

Evie's sob sounded hollow in the small room.

'You could have done the honourable thing, taken the child back to Cedars Road,' Rathbone continued. 'But I think that was too close to home. Give it a few years and that child would be running around near Clapham Common. Mr Matthews might easily come across her, what with his special deliveries and that. She might grow up looking like the spit of you and what then? A big mess, Evelyn. That's what. You're a clever girl. I think that your mother arrived home with a baby and you panicked. Used what was at hand. Sleeping pills, was it? Something you ladies take for your headaches?'

'It wasn't me,' she said, her voice quiet. Defeated.

'D'you think a jury will believe that?' Rathbone was interrupted by a knock on the door. 'I'm busy,' he barked.

The door opened and a young detective poked his head through. 'Sarge, this is urgent. You'd better come.'

Cursing under his breath, Rathbone got up, taking his folder with him. Evie wiped her face and took another cigarette from the packet. If Rathbone wouldn't listen, would anyone else? She'd told so many lies already to so many people. Even Lawrie hated her. Only Ma could help. Would they hang her? Her hand shook at the thought and she couldn't strike the match properly.

She threw down the unlit cigarette and went to the door, thumping on it hard before trying the door handle. It opened easily and Evie peered out into the empty corridor.

'Hello?' she called out, taking a step forward. 'DS Rathbone?'

'Evie?' The voice that replied was familiar but so unexpected that she daren't believe it until Lawrie turned the corner and was there, pulling her into his arms, holding her so tightly she could barely breathe.

'What are you doing here?' she asked.

'Getting you out of here,' he said, pushing her back into the room and closing the door. 'Just stay in here a while where it's safe.'

'Where is everyone? Rathbone was just here but he left. I don't know where he's gone but you should leave before he comes back. He thinks that I—'

'Sit down.' He pushed her to sit and pulled the other chair round beside her. 'There's something I need to tell you.'

His eyes were soft and she knew that he'd been told about Annabel. 'I know. Rathbone told me. About Annabel.'

'I'm so sorry, Evie.' He pulled her close and kissed her forehead. 'Agnes confessed. I found her by the pond and I brought her straight here to Rathbone. They can get the Westlands to identify her as the woman who took the baby.'

'She did it, then?' Evie heard her voice as if from far away. It sounded very small.

'She says it was an accident.' His eyes slid away from hers and she knew he didn't believe it. 'But she's with Rathbone now. It's all over, Evie, you'll be all right. She's been arrested and we can go once Rathbone does the paperwork.'

'Really?'

'Really. We can get on with our lives. Get married. If that's still what you want.'

She nodded. 'But I want to leave here.'

'Of course. We just need to sign something at the front desk and then we can go home.'

'No, Lawrie. I don't mean that. I can't go home. Everyone saw them take me away. Everyone will know by now, and if not then they'll know within a few days once the newspapers get hold of it. I have to leave it all behind. Start again somewhere new.'

He nodded. 'I know somewhere we can go, just until we work out what to do. You think you can put up with Aston for a few days?'

She nodded. She'd be glad to see Aston. She'd be glad to see any familiar friendly face. She felt exhausted all of a sudden, as if a great weight was crashing through her. 'Then let's go.'

'Wait!' Lawrie tried to catch hold of her before she stepped out into the corridor but he was too late.

'Evie?'

She turned to see her mother coming out of another interview room, Rathbone ahead of her. Her legs went to jelly with no warning, Lawrie having to catch her as she slumped towards the floor, her hand pressing against the cool wall as she tried to regain her balance.

'I'm so sorry, Evie.' Ma was weeping now, her voice hysterical. 'I never meant for any of this to happen.'

Rathbone looked angry, his face dark as he dragged her mother towards them, Evie flattening her back to the wall to avoid touching either of them. She could feel the impotent rage blazing from the detective.

'Evie, say something,' her mother begged. 'Say you'll forgive me.'

'You don't have to,' Lawrie reminded her, squeezing her hand. 'You owe her nothing.'

Evie nodded, even though he was wrong, and closed her eyes, refusing to reopen them, despite her mother's cries, until she heard the door close at the other end of the corridor, her mother on her way to the cells.

✳ DECEMBER 1950 ✳

'Day longa dan rope'
JAMAICAN PROVERB

27

She shouldn't have left it until the last shopping day before
Christmas, and had to squeeze her aching body onto the packed
bus. A gentleman at the front tipped his hat as he offered his seat
and she gratefully sank down into it. Lawrie had offered to come
with her but she'd said no. If she'd had the choice she'd have put
off the trip until the new year but she knew that she had a duty.
And once she put it off once, it would be so much easier to do
so the second and third time.

The gates looked just as forbidding as they had the previous
time she'd been to Holloway prison. On that occasion she'd
been accompanied by her aunt Gertie who had been furious at
her niece for running away before they'd even gained entry, the
sudden impulse to throw up overtaking all emotion. Gertie had
assumed that Evie was chickening out and had left her sitting on
the side of the road, her breakfast at her feet. She wasn't sure her
aunt had forgiven her, for that or for the chain of events that had
led to Agnes Coleridge serving a long stretch behind bars, lucky
to escape the death sentence.

Today she felt calmer, no longer nauseous now that her
pregnancy was visible from several paces away. She showed her

identification and waited as the officer checked her handbag and coat pockets. It was busy, as noisy as a school playground because of the sheer number of children. They'd been brought to see their mothers before Christmas, she supposed. The waiting area smelled like a bus station, stale cigarettes, body odour and a faint whiff of urine which she attributed to the children. Some of their faces had that grey pallor that came from a bad diet and infrequent washing.

The doors opened and Evie trailed behind as everyone else piled into the large room beyond, the wooden tables and chairs laid out in an orderly fashion. Evie sat where she was told, leaving her coat on to guard against the chill of the air. A door at the other side of the room opened and Evie dared to look up, waiting for her mother to enter.

She looked old. Her hair was grey and tied back in a greasy ponytail. Her skin looked dry and Evie wished she'd brought some cold cream, though she wasn't even sure if it was allowed. She'd leave some money when she left, she decided, feeling sorry for her mother for the first time.

'You came.'

Evie nodded and fidgeted with one of her coat buttons.

'You look well,' Agnes told her. 'Where are you staying these days?'

'We're still living with Aston and Helene,' she said. 'They've been so kind. The rent is cheap but we'll look for our own place soon. Once the baby's born.'

Her mother gasped as she noticed Evie's belly for the first time. 'That was quick.'

'We were married in May,' Evie reminded her.

The wedding had been a quick register office affair in the end, with a meal at Tony's Italian restaurant in Soho as the reception. With the wad of notes that Agnes had left, Lawrie had agreed to move the wedding up, if only so that Evie could legally cast off the tainted name of Coleridge. Evie had told Lawrie to make a party of it, more to take her mind off her mother's trial than because she felt in a celebratory mood. Their honeymoon had been two nights at the Strand Palace hotel and a theatre show. By the time they returned to Notting Hill, Evie Coleridge was in the past and Evie Matthews had been ready to begin her new life, determined to let her mother fester, out of sight and out of mind. But it wasn't all that easy, she had come to realise.

'I'm happy for you.'

'Thank you.' The words tripped easily of her tongue as though Agnes was a stranger. 'Lawrie's very excited. He can't decide if he'd rather it be a boy or a girl. I'd rather a boy.' She didn't want a replacement for Annabel. She could see that her mother understood.

'You've got a good man there. I'm happy that he's stuck by you. You know, that's all I wanted—'

'Forget it, Ma.' Evie interrupted before her mother could trot out the same old excuses.

'How can I? And you clearly haven't.'

'Are you joking?' Evie hissed, leaning forward before she saw one of the guards shaking his head. She rested back in the chair, shifting her weight to try and get comfortable on the hard wood. 'Ma, I can't do this.'

'Can't do what?'

'I can't talk about it. What you did.'

'So I'm not allowed to have a reason for it? I can't try and explain myself?'

'Not when you try and make yourself out to be some sort of martyr. You're a murderer, Ma, nothing more than that. You're lucky, you know. They fell for it; that you never meant for it to happen.'

'But you don't believe me.'

She chewed the inside of her cheek before taking a breath. 'No. I don't.' She looked up, her mother staring back dry-eyed. 'You had a choice. You could have brought her home and told me the truth. Or you could have taken her to Cedars Road.'

'You'd have her grow up in a home? Your own daughter?'

'Better than being dead, isn't it?' Evie lit a cigarette, her hand steady. 'We gave her a proper burial. Mrs Ryan helped me with the arrangements.' And Lawrie had been so good about it. He even went with Evie every week to lay flowers.

Agnes looked away. 'I didn't know what I was going to do. It was all spur of the moment. I thought I had time.'

'You let me get arrested, Ma. You were going to run away. Did you think Lawrie wouldn't tell me?' Evie pushed back the chair. 'I said we could talk but I'm not sure this is helpful and my doctor says I should watch my blood pressure.'

'If my father had had his way, you'd have grown up in one of those children's homes. Then you'd understand what I was trying to save your baby from.'

'I do understand, Ma. But you aren't God. You never had the

right to make that decision for me.' She squeezed her mother's hand as she watched the tears start to fall, then stood up.

Her chest felt tight as she was checked over once more before she was allowed outside into the frigid air, taking deep breaths as she walked briskly to the bus stop, her head pounding.

She'd forgotten to leave her mother any money, she remembered as she got off the bus, changing onto the tube at Chancery Lane. Funny, but even though the short confrontation had been awful, she felt better. She knew her mother would never admit to whatever madness had been going through her mind when she'd taken her granddaughter. There were days when she wanted to believe Agnes' defence. Lawrie, in his attempts to placate his wife, said that it was for Evie to decide whether her mother was guilty or innocent. She had hoped to leave the prison knowing for certain but even now, even after her mother had seemed to accept the charges laid against her by her own flesh and blood, she couldn't be sure.

As she came up from the underground at Notting Hill Gate she decided to stop off at the bakery. Lawrie had developed a taste for a custard slice and she needed to see that look on his face, the smile in his eyes that he always had for her when she brought him one home.

'Bit chilly out, is it, love?' the woman asked her, spinning the paper bag with one hand to tie ears in it before placing it on the counter.

'Rather. Least it's not raining.' Evie paid and tucked the bag under her arm. 'Merry Christmas.'

Back out on the street she passed a black woman, a new arrival if she had to guess. She said hello and the woman smiled back hesitantly. Those women that Evie had looked for on the Common two years ago were finally arriving. Not everyone was happy about that of course, but for Evie it was exciting. She was no longer the odd one out in her own city. She was part of a new London.

This was a place marred by war; every other woman you passed had lost a husband, a lover, a child. But still they kept going. Evie was no different. This baby wouldn't fix what Ma had done, would never replace the child she'd lost. But they would be loved, as Evie herself felt loved. She just had to remember her own advice: that life didn't always turn out as you imagined… and that it wasn't foolish to have dreams.

The tree was ridiculous, Aston having driven a hard bargain with the street seller that morning. No one else wanted a seven-foot tree, it seemed, only Aston Bayley. Lawrie's arms still ached from the effort of carrying it back to the house. Now that Helene had unleashed her artistic vision, as she called it, he had to say that it looked impressive. A Hollywood sort of Christmas tree, like he'd seen in the movies.

'What time you told them?' Aston walked in, a glass jug in each hand. His infamous rum punch.

'I did say six,' Lawrie eyed the jugs cautiously, 'but I wouldn't bet on them being on time.'

Aston winked as he placed them carefully on the sideboard,

on mats, of course, so Helene didn't scold him. 'Fancy making sure this stuff is all right?'

'May as well.'

A stiff drink would sort him out, he hoped. Stop him worrying about Evie, who'd refused to say a word since she arrived home, just pleaded exhaustion and went straight to bed. He knew she hadn't slept well the night before; neither had he, worrying what would happen with Agnes. He'd wanted to go with her but she refused point blank. It was something for them to sort out between them, she'd said, if they were ever going to.

Aston poured out punch into two crystal glasses that Evie reckoned cost more than she earned in a week. Since she now worked with Helene at the gallery, doing general admin as well as the accounts, she would know. Lawrie flinched a little at the first sip before it started going down smoother.

'You think there's enough rum?' Aston asked, smacking his lips and lighting a cigarette.

'There's rum enough in there to set the house on fire if you hold that lighter too close to it,' Lawrie told him. 'Good, though.'

'We got plenty of beer and Helene bought champagne for the ladies. You think we need more food?'

Helene had ordered food from a catering company, had wanted to book a waiter to hand round plates of food until Evie had stopped her. Lawrie could just imagine Sonny's face, getting offered a plate of the tiny savoury tarts by a man whose suit had cost more than Sonny's entire wardrobe.

'Nah, man.' Lawrie sat down on the wide sofa. 'Just relax. These are *our* friends comin' over, not Helene's fancy acquaintances.'

'True, true.'

They had another glass of punch, just to be sure, and Lawrie's head was a little fuzzy when the doorbell went. Even after almost eight months, it usually felt awkward to answer the door in Helene's house, but not when he knew the crowd outside so well. They'd all arrived together and he could imagine them making the trek across London in convoy, crammed into the vans of Derek and Moses.

He'd never stop feeling grateful to his friends. After Agnes had been arrested Mrs Ryan's doorbell had not stopped ringing for weeks, journalists calling their questions through the letterbox until Arthur had taken to keeping a bucket of dirty water by the door. By the third soaking they'd taken their interrogations up the street, printing local gossip about Agnes and her father that the neighbours were happy to share. *Shame on them*, Mrs Ryan had said, and checked in on Lawrie often, at least once a week. They'd decided between them not to mention any of it to Lawrie's mother. She'd only worry and she didn't need to know.

'Would you look at this place!' Mrs Ryan marvelled as she walked into the hallway, even though she'd been to the house at least three times before. 'I forget how grand you live now, Lawrie.'

'Come in, come in.'

He waved them all on, Aston ushering them through to the living room: Mrs Ryan, who wasn't actually Mrs Ryan any longer. She was newly married to Arthur, who followed her in with Derek. Behind them were Johnny and Ursula, Moses and Al, Sonny trailing in behind. Last were Delia and Sid, holding hands in an awkward fashion since Delia insisted on keeping her left hand tilted so that everyone would notice her new engagement ring.

'Congratulations.' Lawrie stooped to kiss her cheek, shaking Sid's free hand.

'Ta, Lawrie,' she said. 'Where's Evie?'

'Evie? Ah,' he realised guiltily, 'let me go check. She was feeling tired so she went for a lay down. I'll go and see if she's ready.'

Their bedroom was on the first floor, that same room where he had stayed, drunken and desperate, the night before Evie's arrest. Now it felt more homely. Evie had bought some blue velvet from Whiteley's and run up a new pair of curtains to stop the light coming in through the blinds in the morning. Lawrie had found an old armchair at the second-hand shop round the corner and, as Evie said, once the baby came along there'd be all manner of paraphernalia that would mark the space as their own, but with luck they could find their own place before too long. He'd been saying that since May though and, still without a steady job, he wasn't sure when that would be. If Evie hadn't proved such a godsend to Helene in the gallery, they'd only have what Lawrie made with the band.

He found Evie in front of the mirror, sticking a final hair grip into her chignon. He had ordered her to spend the Christmas bonus that Helene had given her on a new dress for herself. She had refused at first, saying it would be a waste when she wouldn't be able to wear it for much longer, but then he pointed out that they had talked about having at least two children, so she would have another chance to wear it. She was wearing it now but he could tell that she wasn't happy with the way it fell over the growing bump. He thought she looked pretty, though the style of it made her look incongruously young.

'Look at the state!' She turned this way and that before the mirror, tugging at the white collar of the knee-length navy smock. 'I look huge. Why did you let me buy this awful dress? I look like a fat old woman.'

'You look beautiful.' He kissed her forehead and put his arms around her. 'You're in a bad mood is all. Because of Agnes?'

She groaned and laid her head against his chest. 'I did what you told me not to. It was awful.'

She hadn't raised her voice but he could hear the tremble of anger and upset, and held her tighter. 'Come on. Come downstairs and have a drink.'

'Is everyone here? Can't we stay up here, just the two of us? Aston can keep them entertained.' She looked up at him and pouted, making him chuckle.

'No! Tempting, but we invited them and it's Christmas. You'll have fun once you get down there.' He kissed her lips, glad she hadn't bothered with lipstick. 'Come on.'

He took her by the hand, and they joined the others in the living room. The punch had already been doled out which was just as well, Lawrie thought, and Aston was struggling to open a bottle of champagne. Mrs Ryan gave Evie a hug and Lawrie smiled to see his wife laugh at one of Sid's terrible jokes, the company of their friends like a magic tonic.

'Give it to me,' Helene ordered, grabbing the bottle and popping the cork out with little effort, much to Derek's amusement in particular.

'See, I had loosened it right up,' Aston claimed. 'But I'll let you take the credit this time, *chérie*.'

Helene kissed his cheek. 'Yes, yes. Now, who wants a glass of this? Much less lethal than that rum concoction.'

Lawrie shook his head, nodding at his glass of punch, but Evie took a flute as Aston stood on a footstool to make a toast. Already a little tipsy, it was a crowd-pleasing speech full of risqué jokes, but Lawrie was only half listening. He wanted to watch Evie, smiling as she laughed at Aston's impression of Arthur in the mornings, heckling as he poked fun at poor Moses who was still having no luck with the ladies – though he did have a fresh bruise on his cheek.

Ever since that night back in the spring, when Derek's intelligence had proved accurate, there had been the odd spot of trouble. Certain pubs it was wiser to stay out of. Talking to the wrong girls or standing in the wrong place could get you a smack. At first, Lawrie had thought that Agnes's arrest would make all that nonsense go away but the baby had just been the first spark. The fire was lit now, but it didn't have to signal an ending to the new life he had come to England to seek. The life that he was finally starting to live.

Someone had put on a record, and as Lord Kitchener's opening bars filled the room Lawrie looked around at the people who were now raising their glasses – the people who were his new family. Raising his own tumbler of rum, he remembered the newspaper they had handed out at Tilbury the day they disembarked from that ship. 'Welcome Home!' the headline had proclaimed.

For the first time, he felt it to be true.

ACKNOWLEDGEMENTS

Huge thanks to my agent, Nelle Andrew, for taking a chance on me when all I had was a few pages and an idea for how the rest would go (mostly that idea was wrong, but I got there in the end!). I will always be grateful to the Lucy Cavendish Fiction Prize for bringing us together.

Clio Cornish, your enthusiasm for this book won me over immediately and I'm so privileged to have called you my editor. Manpreet Grewal and Lisa Milton have been incredibly supportive and I must acknowledge the whole team at HQ – you are brilliant and innovative and there could not have been a better home for *This Lovely City*. Thanks to Claire Brett, Jo Rose, Ammara Isa and Joe Thomas for a marketing and publicity campaign that exceeded my expectations, Rebecca Fortuin for finding the perfect Lawrie and Evie for the audiobook. George Green, Fliss Porter, Darren Shoffren, Halema Begum and Angie Dobbs for all your work behind the scenes. And for the craziest proof drop I've ever seen: Alexia Thomaidis, Hannah Sawyer, Samantha Luton and Izzy Smith.

Any mistakes in this novel are my own and there are far fewer thanks to Jon Appleton and Laura Gerrard. The stunning cover design is thanks to Anna Morrison.

Thanks also to Douglas Richmond and the team at House of Anansi, this novel's North American home.

I will be forever grateful for all that I learned on the MA Creative Writing at Birkbeck, University of London. Julia Bell, Toby Litt, Russell Celyn Jones, Jonathan Kemp and Colin Teevan: I learned invaluable insights through your classes, lectures and tutorials.

All of my friends have been incredibly supportive, for which I am forever thankful, but a few I must mention by name. Harriet Tyce and Maxine Mei Fung Chung, it took a while but we did it! Thanks for all the support and red wine (and gin) over the years. Jane Dumble for reading my first (unpublished) novel and not hating it.

Thanks also to the self-proclaimed Birkbeck #supergroup: Lou Kramskoy, Chris Newlove Horton, Anna Livia Ryan, Peter J Coles, Karen Clark, Ruth Ivo, Arhondia Stickney, Mari Vindis, Abi Dare, Carmel Shortall and Martin Phillips.

To the Pot Tea Posse, Nikki Metcalfe Dermott and Kat Liutai. What happens on tour stays on tour. Thank you for not getting mad when I insisted on bringing this novel on holiday to finish the latest draft.

Last but not least, Mum, Dad and Rob. You inspired and encourage me, even when I believed this may not be possible. I love you.

ONE PLACE. MANY STORIES

Bold, innovative and
empowering publishing.

FOLLOW US ON:

@HQStories